STRANGLED

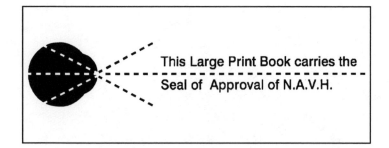

This Large Print Book carries the
Seal of Approval of N.A.V.H.

STRANGLED

BRIAN MCGRORY

THORNDIKE PRESS
An imprint of Thomson Gale, a part of The Thomson Corporation

Detroit • New York • San Francisco • New Haven, Conn. • Waterville, Maine • London

THOMSON

GALE

™

Thorndike Press® Large Print Crime Scene.

The text of this Large Print edition is unabridged.

Other aspects of the book may vary from the original edition.

Set in 16 pt. Plantin.

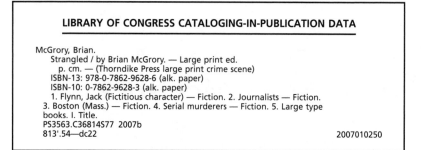

LIBRARY OF CONGRESS CATALOGING-IN-PUBLICATION DATA

McGrory, Brian.
   Strangled / by Brian McGrory. — Large print ed.
     p. cm. — (Thorndike Press large print crime scene)
   ISBN-13: 978-0-7862-9628-6 (alk. paper)
   ISBN-10: 0-7862-9628-3 (alk. paper)
   1. Flynn, Jack (Fictitious character) — Fiction. 2. Journalists — Fiction.
3. Boston (Mass.) — Fiction. 4. Serial murderers — Fiction. 5. Large type
books. I. Title.
PS3563.C36814S77 2007b
813'.54—dc22   2007010250

Published in 2007 by arrangement with Atria Books,
an imprint of Simon & Schuster, Inc.

Printed in the United States of America on permanent paper
10 9 8 7 6 5 4 3 2 1

To Harry, my best friend, and to Pam, the wonderful woman he led me to.

ACKNOWLEDGMENTS

There are many people to thank, but first a little bit of history. My interest in the Boston Strangler case was first agitated back in 1999 when I sat in the living room of a wonderful old Boston cop named Jack Barry who had just retired after fifty-three years on the job. Decades after the last murder, he could still reel off all the Strangler's victims by name.

Unbeknownst to him or me, Boston Police Captain Tim Murray, probably the best cold case cop in the country, had secretly brought some old evidence into the department's new DNA lab to answer one of the most vexing questions in the city's history: Was Albert DeSalvo really the Boston Strangler?

When I wrote that story on the front page of the *Globe,* it shot around the world in what seemed like a minute. Swamped with publicity, the department's higher-ups shut Murray down before he could come up with answers, but the uncertainty over whether DeSalvo was the right guy was out in the open all over again.

Was it DeSalvo? Author Susan Kelly presents the best case that it wasn't, in the exhaustively reported and well-written book, *The Boston Stranglers.* I borrowed liberally from her work in shaping this plot.

Likewise, I thank Casey Sherman, nephew of the last of the Strangler victims, for penning the excellent *Search for the Strangler: My Hunt for Boston's Most Notorious Killer.*

Also, thanks to a legion of *Boston Globe* and *Herald* reporters for their vivid coverage of the crimes while they were happening, and in retrospect as well.

At Atria books, I've been fortunate to be placed in the great custody of Sarah Branham, as probing and as kind-hearted an editor as I've ever met. Thanks as well to editor Emily Bestler for seeing this project through from start to finish.

Thanks to my old friend and constant sounding board, Mitch Zuckoff, a professor at Boston University, for his spot-on final read of the manuscript. The guy could copyedit the Constitution and find a dozen mistakes.

I've been blessed with the best literary agent in New York, Richard Abate of International Creative Management. These novels simply don't happen without him and his team.

Thanks as well to friends and colleagues at the *Boston Globe* for their constant support on these projects, most especially to my own editor, Michael Larkin, and the paper's editor, Marty Baron. The newspaper business is going through hell, but I still have the best job on the planet.

And to family, my most enduring and endearing readers, thank you.

1

Maybe this one would finally be his last. Of course, that's what he thought two weeks before when he stood over the decomposing body of a prematurely aged — and prematurely dead — heroin addict who was found shot to death in an abandoned two-decker in Dorchester. By the time the cops got to the guy's body, the coroner had a tough time telling the needle marks from the rat bites up and down his toothpick arms.

He had as much a chance of solving that homicide as he had of retiring to an ocean-front estate on the Gulf Coast of Florida.

Speaking of which, how the hell was he going to make it all work — not that case, not any case, but the retirement? That's what kept flashing through Detective Mac Foley's mind as he glided through the quiet city on the way to another murder scene, this one maybe the last of his forty-five-year career.

He should have been able to make it work — that's for sure. The pension wasn't bad (actually, he knew it was pretty damned good). The savings should have been there. Then there's Social Security, for whatever that's worth. But he and Sandy had to go off and have a kid late in life. What the hell were they thinking? Now he was sixty-five years old and with a daughter in college, and no, she wouldn't go to UMass like all the other kids in the neighborhood. She needed to go private, and not just any private, but — what is it that her high school guidance counselor had so proudly called it? — an elite school. *Elite* meant there was ivy clinging to the brick buildings and half his salary went to tuition. It meant that he had to take out a second mortgage on their small house. It meant that come next week, the retirement that should have been so comfortable wasn't going to be so comfortable after all.

Not all her fault, though — he knew that. She was a good kid, just getting what was hers. It was him that was the problem, or maybe his damned job. He should have been making more money. Four and a half decades as a cop, and he still held the vaunted title of "detective." No captain, no lieutenant, not even a damned sergeant. Just detective. It didn't matter shit that he was known by anyone who was anyone as the best homicide cop on the force, that he had put eighty-six men and three women — killers all — behind bars for life, that city hall itself once demanded that Mac Foley be put on a case when the mayor's cousin was killed. What mattered was how much money he had in the bank, and right now, staring down the barrel of retirement, he didn't have enough.

He thought again of Hal Harrison, the commissioner. When he wasn't thinking of his own pathetic retirement, he was thinking about the commissioner. They had the same birthday, they started at the police academy on the same day forty-five years ago, they were both elevated to detective the same month, and now they had the same retirement day. After spending his entire career keeping Foley down, making him eat four decades' worth of shit, Harrison was going out on top, with all sorts of fanfare and probably more money than he could ever spend for the rest of his life. And he was probably about to be mayor.

Mac Foley knew the lies that Harrison told to get to where he was. And now he could taste the bile in his own throat.

"Mac, good to see you, old pal. I thought

you'd already been led from the stable out to the pasture."

That was Lieutenant Dan Eldrich greeting him as Mac stepped out of his unmarked car on stately Charles Street on Boston's Beacon Hill. Mac took a quick look around at the typical scenery of his job — the three or four double-parked squad cars with their blue and white flashers cutting through the cold night air and reflecting off the glass storefronts, the foreboding medical examiner's truck idling in the street, the yellow tape, the small crowd of people craning their necks from a nearby street corner to see what was going on.

He looked up and down Charles Street, the main thoroughfare through the most famous neighborhood in the city. Gorgeous. The buildings all looked like antiques, like they were straight out of the age when Paul Revere was galloping around yelling whatever it was that he yelled. The lamps were gaslit, the shops exclusive, and the apartments above the shops expensive. He couldn't remember the last time he had been on Beacon Hill for a murder. The guy who never forgot a murder scene couldn't remember if he had ever been here for a murder, and then he did. It was forty years ago, and he was momentarily surprised at

14

himself that he could ever forget.

"This looks like a strange one," Eldrich said, wrapping an arm over Foley's shoulder as the two of them walked toward the town house building where a pair of uniformed cops stood guard at the front door. "It's why I called you specifically. I didn't want any schmuck on the rotation getting this thing and fucking it all up."

The two of them paused on the sidewalk.

"Domestic?" Foley asked.

Eldrich shook his head. "There's no domesticated guy in her life, what I'm told."

"Then maybe it's a guy who's not domesticated who did it."

Eldrich didn't reply, so Foley asked, "Shooting?"

Eldrich shook his head again. "You'll see in a minute."

"Robbery?"

Another head shake. "Victim's wallet was found in the apartment with all her credit cards and seventy-two dollars inside. And she was wearing a diamond necklace that's still on the body. No driver's license in the wallet, but we think we have a solid identification from other sources. Brace yourself. Pretty girl, approximately thirty-two years old."

"This isn't going to delay my retirement,

is it?" Foley asked. If Eldrich had been paying closer attention, he might have noticed a tinge of hope in the question.

"Never saw a homicide you couldn't solve in a week. You'll get your man and ride off into the sunset. Like a Hollywood ending."

"Yeah, sure," Foley said, turning and walking toward the entrance. He exchanged greetings with the two cops at the door. He saw that the first floor of the brick town house was taken up by a realty office, with advertisements in the big display window for multimillion-dollar condominiums and houses in the neighborhood. Everybody had money but him.

The stairway, he noted, was steep, narrow, and dark — easy to fall down should someone be making a rapid escape. The walls were bare. On the second-floor landing, the apartment door was open, and he walked inside to what appeared to be the living room, where a few fingerprint specialists, a videographer, and plainclothes cops had already set about their work. All stopped when he walked in to offer a greeting. Maybe he didn't have rank, and he certainly didn't have much money, but old Mac Foley still garnered one hell of a lot of respect.

One young cop in uniform sidled up to Foley near the door and said, "Detective, the murder scene is in the bedroom. I've kept it clear until you arrived. I wanted you to have first crack at it."

He said this, Foley noted, in a funny tone of voice, not funny like ha-ha funny, but as if he wasn't sure what had happened and was absolutely uncertain about what was to come.

Foley asked him, "Anything of note yet, Sergeant?"

"There's a lot of note, but you'll see for yourself."

Then the sergeant added, "Her roommate found her. She'd been away for the long weekend. Came in half an hour ago. Apartment was unlocked. There was a light on in the decedent's room. She poked her head inside, saw the body, ran from the building, and called 911 from her cellular telephone. I've had operations pull the tape recording for you."

The sergeant paused and added, "Why don't I show you in, Detective."

Beacon Hill apartments, Mac Foley knew, could be either stately or cramped, depending on whether the occupant was rich or nearly rich. This one was the latter. The living room, while neat, was small and dark. The kitchen, he could tell from a quick glimpse, looked like it hadn't been renovated in twenty years. Obviously a single-family had been cut up into apartments a long time ago, and had barely been touched ever since.

The sergeant led Foley through the living room and down a narrow hallway, past a bathroom, toward the rear of the unit. Where the hallway ended, there were doors — one to the left and the other to the right — bedrooms both. The sergeant, stopping just ahead of Foley, motioned toward the left and said simply and flatly, "In here, sir." Then he quickly got out of the way.

Foley slowly stepped toward the door. He'd been to, what, five hundred murder scenes over his career? A thousand? He hated to admit it, but it was true: after all those years, there was a certain sameness about them. Not only were the neighborhoods usually the same, but so were the streets. The victims were almost always black, with criminal records and substance abuse problems. Witnesses were few and far between — at least for the cops. Occasionally, he'd get the random, unfortunate eleven-year-old gunned down in gang cross fire, or the young woman in a middle-class neighborhood killed by an enraged boyfriend or husband. But they were rare, which was good.

This one, he knew, would be unusual from

the moment he heard the address.

"What's her name?" Foley asked the sergeant.

The sergeant looked down at a small piece of lined paper that he pulled out of his shirt pocket. "Jill Dawson," he replied.

Foley's eyes widened. He stared at the sergeant for a long moment, about to say something, except he didn't. Instead, he hurriedly opened the bedroom door, took one step, and abruptly stopped. He realized immediately that he wasn't just looking at a crime scene, wasn't just looking at a victim, but was also looking at his distant past.

His knees buckled slightly and he leaned quickly, reflexively, against the wall behind him, not even thinking that he might be smudging prints or compromising any other kinds of evidence.

His eyes, though, never left the corpse. She had been a young woman, pretty, with blond hair that had grown past her shoulders. She was naked from the waist down, with only a torn shirt and an unfastened bra on top, revealing her small breasts. She was propped up in her double bed on top of a white comforter, her back against the headboard, her head tilted to one side, her eyes wide open, and her legs splayed apart unnaturally, showing her pubic area. She was positioned so that when you walked into the door, she was staring straight back at you.

Foley took several long, uneasy breaths, steadied his legs, and walked toward the body. When he got closer to the bed, he saw what he had feared most. Around her neck was a ligature, a nylon stocking pulled tight, then tied into a swirling, garish bow under her chin. He saw blood in her left ear — a sure sign she had been strangled.

He'd never seen this woman before, but he'd seen the crime — too many times, forty years before, the Phantom Fiend who had come to be known as the Boston Strangler.

He pulled a pair of latex gloves from his suit pocket and walked from the side of her bed to the foot of it. There, he saw what he had thought he had noticed when he first walked into the room: an unsealed white envelope propped against her foot.

Just as he had about four decades ago, he stood bedside at a murder scene and opened an envelope. He pulled out a sheet of paper — heavy stock, not inexpensive, folded over once — and opened that up as well. With a chill, he read the crudely written words, "Happy New Year." The letters were large and sloppy, each one of them of different size. Right beneath that, the killer had written, "Picking up where I left off . . ."

Foley folded up the note, placed it back in the envelope, and rested the envelope against the woman's foot. He let his eyes roam over her body, and as he did, he felt the past crashing against the present, clouding the future — his past, his future, the commissioner's past, the commissioner's future, his city's past, the city's future. Maybe he should have felt vindicated in some odd way, but anything that had happened, anything that was about to happen, was too late to help him.

He walked toward the door and saw the uniformed sergeant still standing in the hallway, leaning against a wall.

A thought suddenly dawned on him.

"What's the address here again?" he asked the sergeant. He knew the answer already, but he had to hear it said out loud.

"One forty-six Charles Street," the sergeant replied.

The words were like pinpricks in his brain. The last victim of the Boston Strangler, or at least what he thought was the last victim of the Boston Strangler, had been killed in this very building forty years ago.

"Who's been in here?" Foley asked him, nodding toward the bedroom.

The cop ticked off five different names,

hesitating as he went on.

Foley said, "Get everyone assembled into the front room. We're going to need to talk about discretion."

With that, he pulled the bedroom door closed, but the past had already escaped.

2

There are big days and then there are *big* days, the latter totaling maybe a dozen in an entire life. I'm talking about the kinds of days that can be called to mind for better or for worse years after the fact — wedding days, divorce days, birthdays of children, the death days of parents, the days that coveted promotions were given or dreaded pink slips handed out. In other words, transformative days that alter the direction of an entire life.

This, by way of explanation, would be one of those days.

I was scheduled to be married. The lucky woman? One Maggie Kane, who entered my life approximately a year before, and then every bit as quickly fled from it. When I finally caught her in the Sixteenth Arrondissement of Paris in a story too complicated to get into here, I vowed to myself that I would never let her go.

So much for that vow. Now I wanted nothing more than to let her go. Problem was, I was due to marry her in about seven hours. I'm not saying that I'm normal, just desperate, and the whirring hands of Father Time were hardly in my favor.

It was 8:00 a.m., March 21. I stepped from wind-whipped Hanover Street, the main thoroughfare through Boston's North End, into Caffe Vittoria, the oldest and best coffee shop in town and the anchor to my morning routine. I'd order a double cappuccino, take my place at a window table to read the morning papers, listen to some of the ancient goombahs tell me that I write like the Irish cook, and then head off to the newsroom of the *Boston Record,* where I'd spend another day digging another journalistic ditch until I finally had a hole big enough to bury another villain. Next day, I'd do it all over again. It may not be much, but I consider it a pretty good life.

A life, mind you, that I suddenly realized I wanted to hang on to, in all its ever-so-subtle glory and unsubtle individuality.

"You look like a man about to lose his freedom."

That was Kenny, the server who works the espresso and cappuccino machines like Arthur Fiedler used to work the Boston Pops

24

— except Arthur had a shock of white hair where Kenny has none, and Arthur had a refined build, while Kenny looks like he just stepped off the pages of *Steroids Monthly.* At your neighborhood Starbucks, he'd be called a barista, or maybe that's a venti. I don't know. At Vittoria, given that he's about six feet four inches tall and even his eyebrows seem to have muscles, most people simply call him "sir."

"No, just my virginity," I replied.

Wedding day. Virginity. Get it? Everyone in the joint doubled over in knee-slapping hilarity.

Well, okay, nobody doubled over in any sort of hilarity. Actually, they didn't even laugh. Truth is, I've known them all too long and too well, these faux crotchety old guys with names like Sal and Vinny, and they've heard too much of my schtick before. Why I even continue to try is testament to my true spirit of American optimism. Either that, or I can't help myself.

Kenny put a big cup of cappuccino on the counter for me before I even asked, along with my usual bagel, and I retired to my regular table in the window, opened up my *New York Times,* and didn't — or maybe couldn't — read a word. The lead story was about another car bomb explosion at a checkpoint in Iraq that I couldn't pronounce. I scanned down the page and was surprised I didn't see a headline that said something like, "Jack Flynn about to surrender life as he knows it." Drop head: "Is he nuts?"

A guy named Tony, a retired plumber, put his pastry down at a nearby table and called out, "Jack, this is a wonderful thing you're doing. It'll be great to get another marriage under your belt. You'll get yourself familiar with a good lawyer, learn where the best sandwich shop is around the divorce court, the easiest places to park, maybe start a working relationship with the judge. This'll pay off in spades as you get older."

"Thanks, Tony. You're like another father to me."

My name, by the way, is Jack Flynn, and maybe, in fact, I am nuts. But before I could address that question, I had to consider another: Did I love Maggie Kane? The answer: Damned if I know, which may, in fact, be all the answer I would really need.

I mean, I must have loved her when I gave her that ring on Christmas Eve not even three months before, right? She cried, and all right, so did I, and not just over the price. We talked about the life we were going to make, the successes we would see, the kids we might have. And then when we went to bed that night, the last woman I thought of before I drifted toward a restless sleep wasn't Maggie, the wife I was about to have, but Katherine, the wife I had until she died six years before.

Time to get over it, Jack, I kept telling myself these past couple of years. Move on, let history dissolve into the present tense, still there, flavoring life, but secondary to current events.

But this issue was academic. What I had in front of me — a wedding — was ominously more realistic. The only real question I was forced to address this day, it was increasingly occurring to me, was how the flying fuck was I going to get out of it?

Think, Jack. Think.

"Congratulations, Jack, we're all so thrilled for you. We had started to think you were gay."

That was Don, short not for Donald, but Donatello, another member of the daily morning crew stopping by the table to shake hands with the happy groom-to-be.

"Don, I can't tell you how thrilled I am myself. Before Maggie came along, I was starting to think you had a nice ass."

He gave me a funny look, like I had carried the joke one notch too far. He returned to his usual seat, me to my dilemma.

By the way, it's worth pointing out that this wedding was to occur at 4:00 p.m. before a justice of the peace in a conference room of Boston City Hall. There would be no family, no friends, no witnesses, no music, no flowers, no cake, no garter belt, no bridesmaids, no groomsmen, no wedding gown, no tuxedo, no band, no nothing but me and Maggie Kane getting married and heading straight to Logan Airport for our flight to Hawaii and a lifetime of frustration and emotional confinement. In other words, the logistics were somewhat simple in all this. I really only had to inform two people of my absence — Maggie and the JP. But that seemed small solace at the moment. I needed to figure out how.

Think, Jack. Think.

I folded the paper up, having read only about six words of it. I left three-quarters of my cappuccino in the cup and half my bagel on the plate, and I headed into a future that suddenly seemed colder than the worst winter's day.

"I'll see you tomorrow," I said to Kenny on my way out the door.

"No, you won't. You'll be sitting on some island being massaged by native women and oversexed by your new wife," he replied.

No, I'd see him tomorrow. I just wasn't of the mind to correct him right then.

At eight forty-five on a Tuesday morning, the newsroom of the *Boston Record,* the newsroom of any big city daily newspaper, for that matter, is a pretty desolate place. Most self-respecting reporters are still sitting at home in ratty bathrobes chugging black coffee and chain-smoking cigarettes, wondering who they're going to screw that day and how they're going to deliver said screwing by deadline. Or maybe not.

When I walked into the *Record,* only the omnipresent and always nervous Peter Martin, the editor in chief, was in the newsroom, undoubtedly plotting that day's coverage, micromanaging his underlings before they even arrived at work, stressing over events that had yet to occur. I knew he was in the room because about thirty seconds after I had peeled off my coat and taken my seat, he appeared at my desk like a squirrel approaching a chestnut.

"So today's the big day," he said. "The long walk down the short aisle. Do you, Jack Flynn, take this woman to be your lawfully wedded wife —"

I cut him off with a simple "Not now, Peter. I don't think it's going to happen."

He didn't say anything at first, and I thought he might have been thinking about his two wedding days and the failed marriages that followed, and the fact that he wakes up every day now very much alone, married, as the cliché goes, to his job. Instead, he said with an unvarnished tone of hope, "So you mean you might be available to write today?"

Everyone — absolutely everyone — has their own agenda in this breaking story we call life.

"I have to sort a few things through, Peter," I said, my own tone betraying some incredulity that I have not an ounce of doubt he failed to detect. "I'll let you know if I'm up."

He hesitated again, and I saw his eyes form a squint and his lips start to move as if he was about to ask a question, when the aged and lovable Edgar Sullivan, director of *Boston Record* security, ambled through the room and arrived at my desk.

"Special delivery for Jack Flynn," Edgar announced, his tongue inside his cheek, where it often is.

Martin flashed a look of relief over the fact he now had the perfect excuse not to wander into the deep, dark forest of my personal life. Without so much as a good-bye, he spun on his heels and walked quickly toward his office.

Edgar handed me a manila envelope. "This was just dropped off at the front desk."

I looked at the envelope for a moment, bearing only my name on the cover. It wasn't handwritten, but rather in small typeface, which struck me as somewhat odd, but not necessarily alarming. In other words, I was wondering why Edgar had brought it up himself.

Which is when he said, "I hear today's a big day for you, Jack. I couldn't be happier. She's a wonderful woman. You're doing exactly the right thing."

He was standing over my desk. I was sitting. The room behind him was a half-lit haze of empty expanse. I replied, "I'm not going through with it, Edgar."

Without hesitation he said, "In that case, you're doing exactly the right thing." He said this with the slightest little smile forming in the wrinkles around his mouth.

And you wonder why I love the guy.

I leaned far back in my chair as he leaned against my desk. "How long have you been married?" I asked.

"Forty-seven years —" he replied proudly, as he absently stretched his arms over his head and locked his fingers together.

"That's really wonderful," I interjected.

"To four different women," he finished.

Ah. It's probably worthwhile to point out here that Edgar looked like a cross between Ward Cleaver and the Maytag Repairman. I mean, he looked like he had dinner waiting on the table every single night that he walked through the door at 6:00 p.m. sharp. Saturday night, he and the missus would go to a movie. Sunday morning was church. They called the kids on Sunday nights. Needless to say, I was somewhere between bemused and floored, or maybe a combination of the two.

"How long to the current one?" I asked.

"I'm currently between wives," he said, a mischievous look in his eyes.

"Okay, the most recent one."

"Seven years. It was a pretty good run. The one before was my personal record — fourteen years. My first and second ones were thirteen years apiece."

"You have trouble when you get into the early teens, huh?"

"It's hell," he said with a big smile. He stood straight up, slapped my thigh, and said, "Jack, whatever you do today, you'll do the right thing." And he was gone.

As Edgar limped off, I pulled the envelope

open and dumped the insides on a bare patch on my desk. Out slid a folded sheet of paper and a slightly heavier placard of some sort.

I picked up the heavier object, which turned out to be a Massachusetts driver's license for a woman by the name of Jill Dawson, who, if my math was correct, was thirty-two years of age. She wasn't smiling, but she had the kind of practiced close-mouthed camera look that I had been trying to acquire for about thirty years with precisely no success. A good-looking woman, to say the least, with a certain soft-ness to her. She had the look of someone who might volunteer at the local animal shelter while dating the star quarterback of the local NFL franchise.

I looked inside the envelope and saw noth-ing else, so I unfolded the small piece of white paper that was lying on my desk. The words were in the same kind of printed font as my name on the cover.

"You're going to help me get the word out or other women will die."

Two blank lines below that were the words "The Phantom Fiend."

It was written just like that — no com-mas, no periods, no real sense. I read it and then reread it and for good measure read it again. I looked at the envelope for any other markings I might have missed, but saw none. This was likely some stupid prank, yet I felt a pit growing in my stomach, growing into the size of an orange, then a grapefruit, then something bigger.

Obviously, prank or not, a few questions needed to be answered — for instance, what was the word? What other women would die? Who was the Phantom Fiend? Why was he sending this to me? And most urgently, given his use of the word *other,* did this mean that Jill Dawson was already dead? If she wasn't, was she about to become an unwitting target?

Jill Dawson — the name was unsettlingly familiar. I'd heard it. Maybe I had read it. I quickly started typing into the *Record*'s on-line library system, but got one of those maddening dialog boxes on my screen that said it was down for weekly maintenance. So I snatched up the phone and punched out a number to an old source at Boston Police headquarters in Schroeder Plaza.

"Sergeant Herlihy here," the voice on the other end of the line said.

"Reporter Flynn here."

"Mother of God. Let me put you on hold for a sec. I need to call my wife and tell her I'm talking to someone famous."

34

This is the kind of bullshit I put up with every day in my valiant and unswerving pursuit of news.

"If you can knock off the stand-up comedy routine for half a second," I told him, "I have a quick question."

"For a celebrity reporter, anything."

"The name Jill Dawson mean anything to you?"

Sergeant Kevin Herlihy, a longtime source of mine dating back to when I was a young crime-and-grime reporter and he was a cop walking a pretty dangerous beat, mulled over that question for a moment, or at least he mulled over whether he wanted to answer it.

After a moment he said, "Check your own morgue. Murder victim. Found dead in her Beacon Hill apartment on January third. Case unsolved, last that I know. Homicide has revealed very little information, even to us grunts in uniform."

"As always, thank you."

I quickly hung up before he had a chance to take a parting verbal jab.

What had started as a pit was now a watermelon. I was holding the driver's license of a murdered woman, along with a note that said there'd be more victims unless I helped get some mysterious word out.

I hated to say it, but this certainly solved one problem, or, more accurately, delayed it. I snatched up the phone and punched out the cell number to Maggie Kane. I expected to get her voice mail, but instead she picked up on the third ring. I heard an announcer's voice in the background cutting through the din of commotion, telling people something about a final boarding.

"Maggie, hey there." I paused, still listening to that announcer. "Hey, where are you?"

"The Atlanta airport," she replied. Her words came out flat, uncertain.

"Are you traveling on business?" Soon as I asked this, I felt ridiculous. Maggie Kane teaches third grade.

"No, Jack. Listen, I was about to call you."

My head was spinning so fast I thought it might fly off my neck. My vision was actually blurred. On what was supposed to be our wedding day, the happy bride-to-be was sitting in the Hartsfield-Jackson Atlanta International Airport, and I think it's a pretty safe conclusion that she wasn't getting on a plane bound for home. Admittedly, the happy groom was planning to kibosh the whole deal, but that's not really the point here.

"Jack," she said before I could say anything. "Jack, I was about to call you. I'm really sorry. I'm, well, I'm just not ready to go through with this right now."

Just like that.

I mumbled "I'll call you later," and hung up the phone. I should have been relieved. I should have told her that I understood what she felt. But what I really felt was angry, and, surprisingly, a little fearful, though of what, I wasn't exactly sure.

Like I said, I knew it was going to be a big day. I just had no idea why.

3

It's one thing for a reporter to harbor suspicions in a murder case. Hell, suspicion is the backbone of some of the best and most basic newspaper stories. Is the governor right to say she can balance the state budget without raising taxes? Did the president really not have sex with that woman? Did that priest really have all those young boys' best interests at heart?

But it's quite another thing for a reporter to be harboring evidence in a murder case, and evidence was exactly what I seemed to be harboring, as I leaned over my desk and studied the driver's license photograph of a recently deceased woman I never met by the name of Jill Dawson.

She had big blue eyes and shoulder-length dirty-blond hair that looked like it was cut by one of the more expensive stylists — what do they call themselves these days, coiffures? — on Newbury Street. She seemed to have a quiet confidence, like the eldest child of a happily married couple in an affluent suburb like Newton or Wayland. She probably graduated in the top five percent of her high school class, went off to Haverford or Swarthmore, and still takes a vacation with her best friends from college at least once a year. Some guy was probably extremely happy as her boyfriend or husband — unless, of course, that same guy killed her.

Jill Dawson. Yet another woman I met in the past tense. And looking at her, I bet I would have liked her. A lot.

My little newsroom reverie was interrupted by Peter Martin and Edgar Sullivan, who approached my desk the way a cold front approaches New England, which is to say ominously and silently, and beckoned me into the nearby, glass-walled conference room.

"We have the digital tape, but it doesn't show much," Edgar said as he pushed a disc into a DVD player. A plasma television screen mounted on the wall lit up, Edgar pressed a button, and the camera froze on the image of a rather overweight security guard sitting at the front desk of the *Record,* reading — what the hell is this? — the rival *Boston Traveler.*

"Aha, we've finally caught Scully in the act," I said, maybe a little too animatedly. Both Martin and Edgar ignored me, which I guess is their right, impolite as that might be.

Well, not exactly ignored me. Edgar began his brief presentation by saying, "Jack, if you could just put a zipper on it for about three minutes, that might be helpful.

"As you can see, this camera is trained on the front desk in the lobby. A camera mounted on the wall behind the front desk facing the other way, but was out of order this morning, which is, of course, our bad luck."

On the screen, Scully flipped the pages of the *Traveler,* probably from the gossip column to the horse race results. I took Edgar's counsel and didn't say this out loud.

"And here comes our visitor," Edgar said. He now had a pointer in his hand and pointed out the reflection on the shiny tile floor as the big front door opened, then a shadow which was really little more than a fuzzy glare.

The figure seemed to approach Scully from the side of the desk, as if whoever it was had knowledge of the camera angle and was walking outside the line of vision.

"Here's where we see actual flesh," Edgar

said. And just like that, an arm appeared on the screen, handing Scully the manila envelope that was delivered to my desk shortly after. The arm was partially concealed by what appeared to be Scully, who barely looked up from his paper. Maybe he was trying to figure out if he had hit the trifecta the day before. The arm disappeared, and the shadow receded out the door.

"And that's it," Edgar said. "That's our courier."

And probably our murderer, I thought.

Martin said, "We'll have to turn that over to the cops, even though it doesn't show anything. But let's make a duplicate and keep a copy for ourselves."

Edgar nodded and shut down the DVD player. He said, "We could dust that driver's license for prints."

I asked, "You know how to fingerprint something?"

"No idea. I'd send it out."

Smartly, Martin interjected, "Even if we got any prints off it, which is doubtful, we have no database to run them through. It'd be meaningless to us."

I sat back in my chair as those two got up to leave the conference room. I said, "So I call the cops with the news of the license. I offer them the tape. They'll want to talk to

Scully. They'll probably want an original copy of the note. And we get nothing. Peter, right now, I don't even think we have a story."

I swear to God, Martin's nose twitched like the little news rodent he can be, though I'm not sure if it was out of nerves or because he had the scent of something very big. He said, "It's only ten o'clock in the morning. This cycle's just begun."

And with that, prescient as ever, he walked out the door.

My first official call on the case, if there is such a thing that a reporter can make, was to the lieutenant in the homicide bureau of the Boston Police Department, an FOJ (friend of Jack) by the name of Leo Goldsmith.

Leo is just old-school enough that he doesn't have the current-day mentality nurtured in precinct houses and at daily roll calls that reporters are the real bad guys and that the only time you should ever talk to them is to mislead them.

Back in the old days, from what I've been told, cops and reporters used to be comrades in arms. Newspaper photographers and police reporters who cruised the city with a dashboard filled with scanners and a car roof groaning under the weight of antennas would often beat cops to crime scenes. They'd see the same things, crack the same jokes, and at the end of their shifts tell the same stories about the same cases over a pint of beer in some bucket-of-blood bar.

But somewhere along the line, there was a gargantuan split. I think it might be Woodward and Bernstein's fault. After they brought down a president and, more important, had their work glorified by Hollywood, newsrooms suddenly drew a better-educated brand of reporters who hailed from wealthier backgrounds. They didn't carry names like Tommy and Billy anymore, but Jonathan and Eric. They took lunch at fancy joints downtown, which I personally don't have a problem with. But suddenly, the two sides weren't even speaking the same language, or if they were, they certainly didn't speak them with the same words. Suspicion eventually, perhaps inevitably, turned to animosity. Now cops and reporters, often seeking similar truths for the same greater cause, are from two different planets.

Because of this, I take no small amount of pride in my ability to relate to my friends in blue, an ability that I've used to my significant advantage over my entire career.

"I've got something for you, and I'm hoping you've got something for me."

That's how I opened the bargaining session with Lieutenant Leo Goldsmith. He may not have realized it, though probably he did, but a set of negotiations were about to take place, and he represented one side of it.

"What I've got is about one minute," he replied. "We're getting called out on another case."

All right, this wasn't going exactly as planned. The thing about reporting is that few things ever do. The one phone number you need will always be the unlisted one. The crucial official that you need to supply the last key fact in a story is invariably going to be away on vacation, probably in a Third World country, often on a river cruise without any use of a phone. The file you need in federal court is inevitably the one that's inexplicably missing.

"Jill Dawson," I said.

Before I could continue, he interjected. "I've got nothing on that one for you. Absolutely nothing. And take that at face value. I'm not being told anything about the case, and best as I can tell, the decisions on that one are being made way above my pay grade."

"I've got her driver's license," I said. "It

sibility of seeing yourself in those. When the waiter came around, I asked, "Could I have a tall glass of hemlock?"

He looked at me quizzically. Mac Foley actually laughed — as in a real-life, full-on, can't-keep-it-inside laugh. Then I added, "Just kidding."

"I could use a double one of those myself," Foley said to me, leaning in. But the warmth quickly vanished. He stood up, kept his gaze on me a moment longer than I expected, and walked away into an unlit corner of the vast room.

Onstage, Senator Callaghan was describing Commissioner Harrison as a "great American," "civic treasure," and "courageous crimefighter." Forget the hemlock and give me a noose. I couldn't take even another minute of this oral flatulence.

I mean, don't get me wrong. Harrison was a good enough cop, I'm sure. At least the city never seemed ready to tilt out of control under his leadership. But my God, politicians laying it on thick for other politicians — that I've always found to be an unseemly sight.

Across the room, I noticed that Mac Foley had settled into another table and was talking intently to yet another cop in a navy blazer and loosely knotted tie. I think they were talking about me. I think this because at one point, the jackass Foley was talking to pointed right at me and Foley said what looked to be "That's him." I don't think they were trying to pick out the guy in the crowd with the most defined abs. This was most definitely strange.

From the podium, all I heard was more blah-blah-blah, and then amid the white noise and nothingness, I heard a word — or maybe it was a phrase — that struck a nerve. It was as if someone had just slapped me across the face. I quickly dialed back into Stu Callaghan, thinking I must have misunderstood something that he had said.

". . . when the city was in crisis, and he was the one to bring order to it all by cracking that case open like an egg, saving lives and creating calm. He put the Phantom Fiend behind bars for the rest of his dangerous life . . ."

My package. My tip. My note. I looked reflexively toward Mac Foley, who happened to be looking directly back at me, a stern look now, his brow furrowed, his eyes cold. He quickly averted his gaze.

When he did, I got up out of my seat in that crouched way you do when you're trying to be unobtrusive. The crowd was applauding the senator, who was paying tribute to the commissioner. As I slid past Mongillo, I noticed that he was most definitely not clapping. "I'll see you tomorrow morning," I whispered to him. And I was gone. The night had paid off in the oddest way.

5

Once in a cab on Arlington Street, I belted out the number to the *Record* morgue, which isn't really a morgue at all, even if the people in it can seem half-dead some of the time. No, it's journalese for the newspaper library. I asked them to check again what I had already failed to find, which was any reference to the term *Phantom Fiend* in our computer database of *Record* stories.

"Where to?" the cabdriver asked as I flipped the telephone shut.

Good question. I checked my watch — ten o'clock — and thought about how the plane I was supposed to be aboard with Maggie Kane was just touching down in Los Angeles. The plan had been to spend our wedding night at Raffles L'Ermitage in Beverly Hills before grabbing an early-morning connection to Hawaii and enjoying a blissful week of sun and sex at a world-class resort.

And here I was, the brokenhearted pen pal to a possible murderer, sitting in the back of an idling cab with what smelled like a quasi-eaten Big Mac in a discarded bag on the floor.

But back to the question at hand: Where to? My head hurt. My muscles ached. I felt like the entire world was a crowded elevator ride, only the elevator was broken and we were all standing still, looking at the numbers above the doors, frozen in time and place.

"The Hatch Shell, please. Over on the Esplanade."

The cabdriver, an older gentleman with a graying ponytail, turned and looked at me for the first time. "Excuse me?" he asked, not so much curious as incredulous.

"You know, the Hatch Shell. The Fourth of July concert and all that. 'Stars and Stripes Forever.' "

"You're aware that this is March twenty-first, right, not the fricking Fourth of July?"

I replied, "Can you roll the window down? Now that I'm with you, I might as well fling my Palm Pilot away."

Truth is, I didn't actually use a Palm Pilot, but still thought the line was pretty good. He didn't. Rather, he turned back around with something of an eye roll and a huff, and lurched away from the front doors of the Ritz, bound for Storrow Drive.

You see, I had an idea, one that involved exercise for the body and therapy for the mind. My gym was closed at this hour, so that option was taken off the table. Last time I shot baskets at the court near my waterfront condominium, someone nearly shot me, so I preferred not to do that. I was indulging in the next best thing.

My phone rang. It was Howard from the *Record* library.

"I'm getting no hits off the phrase *Phantom Fiend*," he said. He said this in a voice so soft and a tone so flat that I had to wonder if he was taking this morgue nickname to an unhealthy extreme.

I thanked him. He returned to his coffin or wherever it is that he goes between pesky calls from reporters. I looked up as the cabdriver was pulling off Storrow Drive into a little parking area next to the famed Hatch Shell, an open-air stage that sits hard by the Charles River in downtown Boston.

"Where?" he asked, not very polite now.

"Here's fine." I paid him as if this was the most normal destination in the city, and casually got out of the car. He pulled back into traffic. I took a minute to let my eyes adjust to the dark.

The wind was blowing downriver from the west, colder than I had anticipated, but invigorating just the same. To my left was the lawn where thousands upon thousands of people would cram in with coolers, baskets, and blankets for the annual Fourth of July concert and fireworks celebration. At the moment, it was dark and empty, the grass still brown and spare from a long, snowy winter. To my right was the stage that would be filled with the Boston Pops Orchestra on that same holiday night. Now it was vacant and forlorn, looking like the open mouth of a ventriloquist's dummy abandoned in the corner of a dark bedroom. I bundled my overcoat around myself and set off toward the water.

With each step, the traffic noise of the roadway faded, and the sounds of my wingtips on the gravelly pavement grew more pronounced. I felt my muscles start to twitch with adrenaline. I felt my head begin to lighten with the anticipation of exercise.

I approached the old brick edifice of the Union Boat Club, a rare building on the miles-long expanse of the Esplanade, which is the local name for the grassy bank of this storied river. I pulled my key chain from my pocket and fidgeted beneath a floodlight for the right key. I put it inside a rusty lock on a rickety knob, pushed the door open, and stepped inside.

The smell was one of all-encompassing mustiness, like another year, a different season, had sat here frozen in time. I flicked a wall switch and an overhead light came on, illuminating a small, barely furnished office. I had taken up rowing the year before, and the club was nice enough to accept me as a member in good standing.

I opened yet another door and walked into a vast, dark space. Again, I flicked a wall switch and the large storage garage lit up, revealing stacks of sculling boats hanging on all four walls, as well as piles of weathered oars.

I yanked open the garage door, which made more noise than I expected, carried the shell down to the nearby dock, and returned to the building. I grabbed a couple of oars, wriggled into a life vest, donned an old down parka that had probably been hanging on a peg since the first Roosevelt administration, and headed back to the dock.

Let's not kid around here: it was cold out, and given that I had just taken up the sport of crew, I had never been on the water in this kind of weather. For that matter, I had never been on the water this deep into a dark night. But the moon was bright and the sight lines were good and I'd heat up within the down jacket as soon as I began rowing. The wingtips might be a little awkward, but hey, life's a little bit awkward most of the time.

Once on the water, the first push with my legs and pull on the oars felt impossible, like my ribs might crack apart and fall through the black skin of the river. The boat tilted sideways, and I leaned toward the other side to balance it out and pulled on the oars again, a little smoother this time. Still, the boat was wobbly. I straightened it out again and took another pull. Better. And another. Before I knew it, I was thirty yards offshore, the boat's nose heading directly upwind, which was good, because it kept the howling air at my back.

Suddenly, I had movement and a rhythm, thrusting with my legs, pulling with my arms and back, sliding across the surface. Thrusting, pulling, thrusting, pulling. The whole thing was as therapeutic as I had imagined, though I probably could've been locked up in a special room with white padding for being out there at that hour on a March night.

Inevitably, my mind wandered. I thought of Peter Martin pressing me earlier that day for a story that I didn't yet have. I thought of Maggie Kane, wherever she was, running from, well, me. I thought of the Phantom Fiend, whoever he was, and Vinny Mongillo holding court among cops in the ballroom of the Ritz. I thought ahead to the immediate future, how there were too few answers to too many questions on too many fronts — always a dangerous deficit in my line of work. And then my mind wandered far enough afield that I was thinking of nothing at all but my breath and my motion and the little splashes of cold water with each steady row.

Finally, I began thinking of the soft purring I heard in the distance and looked overhead to see if a medical chopper was fluttering down the river toward Massachusetts General Hospital. I saw no lights.

The sound grew louder, grinding closer. I slowed down my rowing and looked to my left, and then to my right, and saw a tiny flashlight hovering over the water about a hundred yards away toward the middle of the river — apparently a boat. I assumed it was a state police trooper on late-night patrol — someone who was undoubtedly wondering what kind of moron was rowing in a scull at this hour.

Sure enough, the sound of the engine got

louder still, the light brighter. I pulled the oars up and rested for a moment, the wind still banging at my neck, the sky unusually bright above. The light continued toward me, close enough that I could hear voices — men, I believe, shouting above the din of the outboard.

About twenty yards away, I could see what looked to be the outlines of a small powerboat, perhaps a Boston whaler. I could make out the silhouettes of two people standing inside it. One of them appeared to be peering through binoculars or some sort of nightscope at me. I thought I heard one of them say to the other, "No life jacket," though I could have been wrong, what with the wind and the engine and my own labored breathing. If he did say it, he was wrong; the vest happened to be concealed by the blocky down parka. I failed to see, it's worth noting, any sort of blue police light on the visiting boat.

At about fifteen yards away, I called out, "Can I help you?" Granted, it was a dumb question; I was in a scull, they were in a powerboat. But I thought it might be advantageous, at least to me, to get a dialogue started.

In response, I got no response, except that the driver of the boat gunned the engine and veered sharply to his left — toward the rear of my shell. He zipped off toward the shore, the boat melting into the darkness.

My shell, meanwhile, rocked violently from his wake, almost to the point of capsizing. I struggled to maintain equilibrium, like a cowboy on a bucking bronco, until the waves settled down and I finally achieved it.

And then came the grinding sound all over again, this time in my face, meaning from the rear of the scull. It got louder more quickly than before, though with no light. Soon I saw the powerboat, first as a hazy form, then in greater definition. It came roaring at me, its speed increasing, and cut just to my right, coming within five yards of the side of my boat. It appeared to be the Union Club's small powerboat that was kept in the storage garage.

Again I surged sideways. I could feel my entire right side up in the air, as if I was on one of those amusement park rides that used to invariably make me puke as a kid. I tucked my head down, preparing to flip over, but miraculously came just short of the tipping point, a phrase I understood more intimately at that moment than I ever intended. I splashed back down on the river, the water hitting my face, my arms, and my hair. I rocked back and forth for another couple of minutes before the waves died down again.

Okay, so these weren't cops. But who?

I could still hear the whir of their outboard motor, but could no longer see the craft. As I held my balance, I started thinking where else a heartbroken reporter amid a potentially huge story would have gone to wash away his sorrow and anxieties. The Bristol Lounge at the Four Seasons wouldn't have been a bad choice; the worst thing that could have happened is that someone might have tipped my wineglass over rather than my scull. But no, here I was in the middle of the Charles River legitimately wondering if I'd ever get back to terra firma alive.

I pointed the boat toward the shoreline and started rowing madly. Louder came the engine. The spotlight suddenly illuminated again, shining directly in my eyes. I heard someone on the boat say, "The bastard's still up." Probably not for long, I wanted to tell them, but didn't have the time. They accelerated toward me from the front of the boat, meaning from my back, veered off again at the last minute, and sped away. And in one giant swell, I flipped helplessly into the water, as if it was my destiny.

I probably don't have to report how cold

the Charles River felt in the middle of an unseasonably cool Boston March, but I will. I will. It was fucking freezing. It was the type of cold that made you believe your fun parts would never again be any fun — in fact, they'd probably have to be amputated in the off chance you got out of this alive. It was mind-numbing, head-pounding, body-enveloping cold.

Immediately, I bobbed back to the surface and resisted the urge to scream for help. The only people who would have heard me were the same people trying to drown me. I treaded water and let my eyes adjust. The scull was but a few feet from me; the shoreline to my right about fifty yards away.

That's when I heard the motor again and saw the light sweeping across the black skin about ten yards to my left. If they saw me, they would try again to kill me. As much as I couldn't believe I was doing this, I dove under the freezing water in the direction of my boat, surfaced just in front of it, jockeyed underneath it, and pushed my face up into the air pocket where I had previously sat.

I could feel my body going completely numb, to the point that I wondered if I would eventually be able to swim for shore. I could sense my head going woozy, as if I might pass out, in which case I knew I wouldn't be getting to shore. I thought of the time I dove into the frigid waters of Boston Harbor after an intruder, as well as the afternoon I had to paddle through a Florida swamp to get away from an attacker who preferred me dead. I spent more time in the damned drink than a trainer at Sea-World. I made a mental note to bill the *Record* for some swimming lessons if I ever got out of this mess alive.

Finally, I could hear the outboard engine sputtering slowly just a few feet away, causing little ripples as it circled the scull.

I heard one of my would-be killers say, "He's in the drink, and he's not surviving more than five minutes in those temperatures."

No kidding.

I heard the second man say, "Let's get out of here." The engine roared, and then quickly faded from earshot. I ducked back underwater, surfaced again in the open river, and thrashed slowly toward the shore.

What seemed like five days later, I made it. I staggered across some large rocks, up onto the grassy expanse, and collapsed onto my knees. I didn't know much about hypothermia, but I did know this: Do not fall asleep. I'd be a goner. So I forced myself up and plodded onward, across a field, along a paved, lighted path, and toward a footbridge over Storrow Drive. The one advantage of being this cold was that I had reached a point of not being able to feel a thing. It was as if I was watching myself amble onward rather than actually doing it.

Finally, I made it over to the other side of the bridge into Back Bay. I lurched down an alley, got to Beacon Street, and began frantically waving at traffic. Within two seconds, a car, a cab no less, screeched to a halt. I fumbled with the door handle. Truth is, my hands were so cold that I had lost any refined motor skills. It took both hands to finally pry it open, and I slumped into the seat with a mix of abject fear and absolute relief.

"Mass General Hospital," I said. I tried saying it firmly, but the words came out as if I was being violently shaken, which I suppose, in a way, I was.

The driver, I noticed through my hazy vision, had a long, gray ponytail. He turned around and gave me a suspicious look, maintaining complete silence. He pulled back into traffic while muttering into the rearview mirror, "I knew you were up to no good."

Then why the hell hadn't he told me?

6

When the telephone rang, I was having a dream about trying to swim across the frigid waters of the English Channel, where my dog, Baker, my wife, Katherine, and my unnamed daughter all awaited my arrival on the other side. I would have liked to have stayed asleep long enough to have our reunion.

"Hello," I muttered into the receiver. It was pitch-black out. My head ached. I was unspeakably tired. My body still felt freezing from the river, especially my farthest extremities.

"You're not answering your cell phone."

It was Peter Martin. I didn't have the wherewithal at the moment to explain that my cell phone was drying out on a radiator next to various articles of clothing, all of them soaked by a pair of men who had tried to kill me on the high seas the night before.

Instead I said, "Long story."

He ignored that, obviously not interested in a narrative of any length. I looked at the red digits of my alarm clock, which told me it was 5:30 a.m. I had only gone to bed about three hours earlier, after persuading the nice doctors in the Massachusetts General Hospital emergency room that I wasn't in any need of further observation and was fine to go. In the age of managed care, they seemed a little too fine with that.

"I just had an idea. We've got to get together and talk. I need you and Mongillo in here as soon as possible. I want him on this story with you."

I cleared my throat and said, "Peter, it's still yesterday, for chrissakes."

He ignored that as well. When Peter Martin gets something in his mind, he's not to be sidetracked. He asked, though not really in the form of a question, "Can you get here in an hour. We need an early jump on the day."

Early jump? There were farmers in Nebraska who would roll back over at that hour. But there wasn't any real reason for me to reply, so I simply hung up the phone.

I lay in bed thinking the same basic questions as I had a few hours earlier when I went to sleep. Who tried to kill me? Was it the same person who sent me Jill Dawson's driver's license? Did the killer have a change of heart and now want me dead? What was with that glare that I seemed to get from Detective Mac Foley at the end of the night, and why was he pointing me out to another cop? This may have been the most intriguing question, because it begged another: Did some cops follow me from the banquet and down to the river? And yet another: Why the hell would police investigators want me dead?

My brain was spinning in more ways than one as I pushed back the covers and struggled to my feet. I lived in a condominium on the Boston waterfront, and had a view of the harbor and ocean beyond, but I don't recall ever having seen a sunrise quite like this one, mostly because I don't recall ever actually seeing a sunrise here. In the distance, across a black expanse of nothingness, was the faint light of morning that quietly announced the start of a new day, one that would undoubtedly be an adventurous, perhaps dangerous, but not necessarily enlightening one.

I showered. I downed a few handfuls of dry cereal — Honey Smacks, to be precise, formerly known as Sugar Smacks before we the people became like we did about what we eat and feed our kids. I thought, of course, about how I should have been waking up in Beverly Hills to a glorious room-service breakfast with my beautiful new wife, getting ready for a week in paradise. Instead, I snapped up the cordless phone on my kitchen counter amid a funereal silence that fit my mood, if not my life, the only occasional sound the wind knocking up against the windows. I didn't imagine it was a warm wind, either. Truth is, I didn't imagine I'd ever be warm again. I tapped out the number to the hotel that we were supposed to be staying at in Hawaii, trying to think of a dignified way to cancel the Honeymoon Package. I really couldn't come up with one, though it didn't matter. The manager I needed to speak to wasn't around.

Well, this was certainly a nice way to start the day. I checked my voice mails. There was nothing good — meaning, specifically, nothing from Maggie Kane.

So at six-ten on a March morning, I was off, the world cold in so many ways. There was somebody out there who was going to be very disappointed that I was still alive today. The key for me was to make sure I was still alive tomorrow.

That's when I saw it on the floor of my entryway, like someone had gained access to my building and slipped it under my door. It was a manila envelope much like the one that was delivered to my desk by the *Record*'s security director, Edgar, the morning before — oversized, with my name printed on it in a blocky typeface. I had my overcoat on by now, over a suit coat, and I stood by the door and held the envelope in my hand for a long moment. I could already feel something of a more substantial weight inside than a sheet of paper. I didn't like where this was going.

I carefully opened it from the top, trying to slice it as cleanly as possible in case any part of the envelope held evidence that I couldn't see. I carefully pulled out a single sheet of folded paper. I opened it and read the note in the familiar typeface. "Back again," it said. "More women will die." On a separate line, the typed signature, "The Phantom Fiend."

I stared at the words until the letters blurred and I was looking at nothing but the page they were written on. Whoever left this for me had gained access to the building, knew which apartment I lived in, and slipped it under the door, apparently fearless about being seen or caught. I wondered if the envelope was already on the floor when I stumbled through the door after my late-night swim at about two o'clock. No way of knowing. In the state I was in, and I don't mean Massachusetts, I easily could have walked right over it. The thought crossed my mind that this envelope was a good indication that the Phantom Fiend was not one of the guys in the boat trying to kill me.

The envelope still had some heft to it, so I reached tentatively inside and felt a small rectangular placard. I had the sense of holding someone's death warrant — or perhaps death certificate. I pulled it out slowly and saw a woman's smiling visage on a Massachusetts driver's license. She had dark hair parted in the middle that framed a slender face with a long jaw. Her eyes were big and blue, her mouth large in that Carly Simon kind of way. She looked like someone who knew what she wanted in this world and wasn't afraid to spend time and capital to get it. Her name was Lauren S. Hutchens, and if she wasn't dead already, she was probably about to be.

The license listed an address in Lexington, a wealthy suburb about a dozen miles northwest of Boston. I ran back to the phone, dialed information, and asked for a Lauren Hutchens in Lexington.

I went through that whole computerized

rigmarole that usually means there is nobody by that name, and then a woman got on the line and told me I was out of luck.

"Any Hutchenses in Lexington," I asked, trying not to sound breathless, though I was of the mind that time had suddenly become crucial.

"I have one, a Walter Hutchens on Dome Road," she said.

I told her I'd take it, and dialed it as quickly as my fingers would allow.

Come about the fifth ring, the sleepy voice of a woman said, "Hello." It was then I realized how early in the morning this was. Didn't matter. I asked for Lauren. The woman hesitated and said, "She doesn't live here."

"Any idea how I might get in contact with her?" I asked.

"This is her mother. She moved into Boston last year. Can I help you with something?"

My heart sank. The truth was not a viable option, not the whole truth, anyway. I said, "This is Jack Flynn, a reporter for the *Boston Record.* I'm trying to speak with Lauren about a story I'm writing."

A long silence, long to me anyway. I wondered if she was about to tell me that her daughter was dead, the victim of a murderer who hadn't yet been caught. Instead she said, still sleepy, "She moved into town a year ago."

"Do you have her number?" I asked, trying to sound neither pushy nor panicked.

"I can call her and pass along your information."

Everyone's suspicious of the news media these days.

I gave her my cell phone and work numbers and asked if she could call sooner rather than later. And with that, I hung up.

I dialed information again, this time asking for a Lauren Hutchens in Boston. There was an L. Hutchens on Park Drive, and I called that number but got no answer. When it kicked over to a recorded greeting, the woman's voice, strong and resonant, sounded like it would go with the picture that I held in my hand. I asked her to call me and gave her my numbers. I had something more than a feeling that she'd never have the chance.

7

Peter Martin and Vinny Mongillo were already sitting in Martin's corner office as I made my way through the darkened, empty newsroom, the Phantom Fiend's envelope in my hand, a little bit of dread in my heart — and maybe a tinge of embarrassment and a bit of excitement over the story that was beginning to unfold.

The two of them were sitting at a small, square conference table when I walked in, Mongillo taking the last bite of a Krispy Kreme doughnut that he had pulled from a half-empty box that sat between them. Truth be told, Mongillo had lost about seventy-five pounds in the prior year and was continuing to lose weight the way Frank Sinatra shed wives, until Krispy Kreme opened its first store in Boston proper. The board of directors of Krispy Kreme Doughnuts, Inc., must set aside ten minutes at their annual meetings just to pay homage to

Vinny Mongillo.

Martin pointed to the chair to his right, in an apparent invitation, though maybe it was a command. I don't know. As I sat, he said to me, "I woke up with a jolt last night. I had this thought that you may not be the only reporter in town that the Phantom Fiend is corresponding with. And if you're not, someone else might get this story into print before us."

He had a point, as he often does, even if it seemed needless to make it at 6:30 a.m. I was already becoming proprietary about the Phantom Fiend. Yes, he may have been a killer, but he was *my* killer, and I'd just as soon keep it that way.

Mongillo coughed hard. I thought I saw a piece of chewed doughnut land on the table in front of me, but didn't want to inspect it too closely for fear that I was right. I asked Martin, "What makes you think that?"

"Wichita," he replied. "The BTK serial killer back in the seventies and eighties. He sent a letter to the local paper that mistakenly got routed to the classified ad department. He was so frustrated that his name didn't get into print that he started writing to TV reporters, radio reporters, the cops. Anyone with a fricking PO box. They lost control of the story. I don't want that to happen here."

I nodded. Mongillo tried to speak for the first time since I arrived, but his voice was choked by the doughnut that he was coughing up. He began coughing again.

I ignored him and pushed the envelope toward Martin. "We've heard from him again," I said.

Martin's eyes shone bright, the same look Mongillo tends to get when you place a nicely seasoned cut of prime rib before him. He tenderly — almost lovingly — fingered the envelope and pulled out the note and driver's license inside. I worried for a moment about contaminating potential fingerprints, but then thought that surely this killer wasn't moronic enough not to wear gloves.

Martin stared at them both in silence. Finally, he looked up and asked me, "Is Lauren Hutchens dead?"

I brought him up to date on my phone calls and concluded, "I don't know."

Meantime, Mongillo was hacking and wheezing and making various guttural noises that are rarely heard beyond the hog lots of Iowa. Finally, thankfully, he stood up and left the room. Martin never even gave him a look.

In Vinny's absence, Martin asked, "Do we

knock on her door or do we call the police?"

An excellent question, one that I had contemplated on my drive into work. The safe thing to do, the responsible thing to do, would have been to call Mac Foley and tell him I was holding the driver's license of a young woman, courtesy of the same person who sent me Jill Dawson's license. The one problem with that scenario was that once I made that call, I would effectively lose control over the story. Foley wasn't of the mind to play much ball with the *Record,* not yet anyway.

But equally problematic was the question of how the paper would benefit if I knocked on Hutchens's door. What could I possibly discover that might outweigh the possibility of somehow fouling valuable evidence?

"I think we have to call the police immediately," I said.

At that moment, Mongillo walked back into the room, a tissue in his hand and his eyes rimmed with red from his coughing fit. He sat down dramatically, turned to me, and said, "Can I see those notes he sent you?"

I slid him the most recent one and pulled a photocopy of the first note from a notebook in front of me. Mongillo read them over in silence. He made a motion with his hand, and Martin handed him Lauren Hutchens's license.

Finally, he looked up at me.

"You know who the Phantom Fiend is, right?"

I shook my head and replied, "I've been trying to find that out for twenty-four hours, but the library has nothing on him."

Mongillo looked from me to Martin and back to me. "It's the Boston Strangler."

The Boston Strangler? My mind began racing like a Chincoteague pony. The most famous serial killer in United States history — though Son of Sam might have an issue with that. He inspired fear, then books, then a major motion picture starring Tony Curtis. Though I knew very little about him, I did know this: He would slip into women's apartments all around town and in the suburbs. He would strangle them with some sort of ligature. He would occasionally leave bows around their necks. And he was gone.

Before either me or Martin could reply, Mongillo added, "The news media back then first dubbed the Boston Strangler as the Phantom Fiend. That's what he was most commonly called at the time. It was later in the murder spree, with all the hype, that his nickname was changed."

That might well be true, but I also knew

something else about the Boston Strangler, or at least I thought I did: He was dead, the victim of a murderer in Walpole State Prison sometime in the early 1970s. Best as I could remember, no one was ever charged.

Which is what I told Vinny. Specifically, I said, "The Boston Strangler was killed, wasn't he? I mean, he's dead."

Mongillo looked back at me and held my gaze.

"No," he said, slowly, firmly, and decisively. "Albert DeSalvo was killed. That's who you think was the Boston Strangler. That's who the public was told was the Boston Strangler. But if you ask almost any good cop who was in the area around that time, they'll tell you that DeSalvo was definitely not the Boston Strangler. The Strangler was never caught. He's still out there somewhere."

He paused here, staring at some distant point, or more likely at nothing at all. I cast a glance toward Martin. Normally, even famously pale, he now looked even whiter than usual. He was staring at Mongillo, his thoughts all but bursting out his eyes and ears.

Mongillo said, "Now he's killing more women. He wants you to write about it. And we've got to get to Lauren Hutchens's place to check it out."

We pulled up in front of Lauren Hutchens's address on Park Drive in the Fenway section of Boston. Fenway Park, by the way, is named for the neighborhood, not the other way around, and Park Drive is named for the Fenway, which is a park, though not Fenway Park. This explanation could probably go on all day, like the fact that South Boston and the South End are two different neighborhoods, and Roxbury and West Roxbury are nowhere near each other. Or that the West End doesn't actually exist. It's a Boston thing. You live in town, you don't think anything of it.

Lauren lived — and possibly died — in a tan-colored cinder-block apartment building that stood seven stories tall, and in stark contrast to the ancient Federalist-style brick town houses all around it. This had obviously been built in the 1950s, as architectural taste had taken a decade-long hiatus while the nation had better things to think about, like family cookouts, the GI Bill, and drinking enough whole milk.

I pulled my Honda to the curb and pulled out my cell phone. "You think I should call the cops now?" I asked Mongillo.

The plan was that we were going to position ourselves as close to Lauren Hutchens's apartment as humanly possible, call the police with the information about the note and the driver's license, then hopefully get a firsthand view of what had happened inside.

"Hold off for just another minute," Mongillo said, taking a long sip of his coffee, which he had insisted on stopping for on the way over. He first insisted on stopping at Starbucks, until I pointed out that a woman's life was potentially hanging in the balance while he waited the requisite twenty minutes for some barrister, or whatever they call themselves, with a nose ring and an art history degree to handcraft his venti, no-foam, whole-milk caramel latte. He agreed to a compromise: Dunkin' Donuts. Henry Kissinger wasn't as good at bringing people together as I am.

We stepped out of the car onto the sun-splashed curb on a still chilly March morning. Across the street, the Fenway — the park, not the baseball field — sprawled bare and brown as far as the eye could see, a lonely place until the April rains and the May warmth would bring this city to life again.

"We have an apartment number?" Mongillo asked, looking up at the building.

"We don't," I replied, striding now toward the glass front doors. Inside, we looked on the row of mailboxes with names written and typed in mismatched hands and scripts, until I found "L Hutchens," neatly scrawled in a black pen. There was no apartment number. We rang the buzzer.

I'm not sure what I expected to happen. Probably nothing. But my stomach tightened as we waited what felt like forever for her voice to come over the intercom, asking who was at the front door. Or maybe she thought she knew her visitor and she'd just buzz us inside. But neither happened. The only sounds in that vestibule were Mongillo's labored breathing and his occasional slurps of coffee.

Another minute elapsed, and Mongillo pressed the button again. I could hear his cell phone vibrating inside his coat, but he ignored it. Still nothing. I looked at the face of my own cell phone and saw that it was 7:32 a.m. Maybe she had left for work already. Maybe she was in the shower and couldn't hear the alert. Or maybe she was dead.

A minute later, it was my turn to buzz. Truth be told, neither Mongillo nor I knew what else to do. The plan was to call the police, but we also realized that standing here in the lobby, the cops would come, they'd deny us access to the building, and we wouldn't see anything of the woman's apartment, including the woman herself. The only thing we'd end up seeing would be several state workers wheeling her body into the coroner's van. This was not a good way to start the day — not for me, but especially not for Lauren Hutchens.

"Fuck it," I said to Mongillo, resigned. "I'll call Mac Foley now. This isn't doing anyone any good."

Before he could answer, a twentysomething guy in a wool ski hat wearing a knapsack slammed open the glass doors from inside the apartment building and continued through the second set of doors outside — obviously a grad student of some sort on his way to one of the nearby universities. As I placed my foot inside the closing door, Mongillo called out to the guy, "Any idea what apartment Lauren Hutchens is in?" It was a Hail Mary question, but sometimes these things pan out.

Without stopping, he turned back and called out, "She's my neighbor, dude. She's in 416."

We were in business. Of course, what kind of business, I didn't know. We took the elevator to the fourth floor. We scouted out

Apartment 416. I looked at Mongillo, standing there in the same durable tan pants he always wore, with a plaid hunting jacket wrapped around his enormous frame. He looked at me. His cell phone was vibrating again, but much to his uncharacteristic credit, he continued to ignore it.

There was no doorbell, so I knocked. Mongillo pressed his ear to the door to listen, but apparently heard nothing. Was she alive? Would a fresh-faced woman named Lauren suddenly appear at the door? If she did, what would we say? Or were we standing just a few feet from a horrendous crime scene that the criminal wanted me to know about first?

A minute or so passed and I knocked again. An older woman in the kind of cloth coat that Richard Nixon's wife once wore appeared out of a nearby apartment. She gave us a suspicious look as she walked past us toward the elevators, but said nothing.

I tried the knob and it was locked. I stepped away from the door, pulled my cell from my coat, and said, "I'm calling." I was surprised at how breathless I had become. Mongillo nodded. I dialed the number to the Boston PD's homicide bureau and asked for Detective Mac Foley.

Last I saw Foley was the night before, first

when he was pleasantly chatting with me, then when he was eyeing me from across the room, pointing me out to another cop. I didn't for a second think he appreciated my unintended involvement in the Jill Dawson investigation, and he certainly wouldn't appreciate my newfound role in the Lauren Hutchens case — if, in fact, there was a Lauren Hutchens case. Most of me hoped there wasn't. Of course, I'd be lying if I didn't admit that some embarrassing little granule deep inside my head was excited about it all, but I tried to splash the cold water of human compassion on it.

I was told by the receptionist that Foley wasn't available, which didn't surprise me. Mac Foley, as I've said, works under the radar of public interest, even as he's working in the public interest. Truth was, he probably also wasn't in yet at this hour. I said, "Would it be possible to page him and let him know that Jack Flynn called. I've received more correspondence that may be of an urgent nature." I left my cell phone number.

Two minutes later, as Mongillo and I lurked in the dimly lit hallway outside of Lauren Hutchens's door, my phone rang with Detective Mac Foley on the other end of the line. I got not one second of pleasantry — no top of the morning, no how are you, no nice to meet you from the night before. This was definitely the second version of Mac Foley.

"What do you have?" he asked abruptly. Same words as Martin always uses, in the same clipped manner.

I said, "Someone slipped an envelope under my apartment door that I found this morning. Inside, a one-line note said, 'Back again. More women will die,' in the same typeface, with the same signature as before. It contained the driver's license of a woman by the name of Lauren Hutchens. Phone listings have her at 558 Park Drive. I've tried to reach her, but with no success."

Just the facts, ma'am. I was only trying to do my job, and maybe save a woman's life, though increasingly, I doubted the latter was possible. I don't believe in the supernatural. I really don't. But I could almost feel her on the other side of that door, and the feeling I had wasn't of her moving about.

After what I thought was a pretty good summation of the situation, I heard silence in response — continued silence from inside the apartment, new silence now from Detective Foley. In a job that relies on people telling me things, silence spells trouble. He finally said, "We'll check it out." He paused, then added, "After we do, I need to see you today, face-to-face, with that envelope in hand. Don't mess it up by letting multiple people touch it. If you think you're going to turn a murder investigation into a fucking media circus, then you need to learn a lesson or two on how we're going to operate here." He hung up the phone without so much as a good-bye.

Mongillo had leaned close to hear both sides of the conversation. I ended up with a craving for pepperoni out of the deal. We both leaned against the hallway wall in silence, though what we were waiting for, I couldn't actually say.

Within about thirty seconds, we heard the faint sound of a siren. Then louder, and louder still. Then we heard something else: a soft tap, followed by a slightly louder bang — coming from the other side of the apartment door. If my heart had been beating any harder, I could have been cited on some sort of noise ordinance violation.

Mongillo looked at me. I looked at Mongillo. I lunged toward the door and banged on it again, saying firmly and authoritatively, "Police on the way. Open up. Now."

Nothing. Nothing but silence. The siren by now was blaring outside the building, stagnant. Mongillo said, "I'm going downstairs to let them in." He hustled to the elevator, oddly graceful in motion for a man his size, and I stood watch over the door, having no idea if it might open, and if it did, what lurked within.

Was she alive? Was she dead? If the latter, was her killer still here?

Before any of these questions could be answered, four cops — two in plain clothes, two in uniform — burst into the hallway, having just stepped off the elevator before Mongillo even reached them.

One of them said, "Hey, Vinny, what's shaking?"

Mongillo said, "For the moment, Woody, just me."

They rushed down toward yours truly. I pointed at the door and said, probably needlessly, "It's locked."

One of the uniformed guys said, "There's a property manager's office in the basement. I'll check for a key."

"We've heard some noises coming from inside," I said.

The other uniformed officer said, "Fuck it. Stand back." He let forth with a ferocious kick just above the knob.

The door exploded open in a haze of splinters and noise. The first sensation I had was that of cold air gushing into the hallway from an open window inside. The second sensation I had was an impulse to vomit. Sitting in a chair angled directly at the door from the middle of the living room was the body of a young woman. She was wearing a nightshirt that was hoisted up around her waist and torn by her chest. She had dried blood around her eyes and on her upper lip beneath her nose. Her legs were splayed far apart. A ligature, which looked to be an electrical cord, was wrapped around her neck and dangled off to one side. And right beneath her chin, a big looping red bow hung toward the other side.

The six of us — two plainclothes cops, two uniformed officers, two reporters — stared inside in collective shock. The bottom of a blind slapped against the corner of an open window — the source of the sound that Mongillo and I had recently heard. At that moment, a figure stepped off the elevator down the hall and shouted out, "Get those fucking reporters away from a potential crime scene." It was Mac Foley. I wanted to tell him that there was nothing potential about this scene anymore.

Instead I whispered to Mongillo, "Take detailed mental notes." One of the detectives, having just regained his wits, yanked the door shut.

Mongillo said to me, "This, my friend, is the work of your new pen pal. God save Boston when it hears what's in our midst."

Foley, close now, snapped at one of the uniforms, "Escort these guys out of here." Which the patrolman did, almost apologetically. And that was it. God save this city indeed.

8

The police commissioner's office looked like it was decorated by a Hollywood set designer — what with the grouping of flags behind a sprawling oak desk, heavy blue curtains, a rich burgundy rug, glass cases filled with Boston Police Department memorabilia, a wall of photographs interspersed with old badges and framed letters of commendation.

I bring this up only because this is where I happened to be sitting a little before noon. Hal Harrison was reclining in a leather swivel chair behind that aforementioned oak desk. Vinny Mongillo sat to my left on the visitor's side of the desk, and Peter Martin, editor of the *Boston Record,* was to my right. It's probably worth noting that I don't think I had ever seen Martin in public when he wasn't sitting at a restaurant table and I was paying for the meal. Smart as he is within the confines of the newsroom, a man of the people he is not.

"You think this is some sort of fucking publicity stunt — another ploy to sell your goddamned paper? That's what you think?"

That was Commissioner Harrison, who had lost all of the confiding charm he had displayed from the podium at his retirement speech the night before. On this day, in the privacy of his office, I'd have to say he was absolutely livid.

So livid that he pounded his fist on the desk, then picked up a pile of papers and tossed them on the floor beside him. His face was beet red, his eyes contorted. Normally a handsome man with silvery hair and a fit frame, he looked like a tired, angry pensioner who had just found out that his Social Security COLA was frozen in the halls of Congress.

Harrison had personally called me the moment I got back to my desk from the Lauren Hutchens murder scene, saying he needed to see me, Mongillo, and preferably the editor of the paper on an urgent matter. I thought he might be prepared to confide information in this investigation. Apparently I thought wrong.

"No sir," I replied. "We didn't ask for these letters. We didn't seek them out. As soon as we received them, we not only alerted your detectives, but we handed over the original copies —"

"As soon as you received them? As soon as you fucking received them?" That was the commissioner again, his voice rising to a whole new level of anger. "When my men arrived at the fucking murder scene this morning, the two of you were already standing outside the fucking door. And you're saying you called us as soon as you received them."

He picked up another pile of papers and flung them on the floor. I've never quite understood the mentality of executives — or, for that matter, of anybody else — who feel the need to rant and throw objects. But I guess that wasn't really the point here. The point was that, well, he kind of had a point. We had waited to call, maybe wrongly so.

I said, "I received the note and driver's license this morning. We called on the way over. We arrived at the victim's doorway at roughly the same time as the police."

Harrison stared at me for a long moment, like he didn't believe what I had just said, his hands first on his cheeks and then sliding absently through his hair. They came to rest on the back of his neck, and he bowed his face in apparent thought. Mongillo and

Martin remained quiet on either side of me — or as quiet as can be, in Mongillo's case. I could hear him breathing out of his nose, the sound like wind gushing through trees.

Finally, Harrison looked up, directed his gaze at me, Mongillo, and then at Martin, and said, "You're not going to report this."

We sat there in silence for another moment until I said, "Not report what?"

"This. For starters, those damned letters. And you're not going to report whatever it is that you saw in the Hutchens apartment this morning."

Mongillo piped in, "Why not?" He sounded sincerely surprised, taken aback.

Harrison directed his gaze at him and said, "Because you'll fuck up this entire investigation. You've got absolutely no idea what you have. You have no idea the meaning of what you saw. You'll send this city into mass hysteria, and you'll get in the way of us trying to do our jobs."

The three of us sat in collective silence again. This time it was Martin who broke it.

"Commissioner," he said, respectfully but firmly, "we regard this as a significant story, and are fully aware of the conflicting interests. Should the public know about the possibility of a serial killer? Will our reportage in any way compromise the integrity of the investigation? We're very prepared to give this some serious thought, keeping in mind at all times that our ultimate responsibility is to our readers."

I first looked at Martin out of the corner of my eye, and as he spoke, I turned my head fully to watch him. When did he grow a pair of brass balls? Actually, I say that in jest. As aggravating as Peter Martin can be to work for, I've never known another newsman who has his ability to reach the right decision for all the right reasons, story after story after story.

Apparently, Harrison wasn't thinking the same thing. He looked at Martin incredulously and all but yelled, "This isn't a fucking journalism ethics class, Mr. Martin. This is real life, and in this case, real death. Debate this all you want. Just don't print it. If you have to, write that a thirty-two-year-old woman named Lauren Hutchens was found dead, and police are investigating the cause."

"Given what we know, that would be a lie," Martin said.

"You don't know that. You don't know if these notes are a fraud. You can't even be sure of what you saw today. You caught one quick glimpse through a half-open door. You know nothing."

Maybe, maybe not. But we knew, like he knew, that these notes weren't likely a fraud. The first one could have been. The second one led us to a woman's body. And through that open doorway we saw a crime scene that was pretty damned horrific, and we saw it long enough, well enough, to record in our heads, and later on notepads, the gory details of a young woman's death.

Harrison bowed his head again. When he spoke, it was in a lower voice, with a calmer tone, as if he was trying to regroup. He said, "Look, there are three potential scenarios that could unfold if you print a half-cocked story. One, whoever sent you these notes will kill again very soon, because he's obviously seeking publicity. The publicity you give him will fuel a desire for more. Two, antithetically speaking, it could cause the killer to not send you any more notes, stunting an opportunity for additional clues. Three, you may prompt copycat killings in the city, which serial killings often do. In other words, frustrated husbands and boyfriends will off their women under the guise of this Phantom Fiend."

He added, almost politely now, "Does this make any sense to you?"

Martin, rising now from his chair, said, "It does, Commissioner, it does. But there's a fourth scenario as well, and that is, if we print the story, we warn people to take proper precautions against a serial killer, and we potentially save lives. Like I said, we're going to give this some very serious thought. We appreciate your time."

I reflexively got up right after Martin, mesmerized by his performance. I'd follow this guy into battle, and actually, I think I just had. Mongillo stood after me and completed the procession.

When you're the commissioner of a major police department, you're accustomed to giving orders, not merely making requests. You're used to people doing precisely as you say, not tabling your demands for further consideration. Poor Hal Harrison. I don't think he knew what had hit him. He was undoubtedly thinking about his mayoral campaign, about a city gripped by fear as the police commissioner tried to make the leap into city hall. What was taking place all around him was not a formula for electoral success.

As the door swung shut behind us, I heard Harrison holler into his phone, "Get me Mac Foley — immediately!" I think I also heard Martin clank a little bit while he walked. The question remained, though: What the hell were we going to do now?

9

I sat at my computer doing exactly as Martin had told me: writing what I knew. Vinny Mongillo stood over my left shoulder, loudly crunching on a large bag of Cheetos.

"Eating helps me think," Vinny said defensively when I first shot him a withering look about the noise. If that had really been the case, he'd be the most thoughtful human being on the planet. I didn't say that to him, but I wanted to.

On my screen, I described the murder scene. I wrote of the two notes that the Phantom Fiend had sent me. I asked Mongillo for more background on the Boston Strangler and included some of that as well. We had other reporters working the story who would be calling in soon from the field, including Jennifer Day, who was pressing Lauren Hutchens's family for information and reaction, and our crime and grime reporter, Benny Simms, who was trolling his sources at Boston PD for any new nuggets.

"It's not art, but it'll do," Mongillo said, now drinking a can of Diet Coke. Someone tell me how that makes any sense: a guy who just polished off a veritable burlap sack filled with processed cheese snacks was now drinking a sugar-free soda.

He added, "Get up for a minute, Fair Hair. Let the master sit down and write."

I stared at his fingertips, which were orange from his Cheetos, and said, "Keep your goddamned mitts away from my keyboard."

"Tough crowd in here," he replied, wiping his palms across his plaid shirt.

At that moment, Martin materialized at my desk the way he always does, right out of thin air. He had a somber look on his face, which I initially attributed to him crashing from the high of standing up to the police commissioner. But he said in a tight voice, "We need to gather in my office. Justine's got some concerns."

Justine, for the record, is Justine Steele, the former editor in chief of the *Boston Record,* now the publisher, meaning she is the paper's chief executive officer, the one who answers to the board of directors and the stockholders, who may or may not understand that good journalism is necessary for good profits. We'd probably find that out very soon.

"The mayor called," she said, as the four of us sat around Martin's table.

I wanted to correct her and say *acting* mayor, but for the second time in a matter of minutes, I contained myself. By the way, the office probably still seemed comfortably familiar to Steele, given that Martin hadn't changed one single thing about it since moving in after her. If Steele had left her family pictures on the desk, Martin would have kept them there as well.

"She's not pleased, and I have to admit, she raised some valid points," Steele said, sighing. "This story is going to trigger widespread panic. We're essentially telling the public that there's a serial killer on the loose, even though police aren't confirming there's a connection between these two killings. On top of that, it has the potential to hinder two murder investigations."

She paused and looked at each of us. "Are we one hundred percent sure what it is we have?"

Maybe I should have deferred to Martin to answer, but I was comfortable enough with Justine to barge right in. I had worked with her when she was editor on some of the biggest stories this paper has ever broken. So I said, "We know we got these letters. We know that one of them led us to a victim that the police weren't aware of yet. We know that victim was strangled to death. We know the writer of these notes uses a nickname that was also used for the Boston Strangler."

Here I paused, then added with a sigh of my own, "I'm not sure what more we need."

"What we need is to make sure we're doing the right thing," Steele replied coolly. "What would your lede be?"

I said, "Right now, the lede is that a thirty-two-year-old woman was found strangled to death in her Fenway apartment yesterday morning after her driver's license was delivered to a *Boston Record* reporter with a note saying, 'More women will die.' "

Okay, maybe Mongillo was right. It's not art, but good newspaper writing rarely is, and it cut right to the bone-chilling point.

I continued, "The second graph would point out that hers was the second death of a young woman in which the victim's driver's license was sent to the *Record* reporter, accompanied by a note. Both times, the note was signed 'The Phantom Fiend' — the same moniker that referred some forty years ago to a serial killer better known as the Boston Strangler."

As I talked this through, I was feeling a rush of adrenaline. In a perfect world, reporters aren't supposed to be part of the story, though the mere fact that a reporter covers a story makes him or her an inherent part. People change their actions when they know there will be public awareness. Politicians preen. Lazy bureaucrats suddenly rush. Businessmen become uncharacteristically concerned about the consumers they're supposed to serve.

But if we printed this story, I wouldn't merely be a part of it. I'd be dead center — pardon the term — especially given what happened on the Charles River the night before. A serial killer was communicating with the city he was terrorizing through a senior reporter at the largest newspaper in town. Sickening? Maybe. Intoxicating? Definitely. And this from someone who once found himself front and center in an international story when I was shot and wounded in what appeared to be a presidential assassination attempt. That's an entirely different matter — though it does explain my fear of loud noises and presidents.

Steele said, "We don't know definitively that it was a strangling, right? The cops aren't confirming the cause of death yet.

There is no coroner's report. Things aren't always as they seem."

No, they're not; she was right. But before I could reply, she said, "And the Boston Strangler — he's dead. We know that for a fact."

Mongillo interjected, "No, we don't know that for a fact. Albert DeSalvo is dead, but he was never charged or convicted in any of the stranglings. There are a lot of people who never believed that he was the Boston Strangler."

Mongillo said this with unusual intensity, much as when he corrected me on the same point the day before. His words were so heartfelt, I could even overlook the orange Cheetos crumbs that had taken residence on the side of his lips.

Steele said to Mongillo, "You're not suggesting that the same Boston Strangler from the sixties is killing these women now?"

Mongillo shook his head slowly. A crumb fell from his face to his lap. He said, "I'm not saying yes and I'm not saying no. I'm only saying that our job is to keep an open mind. Life is strange."

Life is strange. Tell me about it. I was supposed to be spending this day stretched out on a comfortable chaise lounge on a warm Hawaiian beach beside the woman I would love for the rest of my life — all the while with a paperback novel in one hand and a frozen strawberry concoction in the other, listening to the tranquil waves lap lazily against the Pacific shore. And here I was in Boston writing a story about a woman who apparently had been raped, then strangled in her Fenway apartment by a killer who had personally revealed his vile acts to me.

Yes, Vinny, life is definitely strange.

Steele said, "The thing that I have to keep in mind, that we have to keep in mind, is how do we do the most public good. Mayor Laird tells me that the police have made major progress in the investigation, and that publicity, and the resulting public outcry, could hamper the case."

Martin interjected, "Or do we do the most public good by warning readers there is a serial killer in their midst who has told the *Boston Record,* and I quote, that 'more women will die.' "

Steele shot him a look that wasn't just cool but arctic. I mean, you could get freezer burn, that look was so cold. I had to wonder if the acting mayor had gotten to her. I'd read in the *Traveler*'s gossip column that the two were becoming buddies, seen together at a play one night, and in the *Record* luxury box at a Patriots game in December.

I've never even sat in the *Record*'s damned luxury box. Did Steele leave her news judgment on the newsroom floor when she got promoted to the front office?

Martin ignored her look, or maybe he wasn't aware of it. He added, "We could actually save lives."

Steele replied, "Or the police could save lives by cracking the case faster without our interference." Each word came out of her mouth with icicles hanging from them.

Then she looked at me, even sterner now. "Jack, you guys write up what you have. I want to see it before we make up our minds on this thing. It's not an easy decision. But it's one that I feel I have to personally make."

Not easy? In the last thirty-six hours, I've had my fiancée flee the state on our wedding day. I'm on the friends-and-family list of a serial killer. And someone tried to drown me in the freezing, fetid water of the Charles River the night before. And she's telling me that the decision she has to make in the comfortable confines of her fireplaced office is not an easy one? I made a mental note to land myself a job in management. It was starting to feel like the right time.

Of course, what we didn't know then was that it was about to become even less easy.

■ ■ ■ ■

I filed the story at 6:00 p.m., after taking feeds from reporters Jennifer Day and Benny Simms, neither of whom had a whole lot to offer, but just enough to help round things out. Just before I hit the Send button, Mongillo leaned over my desk, kissed the computer screen, and said, "I'll see you in tomorrow's paper. Please, story, please, get yourself into tomorrow's paper." And just like that, it was out of our hands.

I leaned back and thought about the voice mail I had received from the general manager of the Hawaiian resort that I should have been staying at that night but wasn't. He expressed deep regret over my circumstances, and slightly less regret over the fact that there was nothing he could or would do about a refund on my significant deposit. I was, in a word, completely screwed — though I guess that's two words.

Right now, I just craved a steak — a fat, juicy, dry-aged sirloin sizzling in its own juices on a warm plate that would also carry some home fries and grilled asparagus.

I was punchy. I was tired. I had precisely three hours of sleep the night before. And what I craved wasn't what I needed, because what I needed was a crash course on the Boston Strangler and Albert DeSalvo, and why the latter was believed to be the former, and why it was that Vinny Mongillo didn't think it was necessarily so. So I did something that no right-thinking reporter in any newsroom in America ever wants to do. I walked into the morgue, asked them to set me up at a table, and began my own exhaustive research.

Soon enough, a nice man by the name of Chadwick — or maybe it was Chad Wick, I really don't know — delivered to me about a dozen musty manila folders, all of them crammed full of the yellowed news clips of the *Record*'s coverage of the Boston Strangler killing spree and DeSalvo's confession about a year later.

Poring over the stories, I quickly learned this: There were eleven murders in all from the summer of 1962 through the very early winter of 1964; the first victims were women in their fifties and sixties who typically lived alone, the later victims women in their twenties and thirties; the killer often left semen on their bodies — in one case, on the victim's chest, in another, around her mouth; sometimes the killer left garish looping bows around the victims' necks, not unlike the one I saw earlier that day on Lauren Hutchens; sometimes the victims were ghoulishly positioned to greet investigators as they came onto the crime scenes. Again, see: Hutchens, Lauren. All of the women were strangled to death.

The city had been panic-stricken, just as Justine Steele predicted it would be again. Dog pounds were cleaned out. Locksmiths worked twenty-hour days. The streets emptied after dark. Single women set up phone trees to check on one another's safety.

The investigation, at least on my first, brisk read, sounded like a mess, led by then state attorney general Stu Callaghan, who used his success on the Strangler case to win election to the U.S. Senate, where he remains. The Suffolk County district attorney's office fought with the state attorney general's office, which fought with the Boston Police, which fought with the state police. There was so much fighting I'm surprised the Strangler's victims were the only ones who wound up dead.

Then in 1965, more than a year after the last of the killings, Albert DeSalvo, a smooth-talking laborer who was described in stories as having the odd gift of being able to slip into a crowded room completely unnoticed, confessed. He was being held in a state prison for sexually dangerous convicts at the time. He had never been a suspect. In the company of his now-famous lawyer, H. Gordon Thomas, he provided cops with vivid details of many of the crime scenes. Like Mongillo said, he was neither charged in any of the slayings nor convicted. Instead, he was sentenced to life in prison on an unrelated rape charge. He later recanted his confession when he learned his family could not profit from any of the book or movie deals that the Strangler killings had spawned.

He was stabbed to death in prison in 1973 by an unknown killer on the day before he was to meet with his lawyer to provide what he had described as an important revelation. Reading between the yellowed lines of these old stories, it didn't look like authorities had busted a gut trying to crack Albert DeSalvo's murder.

I opened up a folder of newspaper photographs from the era and saw a much younger version of now police commissioner Hal Harrison — then a police detective — sitting beside Senator Stu Callaghan, who was then the state attorney general, at a press conference announcing DeSalvo's confession. I saw multiple shots of DeSalvo in various settings. I saw a shot of a Boston PD detective identified in the caption as

Bob Walters walking out of a Charles Street apartment building that was the site of the last strangling attributed to DeSalvo.

That last photograph stopped me cold, though at first I wasn't sure why. I stared at it longer and harder, harder and longer. And then it struck me — hard. Charles Street. Beacon Hill — the site of the Jill Dawson slaying. I strained my eyes to see the address above the door on the brick town house, but the picture was too grainy to clearly see the numbers. I was peering so close that my forehead banged against the table, making me reflexively jump back in surprise. I leapt up and ran over to the counter where Chad or Chadwick or Chad Wick was chortling through his nose at something he had just read in *The Economist.*

"Do you have a magnifying glass I could borrow?" I asked.

He shot me a look like I was an idiot. Do they have a magnifying glass? It's their weapon of choice in the *Record* morgue. He opened a drawer and asked in a nasally voice, "How strong do you need?"

How do you answer that? I hesitated and replied, "Pretty strong."

He seemed to understand and handed me a perfectly nice magnifying glass, handle first. I headed back over to my conference table and held the glass about two inches above the photograph. I immediately saw the number clear as day, even though in the photograph it was night — 146; 146 Charles Street, Boston, Massachusetts. I thought I knew what I had, but to be sure, I snapped up the phone and called up to the newsroom.

"Mongillo here."

"Flynn here."

"I'm on the other line."

"Doesn't matter. What was the address of the Jill Dawson murder earlier this week?"

"One forty-six Charles Street."

"You're an animal."

"You're my bitch."

I'm not sure his salutation was really necessary, but I got what I needed. I riffled through the files again, looking for stories on the other murders, until I finally found one from the Fenway — 558 Park Drive, to be exact, the same location where we found Lauren Hutchens's strangled body that morning. The modern-day killer was retracing the steps of the old Strangler — a discovery that sent one of those electric chills up my back and into my neck.

Something else kept nagging at me about that Charles Street photograph as well —

something about the scene, or the people in it. I placed the magnifying glass over the shot again and scanned the sidewalk, inside the windows of the awaiting police car, the street — until there it was: the young, handsome face of one Hank Sweeney walking several paces behind Detective Walters. Hank Sweeney is a retired Boston Police homicide detective. Far more important to the point of this story, he was also a very good friend who owed me a very large favor.

"Thank you, Hank Sweeney," I murmured to myself.

I picked up the phone again and called Hank's cell, a number I knew by heart, even if I hadn't called it in over a year.

He picked up on about the third ring, his voice as smooth and calm as ever.

"Hank, how's about I buy you the best steak at Locke-Ober in thirty minutes?"

"That place is so ten minutes ago, Jack. How's about I meet you over at Grill 23 instead?"

That's really what he said. The guy is in his mid-seventies and he's talking like a sophomore coed at Wellesley High. Beyond that, he's questioning my taste in restaurants. And beyond even that, maybe he could act a little more excited about having the pleasure of my company again.

"No, Locke-Ober," I replied. I mean, you can push me around on a lot of things, but not about restaurants. "I'll see you there." And just like that, I was on my way — hopefully for a lot more than a good meal.

10

Tony, the world's most hospitable maître d', greeted me at the door of Locke-Ober as if he hadn't seen me in months — mostly, I suppose, because he hadn't. Life sometimes gets in the way of fine dining, tough as that fact is to accept.

"I was starting to think you went out and bought an oven," he said, giving me that low-lying handshake that is his trademark.

"I did, but then I couldn't get a license to operate it," I replied.

He laughed, God love him. Then he asked, more confiding now, "Everything all right?" I merely shook my head and flashed a smile of futility. He nodded in agreement.

A word about Tony: solid. And another: knowing. He's stood at the host's podium of Locke-Ober for forty years, which makes him a relative newcomer at the restaurant, but still an institution in the town. He has seated kings and Kennedys, tycoons and tyrants, always with a gracious demeanor and just the right amount of solicitude.

"I hear you've gotten married," he said. "That will always shake things up a bit."

I shook my head again and smiled with even more futility. "I walked to the brink of the altar before I realized I was standing in the wrong church," I said.

Tony nodded, looking away from me, not betraying even a hint of surprise.

"Smart boy," he said. "I've got three weddings behind me already, and I'm thinking of a fourth."

"How's biz?" I asked.

He looked behind him into the three-quarters-filled dining room and said, "Can't complain." And he didn't. It wasn't his style, even if he had something to complain about.

I said, "I'm meeting a gentleman, which might be the most liberty that's ever been taken with that term, by the name of Hank Sweeney. Tall, dark, and not particularly handsome. A retired member of our distinguished police force. Have you seen him?"

Tony nodded back into the room. "He's sitting near Yvonne, drinking on your tab as we speak."

I poked my head around the corner and sure enough, there was Hank Sweeney, with a lowball glass containing what looked like a Tom Collins in his hairy hand, lounging in a chair at a table pushed up against the wall beneath the famous portrait of a woman named Yvonne.

As I previously mentioned, I hadn't seen Hank in roughly a year, a fact I immediately regretted upon seeing him again. He pulled himself to his feet with a look that was equal parts appreciation and warmth, and as I walked toward him, he wrapped his arms around me in a long and wistful hug. When he finally spoke in that whiskeyed, raspy voice of his, he said, "Like it was only yesterday."

I replied, "We let too much time get away from us, Hank. Too much time." He gave me a hard, final slap on the top of my back, and we both took our seats.

Hank, for those keeping score, is one of my favorite people in life. About a year earlier, I wrote a story that led to the mayor's resignation. In my reporting, I came to learn that Hank, my Hank, had been compromised many years ago in a scandal involving the FBI and the Boston Police. I conveniently left that part out of print. He conveniently helped me with key information. After I filed, I didn't call him the next day, nor did he call me. A day turned to a week turned to a month turned to a year, two great friends floating foolishly apart. Maybe I was disappointed in him. Perhaps he had been angry at me or embarrassed by what I learned. Whatever it was, all of it washed away in the dining room of Locke-Ober in that split second when we came together again.

Hank had thrown on a sport coat and a tie for this occasion, which I knew he would. I noticed he had slimmed down quite a bit, nearly to the point of being svelte, and I told him so.

He laughed softly, that laugh that begins inside his chest, shakes his shoulders, and makes his head bob up and down a little bit. "Son, if I start looking and acting my age, then I might as well just hang the whole thing up and go back to that pit in Florida where you found me."

He was referring to the time I knocked on his door in some godforsaken retirement community in inland Florida a few years before because I figured he'd have some information on a story I was reporting. He did, and he helped me, but even better than the insight he provided, he gave me friendship. Hopefully, he was about to give me both of those all over again.

The waiter, Luis, twenty-four years in the

café, came over with menus, a fresh drink for Hank, and a Sam Adams for me. "Compliments of Tony," he told me solicitously.

"Please tell Tony that I thank him for the compliment," I replied.

Hank and I made some standard-issue bullshit, which felt good. We both ordered the signature lobster bisque, along with dry-aged sirloins, some hashed browns, and a plate of asparagus that I already knew Hank would drench in hollandaise. When the food arrived, I met his eye across the table and said, "I need you on something again."

"Always needing something," he said, feigning annoyance, but I could see it all over his face that he was anything but annoyed.

I said, "Was Albert DeSalvo the Boston Strangler?"

He took two big spoonfuls of what it's worth pointing out was an absolutely delicious bisque, put his spoon on the plate beneath the bowl, wiped his lips, and asked, "Why?"

A fair question, and I say that as someone who generally hates it when my inquiries are met with inquiries rather than answers. Still, I said to him, "I'll tell you in a minute. First, answer me."

He took a sip of his drink. He looked

down at the table where the breadbasket sat, though I was sure he wasn't really looking at the bread. Then his eyes settled on mine again and he said, "Depends who you ask."

"I'm asking you."

"I don't really know. I was a junior detective then. I made detective about halfway through the killing spree and was put straight into homicide because they were stretched so thin and because the whole city was so damned scared. My role was minimal."

"But Hank, I know you, you're a good listener. What were your superiors saying? What did your gut tell you?"

Hank took another spoonful of bisque, a little more relaxed now. He said, "That's what I mean when I say it depends who you ask." He paused again before asking me, "You want the elaborate answer?"

"I want the best answer, yeah."

He sighed deeply, as if he was collecting himself, then began. "There were three lead detectives on the case. Each one had their own theory.

"The most senior guy was Lieutenant Detective Bob Walters. He was always something of a mentor to me. He believed that there might have been a serial killer who offed a few women, maybe three, maybe four, maybe five — six tops. I think he might have even had a suspect in mind by the end. But he always believed that the last six or seven murders were either the work of a second serial killer, or a bunch of copycat killers — disgruntled husbands, angry boyfriends. They know there's a serial strangler out there. They realize if their wife or girlfriend shows up dead, she's immediately going to be lumped in with the other victims."

"Did you have proof that some of these were copycat killings?"

"Nothing forensic, only circumstantial. The reality is that serial killers, especially in sex crimes, virtually never dramatically change the profile of their victims mid-spree. The Strangler did. He started with older victims who almost always lived alone, and by the end, his victims were twenty, twenty-five, thirty years younger, many of them living with other people. It never made any sense."

Luis came and hurriedly cleared away our soup bowls, dropping off two fresh drinks in the process. He was followed by a second waiter, delivering the steaks, starch, and asparagus. Sweeney surveyed his plate, then the rest of the table, and said, "The thing about not hanging out with you over the past year is that it allowed me to lose about fifteen pounds."

We both lit into our beef. I said, "Go on."

Hank swallowed another bite of sirloin and began anew. "The second detective you may or may not know. Name of Mac Foley. A damned good homicide investigator. He was a young upstart back then, put on the case for his sheer brains. He never believed DeSalvo was the Strangler. Didn't think he had it in him to commit murder. Thought his confession was too pat. Never bought into any of it."

I asked, "He thought they were a bunch of copycat killings and that the Strangler was a myth?"

"No. Maybe he thought one or two of them were copycats, but everyone thought that. He had another suspect in mind. He chased that theory to the ends of the earth trying to prove that he was the killer. I remember him being damned close, too. And then one day DeSalvo confesses and the books get shut and all the detectives get sent home, case closed, thank you very much."

I asked, "And the third?"

"You've heard of him. Hal Harrison, then another young, upstart detective. I have no idea what he believed during the killing spree, but when DeSalvo confessed, he bought hook, line, and sinker into that — along with another guy you've heard of, Senator Stu Callaghan, who was back then the attorney general. They never seemed to question it, never looked at any other possibility. If DeSalvo said he was the strangler, then in their heads, he was the strangler all right."

A busboy, who hadn't been a boy in about five decades, silently cleared the plates, then made way for Luis, who cleaned up our crumbs and presented dessert menus in one seamless exercise. Hank ordered a glass of port; I asked for a plate of the macaroons. Dining at Locke-Ober without having macaroons is like going to Italy without eating pasta.

"Which camp were you in?" I asked.

Before he could answer, my cell phone vibrated in my coat pocket. Normally, I wouldn't talk on the phone in this dining room. It just didn't seem right. But given my current circumstances, I apologized to Sweeney and quietly answered the call, which was from Peter Martin.

I hadn't even offered so much as a hello when Martin said, "Bad news. Justine's made up her mind. She wants that story held for at least one day, maybe two. I think the acting mayor got to her again and pleaded for more time. I tried like hell."

I was too stunned to argue and too angry to try. So I said, "Big mistake. We'll talk in the morning. Hopefully, we're not playing catch-up when someone else reports a serial killer."

Martin said, "I know. Believe me, I know. I'll see you here early." I looked at my watch — 10:40 p.m. — and knew that Martin was still in the *Record* newsroom. He had probably been there, no exaggeration, since his call to me at about five in the morning, and didn't have so much as an exclusive story to show for it in the following day's paper. Sometimes the news business really sucks.

I hung up. Sweeney said to me, "Good God, son, it looks like the gypsies just ran off with your dog and your baseball glove. What's going on with you?"

I told him. I told him about the notes from someone identifying themselves as the Phantom Fiend. I told him about the visit to Park Drive that morning, seeing the strangled young woman sitting in a chair, a macabre prop in some madman's game. I told him about the incident on the river the night before, the anger in the police commissioner's voice that morning, the fact that

Mac Foley was proving to be anything but helpful.

He nodded all the way through, until finally I asked him, "So which camp were you in, Hank?"

"Doesn't matter who I was with," he said in that raspy voice. "I was a nothing back then, as junior as an April bud on a New England tree. But if I were you . . ."

He stopped here, took his first sip of port, gave an approving sigh — suddenly, everyone's a vino critic — and continued. "If I were you, I would track down Detective Walters, a man who I respected very much — and still do. I would ask him why he believes DeSalvo wasn't the Boston Strangler. I think you might find what he has to say to be of significant interest."

He sipped his port again. I said, "I will. I absolutely will. But regardless of what he has to say, how can you ever prove a negative? How can you prove that a dead man wasn't the killer that everyone believed him to be?"

Hank smiled, his smile turning into a soft, knowing laugh. "That's easy, son. Easy. Forensics. Science."

I tapped the table a couple of times, trying to get my mind around what he meant. These murders occurred some forty years

139

ago, back when they used fingerprints, not sophisticated DNA testing, to match murderers to crime scenes and prove guilt beyond any reasonable statistical doubt. Hank saw the look on my face, one of confusion, and continued.

"The killer left his semen — his DNA — at the crime scenes. I'm betting it was pretty well preserved."

I replied, skeptically, "Okay, but DeSalvo's dead and buried. Even if you could find those DNA samples, how would you match them to his?"

Hank drained his port and said, "That should be the easiest part of all. The knife."

He let that linger there for effect before adding, "The knife that was used to kill Albert DeSalvo has his blood — his DNA — all over it. The question everyone's been wondering for a whole lot of years is, where is it? It was left beside his body by whoever killed him in jail. Evidence in a murder case isn't supposed to disappear, but my understanding is, this evidence did."

Another pause, to even greater effect. Say what you will about Hank Sweeney. Call him dramatic. Call him melodramatic. But the guy knows how to hook an audience, which in this case was me.

"Find the knife," he told me. "Find the

knife and you're on your way to answering the most enduring and troubling question in the history of Boston law enforcement: Was Albert DeSalvo the Boston Strangler?"

I thought of the look on Mac Foley's face from across the room the night before, the fury in Commissioner Harrison's voice as he warned us off that day, the grotesque way in which poor Lauren Hutchens was splayed across that chair, the notes that were so brief but said so much.

And I thought too that a knife, any knife, especially this knife, was like that proverbial double-edged sword. The closer I got, the more danger I would undoubtedly find myself in.

11

I was in the middle of this dream when I was awakened by the ringing telephone. I looked at the digital clock beside my bed and it said 5:40 a.m. The first thing I thought was that I had to get myself to Suffolk Downs that day and bet the trifecta, my mind was working on that kind of level. I mean, this was a very meta moment, but meta what, I wasn't sure.

Second thing I thought of was that I was going to ring Peter Martin's scrawny little neck, because there was absolutely no one else in the world this could be, and there was precisely no good reason for him to call. I reached for the cordless phone and mistakenly knocked it to the floor, where it kept ringing, ringing, ringing — the sound penetrating through my eye sockets and into my skull. When I finally grabbed it and said hello in a voice still thick with sleep, all I heard in return was a dial tone.

I flopped back down in the dark room, muttering to myself, "That goddamned bastard." In other words, a terrific way to start the new day.

Seconds later, the phone rang anew. "What," I said.

"Turn on the radio."

It was, as predicted, Peter Martin, failing in what was becoming too typical a way to wish me a good morning or to inquire about my relative health or spirits, or even offer an apology for not prevailing on the publisher to run the most important story in the city that day. No, just an order to listen to the radio.

"There's a lot of stations on the radio," I replied, caustic now. "Any special one I should find?"

"FM 99. The Barry Bor Show. Hurry up."

Even in my foggy state, I didn't like where this was heading. Barry Bor was a dim-witted cross between Howard Stern and Bill O'Reilly, minus their refined manners and classic good looks. He made hundreds of thousands of dollars every year by basically insulting people and saying outrageous things. He was a hero to morons; a guilty pleasure for quasi-smart people on their morning commute to work; a torturer of politicians; a flagellator of the rest of the

Boston and national press. Everyone, in his mind, was stupid — everyone, of course, but him.

I'll put aside the obvious question of what in God's good name Peter Martin was doing listening to Barry Bor at five-forty on a weekday morning. The guy needed more help than was probably possible — Martin, not Bor, though probably Bor as well. I quickly hung up the phone, grabbed the remote to my Bose clock radio, and turned to FM 99.

"Ladies and gentlemen, you are the chosen ones who know intuitively when you tune into this show each and every morning that you're listening to something special, something that only the elite thinkers in this city can truly comprehend. And now you can be more assured of that fact than ever before. Could I ever possibly feel more vindicated?"

Lying in bed, Bor's admittedly sonorous voice filling the room, I felt a pit in my stomach. Whatever this was, it wasn't going to be good.

"Before we go on, let's make a few stipulations. Let's accept as fact that what the stupid analysts on all those fatuous cable shows call 'the mainstream media,' let's accept that it's really not all that mainstream anymore. What those liberal blowhards at papers like *The New York Times* and *The Washington Post* and the *Boston Record* and at the network news shows like CBS and NBC, what they are is tired, old, biased curmudgeons — liars, plagiarists, unreliable navel-gazers who wouldn't know a piece of news if it crawled up their fat asses as they sit at their desks reading *The New Republic* and waiting for Hillary Clinton to call them back to tell them what to say and write.

"They're all done. They're part of a dying industry. And I have the goods to prove it now. I'm one-stop shopping — politics, news, analysis, anything you need, right here on the Barry Bor Show. And this morning, we're about to break brand-new ground yet again.

"Ladies and gentlemen, I received a telephone call this morning. It was a very important call. . . ."

Oh fuck. Before he even said it, I knew what it was. My pen pal, the Phantom Fiend or the Boston Strangler or whatever it is that he turned out to be, became undoubtedly frustrated with my inability to get his story into print, so he went to the Barry Bor Show on FM 99, where he knows that anything goes. Think about it. Why was this guy writing to a reporter, except that he wanted publicity? And what was I not giving to him? Anyone? Anyone? Right, publicity. I slammed my fist against the mattress, but all I could do was listen to my own ineptitude — or rather, that of the paper. Maybe Bor's diatribe, sickening as it was, was actually right, and that's what made it all so awful.

"A murderer called me. We're not going to glamorize him just because he had the intellectual firepower to seek out Barry Bor. After all, even though he's one of the chosen ones, he's still a murderer, and though we can forgive a lot, we can't quite forgive that — not unless it comes out later that he was only killing abortionists or stem-cell cloning scientists or anyone supporting the Social Security system exactly as it is now.

"I'm kidding, chosen ones, I'm kidding, so before any of those waddling, fat-assed critics at the *Record* start hassling me again, well, I've got something you don't. I've got you beat on a crime story.

"So back to it. This murderer, he called me here at the Barry Bor Show as we were getting ready to go on the air this morning. I talk to a lot of people during show prep, as you can well imagine — congressmen and senators and sitting governors and retired presidents and big-time consultants.

Rarely do I talk to murderers — except when the stray Democrat gets through on the line."

By this point, I was up out of bed and getting dressed, only because I needed to move, to expend energy, while I listened to this pathological idiot prattle on about himself as he held information on a story that should have been exclusively mine. Here I was, at five forty-five now in the morning, listening to my own failure get broadcast across the city.

"He called me and referred me to a blog, but only under the condition that I not publicly reveal the address of the site, which I won't. Barry Bor keeps his word, even to murderers. When you talk for a living, your word has to be gold, and mine is.

"On this blog were pictures of a young woman whose name is Lauren Hutchens. I'd be remiss in not informing you that she is quite a looker. But in this picture that was posted online, she also appears to be dead, with a cord around her neck. The site also contains a photograph of her driver's license.

"I personally checked police records on-line, and have come to learn that a Lauren Hutchens was recently found murdered in the Fenway section of Boston. No one has been arrested in the crime. Whoever should be, that person is busy calling me. Ladies and gentlemen, I, Barry Bor, am in touch with a murderer, and the most chilling part I've yet to tell you. I will — right after this commercial message."

"Fuck. Fuck. Fuck."

That was me, yelling at the damned Bose radio that sat on a small armoire in my room — such an innocent object, such a bearer of bad news on this morning.

The phone rang again, undoubtedly with Martin on the other end of the line. I picked it up with a clipped "I can't believe we screwed up this badly."

There were a few seconds of silence in response, which instantly struck me as bizarre. When there was still no response, I said, "Hello. Peter?"

The caller asked, "Are you listening to the Barry Bor Show?"

Whoever asked that question asked it in a voice that sounded in some way automated — as if he was talking through a scrambler or a synthesizer.

"Who's calling?" I asked, blurting out the words.

"Are you listening to the Barry Bor Show?" Again, the words had that slightly synthetic quality to them.

I said, "I am. But who is this?"

"Why didn't you write about me in today's newspaper?"

Now my shoulders reflexively shuddered and my head clouded anew. I kind of knew how Barry Bor felt. I've talked to presidents and senators and even killers after the fact. But I've never talked to an unknown murderer who was vowing to kill again.

I said, "I was trying to get you in today's paper. We didn't think we had enough information."

"You know Lauren Hutchens is dead. I killed her. You know Jill Dawson is dead. I killed her, too. And I'm going to kill again."

The way he said *kill,* the *k* tripped over itself and the *ll* had a long echo to it, making it sound somewhere far beyond macabre, especially since I was reasonably sure he would follow up on his threats. I shook my head and pushed my shoulders back, silently attempting to get a grip on myself, and I said, "Why did you call Barry Bor?"

Now, I'll admit, there were a lot of lead questions I could have posed to this admitted murderer, not the least of which were: Why are you killing? When will you kill again? Who will you kill? Will you give yourself up? I could have even asked the completely self-interested question: Did you try to kill me, or if not, do you know who did? But here I was, worried not so much about the safety of Boston's female population as I was about the competitive position of the *Boston Record.*

The caller replied, "I contacted you first. You ignored me."

"I didn't ignore you. We need more information from you. I'm not a damned radio talk show. I deal in facts, and I need more of them." I hesitated here, hesitated at the thought of what I was about to do, then said, "And we need you to work exclusively through the *Record.*"

I used the word *work,* as if what he was doing was political fund-raising or maybe whistle-blowing on some unraveling government project, everything polite and aboveboard and squarely on the side of virtue. But the reality was that I was trying to sell my paper and myself to a killer so we could get the exclusive story. There are some days I think I probably would've been better off if I had followed an old girlfriend's advice and gone to law school. This day was foremost among them — and it wasn't even six in the morning yet.

He remained silent, so I filled the void with "We can work together, but that won't happen if you're talking to inflammatory talk show hosts who aren't going to treat your information with the respect that the *Record* would. And because you're dealing through a medium that no one takes seriously, people, the public, aren't going to take you seriously."

Here I was, giving my full-on sales pitch to a guy who had strangled two women, actually stood there tightening a ligature around their necks and watching the life leave their panicked eyes. And I was trying to sell him on a relationship with the *Record.* I made a mental note that I was a complete asshole.

"What kind of information?" he asked.

Good question. What was I going to say, Hold the line while I call the damned publisher and ask her what the hell else she needs before we put this story into print? I wisely, even uncharacteristically, bit my tongue and instead asked, "Are you the Boston Strangler? And why are you doing this?"

The caller said, "Go to the bench in the northwest corner of Columbus Park at nine a.m. Don't get there a minute beforehand or you'll never hear from me again. Don't call the police or you'll never hear from me again. Bring your cell phone."

He hung up. I could still hear the *n* vibrat-

151

ing on the word *phone* because of the synthesizer he was using.

As I put the receiver down, I listened to Barry Bor say on the radio, "Ladies and gentlemen, the chosen few, you are listening to talk radio history here today. We, meaning you and me, are making history. I have been talking to a gruesome murderer who is vowing to kill again, and will tell us where and when he strangles his next woman . . ."

I flipped the stereo off and the room went quiet except for the sounds of the ocean breeze pushing against the outside window — at least I hoped it was the breeze that was nudging the window. Who knew anymore?

Pleading with a killer for an exclusive story. Another day in the life of the intrepid reporter, and it would quickly get worse from there.

12

The day came bright and breezy, the breeze carrying with it more than a hint of spring. The sun caressed my cheeks with its golden fingers. The grass was even turning from winter brown to a pale shade of green.

So why, then, did I still feel such doom as I strode from Atlantic Avenue into Columbus Park at about two minutes to nine on this Wednesday morning? Well, first off, there are the obvious answers. I suspected the day would bring with it more death, most likely of yet another innocent young woman long before her time.

Second, I was still infuriated at my own newspaper for blowing a blockbuster story and putting me in this kind of bind with an admitted killer. And I wasn't exactly pleased with myself over the unseemly telephone negotiations that I carried on that morning with this man who called himself the Phantom Fiend.

Third, there was no small amount of trepidation that I was being set up here on this park bench by whoever tried to kill me on the Charles River two nights before. Or maybe that's *whomever.* I can never figure these things out. That said, I hoped that since he picked a place so prominent and a time so public, he wouldn't be trying anything funny.

Finally, this was the park where I used to bring Baker virtually every day for the past many years to romp and fetch a tennis ball until his tongue was hanging to the ground. Baker was my old golden retriever, dead a little more than a year now, but never a flicker of the memory from my mind. We always saw the first red leaf of autumn together, the first flake of winter, and the first bud of spring. We were an item then, and I thought we always would be, until the day when he was diagnosed with advanced cancer at Angell Memorial Hospital and taken from me before I barely had a chance to say good-bye.

Okeydoke. So, we're off to a perfectly terrific start to yet another wonderful day, one that would surely include murder and at least a little mayhem, as well as lame excuses from my newpaper higher-ups for their colossal screw-up, pleas for dinner invitations from Vinny Mongillo, and maybe a face-to-face meeting with a past and present serial killer who calls himself the Phantom Fiend. What was my alternative — to have gotten married to a beautiful woman and jetted off to a resort in gorgeous Hawaii? Then again, Maggie Kane hadn't left that alternative on the table for me, not as she was fleeing on a connecting flight through the Atlanta airport to God only knows where. Maybe she was in Hawaii, which wouldn't necessarily be a bad thing, because at least someone would be getting use of a hotel that I had already paid for.

Ah yes, a great day getting even greater.

I found my way to a bench in what I believed was the far northwest corner of the park. It looked out over the grass, through a bare trellis, toward a part of Boston Harbor where I once swam in pursuit of an escaping intruder in the middle of the night, in what I guess I'd now refer to as the good old days. Now that I thought of it, I should apply for hazardous duty pay. Either that or enroll in swimming lessons at the YMCA and send Peter Martin the bill.

So there I sat, thinking, waiting, and wondering. I wasn't there but two minutes when my cell phone chimed. When I answered, all I heard was silence.

Well, not exactly total silence. I heard what sounded like a young calf chewing on its cud.

"Mongillo?" I asked.

"Oh, hey, sorry, Fair Hair. I'm on the treadmill and didn't hear you pick up."

"Are you eating and running? Isn't that illegal?"

"Just a PowerBar. And no, I'm being careful."

He was out of breath, I noticed. I mean, really out of breath, as in, I was half tempted to ask him if I could be the beneficiary on his 401(k) plan and hold a microcassette up to the damned phone.

He said, "Did you hear your boy on the Barry Bor Show?"

Jesus, the whole world listened to that stupid call-in program at that ungodly hour. I replied, "Me and everyone else in Boston. We really fucked up."

"That we did, but nothing more you or I could have done to prevent it. Listen, I have a pretty good guess where the next murder is going to be. How about we meet for lunch to talk about it."

"You're saying you know who he's going to kill and you want to go have lunch?"

"No, I'm saying I think I know what neighborhood, or even street, he might kill next. And yes on lunch. Nice of you to ask."

"I've got a meeting. I'm not sure if I'll be out. But I'll call you."

He asked, "Who's the meeting with?"

"The Phantom." Then I added, "I've got to leave this line open. Call you soon."

He was whistling as I hung up the phone — chewing, panting, and whistling.

A moment later, an elderly man ambled past, still dressed for winter in a long wool herringbone coat, even though the day was screaming spring. People are like that in this town — suspicious of the weather, slow to acknowledge that the season is really changing, always believing that the next wind is going to send another cold front or storm system our way.

This old man, though, he was looking at me, almost studying me, and the truth is, he looked familiar.

He stopped short and said, "Excuse me, but did you used to have a dog?"

I wondered if that was some sort of code for "I'm the Phantom Fiend and I just committed another murder." I replied, "I did, but he died about a year ago of cancer."

He nodded slowly and said, "I used to watch the two of you play fetch out here in the mornings. You were quite a pair."

Well, okay, I wasn't sure I knew how this

morning could get any worse. I said, "Thank you," but he had already turned and was walking off.

My phone chimed again.

"Any luck?"

It was Peter Martin, once more not seeing the need for the kind of manners that separate human beings from lower forms of life.

"It depends what you call luck. If you're asking if I've been approached yet by a serial murderer and asked to go take a car ride to a dark warehouse where my life will be immediately endangered, the answer is no. But in that same regard, I also feel kind of lucky, so the answer would be yes."

He dismissed that line without even seeming to think about it.

"No sign of him yet?"

"No."

"Keep me posted."

We hung up. I scanned the park. There were a few young mothers pushing strollers together on the cement path closest to the shoreline. Businessmen and -women were coming and going in either direction. A maintenance worker was spearing loose litter with a sharp-edged pole and placing the trash in a plastic bag.

In other words, there were abundant witnesses to anything that might happen here, which was a relief, but which also made me wonder if the Phantom or the Strangler or whatever he might like to be called would be frightened off by the exposure of the venue. But he's the one who picked the spot.

I should also mention that Edgar Sullivan, the *Record*'s aging but no less relentless director of security, was somewhere with a view of this park, if not actually in it, per Martin's orders. We had discussed calling the police, but immediately dismissed it because of the myriad possibilities that they would screw things up.

My phone chimed anew.

"Flynn," I said.

"Go into the trash can to your immediate right and pull out today's *Boston Traveler*. Open up to page thirty-eight and see the destination written across the top of the page. Place the newspaper back in the receptacle, do not pick up your phone again, and take a taxi directly to the location that is written down. If you use your phone between now and the time you get to the location, either you will be killed or you will never see me again."

It was that same slightly synthesized voice, the words fringed by just a bit of static, as if someone was speaking through a machine set on its lowest level of alteration. By the way, who uses the word *receptacle* except for maybe a junior high school vice principal or a bureaucrat with the city sanitation department? I thought better than to question him on his language usage and instead said, "I'll do exactly as told." For kicks, I added, "Is there a number where I can reach you if something goes awry?"

By the time I got that request out, he had already hung up. They say that jokes are all about timing, and I'm starting to think they're right.

I stood up and walked to the green barrel to the right of the bench and saw a copy of that day's *Traveler* lying near the top. I say near because on top of the paper were several plastic bags filled with what could politely be called dog waste. As I pulled the paper up, one bag spilled open and the, ahem, waste dripped onto the front page. Now, I'm not saying this is an inappropriate substance to appear on the front of the *Traveler;* God knows they've published worse. But I am saying I'd prefer it wasn't on a paper I had to read.

I carefully flipped the paper open to page thirty-eight while trying to avoid getting dog shit on my hands. The smell wasn't entirely pleasant. It always seems fine when it's your

160

own dog, but someone else's, it's completely gross. It wouldn't happen this way in the movies, with the handsome hero trying to avoid the animal feces as he's working toward saving the city — that I knew for sure.

Anyway, I got to the appropriate page, and written across the top in pen were the words "Prudential Skywalk. Telescope in the corner pointing toward Charles River and downtown Boston." And that was that. This Phantom definitely had a flare for the dramatic.

I placed the paper back in the barrel, as ordered, making a mental note to call Peter Martin at the first available opportunity and see if we could get a handwriting analyst to look at the paper before the garbagemen came. I walked back out onto Atlantic Avenue and flagged a cab that happened to be passing by.

The Prudential Skywalk, for the uninitiated, is the pavilion on the fiftieth floor of the Prudential Center, for a while the tallest building in town, but now eight floors shorter than the nearby Hancock Tower a few blocks away. The Pru, as Bostonians tend to call it, is a remarkably ugly structure, boxy and boring and nearly a blight, except it's our blight, and for that, the city loves it.

I got out of the cab on Boylston Street, reflexively looked straight up at the top of the building in the way that tourists from New Hampshire probably do, and took the escalator up into the mall that wraps around the skyscraper. The streets and mall passages were busy with late-arriving workers and early shoppers, and I looked around in quasi-wonderment at whether I was being followed. I assumed that the Phantom was probably already in the Skywalk, though if he was, what was with all the taxicab stuff? Why not simply sit on the bench with me in Columbus Park?

The elevator ride made my ears pop, as elevator rides generally do. At the top, I paid the nine-dollar admission fee and pictured Martin quibbling with me when I submitted the expense. He'd argue that I should have been able to talk my way in for free because I wasn't actually going to see the view.

As I strode out onto the glass-enclosed Skywalk, the first sensation was that of light — light everywhere, streaming through the windows, reflecting off the floors, dancing along the walls, glistening off the telescopes that were pointing at the Financial District and the harbor beyond.

The second sensation was that of space —

space everywhere. I don't care how old I am, I don't care how many times I've sat in offices or dined in restaurants atop high-rise buildings; whenever I do, the feeling is one of being above it all, figuratively as well as literally. The city below is minuscule, as are all the little problems of everyday life, things like traffic and litter and crowds and late appointments. High in the sky, you're above the daily grind, free to contemplate the larger issues of life.

Which I don't necessarily think was good at the moment, because what I had to contemplate were hardly the issues of soaring dreams. A broken marriage before the vows were ever recited, two dead women, a newspaper publisher with no balls, a serial killer who regarded me as his confidant, and some unknown would-be assailants who seemed to want me dead. I think I'd have to be soaring around the earth in a space shuttle for these problems to appear small at the moment, but maybe that's where the Phantom would send me next.

Speaking of which, I didn't see him. Of course, I didn't expect him to be padding around the Skywalk with one of those stickers on the front of his jacket that says, "Hello, my name is Phantom Fiend." But I didn't see anyone who looked the part.

Actually, I didn't see anyone at all, which didn't entirely thrill me.

So I went to the assigned telescope, which, as described, was tucked into the corner overlooking both the Charles River and downtown Boston. The morning sun sparkled on the calm skin of the water and flashed on the distant office towers. In the distance, the newly clean water of Boston Harbor looked nearly turquoise.

I had no change for the telescope and wasn't of the mind to walk back into the lobby to get any, so I stood and drank in the view with my bare eyes. Vehicles in miniature dawdled down Boylston Street fifty stories below, reminding me of the Matchbox cars my father used to bring home for me when I was a kid. Down on the street, people were but insignificant little specks flitting about, and I couldn't help but think that's how the Phantom regarded them in life as well as in death — as insignificant, a means toward a very temporary gratification, or maybe just a step in his pursuit of fame.

I wondered if on a clear day you could see Hawaii. Probably not. And then I realized I was facing the wrong way, which I deemed to be something of a metaphor, though for what, I wasn't exactly sure. I did know one thing for certain: it would be nice if Maggie picked up the phone and gave me a call. That said, I hadn't actually broken a finger dialing her cell phone number, either.

Just then my phone rang. I looked at the incoming number and saw it was "Unavailable." I answered with my trademark, clipped "Jack Flynn here."

"I told you to go alone and you're not," the Phantom said.

I looked down the long, sun-soaked expanse of the Skywalk in both directions and saw an older man in a Red Sox cap and sunglasses peering through a telescope. From the way he was standing, favoring one leg, I assumed it was Edgar. I replied, "I wasn't followed, and I haven't used my phone."

The Phantom didn't respond directly to that assertion. Instead, he said without a hint of impatience, "Leave the Prudential Center complex. Drive by taxi to the September 11th memorial in the Public Garden. Go there right away. Again, do not use your cell phone or contact anyone about anything. I will meet you there."

This Phantom was lucky I had a lot of time on my hands. Truth is, I was starting to doubt his last assertion, that he'd meet me there, and was wondering if this might be some sort of wild serial-killer chase, meaning I was going to come away empty-handed and still without a story for the next day's *Record*. That being the case, I suspected good old Barry Bor would be getting another call on his show, and I'd have yet another miserable morning to follow.

I did as told again. Should I ever reunite with Maggie Kane, this was probably pretty good practice at being married. Again, a cab happened to be out front, but I was less suspicious because it was an actual cabstand. I rode the six blocks down to the Public Garden in anxious silence, got out at the corner of the park, and walked along the sidewalk of Arlington Street toward the main entrance at the base of Commonwealth Avenue.

This park was also familiar ground. It's where I got engaged to be married, where I first told a former live-in girlfriend named Elizabeth Riggs that I loved her as we tromped through the sunlit snow one Sunday morning in the calm aftermath of a bad blizzard, where I last saw former *Record* publisher Paul Ellis alive the morning he was murdered in the parking lot of his newspaper. And now I was heading for this memorial built in honor of 202 Massachusetts residents killed in the attack on the

World Trade Center in New York; many of the people were aboard the two planes that were hijacked shortly after leaving Logan Airport on the morning of September 11.

When I was about thirty yards from the park gates, I saw a cab roll to a stop at the entrance. The door flung open and a well-dressed young man — I say well dressed and young because he looked similar to me — stepped out and strode purposefully inside the park in the direction of the September 11 memorial. Across the wrought-iron fence and through the defoliated trees that separated the Public Garden from Arlington Street, I could see the man sit on one of the stone benches facing a memorial wall etched with the names of all the victims. I slowed down, curious. He slouched with his two hands folded under his chin. He then hung his head low, his hands holding the back of his neck in what I guessed was sad contemplation.

I kept walking toward the gates of the Public Garden, but slower now. I didn't know if this was the man I was supposed to meet. If it was, I was shocked at his age, which, like I said, was close to mine. I had anticipated someone much older, from the voice on the phone and the fact that the original Boston stranglings had occurred forty-plus years before. More likely, the guy was simply a visitor to the memorial, and a visitor who looked like he wanted some time alone.

It was when I was walking through the grand front gates, toward the memorial, that I heard what could have been a car backfiring, or someone setting off firecrackers, but I knew instantly to my core that it was something else entirely: gunshots. Reflexively, I ran my hands down my arms and torso to see if I had been the target. I felt nothing liquid, which was good. I also didn't feel any pain, which was better. The sound had come from the area of the memorial, so I instinctively hunched low along the evergreen bushes and trotted along the cement path toward the man I had seen earlier.

I had run maybe twenty yards when, without warning, a figure in black blasted from one of the bushes and slammed directly into my face and chest with such ferocious force that we were both knocked to the ground. My head bounced on the pavement, causing me to see the clichéd stars of comic-book fame. More to the point, I also saw a handgun clank on the ground a few feet from my left arm. Without thinking, which is probably why I did it, I lunged for it, but the guy who knocked me over had already scrambled to his feet and dove on the weapon just ahead of me. He then leapt back up and sprinted toward the park entrance. I climbed unsteadily to my feet and set off in an uncertain pursuit.

I had staggered but a dozen or so steps when I saw the guy fling open the back door of an awaiting van along the curb of Arlington Street. I saw the van peel away. I heard a woman wailing in the distance, "He's bleeding to death. Someone call for help. He's dying."

The next day's paper would identify the victim as Joshua Carpenter, the husband of a flight attendant who was killed in the September 11, 2001, attack. His family would be quoted saying that, without the actual body of his wife, without a gravestone to mark it, he visited the memorial every morning to mourn her. Police would say that he was the victim of a brazen daylight robbery, and that uniformed officers and plainclothes detectives were calling in all their informants and scouring the city's most drug-addled sections for any tips on the killers.

I knew it wasn't a robbery. I knew this poor man wasn't the intended victim. And I knew as well that the cops would never find the killer.

But that's all I knew, and that was a huge problem.

13

My plane bounced down at McCarran International Airport in Las Vegas, as if the pilot was in as big a rush to get to the tables as everyone else. Everyone but me, that is. I had come here to gamble, though not in the same way that my fellow passengers likely would. No, I was in Vegas to pay a visit to one Bob Walters, once one of the lead investigators on the Boston Strangler case, a lieutenant detective now retired from the Boston Police Department for some twenty years.

I'll admit, it would have been a hell of a lot easier to have called him on the phone instead of flying nearly three thousand miles to knock on his door, except that I subscribe to the theory that in newspaper reporting, and life in general, it's always better to show up. If there's only one thing I've learned in twenty-plus years in the information negotiation business, it's this: People tell you things in person that they wouldn't on the phone. They're not as likely to slam a door in your face as they are a receiver in your ear. They admire the effort made in pursuit of knowledge, and generally reward it.

I also thought it was a pretty opportune excuse to get the hell out of Boston, given that people kept dying the worst possible deaths, with at least one of those deaths apparently intended to be mine.

The day had been a tense one. Peter Martin, Vinny Mongillo, and I listened to Justine Steele's rationalization for not running the story that morning, reporting the fact that a serial killer named for the Boston Strangler had murdered at least two women and reached out to a *Record* reporter to warn that more deaths were on the way. I guess being publisher means, among other things, never having to say you're sorry, because an apology she did not give. What she did give, though, was a promise to run the story the following morning.

That led to the question of whether to report the fact that I had been contacted by someone claiming to be the Phantom who directed me to go to a location — the Boston Public Garden — in which someone was murdered. On this we collectively decided to withhold information, based on reasons I thought were just. It was all too circumstantial. It looked like we were trying too hard to inject ourselves into the story. And the tipster may not have been the Phantom at all. Truth be told, I didn't think he was.

Which brings me to the most significant question in all this, at least in regard to me: Who wanted me dead, and why? I was reaching the conclusion that it was preposterous, if not downright impossible, that the same figure tipping me off about the strangulation deaths of young women was also trying to kill me. Why guide me with letters and try to kill me in person?

So I updated the story for the following morning's paper to include the fact that the Phantom had also contacted radio host Barry Bor and led him to a website that contained photographs of a murder scene. That done, I sneaked to the airport in the back of Vinny Mongillo's car and boarded a nonstop Delta flight for Vegas. Normally I'd be over the moon about an all-expense paid trip to Sin City — a couple of nights in a five-star hotel, dinner at Craftsteak, black-jack at the Wynn Las Vegas, maybe a cocktail or two at the Ghost Bar. But on this particular trip, all I wanted to do was get safely to

173

my room, sleep for seven hours, and make it to Bob Walters's house in one living piece the following morning.

On Walters, I had an address, courtesy of Hank Sweeney, also retired from the Boston Police Department. I had a brief description that he could be ornery and impatient, but was also regarded as brilliant in his day. I think that actually describes me as well. I also knew that he was eighty-five years on this earth, not all of them particularly good to him.

Once in my room at the Venetian, I gave myself a little tour of the various luxuries, from the motorized drapery opener in the sunken sitting area to the bathroom that was roughly the size of my condominium on the Boston waterfront. I ordered a twenty-seven-dollar-room-service hamburger. I could already hear Martin asking if I paid for the entire steer. I checked my voice mails and realized with another pang of depression that Maggie Kane had not yet bothered to call. In a fit of either whimsy or impatience, I dialed her cell phone number with no idea what I was going to say. Fortunately or unfortunately, it kicked directly into her voice mail. I listened to her recording for several long seconds and hung up.

Nothing from the Phantom, either, by the way.

I fired up my laptop and checked my e-mail. Again, nothing from Maggie and nothing from the Phantom. I flicked on the television, but all the March Madness NCAA basketball previews were over for the night. The most interesting thing on the tube was a hotel video of a dealer giving a lesson in baccarat, which I figured after about a minute of watching him would take me roughly six years and a million dollars to learn.

I hit the Off switch on the TV's remote and turned my attention back to the computer as I bided time waiting for my gold-plated burger. I absently flipped back through my laptop's remote e-mail account and inexplicably clicked on a note that Maggie had sent me eight months earlier.

In it, she was talking about an award she had just been given as the teacher of the year at her school, and what it meant, and why she believed in her heart that the reason she had just won it was because she was a better teacher and a better, happier person since she met me — that the pain in her life, the loss of a child, the breakup of a marriage, the death of her sister, had lessened since she met me. I read the note a second time, this time with a lump in my throat.

I clicked on another e-mail from her about a month later. This one was a short, chatty, flirty little missive. I was on a work trip to New York, due home that night. She asked me to try to get on an earlier shuttle because she didn't think she could wait another minute to have sex.

I opened up another that said, simply, "I love you." I clicked on one that she had sent a few minutes later that said, "I want you." And a couple of minutes after that, she wrote, "Now."

I couldn't help but smile, sitting in a dark hotel room that was illuminated by a low-hanging desk lamp and the bright neon of the strip shining through the picture window. It was a smile, yes, but a rueful one. Not for the first time, I thought how tough it is at the beginning of something good to remember that it's probably going to end bad, such being one of the overriding lessons of my life.

In those first, heady weeks and months of a relationship, it's impossible to think that the whole thing will fall apart with a phone call made from the Atlanta airport on what's supposed to be your wedding day. When you start a new job, it's impossible to picture the day your company is sold and you're summoned down to the human resources department and told you'll be given two months' severance, but they need all your stuff out of the building by the end of that day. When you watch a new puppy romping around the house, you can't foresee the day you're lying with him on the floor of a veterinary office while the doctor sticks a needle in his leg that will forever relieve him of his pain.

But that's the thing about beginnings — they inevitably, invariably, lead to endings. Jill Dawson and Lauren Hutchens couldn't foresee their end coming with a ligature around their throats and some freak watching the life vanish from their panic-stricken eyes. That poor widower in the Public Garden, Joshua Carpenter, couldn't have imagined that his end would come with a bullet to the head while he mourned the loss of his wife, whose ending itself he could never have foreseen. And I never in a million years imagined driving to the hospital with a pregnant wife that morning too many years before and returning home alone that night, completely alone, because Katherine and the daughter I never knew died in childbirth.

I scrolled upward on my computer until I found the name of Elizabeth Riggs, the one

I let get away, despite the fact that every sane cell inside of me screamed for me to hold on for the rest of my life. I clicked on the e-mail and it simply said, "The two of you were snoring in stereo."

That one line just about jumped off my computer screen and kicked me in the gut. I knew instantly what she meant, even if the note was sent some three years before. She had been complaining to me, tongue in cheek, about the lack of sleep from the night before, not because of any wild circus sex, but because I was on one side of her and Baker on the other, both of us with colds, snoring in her ears. I even remembered that night, stretched out long and comfortable in my bed with a woman and a dog I would always love, having no idea that everything — everything — comes to an end.

And then it did, the day she walked down the jetway to board a flight for San Francisco. She told me she loved me, but she knew I couldn't love her back, not the way she needed me to. And all I could do was stand there like an idiot and mutter goodbye. Very rarely, too rarely, endings come with warnings, but far more often they don't.

Someone rang the doorbell of the hotel room. I jumped up, startled, then heard a man's voice call out, "Room service." When I opened the door, he rolled in a cart and reached into a warmer. For a fleeting moment, I thought he might pull out a gun. Instead, he held out a plate with my hamburger. We exchanged pleasantries, I signed the check, and he left. I took a bite of the burger, which was good, though twenty-seven dollars' worth of good, I doubted. Of course, at that moment, it could have been the best burger ever and I don't think I would have tasted a thing. I dropped it back on the plate with a quiet thud and pushed the cart back toward the door.

I looked around the empty hotel room and thought about my empty apartment back home. Had I been the one to die in the Public Garden that day, I wondered how many people would have really, truly cared. Would Maggie have come back for the funeral? Elizabeth? Is that what it would take to be with them again, to finally be at peace in our relationships, for me to be dead?

Wait a minute. This wasn't me. This wasn't how I thought. This wasn't how I looked at life.

I flicked off the desk lamp, leaving the room with just the glare of the red and blue neon outside. And with that, I climbed slowly into bed.

14

The day dawned with a chain saw ripping through the darkness and heading toward my handsome head. I bolted upright to see who or what was attacking me, and for that matter, where I had been taken hostage, when I realized I was in a hotel room, a pretty nice one, actually, and the urgent sound emanated from my cell phone, which was lying on the nightstand. I squinted at the alarm clock's lighted red numbers and saw it was 3:15 a.m.

"Peter, it's the middle of the fucking night here," I said, my voice still thick from a sleep that had barely begun.

In response, I heard no response, just silence. I said, "Hello?"

The caller cleared his throat, hesitated, and asked, "Is Jack Flynn there, please?" It was one of those deep voices that called attention to itself, like Ted Baxter's on the old Mary Tyler Moore show, but with more of an edge.

I replied, "He is."

Again, no response, not immediately, anyway. The caller cleared his throat again and said, "May I please speak to him?" He calls me at three-fifteen in the morning and he keeps using the word *please,* as if he's being polite.

I said, "You are."

"Great. Jack, if I may call you Jack, this is Walt Bedrock from the WBZ-TV morning show. Terrific story in today's *Record.* Terrific read. We're interested in getting you on the air so you can tell people about it."

The name was familiar to me in the way that the names of dozens of lightweight television reporters and anchors are familiar to me, which is to say it was barely familiar at all. Put them all in a room together and you'd discover an immediate cure for even the worst TV addict.

I asked, "Didn't I already tell people about it — in the *Record*?"

Again he hesitated. Sometimes you're on someone's wavelength, other times you couldn't possibly be further away. Walt Bedrock and I, it was immediately apparent, were like fire and ice, though it was either too early in the morning or too late at night to tell who was which.

"Possibly," he said, "but —"

I cut him off and asked, "Walt, if I may call you Walt, what's your viewership over there on the WBZ-TV morning show?"

Don't ask me why I was this angry at this hour. Maybe because of the hour, though poor Walt Bedrock didn't know I was trying to sleep 2,800 miles and three time zones away, and he never would. More likely it was my visceral disdain for reporters interviewing reporters, an increasingly common practice among the laziest denizens of my world.

"We are watched in a hundred and ten thousand households a morning." He said this proudly.

I replied, "The *Record* prints five hundred and twenty thousand papers each day, with an average readership of 1.7 people per paper. Plus there's however many hundreds of thousands of people who read the *Record* online, freeloaders that they are. Why don't I just stick with my medium and you stick with yours?"

He hesitated yet again, and then said, "Because this is TV."

Good answer. Perfect answer. Couldn't have imagined a better one coming from a guy who undoubtedly sits in a studio for his entire three-hour workday, reads a script, and moves his hands and facial muscles exactly like the producers tell him to through an earpiece that's never as well hidden as they think.

I said, "Walt, I'm going to do you a favor. We've never met, but I've got the kind of face that was born to be in newspapers. Trust me, you put me on the air and you'll shrink to sixty thousand viewers that day, most of whom would have the last name of Flynn. And it's not a particularly desirable demographic for advertisers. Thank you anyway."

And I hung up. No sooner than I had sprawled out anew did the phone ring again.

"Jack Flynn here," I said.

"Jack, you're a superstar. You're a real fucking superstar, but you probably know that already."

"I do. Who's calling?"

His voice, by the way, was inexplicably strong and nasally at the same time, like a football player addicted to Afrin.

"It's Brett. Brett Faldo. Senior producer from the *Today* show. Meredith and Matt asked me to call you. They absolutely love your story in today's paper. They want to get you on the air ASAP, as in this morning. We're not even going to make you go into the remote studio. We'll send a crew over to your place to make this easy on everybody."

"Who are Meredith and Matt?"

He laughed his nasally, jocular little laugh, incredulous, as if I had asked who Christ was. He said, "Just give me an address. You're a hero, and you're going to make this a great show."

I'm a hero. I'm a superstar. A killer emerges from a four-decade hibernation, or maybe a new killer comes along with a passion for history, decides to contact me with a couple of cryptic notes and the driver's licenses of a pair of dead women, and that makes me, in the eyes of the broadcast-news media world, not merely a superstar but a hero as well.

I should have anticipated this, and I guess to a certain extent I probably did. But there's a difference between anticipating something and preparing for it. I had no set answer, which may have been just as well, because that brought me to my default answer whenever a television show asked me on as a guest, which was, in a word, no. What I had said to Walt Bedrock about having a face meant for newspapers wasn't entirely untrue — though maybe a little bit so.

I said, "Meredith and Matt, they're on

185

really early, right?"

"Every day, yes." Proud of this. Very proud.

I said, "The problem is, I don't get up that early."

He gave me that same laugh. I'm betting he used to give Tom Brokaw that same laugh regardless of how bad the jokes may have been. Brian Williams, that's probably a different story; he's supposed to be legitimately funny, though I bet Brett, his nose constantly twitching for the next story or office politics vibration, can't tell the difference.

"Like I said," he said, his tone clicking ever so slightly from solicitous to demanding, "we'll make this easy on everyone. Meredith and Matt really want this to happen. I'm not going to tell them it can't. I'll have a crew over to your place in thirty minutes. Just tell me where."

"I could, Brett. But the problem is, I'm not there. I'd love to help you, Meredith, and Matt out, but I'm working on a story for tomorrow's *Record*. I've got my own job to do, Brett. As a matter of fact, I've got to run and do it now. Thanks for your kind offer."

I heard him whining into the phone as I hung up.

Not ten seconds later, the phone chimed again.

"Yeah, Flynn here."

"Jack, Regis Philbin here . . ."

Seriously, it was Regis Philbin. I love the man, I really do, but now was not the time to profess it. I write a story destined to rock my native Boston right to its parochial core, and this is how it begins to unwind, with a bunch of TV people wanting to piggyback on what they don't have. And I thought it was newspapers that were in trouble. Well, okay, maybe we are as well, but at least there's some honor to it.

As soon as I extricated myself — politely so — from that offer, I turned my phone off, rose from bed, and gazed out the window at the flashing neon up and down the Vegas strip — Paris to my left, New York–New York and the Bellagio across the street, the outdated Bally's to my right. I wondered if my gamble would pay off today, not just for me but for women I didn't yet know, women who were marked to die. Which is when it hit me. Most stories, truth be told, were little more than an exercise in this grand and illustrious business of reporting. If you get it, terrific, you make a splash, maybe cause some humiliation, perhaps even a resignation. Believe me, been there, done that, with mayors and governors and even a president. But this one, this one was different. People's lives were on the line, people I didn't know. A killer might have been playing games with these notes and driver's licenses and all that, but it wasn't a game at all. I was in the middle of it, but felt like a mere conduit, working on behalf of people I would probably never know.

I did know this, though: I needed a good hand, I needed it fast, or more people, myself possibly included, were destined to die.

15

At about nine o'clock, I slowly drove down Rodeo Road, a street, I'm fairly certain, that was pronounced like the sporting event with the cowboys on the bucking broncos, and not the more affected shopping boulevard that runs through the heart of Beverly Hills. I once quite literally bumped into Angelina Jolie on that boulevard, but that's not really the point here. I'd bet Mongillo's lunch money that I wasn't going to run into her today.

Still, the houses surprised me for their size, which is to say they were large, as well as for their condition, which was well kept. These were nice homes painted in subtle, sophisticated colors with wide, irrigated lawns and freshly trimmed fauna. All very un–Las Vegas — although what did I expect, giant lighted flamingos in residential developments? Some of the houses had big bay windows, others had triple-car garages. It appeared very quiet, this neighborhood, meaning there weren't kids running around the streets playing kick the can, but maybe that's because kids don't play that anymore.

Anyway, 284 Rodeo Road was a gray center-entrance house with two levels and a brick driveway. More important, it was also where Bob Walters had come to live after retiring from the Boston Police Department, which gets back to the point about me being surprised. This didn't look like the kind of street where old men on a public-service pension could afford to retire, but maybe he bought at just the right time, as it was being built, or maybe he had family money on one side or the other. People and money, I've learned in life, will always surprise you in ways good and bad.

I glided past the house to get a sense of what I was dealing with, as well as to stall for a little more time, and a block or two down pulled a U-turn and circled back. The garage doors were closed, as was the center door. The windows were all pulled shut, some of them darkened by drawn shades or curtains. The sprinklers were not on, but then again, they weren't on any other lawns, either. Maybe that whole thing about not watering the grass while the sun beats down on it is true. But how would I know? I live in a downtown condominium.

All of this is to say that it didn't look like there was anyone home, or if there was, it didn't appear that they had jumped out of bed and happily embraced the new day, as I had nearly six hours earlier. I knew Walters's phone number and could call, but why would I do that after flying all the way across the country to knock on his door? If he wasn't home, I wouldn't leave a note, because the element of surprise was an advantage I wasn't ready to cede. No, I'd end up staking out his place for pretty much the entire day if I had to. The big problem would come if he and his wife were away on vacation, but they already lived in Vegas — where the hell would they go?

I pulled up to the curb next to the neat sidewalk and parked. "Hello, Detective, Jack Flynn, it's an honor to meet you. I've come a long way to ask you a few questions and am hoping you can be of help."

That was me, practicing. I don't usually do that, but I was uncharacteristically nervous over this encounter, if they were home to have one. I needed to get this right.

A couple of more sessions like that, and then I opened the door, pulled myself out of the rental car, and walked up to the house, carrying just a blank legal pad in my hands. The day, by the way, was nothing shy of brilliant, with a big sun floating in the shallow blue sky and temperatures that felt like the low seventies, cooled with just a whisper of a desert breeze. Beats the hell out of a Florida retirement, that's for sure.

I rang the doorbell but didn't hear the chiming sound inside, so I wasn't surprised that it didn't get any sort of response. I stood for several long seconds waiting, then opened the screen door and knocked.

Nothing.

I knocked again. Still nothing. No dogs barking, cats meowing, home owners threatening me to get off their property. Just empty, dead air, sonorously punctuated by a few birds chirping from a distant tree.

I knocked a final time, to the same lack of response, so I shut the screen door and walked back to my car. I didn't like the feel of this, but couldn't figure out why.

I fidgeted with my cell phone, wondering if I should call Walters's number to make sure he wasn't home. He was probably running errands with his wife, or at a doctor's appointment. My worst case, he was on that vacation I feared, maybe off visiting a grandchild back in Massachusetts. We could have passed each other at the airport here or in Boston, or maybe our planes roared by each other thirty-three thousand feet in the sky. If so, at least I got the frequent-flier miles out of the trip.

Then something occurred to me: Maybe he was inside, dead. Maybe whoever had been trying to kill me killed him. It wasn't necessarily a rational thought, but these weren't necessarily rational times. People kept indiscriminately dying, or, as in my case, nearly dying, and there was no logical reason to think that pattern was about to stop or change.

I started to punch out his phone number, urgently now, when a red van pulled up to the curb behind my car, stopping abruptly a few feet from my back bumper. For some reason, it made me think of how I had declined the insurance at the car rental counter, because I'm told that's what you're always supposed to do. Anyway, the driver's-side door flung open and a twenty-something kid, a guy, in loose jeans and a T-shirt, trotted up to the front door holding a small brown paper bag. He opened the screen door and left the small bag in the gap between the doors. Two seconds later, he was gone.

I sat in my idling car with the cell phone in my hand and my sunglasses off, wondering what to do next. I didn't wonder for long. Maybe a minute later, the heavy storm door opened about halfway. I could see the face of an older woman through the screen. She looked around her yard quickly, picked up the bag, and shut the door tight. That was that.

I jumped out of the car, walked briskly back to the front door, and knocked. Again, no answer. So I knocked louder. No answer. If I'd knocked any louder, I'd have ended up knocking the fucking door down, so I backed off, quite literally, and walked across the lawn and around to the rear of the house.

I'll be honest here: I wanted to look in the windows. If you look in the front windows and a neighbor happens to see you, you're what's known as a Peeping Tom. If you look in the back windows where no one sees you, you're what's known as an intrepid reporter. They don't teach you these things at the Columbia School of Journalism, though they do at my alma mater, the School of Hard Knocks.

The backyard, by the way, was as lush and well kept as the front, with a carefully edged garden tucked close to the foundation of the house, and a stone patio leading to the back door. I walked up to the door, which, unlike the front, had two big windows, and looked inside.

I was looking into the kitchen, which seemed to be in need of some updating. My eyes were scanning along the cabinets and countertops and appliances when I saw a flash of movement. Sitting at a small table pushed up against a wall was a woman, undoubtedly the same one who came to the front door. She was sitting alone, sipping from a glass.

On the table before her was a bottle that looked to be vodka, and not one of the fancy new labels from countries I've never been to, but some plain old call brand. Beside the bottle was the brown paper bag on its side. The delivery had been from a local liquor store. I gazed back at the counter and saw that a similar but empty bottle sat next to the sink.

As I watched, she unscrewed the bottle and refilled her lowball glass, taking a long swig as she stared straight ahead at the pale green wall. I noticed on the wall some sort of embroidered poem that involved the words *home* and *love,* a piece of household kitsch, but was too far away to read anything more.

I stood in the back doorway, the warm desert sun on my neck, playing the unintentional role of the voyeur in what I immediately understood was this woman's sad and painful life. If anyone saw me, I was as good as arrested, though maybe the Las Vegas jail might be the safest place I could be. I watched as she finished off her drink and tilted the bottle into her glass yet again, spilling a few drops of vodka on the wooden top of her table. She drank again as she stared at things I would never be able to see.

I knocked. It was a soft knock at first, three times against the window in the door. I didn't want to startle her, and I didn't. She slowly turned her head in my direction. When her gaze set upon the door, she squinted as if she couldn't understand what she saw. She didn't move, though.

So I knocked again, a little harder this time. She slowly pulled herself to her feet and walked unsteadily across the tiled kitchen floor. She was wearing that kind of floral housedress that old ladies tend to wear, formless and unstylish. My guess was that she hadn't been planning on seeing anyone that day.

When she got to the door, our eyes met through the glass. Hers were bloodshot, exhausted, and slightly confused — yet still oddly serene. She looked at me for a long, awkward, silent moment, and then simply opened the door.

"I thought I left my MasterCard number with the clerk," she said. Her words were soft yet lurching, the end of one running into the beginning of another.

"I'm not with the liquor store, Mrs. Walters."

Unfazed, she said, "Come in." She walked unsteadily back to the kitchen table, took her seat, and asked, "Then who are you?"

I was still standing awkwardly in the doorway. I asked, "Do you mind if I sit down?"

She motioned to the chair. I sat and gave her my whole Jack-Flynn-from-the-*Boston-Record* thing. She remained entirely unimpressed, with my presence, with my position, with the distance I had traveled to be here.

"What is it you want?" she asked.

Her words came out lazy and a little bit warped. She took a sip out of her glass, the bottle still tall before her, doing nothing to hide the fact she was drinking vodka, straight up, at nine-thirty in the morning.

"I was hoping to talk with your husband," I said.

This finally got a rise out of her.

"My husband," she said dramatically, slurring even more the louder she spoke. She squinted at me and added, "You want to speak to my husband?"

Sometimes, in journalism, you have to play along, so I nodded and said without an ounce of disrespect, "Yes, Mrs. Walters, I was hoping to have a word with your husband."

She took a long gulp of vodka and refilled her glass, never offering me any, not that I would have accepted. She was looking down at the table for so long that I was starting to think I had lost her. Then she cast a glance at me and said, "About what?"

"The Boston Strangler."

I mean, why lie? Why wander down all sorts of hazy dead-end avenues with a woman too drunk to guide me on a clear path to the place I needed to go? At least the truth would set me forth in the right direction.

Well, maybe not. She coughed loud and hard, reflexively grabbing at her chest in that melodramatic way some people have of showing their distress. When she collected herself, she walked over to the kitchen sink and poured water from the tap into a glass. When she got back to the table, she put the glass down, untouched, and took another sip of booze.

Finally, she said, "You want to speak to

my husband about the Boston Stra...

Her face was contorting as she spoke, ... words slurring more now than the few minutes before when I arrived. This was not going as planned, but should be just a small obstacle, provided I didn't lose patience.

"Yes, ma'am," I said. "That's why I came out here from Boston."

"What about the Strangler?" she asked. Her words were so wobbly, they almost fell out of her slanted mouth and smashed on the floor.

I fidgeted now, growing uneasy, thinking for the first time that Mrs. Walters might prove to be a bigger obstacle than I had anticipated. I said, "Lots of things, ma'am. I'd rather just ask your husband."

In one shockingly smooth motion, she picked up her lowball glass and flung it across the kitchen. I whirled around to see it explode against her wooden cabinets, the force sending a spray of booze and shards in all directions.

She screamed, "Damn my husband. Damn the Boston Strangler. And damn you for asking about them."

All right, so this wasn't precisely the reaction I had expected to get. I had expected to be greeted at the door by a diminutive elderly woman who would show me into a

…ı where her husband, a retired …e detective, would pull out his …s and relive the case with me as …readied us some raisin scones in …chen.

…wanted to get the hell out of this house, and, for that matter, get the hell out of Vegas, but I sure as hell wasn't in a position to do that now. I said, "Mrs. Walters, I'm sorry for upsetting you. But what is it? What about the Strangler upsets you so much? That was forty years ago."

As I was asking this, it occurred to me there might be an obvious answer: He killed people. He violated the civility and livability of a city. He defeated her husband. Maybe she meant all that, but here's what she said: "He ruined my life." And after she said it, she looked down at the top of her wooden table and began to sob — one of those tearful, shoulder-shaking sobs that can't be comforted.

A moment later, she looked back up at me with glistening eyes and said, "He ruined my whole damned life. He took my husband from me. He took my marriage from me. He left me with nothing to look forward to but my next glass of booze."

"How, ma'am?"

She raged, "Fuck you. Fuck you for coming into my life and questioning what I have to say." Then she sobbed again.

I asked, "Ma'am, is your husband here?"

"Fuck him, too. Go tell him you want to talk about his Boston Strangler. Go tell him that. And tell him that they ruined my life, both of them."

"Where, ma'am? Where can I find him?"

When she looked at me, there was fury in her eyes. I feared that she might throw her water glass, or even the half-filled bottle of vodka.

"He's upstairs. Go tell him that they ruined my fucking life." Then, screaming, "Now. Tell him now."

I got up and walked from the kitchen, legal pad still in hand, my shoes crunching over broken glass, looking for the staircase, hoping though not hopeful that I wouldn't get a glass in the back of the head.

Behind me, Mrs. Bob Walters began crying again, crying hysterically, her head down on the table, her back quaking in uncontrollable spasms over a series of murders committed forty years before. Sometimes the past never lets up. That's a fact I know all too well. But I suddenly realized, with no small amount of hope, that there was something else at play here, something that might explain what had been going on in Boston the past week, something that might help me bring it to an end.

16

Bob Walters was propped up in a hospital bed watching a game show on a big, clunky television that was on the other side of the small room from the door. The shades were drawn tight. The nightstands on both sides of the bed were covered by used glasses and dirty dishes. A portable oxygen machine stood on the floor on the near side of the bed, its mask lying haphazardly on the rumpled blankets. The place reeked of disinfectants and the faint odor of illness, which the chemicals failed to cover up.

I stood in the doorway, undetected, instantly depressed over this little world I was about to enter, not to mention amazed that *The Price Is Right* was still on the air. Come on down, or in this case, come on in. No one had invited me, though, so I cleared my throat loud enough for Bob Walters, the former lieutenant detective with the Boston Police Department, to realize I was there.

"Where the fuck have you been?" he said, his words, though not loud, were as sharp as the broken glass that was strewn across the kitchen floor downstairs. He said this without ever moving his gaze from the television set. "This place is a fucking mess and you're sitting down there getting smashed, you drunken bitch."

Okay, so not everyone can be Ozzie and Harriet, but the Walters might have been carrying this to an antithetical extreme.

I cleared my throat again. Walters said, his voice no louder and every bit as sharp, "Get some of this crap out of here before you're too drunk to get up and down the stairs."

I said, "Lieutenant Walters?"

He pivoted his head on the pillow so that he was facing me. His eyes were the first thing I noticed. It was almost impossible not to. They were big and yellow and sunken deep into his bony face, vacant eyes that had seen so much of life but now rarely saw anything outside of the four dreary walls of this godforsaken little room. They were the eyes of a man resigned to misery.

The next thing was the stubble, coarse and gray, all along his jawline and neck, most pronounced on his upper lip and chin. He hadn't shaved — or been shaved — in at least a week, probably longer. Then his hair, all silvery black, mussed in the back, greasy and matted down on his forehead in the front.

And finally his skin, sallow and veiny, more of it than he needed in his current state — the skin of a dead man, really.

He said to me, "Who the hell are you?" His voice was old, tired, raspy, and world-weary, like warm water flowing through sand.

"Sir, I'm Jack Flynn, a reporter for the *Boston Record.* I've flown out here to ask you a few things about the Boston Strangler case. I'm wondering if you have the time to help me out."

Of course he had the time, I mean, unless he couldn't bring himself to miss a single glorious episode of *Let's Make a Deal,* which was probably on next. The more important question was whether he had the inclination. It's probably worth mentioning again that a lot of cops, active or retired, are particularly leery of newspaper reporters. Actually, forget leery. They hate reporters. We do the same basic thing, which is try to pull layers of lies away from essential truths, but we go about it in remarkably different ways. The cops do it mostly in the privacy of interrogation rooms or at crime scenes, or in the heat of violent moments when no one is watching but the suspects and God. Reporters, we're more public, tending toward documents and interviews that will be splashed on the pages of our newspaper.

The biggest schism comes from the fact that reporters tend to get particularly gleeful over policing cops, catching them in penny-ante shenanigans — the vice cop looking the other way on a prostitute because he's getting free oral sex in the back of his cruiser; the street-crime officer who grabs a couple of thousand dollars in tainted cash when he raids the house of a heroin dealer. On the flip side, cops don't police reporters; the best weapon they have against us is mere silence, which can be a dangerous weapon for all.

"The Boston Strangler? You want to ask me about the Boston Strangler? A reporter for the *Boston Record* came all the way out to my castle here to ask me about the Boston Strangler?"

His words were as slurred as his wife's had been, but I had a feeling that it was caused by either pain or a medication to treat it.

I decided not to mince words or motives. I mean, it looked like any word this guy uttered could be his last. Given that the original stranglings occurred forty-two years ago, I probably should have been prepared for the fact that the people who possessed the most intimate knowledge of them were going to be pretty damned old by now, possibly even infirm, but I wasn't. Not prepared enough, anyway.

So I said, "Sir, if I can talk honestly with you, I think the Boston Strangler might be killing again."

This declaration didn't seem to faze him one tiny bit. He continued to look at me through those distant eyes, his mouth slightly agape, as an announcer on a television commercial was prattling on about the cooling relief of Preparation H. He just kept looking, saying nothing, not at first, anyway.

When he ultimately did speak, he said, "What the hell took him so long? They must have kept him in prison for a long, long time."

I said, "But Lieutenant, I thought the Boston Strangler was murdered in prison. Albert DeSalvo was stabbed to death more than thirty years ago."

"That's right, kid. Albert DeSalvo was stabbed to death in prison. The Boston Strangler wasn't."

By now, I had walked into the room and approached the side of his unkempt bed. This far in, the room was even more of a pit, with crumpled old issues of *TV Guide* and *Reader's Digest* strewn about the floor around the bed, old food wrappers on top of the discarded magazines, and stains on the sheets. Outside, it was gorgeous and vibrant, spring in the desert. Inside, the shades filtered out any sense of the world, casting the walls and furniture in a colorless haze.

I nodded. "That's what I've heard. As a matter of fact, I'm starting to hear that more and more."

He laughed a shallow laugh and turned his head back to the television to see a commercial for a soap opera that was going to be on later that day. Then he focused again on me.

"Stranglings?" he asked.

"Two young women so far."

"The cops making the link from the old serial killer to the new one?"

"Absolutely not."

He laughed again, this time louder and more gutturally, and that caused him to descend into a coughing fit, which spurred him to stick the oxygen mask over his mouth for several long, deep breaths. As he breathed, his blank eyes stared straight ahead at nothing, a total acceptance of this as his human condition.

When he pulled the mask away, he said,

"They wouldn't, would they?"

"Why not?"

He looked at me like I was a bronze-plated idiot, and maybe I was. But sometimes these are the kinds of questions you have to ask in this grand business of information acquisition — questions that might seem obvious to everyone but the person asking them.

He asked, "Why would the brass want people thinking that the Strangler is killing again? That would be an admission that they didn't get the right guy back then. That would mean that the grunts, people like me, were right, and that the higher-ups, they were wrong. Why would they want you to think that?"

As he spoke, he grew more animated, even agitated, moving his arms out from under the unwashed sheets. He fell into another coughing fit, then climbed his way out of it by sipping water from a badly smudged glass on the other side of his bed.

When he collected himself, I asked, "All these many years later, the brass is still sensitive about it?"

He shot me another one of those looks that made me feel like the stupid kid at the fifth-grade science fair. You know how they say there's no such thing as a dumb question? In Bob Walters's presence, I was the exception to that rule — a living, breathing asker of the dumbest questions he'd ever heard.

Still, he contained himself and said, "Think about who's where. One of the lead detectives on the case is now the police commissioner, and from what I hear from the few friends I still have on the force, he wants to be mayor. The U.S. senator from your state was the attorney general heading the Strangler investigation. These are just two guys who have staked their whole fucking careers on that one case. And they're not done yet. Think, kid, think."

I was, but to no avail. I said, "Tell me about your role. You headed up the investigation, right?"

He swallowed hard. His eyes were transforming right before my eyes, sharpening. He laughed softly and said, "Yes and no. A lot of people headed up that investigation. After DeSalvo confessed, there were probably forty people who claimed to have led the case, every one a fucking tactical genius. I was just one of them."

I said, "Save your false modesty for your lovely wife. Tell me your role."

He looked at me — both surprised and amused.

"I headed homicide at the time, so yeah,

it was my case. The whole fucking world was coming down on us. Boston had four newspapers at the time, every one of them going crazy with this thing. The Phantom Fiend, the Boston Strangler, another woman dead, read all about it. Women were locking themselves indoors. The mayor was having fits. The Strangler didn't care about city and county boundaries, and the other police departments and prosecutors were being real pricks.

"And then you've got the state attorney general, the most ambitious prick in the world, taking over the case and putting some sham group together called the Boston Strangler Commission, trying to make it all go away in the best possible way so he could have a campaign issue when he ran for president. And my own fucking cohorts in homicide were sticking knives in each other's backs to get in the next day's paper. The thing was a pure fucking disaster from the day the first broad was found strangled in Back Bay."

He paused and took another long sip of water. He pivoted his head along the pillow again, looked at me, and said, "So you want to know my role? That was my role. Bring order to total fucking chaos. I thought I had succeeded until the day I failed, and when I

211

failed, I failed big."

He shut his eyes and seemed to rest for a moment. I stood in silence on the side of his bed. When he looked at me again, I asked, my tone softer now, "What's got you laid up?"

"I'm old, kid. I'm old. That's my problem. You'll be old someday too, and it sucks."

Before I could respond, he added, "And I have diabetes, which prevents me from walking. I haven't even tried taking a step in a year. I get out of here maybe once a month in a wheelchair, when I can get someone over to carry me down the stairs. The doctors want to amputate both my legs. I'm on borrowed time down there. And I've got emphysema, which is what's causing this fucking coughing all the time. I guess I'm on borrowed time everywhere.

"And I've got a miserable drunk of a wife who doesn't give one flying fuck whether I'm dead or alive. You know what, never mind that. She'd much prefer if I was dead so she wouldn't have to deal with all my bullshit. Kid, I hope your wife is someone special, because like I said, growing old sucks."

I asked, "If not DeSalvo, then who's the Strangler?"

"Nobody's told you that already?"

"I haven't really asked anyone until now. All respect intended, sir, you were the guy who knew the most back then, the detective that all the other cops looked up to. Speaking of which, Hank Sweeney says to say hello."

He didn't, but he probably should have. And far more important, I had a strong sense that dropping his name, showing that I already had easy access among favored members of the fraternity, would help my cause here at a level that I hadn't yet explored.

Bob Walters brightened at the mention of Hank and said simply, "A good man. An excellent man. Broke barriers and broke cases. You can't beat that combination."

I said, "Who is it?"

He lay in silence for another long moment, his gaze moving from me to some faraway place I couldn't see.

Finally, he said, "A guy who was never on my list until long after the stranglings stopped. A brilliant guy. Pure evil. Poor Boston if he's back."

"You're not helping me," I said.

He laughed again. Our rapport was growing easier, even as he seemed to be growing tired again.

He said, "DeSalvo was arrested on a rape

213

charge, actually, a string of rape charges, and sent to the Bridgewater Treatment Center for Sexually Dangerous Persons while he awaited trial. He wasn't a suspect in the stranglings, either. But one day, he just ups and confesses. He gave details of each of the murders that impressed the hell out of Stu Callaghan and a bunch of his people. Callaghan was so excited about the confession, about bagging the Strangler, that he never let any of the hands-on detectives interview him, because he knew we had doubts and he was afraid we'd ruin his moment and all the fawning press coverage that went with it. So he only allowed access to DeSalvo to a bunch of his pissant, know-nothing administrators who wanted nothing more than to close the books on the whole thing."

He paused, then said, "Trust me, Albert DeSalvo couldn't hit a dog, never mind kill a woman. He was not the Boston Strangler."

I said, "But the killings stopped as soon as he was arrested."

"You're right. They did," he said. "It ends up that DeSalvo's cellmate in Bridgewater is a guy named Paul Vasco. Ever hear of him?"

I shook my head.

"Vasco's got an IQ of 158. I wasn't kidding when I said he was a genius — an evil fucking genius. Diabolical. And cold-blooded. He had beaten a murder rap years before on a technicality. Robbed a gas station. Drove halfway out of the parking lot, flipped his car in reverse, went back inside, and shot the clerk in the head just for kicks. Then he left. This was in the 'burbs, and the damned cop forgot to read him his Miranda when he pulled him over later that night and found powder burns on his hand and blood on his shirt. So he walked.

"Anyway, Vasco's arrested at just about the same time as DeSalvo. They spend months in Bridgewater together, walking this route up and down a corridor heading from the cell block to the rec room. Other prisoners I interviewed said that's all they did, walk and talk, day and night, week after week, walking and talking.

"When DeSalvo confesses and starts reciting details from the crime scenes, everything he knew he learned from Vasco. DeSalvo's famous for having this photographic memory. But it wasn't really photographic. He didn't have to see things to remember them. It was just a fabulous memory. And everything that Vasco told him about the crime scenes, DeSalvo committed to memory and recited for Callaghan's lame-brained bureaucrats who were allowed to interview him."

By now, retired Lieutenant Detective Bob Walters was on a roll, and the look on his face didn't make him look so old and frail anymore, as if he was back on the job, running a crime scene, drawing out a witness, intimidating a suspect into confessing to some heinous crime.

I asked the obvious question, which, again, is something we sometimes do in my line of work. "If he didn't kill these women, then why confess?"

Walters looked at me in silence for a long moment, his head still resting against two propped-up pillows, his weak chest and useless legs spread beneath his graying sheets.

"That's what we spent a lot of time trying to figure out," he said. "You've heard of professional confessors, right?"

I had, but wanted to hear his definition, so I said nothing.

He continued, "They're people who get their rocks off confessing to crimes. Don't ask me why. They like to be in the middle of things, but their own lives are too pathetic to ever put them there. Don't know. It's why we usually hold something back from you guys at the paper, some key fact that only a person at the crime scene would know about. In this case, we held something back that was pretty big."

He paused and looked away for a moment, as if recollecting events that didn't, to him anyway, seem all that long ago.

"DeSalvo didn't really fit the bill as one of those," he said. "He was a rapist, or maybe just a groper, so why bother confessing to murders? So we counted that out. Then we — we, like Boston PD — interviewed a bunch of other prisoners. Ends up, they said DeSalvo thought he was going to make a fortune for his family from a book and movie deal if he was the Boston Strangler. He knew that he'd be going away for a long time on the rape charges, so what was the difference if he was a murderer, too. Then he got this high-powered lawyer to take his case, H. Gordon Thomas. And Thomas convinced him that if he confessed to the stranglings, he could plead innocent by reason of insanity to the rapes. Thomas tried telling the jury that anyone who committed all those Boston Strangler murders must be crazy. The jury, though, saw right through it.

"Guilty, and sentenced to twenty-five years in Walpole. And trust me, you wouldn't want to spend twenty-five minutes in Walpole."

This from a guy who was confined to his own little prison, life without parole sprawled on a bed in a dreary room with a wife downstairs who drank herself into oblivion every day of the week. I don't take credit for it, but this conversation seemed to be a furlough for him, a brief respite from his disease.

I asked, "Why do you think Vasco did it?"

He said, "I just do. You develop a sense of people in my business, probably the same as in your business — when people are lying, when they're telling the truth, when they're hiding, when they're exposing. I asked him once, put it right to him: 'Hey, Paul, DeSalvo's gone. The case is off the books. But we had the wrong guy, didn't we?'

"You know what he said?"

He didn't wait for an answer here, in the way that people in charge aren't really seeking answers when they ask questions. It's just part of their show.

"Nothing. Not one fucking word. You know what he did? He smiled at me, this evil fucking smile, his eyes locking on my eyes, his teeth like a wolf's, just sitting there smiling. I swear to God, I wanted to grab his throat and choke the guy and ask how it fucking felt as his eyes bulged out and his ears filled up with blood because his damned eardrums burst. But I didn't, and that look has stayed with me ever since, the look of defeat in the biggest case of my career."

He added softly, "That's why I think Paul Vasco was the Boston Strangler."

I nodded. What else could I do? What was I supposed to say? How do you tell a guy it's going to be all right when it's not, when his wife is downstairs probably passed out by now, when he's never going to get out of bed, when the guy he thought was a killer forty years ago could very well have been killing again?

Finally I asked, "Given the advances in DNA, shouldn't forensic scientists be able to prove or disprove whether DeSalvo was the Strangler?"

"Kid, so much of this science is more like science fiction to a sick old man like me."

I said, "When DeSalvo was murdered, he was stabbed. There was obviously a knife involved, covered in DNA, his DNA. Where is it?"

He smiled again, a long, remembering smile, and rolled his head from me toward the wall on the other side of the room, that smile never fading from his mouth. After a few moments he said, "The murder was committed outside of my jurisdiction, in another municipality and a different county. The attorney general's Strangler task force had already been disbanded. Hell, the attorney general had already gone on to bigger and better things — mainly the United States Senate. But I got one of the state police detectives to get me the knife."

I was stunned. The knife could prove to be the Holy Grail in the Strangler case. According to Sweeney, if you found the knife and placed it in the right hands, you could determine that DeSalvo was not, as many people suspected, the Boston Strangler. This, in turn, could possibly mean that the new serial killer in Boston was, in fact, the old serial killer.

I blurted out, "You have the knife?"

As I asked this, I began picturing the burgundy-stained blade sitting in a Tupperware container in the bottom of a box in a corner of Walters's cellar or garage. Hopefully his old lady hadn't spilled vodka or gin all over the damned thing and destroyed the most important evidence in the annals of Boston crime.

"I had the knife," he replied. He paused and added, "I gave it away."

"You gave it away?" I mean, what the hell, did the old guy sell the Strangler knife on eBay, for chrissakes? Was that how he was living in this house?

"I gave it to the family of one of the victims."

"You gave it to the family of one of the victims."

He said, smiling again, "Is there an echo in here?" It was his first token attempt at humor, and for that reason and perhaps that reason alone, I obliged with a laugh.

But quickly I asked, "Why?"

"It gave them closure. That's a fancy word that all the victim advocates use for helping them get over the fact that the human race sucks. That knife wasn't doing me a damned bit of good."

It would now, but I let that obvious fact remain unstated. Instead I asked, "Which family?"

"It was —" And before he could get the words out, he started to cough, that deep, penetrating cough. He reached for his glass again, but the water was gone. The cough was getting harder and longer. He pulled his mask desperately to his face.

At that exact moment, a woman behind me said, "Who the hell are you?" She wasn't yelling, but each word was as firm as a rod of steel.

I whirled around to see an overweight

fiftysomething dark-skinned woman in those green medical scrubs that were fashionable to wear many years ago, though I suppose they don't go out of fashion if you're in the business of making people well. Sometimes I feel like I'm in the business of making people unwell, or even dead, but that's a concern for another time.

I gave her the whole Jack Flynn thing. She was uniquely, and might I add bizarrely, unimpressed.

"He can't be bothered by no reporter." She said *"reporter"* as if she was spitting on an already littered sidewalk. I could have pointed out that, in fact, by talking to that reporter, Bob Walters was probably happier than he had been in months or years. I could have said that I, like her, was in the business of saving lives, and Bob Walters was helping me do it.

Instead I said, "We were just wrapping up. If you could excuse us for a moment."

Walters was still coughing, though not quite as loud or hard as he had been, and he continued to hold the mask over his face. The health worker walked around me to the oxygen tank, turned a knob, and more oxygen came out into the mask with a large swooshing sound. Walters closed his eyes in relief.

She said to me, "He's done. Get the hell out."

Maybe she was right, maybe he was done, but the problem was, he had left one key fact dangling at the end of an unfinished sentence. I turned back toward Walters and said, "Sir, the name of the victim's family?" He pulled the mask off his face and let forth with a phlegm-covered rapid-fire coughing fit. The health worker shot me a look that would kill a weaker man and shrieked, "Get the hell out. Now!"

I looked at Walters, but his eyes were deadened again, staring straight ahead. His body was convulsing in coughs that he was trying unsuccessfully to contain. "I'll drop by later, Lieutenant," I said.

He didn't say anything or do anything in response. He didn't even look at me. As I walked out the door, I dropped my business card on his soiled side table. He seemed to be in an ongoing struggle for his life.

Downstairs, Mrs. Bob Walters still sat at the kitchen table, staring now at an empty bottle of vodka. I didn't say anything. Really, I couldn't say anything. As I walked out the back door, she never even looked up.

17

I had twenty-eight voice mails on my cell phone when I dialed in from the rental car, and immediately assumed that twenty of them were from Peter Martin. Ends up I was wrong. Twenty-one of them were from Martin. By the fifteenth one, he was reduced to pleading: "Call me." Voice mail sixteen: "Call me now." Voice mail seventeen: "Fricking call me now." Voice mail eighteen: "Fucking call me or you're fired."

Voice mails nineteen and after continue in that same general tone and theme.

I got five messages from other media outlets, including *The New York Times* and *The Washington Post,* wanting to interview me about my correspondence from the Phantom Fiend. There was a message from Boston Police Detective Mac Foley, sounding anything but happy with my reportage in that morning's paper. The one remaining voice mail came from Vinny Mongillo, providing me a list of his favorite Vegas restaurants and offering — or was it threatening — to fly out and join me for what he described as "a little dinner and an evening of gaming." Such is the adventurous life of an intrepid reporter on the road.

None of the messages, perceptive minds might note, were from anyone identifying themselves as the Phantom Fiend. For that matter, I was also lacking a voice mail from one Maggie Kane, who almost became Maggie Kane Flynn, though not really.

I was about thirty minutes from the Strip, not including traffic, so it wasn't worth my while to go back to the hotel. Instead, I pulled off the road into the parking lot of a lush golf club named Dunes East, even though there wasn't a dune within a hundred miles of the place, and called Martin back. He, of course, picked up the phone on the first ring and promptly explained that the city of Boston was unraveling at the seams.

Police, he said, held a press conference at Schroeder Plaza to say they were unconvinced that a serial killer was on the loose, and publicly complained that the *Record* had published its story before any of the correspondence could be — their word here — "authenticated." I'm not really sure how you authenticate a note from an anonymous person, and I don't think they knew either. But you can bet that the blow-dried reporters on the six o'clock newscasts wouldn't be probing this particular point as they repeated the complaints verbatim. Also, you can bet that Jill Dawson and Lauren Hutchens wouldn't have had any doubt about the existence of a serial killer, if they were still around to have doubt, which is once again the point.

Those aforementioned television reporters were chronicling a massive run on pepper spray and mace by women, as well as a surge in demand for area locksmiths, according to Martin. One particularly creative reporter even did a stand-up from the Animal Rescue League's dog shelter, where she reported a sudden spike in dog adoptions by the city's female population.

There weren't any other new developments on the story, Martin said — no more calls to the Barry Bor Show that morning, no blog postings, no new deaths — at least none we knew about yet. Maybe the Phantom was all mine again. We can only hope, right?

Martin told me that Edgar Sullivan wanted to speak to me, but was in a meeting for the next twenty minutes and would call back. I briefed Martin about my Walters meeting and promised to be on an eastbound plane by nightfall.

I then called back a few of the print reporters who had left me messages earlier in the day. To each of them I explained off the record about the various notes but said I was forbidden from talking for attribution, which in a way was true; I had forbidden myself. The TV people I didn't bother with, knowing full well they wouldn't have bothered with me.

And I hung up. I checked the dashboard clock and it read 10:50 a.m. I figured it would be safe to return to the Walters's house at about noon — safe meaning that the Abu Ghraib guard who doubled as his home health care worker would be gone by then. At least I hoped she would be.

I listened to more voice mails on my work machine, but again, nothing from the Phantom Fiend or my phantom fiancée, though I wonder if that title expires with an unrealized wedding day, or whether, like retired ambassadors, we carry the moniker for life. I kind of doubt that, but the thought made me realize I was getting punchy.

Sitting in the front seat of my rental car, I had nothing to do but wait, and as I did just that, temptation finally overwhelmed me, sending me in the direction of the immaculate driving range where half a dozen or so guys were hitting golf balls. I grabbed a five-iron out of a bag of extremely expensive demo clubs, approached a pile of golf balls stacked into a pyramid, and began to hit.

My first shot of the new golf season faded hard to the right, but it didn't feel bad. The second was a little fat, the third a bit thin. The fourth shot clicked effortlessly off the clubface, long and straight, as did the next, and the one after that.

The morning sun was high in the sky, warm without being overwhelming. The air was clean and crisp, the sky an ocean blue, dare I say the color of my eyes. I was starting to feel pretty damned good.

I traded in the five-iron for a pitching wedge and lobbed balls at a flag about a hundred yards away, one after another falling just to the right or the left — not bad for a New Englander swinging for the first time at the end of a brutal winter. I thought of so many of my more memorable rounds — my father teaching me the game on the tenth fairway of the Number Two course at Ponkapoag outside of Boston; the day at Congressional Country Club in Maryland with the president of the United States when shots rang out and we both ended up bloodied in the sandtrap on the sixteenth hole; the late Sunday afternoon shoot-out on the hallowed links of Pebble Beach with my best friend, Harry Putnam, as we celebrated his impending nuptials.

My father was dead. The president was retired. Harry was married now to a woman that neither one of us particularly liked, but he said he was sticking it through for the sake of his young son and daughter. The world, I thought, is an ever-changing place, but too rarely for the better. It also seems to be a diminishing place; the people you love most tend to leave you too soon.

So much for my rising mood.

A young man came sauntering toward me in a pair of golf cleats and a shirt with an insignia that said "Dunes East."

"Sir, are you playing with us today?" he asked, politely more than accusatorily. I apologetically explained that I was out from Boston on business, was returning a few phone calls from the road, and was just hitting a few shots before I got back to work.

"Ah, Boston," he said. Usually this line preceded what used to be a crack about the Red Sox, but was now more along the lines of congratulations. Instead, though, he continued, "That's crazy with that new serial killer you've got, huh? Have you read about it?"

Try written about it, but I wasn't going to tell him that. Before I could reply, one of the guys hitting balls a dozen or so yards away looked up and said, "I saw that on CNN this morning. That's really scary, no? This new killer is like the old killer from back in the seventies."

It was actually the sixties, but again, I wasn't of any mind to correct him. Instead, I asked the young assistant pro, "What's the latest?"

"You know, cops saying they're not sure whether the whole thing is a prank. Two women dead. The newspaper there getting anonymous letters when someone is killed. Pretty damned spooky, if you ask me."

I hadn't, but still found his take interesting. There are some stories, very rare stories, that transcend gender and geography, class and race, and serve to bring people together in conversation and speculation, sometimes in hope, other times, like now, in fear. This was one of those stories, and I was in the absolute middle of it.

As we talked, my phone vibrated in my back pocket, and I could see on the caller ID that it was coming from the *Record.* I quickly excused myself and walked back to the car. It was Martin. He said he had Edgar Sullivan and Monica Gonsalves, the paper's technology guru, on a conference call. They both said hello. I barely knew how to use call waiting, and made a mental note to get a session in telephone operations when I got back east.

Edgar said, "Jack, we've been monitoring your incoming mail for obvious reasons. I hope you don't mind. First off, I want to be on record as saying I think it's fine that you're the New England chapter vice president of the Martha Stewart Fan Club."

That Edgar, such a card. This, for whatever reason, made Monica laugh uproariously. It's probably reasonable to note here that since Monica works in IT, almost anything could make her laugh uproariously.

Edgar continued, "You received a disc in this morning's mail, an unlabeled DVD in an unmarked envelope with a Boston postmark. I opened it. There was no note included. I didn't feel right invading your privacy by viewing the DVD, but I did take the liberty of having Monica upload the contents into the computer system. She, in turn, is going to e-mail it to you, and you can view it and determine whether it's got anything to do with this Phantom Fiend business. It probably doesn't, but I don't want to leave anything to chance right now."

Edgar is how old? Sixty-five? Seventy? Older? And here I am, somewhere in the middle of my life, and I lost him at *DVD*. I said, "That's great, but I'm not near my hotel at the moment to view it."

Monica chimed in. "Jack, Monica here." She said this even though she was the only woman on the call, as if I was an absolute idiot. I guess maybe when you work in IT, you grow accustomed to the idea that everyone around you is an idiot. "Do you have your laptop with you?"

"I do."

"You can receive your e-mail right from your laptop."

I went into a long explanation of how I couldn't, because I wasn't wired into anything. She went into a longer explanation on how I didn't have to be because of something called an air card that she had installed in my machine a year ago when she had it in for maintenance. I explained that she was wrong. She asked me to press a couple of buttons and proved that she was right. All in all, this is why I don't make my living writing manuals for IBM, though that would probably pay more and prove less hazardous, at least compared to my professional life at the moment.

We hung up so I could deal with the DVD. I called up the e-mail with the video clip, expecting it to be another piece of schlock from an independent film producer desperately looking for a few moments of free publicity that would allow his arty movie to take off in the direction of *The Blair Witch Project.*

As the video was downloading, my phone rang again.

"Hey, Fair Hair, I hope you're about to tell me you won a million dollars at the craps table, spent the night having wild sex with a pair of thousand-dollar-an-hour escorts, and are about to quit journalism to pursue your dream of being a hydroponics farmer."

It was my mother.

Just kidding. It was Mongillo.

I said, "You're using spy satellite photography to monitor my every move, aren't you?"

With the halfhearted attempts at humor out of the way, he asked me how I was doing. I, in turn, told him about my meeting with Bob Walters and his information about Paul Vasco.

I said, "I don't even know if he's still alive, but my gut says he's the key."

Mongillo replied, "Best that I know, Vasco is alive and well."

As he was talking, the video began playing on my laptop screen, a very methodical tour of the inside of a reasonably nice apartment. The camera proceeded slowly around the living room, pausing at an ornate marble fireplace, scanning the coffee table, which held some magazines and an unlit candle, glancing past a chunky contemporary couch in what a designer might describe as an aloof shade of gray. The tape looked to be nothing more than a particularly aggressive Realtor trying to sell an upscale condominium.

I said to Mongillo, "Oh yeah? Walters was adamant about it. We need to track Vasco down and double-team him. I'm going to be back east sometime later tonight, not in time to do us any good for tomorrow's paper. It would be great if we could see him by tomorrow."

As I said this, the camera proceeded from the living room to the small kitchen, the angle drifting over the appliances to a stainless-steel kitchen door that had a photograph of a tanned thirtysomething man in a blue blazer and open collared white shirt with his arm around a smiling woman in a yellow sundress.

Mongillo said, "Your wish is my command. Can you invite a murderer to lunch, or is that unseemly?"

Whoever was carrying the camera was now walking it down a narrow hallway that seemed to connect the front of the apartment to the back, the picture growing darker without any ambient light. I could make out a collection of old maps on the hallway walls, and at the end of the hall was a giant vintage poster, an advertisement for a trans-Atlantic voyage on board the *Queen Elizabeth II*. Very stylish. Maybe I'd buy the place. I wonder if I could get it furnished.

I said to Martin, "Why don't you just find out where he is, for starters. We'll figure out tomorrow's lunch plan later."

He hung up. The camera took a left into a rear bedroom of what Realtors call a floor-thru apartment. For whatever reason, I became instantly drawn in by the image, my spine feeling a slight chill. I wasn't entirely sure why until I took a harder, more focused look. Unlike the front room and kitchen, the bedroom was in a state of disarray, as if it had been ransacked. Items had been knocked off a bureau and could be seen scattered on the carpeted floor — loose change, a makeup kit, a jewelry chest. A closet door was ajar. Clothes were flung here and there. A desk chair had been flipped on its side. If this was a real estate promotion, I'd want a new Realtor.

That's when the camera casually but abruptly focused on the rumpled bed, and clear as day, which is when this shot was taken, I could see the woman who had been shown in the photograph on the refrigerator door.

She was sprawled on top of a white comforter, dead, her eyes wide open, her tight purple tank top lifted above her bare breasts. She was completely disrobed from the waist down. She had her head propped up on a pair of pillows. Her bare legs were parted wide, one of them bent awkwardly under her at the knee. She had what looked to be a pair of nylons wrapped around her neck in a ligature, tightened into a knot, and then tied into a looping bow just beneath her chin. I could see blood in her right ear, and drops and smears of blood on the sheets. Her face looked unsettlingly serene, as if death came as a relief from what she had gone through in the moments before it.

The camera casually lingered on her body the same way it did on the coffee table and the refrigerator door, as if this body was nothing more than another inanimate object in what was now a completely lifeless apartment. And then the image simply went blank, a circle appearing in the screen where the video had just played. My eyes remained frozen on it, as if at any moment anything else could appear. After a few long seconds, I clicked the video player off, placed the laptop on the passenger seat beside me, and took a couple of long, deep breaths. When I shut my eyes, I could see the woman's face, her brown hair matted against her right temple, her sharp blue eyes, her slightly chubby cheeks. Someone's girlfriend, someone's daughter, someone's friend, maybe someone's aunt. And my bet is, I was the only living person besides her killer who knew she was dead.

I pounded out Martin's number. He, in turn, put Edgar on another conference line, as well as Vinny Mongillo and Monica Gonsalves. She e-mailed the three of them the link, and all three watched it in silence as we stayed on the line. Well, almost silence. At the key moment, I heard Martin mutter, "What the frick." Mongillo gasped. Poor Edgar simply said, "Dear Jesus."

Martin cleared his throat and asked, "Okay, now what?"

I replied, "The Phantom has struck again. Problem is, we don't know where. He didn't give us any indication here."

"Much as I hate to let this story get away from us, we need to get a copy of this to the cops, right?" Martin asked. .

Before I could say anything, Mongillo said, "This will at least prove that we were right in reporting the likelihood of a serial killer in today's story."

Mongillo was right. So was Martin. I offered to get the police a copy of the e-mail, because I had to return Detective Mac Foley's call anyway.

Martin was adopting that calm tone he gets as a story grows more chaotic. He said, "My impression is that this is a reportable event, this video. We opened the door today. We can't shut it on more news now."

Mongillo said, "Unless we start getting every two-bit prankster in the world. How do we prevent that, and how do we know beef from baloney?"

Martin asked, "Why the frick didn't the person who sent this disc give us a fricking address?"

Before I could say anything, Edgar cleared his throat and announced, "He did."

There was a moment of silence as Edgar — intentionally, I suspect — let the drama build. He finally continued, saying, "The cameraman scanned some magazines on the coffee table. He more than scanned them, he lingered on them. While you gentlemen were discussing the story, I pulled that part of the clip out, froze it, and magnified it on my screen. If you look closely at the magazines, they all contain the same name and address on the front: Kimberly May at 284 Commonwealth Avenue in Boston." He paused, then said, "It's in the Back Bay."

Where was Edgar Sullivan before he came to the *Record,* at Scotland Yard? Make him a reporter and we'd be a virtual lock on a Pulitzer Prize.

"I'll shoot it over to police," I said.

Mongillo added, "I'm on my way to the scene. I will not get in the way. I will not get in the way. I will not get in the way."

Rest assured, he was about to get in the way.

Martin said, "Flynn, get your ass in the seat of a plane. I don't care what it costs."

Those are words he had never before uttered.

"Peter, are you all right?" I asked.

His tone was calm, but his words were not. "No," he said. "This story's about to get a whole lot bigger before it goes away. We've all got to be ready for that."

He was right, as he usually is. We hung up. I threw the car into drive. I still had one more stop to make before the long journey home.

18

I'm trying to remember what life was like before cellular communications, back when we thought the earth was flat and the Celtics would forever be a dynasty and the afternoon paper would always be people's primary, if not only, source of news. Times change. The NASDAQ, it ends up, can also go down. The Red Sox can win a World Series. And you don't need to be particularly bright or enlightening to make it as a star political analyst on cable TV.

But where were we before the cell phone, besides listening to eight-track cartridges of Barry White and thinking they'll never make another show funnier than *Laugh-In,* which maybe they haven't, though that's not really the point. The point was that out here in the Nevada desert, Verizon and all its technological marvels had instilled in me a certain amount of freedom, and I chose to use that freedom to place a call from my rental car to Mac Foley of the Boston PD.

A rather gruff gentleman answered the phone and tersely announced, "Homicide."

"Is Detective Foley in, please?"

"No."

Silence. And some people wonder why reporters and cops generally have such a tough time getting along. If you strip everything else away, I think it's because reporters, by their very nature, like to communicate, to put their thoughts into words and use those words to enlighten. Cops, at least the ones inevitably assigned to answer the phones, don't like to talk — except, maybe, to one another.

I said, "Could I leave a message for him?"

"Sure."

I'd like to see this guy consoling the grieving relatives of a newly made victim. The odd thing is, he was probably pretty good at it, all his emotions spare but heartfelt.

"Could you tell him that Jack Flynn called."

"Hold on."

He didn't, though, bother putting me on hold. Instead I heard the receiver clank on what sounded like a metal desktop. Then I heard him yell, "Hey, Mac, the asshole is on line one."

I could vaguely hear a distant voice reply,

"Which asshole?"

"The big one."

The phone clicked and another voice came on and announced, "Foley here."

"Jack Flynn calling."

"Jack," he said, his tone surprisingly upbeat, "you outdid yourself. I thought I'd seen a lot of bad, sleazy reporting in my forty-something years on the job here, but in today's fish wrap, you turned sleaziness into an art form."

I said, "Thank you. God knows we try."

Actually, that's not really what I said, though I might have, if he had given me a chance, which he didn't. As he spoke, the scrub of the Nevada desert washed by me on either side of my car as I barreled back down the same interstate highway destined for Bob Walters's house to try to wring out that one last piece of information: Who had the bloody knife? I use the descriptive *bloody* not like a Brit might, but in the most literal way possible.

Foley continued, "That was really a pile of shit, Jack. You were used by some fucking kook. You violated the privacy of two different families. You needlessly scared the crap out of an entire city. And you got in the way of a police investigation that is now stalled in its tracks because you and your fucking editors are desperately trying to sell newspapers on the misery of others.

"Otherwise, great job, you asshole."

"So you liked it?"

That I did say, though he didn't respond. I think he was too busy disemboweling a bunny at his desk or something. I was also starting to rethink my theory that I was uniquely capable of maintaining great relationships with law enforcement types, mostly because I could relate to them so well. If this was an example of a great relationship, then Michael Jackson and Lisa Marie Presley had a terrific marriage.

I said, "So you don't think there's a serial killer in town?"

He responded, "I'm not saying a fucking word to you, except that by rushing that story into print, you just validated that lunatic talk-show host. And if there is a serial killer in town, you just made it one hell of a lot harder for us to catch him — and you can quote me on that, but you won't, because you're too chickenshit."

Don't bet on that. His answer was interesting, though, the profanity aside, because it represented what former *Washington Post* editor Ben Bradlee famously described during Watergate as a "nondenial denial." Mac Foley wasn't actually denying the existence of a serial killer. What he was saying is that by reporting on it, I was making his job tougher — which I hate to say, or maybe I don't, wasn't really my concern. Because by reporting on a serial killer, I was also prompting hundreds of thousands of women in the city to take precautions, maybe saving lives. I'm not saying police wanted him to kill again, but every murder provides them with fresh possibilities for clues, and unreported or underreported murders allow police the luxury of time to find out who committed them.

I said, barely able to conceal my increasing disdain, "If you can hold yourself together for a moment, I wanted to share with you some new correspondence from the Phantom Fiend."

Silence. I can only imagine how much he hated the fact that his investigation was dependent on a reporter for information — an investigation that would now fall under intense scrutiny because of that same reporter. Actually, I can more than imagine, because here's what he said: "Flynn, if you try playing any games with me, if you so much as hiccup before you get me every tiny little piece of information that comes your way from whoever this is that's calling themselves the Phantom Fiend, I'll have you grabbed off the street and thrown in front of a grand jury so fast that you won't be able to change out of the panties that you fucking reporters probably wear. And that's if I'm in a good mood. If I'm in a bad mood, you'll end up spending some time at the county jail."

I rolled my eyes, even as I admired his ability to put his thoughts into words. This was why he wasn't in charge of answering phones, I'm sure. I asked, "What's your e-mail address?" He gave it to me. I told him I was sending him a video that had been mailed to the *Record,* that he could have the hard copy, and that our own investigation showed the address to be at 284 Commonwealth Avenue. We both hung up without saying good-bye.

I came around the corner of Rodeo Road and blinked at what I saw: straight ahead, several blocks away, the pulse of red and blue police lights from squad cars idling in the otherwise empty street.

I reflexively hit the gas, which I suppose isn't something you should do with cops around. As I got closer, my fears compounded with every passing house. The police cruisers were parked in front of Bob Walters's house, and they were parked alongside an ambulance, which, in turn, was idling next to a black van. This was not good.

As I pulled up, I saw that there was no yellow police tape, meaning the authorities weren't treating this as a crime scene, meaning, hopefully, that maybe this was merely a matter of the sickly Bob Walters suddenly needing some medical attention and now everything inside was just fine. Couple of aspirin, maybe a catheter, and the guys in rubber gloves are on their way out the door. Or better yet, and I should probably be embarrassed for even thinking this, but maybe it was his wife in physical distress. Slouched on the kitchen table amid a puddle of vodka and glass fragments, she was hardly the picture of long-term health.

But as I left the air-conditioning of my car for the growing heat of a late desert morning, I saw with a start that the black van had the words, in sterile type, COUNTY CORONER on the side. Still, I thought, maybe Mrs. Walters had killed herself or died of a heart attack or sudden liver failure.

There were a couple of uniformed Las Vegas cops chatting with each other on the front lawn. A team of paramedics came walking out of the front door of the house empty-handed. Well, not entirely empty-handed. They each carried what looked to be a briefcase in their hands.

By now, sweat was dripping down my forehead and across my cheeks, and not from the heat, either. I didn't want to look panicked, but didn't know how to stay cool. I noticed that a few neighbors were looking on from their respective yards. I saw through the glare of the front outer door that uniformed men were crouched over, tending to something inside the front hallway. A man in a suit with a stethoscope around his neck came walking silently out the front door, got in an unmarked Ford Expedition, and drove away.

I left my notebook behind in the car. I wiped the sweat off my face with my sleeve and walked across the lawn toward the cops, who kept talking to each other. As I got near I announced, "I'm a friend of the Walterses. Can I ask what's going on here?" Easy does it, no panic, just projecting true, heartfelt concern.

Both cops, young guys, turned to me with casual, even friendly looks on their faces.

"What's your name?" one of them asked, not accusatorily, but so he could have a point of reference as he gave me what was undoubtedly bad news.

I told him. Before he could say anything

else, the front door opened again, and a man in a white lab coat backed out of it carrying the front end of a stretcher, another man in a white coat picking up the rear. They carefully descended the two front steps, pulled on a bar at the same time beneath the stretcher, and a set of poles and wheels protruded out. They dropped the stretcher with a bounce and rolled it toward the awaiting van.

On the stretcher was a long form wrapped in a black body bag, zipped from what I assumed was head to foot, shining in the midday sun. I watched in silence, as did the two cops, watched as they slid the bag into the back doors of the van and shut them with an aching thud. Still, some part of me thought that without Mrs. Walters around, maybe it was her in the bag. After all, if it was her husband, wouldn't she be witnessing this scene, even if only with fake tears?

My hopes were raised further when the two paramedics went walking back into the house carrying a portable stretcher. At the same time, one of the cops put his hand on my shoulder and said, "Sir, how do you know the Walterses?"

I said, "He's a retired cop, Boston PD. I'm visiting from Boston." There wasn't a lie in either sentence.

The same cop put his hand on my shoulder and said, "There was an accident this morning —"

Before he could finish, the front door opened one more time. This time, a paramedic backed out lugging a stretcher, which seemed to take forever getting through the door. They came slowly down the steps. I strained my eyes. There on the stretcher was Mrs. Bob Walters, her eyes open and blinking, her lips moving, nothing more than incoherent blather coming from her mouth. I hung my head in sadness — for Bob Walters, for the victims he couldn't help in Boston, and yeah, a little bit for this reporter who didn't get the full benefit of his knowledge.

The young cop was still talking. "He was very frail, as I'm sure you know. He fell down the stairs sometime this morning. The mailman saw him through the front door on his daily delivery and called 911. By the time we got here, he was dead."

Fell down the front stairs.

I haven't even tried taking a step in a year. That's what Walters had said to me less than two hours before. He didn't suddenly get out of bed and try his luck hobbling around the house. He wasn't anywhere near the stairs under his own power. He didn't fall by accident.

And I also knew something else: his wife had been too drunk to get herself upstairs, drag him out of bed, and push him. She probably wanted to do just that. She probably spent entire days dreaming of this scenario. But it didn't happen like that, not here, not this morning.

Of course, I couldn't tell the cops any of this. If I had, they probably would have thought I was some sort of kook — the word that Mac Foley had used to describe the Phantom Fiend. And if they didn't, they would have wanted me to go downtown to answer questions, and as anyone who knows anything about Vegas knows to their core, you never want to go downtown. Especially me, especially now, when I needed to get back east to deal with the new case of Kimberly May.

So I solemnly nodded to the young cops and told them thanks. I got back in the car and carefully navigated around the emergency vehicles and the coroner's van, which was also pulling out. I thought of Jill Dawson and Lauren Hutchens and Kimberly May, and wondered what their lives were like before they didn't have them anymore. I thought of that poor man, Joshua Carpenter, mourning his wife in the Public Garden, wrong time, wrong place, and now he too was dead. And Bob Walters, just an old retiree with a lot of regrets and a reservoir of knowledge that he had been waiting forty years to share. I got almost all of it, but not enough.

I drove off toward the airport. Success and failure seemed inextricably intertwined, as if good and bad were forever linked. I wondered if most of life was like that, and feared that maybe it was. I had to get back to Boston to figure out how to separate the two.

19

I was in San Francisco International Airport when I saw her. Specifically, I was sprawled across a chair in one of those generic lounges with the floor-to-ceiling windows overlooking the departing and arriving planes, waiting for my connecting flight to Boston, because the only nonstop out of Vegas with any available seats was the red-eye, and civil people, it must be said, don't fly on red-eyes. My shirt was untucked. My hair was mussed up. I had circles of worry and exhaustion under my sky-blue eyes. I had my cell phone plastered to my ear, listening to Vinny Mongillo explain that he had once again proven himself to be the world's most tenacious and talented reporter by producing, in a mere three hours, Paul Vasco's entire criminal record, his incarceration history, and, most notably, his most recent release date, which, not by coincidence, happened to be six months before. He also had Vasco's current home address, a nugget of information he said would cost me dinner at a major Boston restaurant or, better yet, a private club, for him and the state bureaucrat who provided it. I couldn't even imagine how much fun that would be.

When I was done with the requisite congratulations, promises, and thank-yous, Mongillo said, "Now let me tell you about Kimberly May."

And that's when I saw her, sauntering down the airy walkway amid a cluster of humanity that had apparently disembarked from the same plane and were heading for the exits and for wherever else after that — great hotels, bad motels, overseas flights, the warmth of home, the stone-cold reality of a failing marriage. Wherever. I noticed first the achingly familiar walk, the swivel of the hips, the fit of her jeans, the way her long brown hair swished back and forth. Then I saw the unmistakably beautiful shape of her face, the deep-set eyes, and the perfectly proportioned nose. All those people walking by, maybe a hundred a minute at least, and my eyes naturally fell on her. I swear to God, you could see the person you truly loved in a pitch-black room.

And not that I'd make too big a deal of this, but there must have been eighty people sitting in the waiting area for the flight to Boston, and out of all of us, her look naturally came to rest on me. So she came walking over, calm and casual, unflustered, as if I'd been her destination all along, like something prearranged, not in the slightest bit surprised to see me. She had an overnight bag slung over her shoulder and a computer satchel in her hand. She placed them both on the floor, sat down in the empty seat beside mine, and said in that somewhat husky voice, "Come here often?" And then she smiled that crinkle-eyed smile that I don't think has ever fully left my thoughts, or, in my more honest moments, my hopes.

It was Elizabeth Riggs, a woman I once thought I'd marry and probably should have married, but never did, mostly because, I've come to convince myself, she came into my life at exactly the wrong time.

She knew her line was weak, and so did I, but I let her off the hook with the following pale little offering of my own: "Only when I'm flying."

I remained slung across my chair, my neck supported by the top of the backrest. She reached out and touched the side of my face with her hand — no hesitation, no qualms, no forced display of formality. It's just what came to mind or body, so it's what she did.

Her touch, by the way, was warm and soft, casual yet luxurious, like a cashmere blanket flung across an aging couch. I wanted to wrap myself in it, to take shelter from the cruel world in it. Instead, I took her hand in mine, kissed it once, and placed it back against my cheek. Given how attractive she was, anyone who was watching, and there were probably more than a few people who were, would have assumed that we had been lovers for a long, long time. And in some odd way, they were right.

"So I get to the building about ten seconds ahead of the first screaming patrol car . . ."

That was Vinny again, his voice still coming into the forgotten phone that remained absently against my ear. I said, "That's terrific. Call you back in a little while."

I flipped the phone shut and said, "That was Vinny."

She nodded, her gaze hanging on mine in a spell of silence. She said, "You look good."

I didn't.

"So do you," I said.

She did.

Her hands were now resting on her thighs. I asked, "Where are you coming from?"

"LA. I was down there visiting a friend for a couple of days."

A friend. There used to be a day not so long before that I knew every one of her friends and she knew every one of mine. Times, quite obviously, change, and a friend in this case could mean absolutely anything.

She asked, "Are you heading back to Boston?"

I nodded. We looked at each other again, undoubtedly both racking our overwhelmed brains for more banal questions.

They write songs about these kinds of encounters, particularly bad songs, actually. Wasn't there an especially awful one about a pair of former lovers who ran into each other on Christmas Eve in a grocery store, or some similarly regrettable time and place, shuffling their feet in the frozen foods aisle as they tried to stem the flood of memories?

She finally moved beyond the realm of verbalized politesse and said, "I heard you were getting married. I've been meaning to call and congratulate you. But you know, you violated our agreement. We're supposed to inform each other of moves, deaths, marriages, and births."

I didn't remember any such agreement, though I kind of liked the sentiment. I smiled a weary smile and thought about the number of times we'd sat on the couch together, or lain in bed, or faced each other on bar stools, sitting close, one of us telling of a recent failure, the other there to do the propping up, always successful until the day it wasn't, and then the relationship wasn't a relationship anymore.

I said, "But you didn't read the follow-up story of me not getting married?" I shook my head self-consciously, expressing, or at least trying to, the full depths of my idiocy in male-female relationships.

She looked surprised without being particularly disappointed, though maybe I was reading too much into that. "Um, why not?" she asked.

Blunt now. She pulled her hair back with both arms in that way she always did, getting it out of her face, getting ready to have a serious talk.

I said, "You know. Life."

"Or death?"

Clever, her referring to my wife's death six years before, something that Elizabeth ended up believing would color me for the rest of my days, making it impossible to have a normal, healthy relationship with a normal, healthy woman.

I leaned forward now, my elbows on my knees, looking at her with a cocked head. I said, "No, I'm pretty sure it's life. You know, sometimes two people aren't meant to get married, even if they first thought they were, and it's not because the guy's wife died."

She nodded. "Point taken. What went wrong?" Not dropping it, and unapologetic in her pursuit of facts.

"I'm not really sure. I haven't talked with her."

She looked at me with a flash of incredulity and bemusement. "So how did you tell her you didn't want to get married?"

"I didn't."

She guffawed, which probably wasn't the most endearing or empathetic reaction to this revelation. Then she said, "She called it off, not you?"

"Long story, though I guess not really. I was sitting down at Caffe Vittoria that morning trying to figure a way out of things. I mean, the woman is terrific — for somebody else. I swear, someone's going to marry her someday soon and think they've hit the fucking lottery.

"We were going to do a little justice-of-the-peace deal and then head to Hawaii, you know, everything very low-key. So I finally get up the guts to call her, and when I do, she tells me she's in the Atlanta airport. It's five hours before we're due to be married, maybe less. I say, 'What are you doing down there?'

"And she comes back with, 'I'm so sorry, Jack. I was just about to call you.'

"She literally fled town. I haven't seen her since."

Elizabeth looked at me incredulously. "You're sure you didn't pull a Jack on her without realizing it? You didn't send her signals? You didn't drive her away? You didn't do that thing where you kind of cut her off from everything you're doing and thinking because you're afraid to let someone else in?"

Pull a Jack. "That's real nice," I said. "Thank you for your heartfelt sympathy in this most trying time."

I said that last part with intentional, mocking formality. She laughed and absently dropped her hand on the outside of my leg like she always used to do and said, "I'm sorry, but come on. You know how you can be."

"And I know how you are, which is not very nice."

Past the awkwardness, everything very familiar again, comfortable.

She asked, "And you really haven't talked to her since?"

I shook my head.

"What are you doing out here? Don't tell me you went on your honeymoon on your own."

I smiled and said, "No. Story." I didn't tell her what, and she had obviously been too busy with her friend in LA to have read the *Record* online.

She said, "At least you picked a honeymoon destination that we'd never been to. I would've killed you if you went to Turks."

The Turks and Caicos Islands, amid a stretch of too much arguing, near the end of a bitter winter. We were having yet another senseless fight over something we wouldn't be able to remember the next day when she glared at me and said, "You know what the problem is with us? We don't spend enough time together." I mean, I always knew she could be counterintuitive, but this was the biggest bit of counterintuition that I had ever heard.

That's when she flipped open the morning *Record,* pointed to an airline ad, and said, "We're going here."

"Where."

"Providenciales."

"Where's that?"

"I don't know. Um, says here, the Caribbean."

"When."

"Tomorrow morning."

And sure enough, there we were at the airport the following morning, bags in hand, frequent-flier miles drained out of our accounts, with two round-trip tickets to the Turks and Caicos Islands and a reservation for three nights at a beachfront guesthouse named Jose's Place. I had created a rule for myself about never staying at a place named for the owner, unless it was Donald Trump or Steve Wynn. But in this case, every decent resort on the island was booked. Jose's, for every good reason, wasn't.

After Jose himself proudly showed us to our room, with the torn shade covering the single window, the scraped tile floors, the refrigerator-size closet, the Third World bathroom, we looked at each other, wondering what the hell we were going to do.

Ends up, we decided pretty quickly: we had sex. We had it in the room, immediately and urgently, then later, constantly. We had it that evening on a blanket under a coconut tree on the pristine beach as insects the size of dairy cows chirped in the nearby brush. We had it in the handicapped restroom of a very swank resort before the dessert course of our dinner the following night. We had it in the middle of the afternoon under a blanket on a dock during a passing rainstorm.

Not that I'm proud of any of this. Well, okay, maybe I am a little.

We also talked. We talked about the past, mine and hers and ours. We talked about the present. And we talked about the future, always as a couple, the challenges we'd face, the marriage we would undoubtedly embrace, the babies that would someday pop into our lives. And then we had more sex.

She wore a flower in her hair. The tops of our feet got brown. We'd walk the beach and look at the silent, sullen couples sunning themselves on the expensive chairs at their luxury resorts, knowing that our little eighty-five-dollar-a-night prison cell of a guest room back at Jose's was the most perfect thing we could ever have imagined.

"I wouldn't have gone to Turks," I told her, solemn now. "That's off the list."

She squeezed my thigh. "Good," she said. "Same here."

We fell silent for a minute. Finally, I looked her square in the eyes and asked, "What went wrong?"

When she looked back at me, her eyes were glistening like the top of a pond after a hard rain, like they might spill over in even the slightest breeze.

She swallowed and said, "Life went wrong, Jack. Life. We didn't share enough of it. You spent too much time looking at the past — understandably so. I spent too much time worried about the future — maybe just as understandably. And the moment kind of passed us by. Before you knew it, you and I weren't really you and I."

I saw a tear fall from her left eye to her cheekbone, then begin the long descent toward her neck. My reflexes wanted me to reach out for her. My brain kept everything still and in its proper place. Brains can be stupid sometimes, especially mine.

She added, "The thing with you, Jack, the thing with you, is that the dead people in your life keep on dying."

She paused after this declaration, causing me to replay it in my mind. *The dead people keep on dying.* She always did have a pretty amazing way with words, as well as piercing insight. The problem now, though, was that even people who had never been in my life kept on dying.

"It's completely understandable," she added, "but the fact that it's understandable doesn't make it any easier on the living people in your life."

I said, "You're over us?" I don't know where I got the guts to ask that question, but I did.

She replied, "Some days, yes. Other days, not really. You?"

I bit my lip and replied, "That about sums it up here as well."

"I miss you," she said.

"I miss you, too."

A woman's voice over the PA system announced a preboarding for the flight to Boston, which brought me back to that awful day at Logan Airport when she first left for her new life in San Francisco. I should have stopped her. I could have stopped her. And I didn't.

She flashed me an odd look, the two of us sitting there amid the soft commotion of passengers all around us rising to their feet and grabbing their purses and computer cases and carry-ons. She said, "I had planned to tell you this if you ever got around to calling me to let me know you were getting married —"

"I didn't get married," I said, cutting her off.

She smiled wanly and continued, "But I might as well tell you here." She paused and gave me a long, familiar look of mild trepidation mixed with excitement, and then said, "I'm pregnant."

Did someone just set a bomb off? What

was that intense white flash? Was I asleep? Would I at some point awake? Any reason I should be this inwardly distraught over a two-word sentence uttered by a woman I hadn't been involved with in the biblical sense in at least a year?

I said, slowly, calmly, forcing a smile, "I thought you had a glow to you." I don't know if she did or didn't, but it was a pretty good line for its magnanimity and the fact it bought me a little bit of much-needed recovery time.

She smiled in return and said, "I'm not really showing yet, not unless, well, not unless you look really hard. I've been a little bit sick, but not too bad. I'm pretty nervous. And I'm really goddamned excited."

She rolled her eyes toward the ceiling and smiled more broadly — unrestrained happiness all over her face.

I squeezed her hand and said, "I'm really thrilled for you." Was I? I didn't know.

Passengers were filing past us, lining up for the boarding call, riffling through their coats for tickets and IDs, completely unaware of the minidrama unfolding in their midst. Or at least I think they were unaware.

I flashed to a scene a few years before, a summer's evening at a traveling carnival in a small town in Maine. Her hair was wavy from the sun and her tan skin untouched by makeup. She had just nervously told me she thought she was pregnant, and I scooped her up in my arms and paraded her around the grass parking lot, thinking we were going to be parents together, that we were going to spend the rest of our lives together, that I was going to have what was taken away from me before, or at least some sort of approximation of it.

Instead, the tests came back negative, the relationship eventually soured, and, well, here we were. Imagine if I could have looked into the future that night in Maine, and this scene at the San Francisco Airport is what I saw?

Of course, I hid all these feelings and recollections, or at least I hid them as best as I could. I said, "I'm really thrilled for you. And in all seriousness, you look spectacular."

She beamed.

Left unasked, unanswered, and entirely unstated was the issue of paternity, which, for every logical and illogical reason, I was dying to know, though damned if I was going to bring it up. I did a double-check on her left ring finger and saw nothing but skin. I pictured a tall guy, dark hair, probably an investment banker, maybe a venture capitalist, every bit as thrilled as I was that night in Maine when we had that false alarm. That expanse I was suddenly feeling in my chest was what's known as emptiness.

She said, "It's all pretty overwhelming, you know?"

Well, yeah, I did know until I didn't, which happened in a hospital when Katherine and our daughter died during childbirth. I guess this is exactly what Elizabeth means when she says the dead keep on dying in my life.

The line all around us had receded to a few stragglers, and the hum of activity had lessened to a vague sense of quiet. The gate agent announced over the PA system, "Final call for Flight 423 to Boston. This will be the final boarding call. All ticketed and confirmed passengers, please get on board now."

A deadline, so I asked, "Are you planning a wedding at the same time?"

Tactful, even if it wasn't.

Without missing a beat, she replied, "That's what's so overwhelming about it. I'm doing it on my own. I'm using a friend's sperm. He signed away all rights; I freed him of all obligations."

It's always something with this woman, always another surprise around every terrific curve. My mood lightened, though I tried to hide it. I asked, "Why?"

The gate agent approached us and asked, "Are you guys on this flight?" You guys — everyone assuming we were a couple. I looked around the waiting lounge and saw only one man in the distance reading a newspaper.

I said, "I am. Do I have ten seconds?"

"How about five."

Elizabeth said, "Because I was writing about other people's lives and not living my own. Because time was passing me by. Because it's something I've always wanted, and I don't have the luxury anymore to sit back and wait."

I looked at her and she looked at me and the gate agent looked at both of us.

"Congratulations," I said. "I'm really thrilled for you, and don't take this the wrong way, but proud of you as well, even if I no longer have the right."

I kissed her on the cheek, turned around, and walked toward the jetway.

Me and Elizabeth Riggs — we were always parting ways.

20

There was very little rhyme and virtually no reason to the killings to which Albert DeSalvo confessed some forty years before. The victims were all women, they were all single, and they were all strangled. The similarities stopped there.

Sometimes the killer strangled two women in a single week. Other times, he went a month or more without killing anyone. Usually he killed within the borders of Boston, but he also traveled as far as Lowell and Lawrence to commit murder.

His first half-dozen women were into their middle or later years, some of them pretty divorcées, others spinsters. Later, his victims grew younger in age. One black woman was killed, though it was never clear whether she was part of the spree.

Sometimes the killer left big looping bows around their necks, usually tied from the victim's own hosiery. Other times he didn't.

Occasionally he left them in ghoulish positions — sitting in a chair facing the door, for example, or propped up in bed just so, once in a bathtub. Other times they were left haphazardly where they died.

He left semen on various victims' crotches, mouths, and chests. Some were vaginally raped, others not. One woman seemed to have been the subject of the killer's necrophilic fantasies. Other women showed no sign of sexual assault.

He left a note — a card, actually — propped up against the foot of his final victim, but he hadn't left anything like that with any of the victims before. He never had any contact with the news media, never reached out to the police, never intentionally left clues at any of the scenes.

When Albert DeSalvo confessed from the dank environs of the Bridgewater Center for Sexually Dangerous Persons, he poured out his soul, providing intimate details of each and every crime scene, as if he had so reveled in every murder that the sights, sounds, and smells would never leave his mind. Either that or, as Bob Walters seemed to believe, he committed someone else's impressions to memory.

This is what I learned from my reading on the evening flight from San Francisco to

Boston, which was also spent knocking back a couple of Sam Adams with a stewardess — ah yes, flight attendant — who invited me to join her for a drink at her, ahem, hotel bar. That wouldn't happen, despite my best intentions, for a reason that can be summed up in two words: Edgar Sullivan.

You see, Edgar was there to greet me at the gate at Logan International Airport, along with a member of the Massport security team. It was nearing midnight. I think Edgar was up about five hours past his bedtime, though he didn't seem to mind. He never seems to mind anything. The two guys silently hustled me down an escalator, past baggage claim, and through a set of double doors that I never knew existed. I thought they were leading me into some vault where frequent-flier miles are kept, but no, we were on the ground floor of a concrete garage.

Edgar had an SUV waiting, the kind of vehicle that celebrities are always getting into the moment they leave the courthouse where they face various securities or molestation charges. We climbed into the back. The driver I didn't recognize. Edgar simply said, "Over to the *Record*," and we were gone. To me he said, "Welcome home. Peter and I agreed that this was the best way to assure that you would get safely back into town without being followed. Toby here" — the driver, a balding and rather burly man, turned around briefly and waved — "is a former linebacker for the Chicago Bears. He'll accompany you wherever you need to go for the time being."

Truth is, I didn't mind. Every once in a while, I still shivered from that night earlier in the week spent flailing in the cold, murky waters of the Charles. And I don't think I'll ever get the sound of the gunshot out of my head that killed that innocent guy in the Public Garden two days before, then the woman screaming that he was dying, her voice rising in the early spring air before fading into the wind.

By the time I walked into the *Record,* it was nearing midnight. Didn't matter. Peter Martin arrived at my desk about a minute after I did, though rather than being a bundle of jangled nerves, he was in that zone of calm that he gets into when the world around him gets particularly frenzied.

"Welcome back," he said. He said this in the same mechanically calm tone that one of the Stepford Wives might use to welcome her husband home from work.

"Thank you. Are you okay?"

"Fine, yes. Just fine. We need to go over

some things."

He pulled up a chair next to my desk.

He said, "Okay, the cops went to Commonwealth Avenue. Kimberly May indeed lived there. Second floor."

Already, I'm thinking to myself, life in the past tense. This wasn't going to be good, not for Kimberly May, not for the women who would inevitably cross my desk after her.

He continued, "No answer at the door, so they knocked it down. Mongillo was downstairs and could hear the whole thing. They found Kimberly exactly as she was shown on the video sent to you, dead for what they think was at least a full day, maybe two."

I asked, "We're going with it for morning, right?" That was newspaper speak for the next day's paper.

Martin replied, "Full bore. Leading with the murder. Second graph is the fact that *Record* reporter Jack Flynn was sent a videotape of the apartment and the body by the person who apparently committed the murder. Flynn, in turn, contacted police. Police rushed to the address supplied by the *Record* and discovered the body. *Record* saves the day, though we don't use those exact words."

I said, "Not for Kimberly May."

He nodded. "Point taken," he said.

He added, "Then the issue became, do we post the video online?"

"What the fuck?"

Martin said, "It's a tough market out there. We have a video of a murder scene given to us by a murderer. We shade out the actual corpse. Why not get it out there? It has a hell of a lot of value."

I said, "Value to who? What kind of value are you talking about? Allowing people to be voyeuristic? To see a dead woman's apartment, the place where she was killed? Like I said, Peter, what the fuck?"

Martin said, "Yeah, that's why we didn't do it. But bet the farm the *Traveler* would if this video was sent to them, and that's my fear. You know, the Phantom is upping the ante here, from driver's licenses to real visuals like this video. He may want this thing in the public realm. By us not putting it there, he may shop it around somewhere else."

That kind of talk reminded me of my conversation with the guy on the phone who claimed to be the Phantom the morning before, my pleading with a murderer to avoid talk radio like the Barry Bor Show, to not post his stranglings on a blog, just to deal with me and the *Record*. I'd burn in hell for that, but at least I'd have the story first. Hopefully.

Martin added, "Your reaction was my reaction, but it might not be the right reaction. You and I might be too old-fashioned in the age of FOX News and the Internet. And this may not be the last of it."

We both sat there in the middle of the newsroom, quietly now. In the distance, the copy desk was in the throes of another deadline, with pasty-faced copy editors nearly delirious in the discovery of a misplaced semicolon or a wrong middle initial.

Martin said, "There's word of a press conference tomorrow morning at police headquarters. Nine o'clock. I think you'll want to be there. Tomorrow's going to be a big day."

At that point, neither one of us had any idea just how big the day would be.

21

If there was ever a moment's doubt about the national appeal of the Phantom Fiend story, it was rapidly put to rest when Toby glided up to the front of Boston Police headquarters at Schroeder Plaza at 8:45 in the morning to drop me off for the commissioner's press conference.

Television satellite trucks lined Tremont Street on the outskirts of Boston's Roxbury section, long trucks, huge trucks, with the outsized insignias of various networks — from CNN to FOX News to the big three of NBC, ABC, and CBS — emblazoned on the sides. In the narrow gaps between satellite trucks were the smaller vans owned by affiliate stations in Boston, Hartford, Springfield, Providence, and Portland, Maine.

I swear to God, it was all part of one huge traveling carnival, same trucks driving the same people facing the same pressures to cover the same stories. The only thing that changed was the location, whether a remote Indian reservation in Minnesota for a school shooting, or an Atlanta suburb for a missing bride (not Maggie), or the California coast for the guy who murdered his pregnant wife. Could be Waco, could be Ruby Ridge, could be wherever — and it always was. The only guarantee in this media age is that when one blockbuster story is ending, another one is just gaining legs someplace else. There's no other choice: the executives at MSNBC aren't going to broadcast ten hours a day of nothingness, even if it sometimes seems like that's exactly what they do.

And now the show had traveled to my backyard, courtesy of, well, me, though not really. I was an incidental, if somewhat pivotal player, an unintentional conduit between a murderer and the city that he seemed to be killing off one woman at a time. As I stepped out of the Navigator, I hoped my colleagues from the national press corps could and would leave me the hell alone. I really did. Many reporters — hell, most reporters — would bask in the limelight created by the Phantom Fiend. I didn't need it. I didn't want it, not least because I really do have a face made for newspaper work. I would only put up with the publicity if it furthered the cause of me breaking more news.

The sidewalk along Tremont Street outside the glassy headquarters was a sideshow in that aforementioned carnival. One man with hair like Johnny Damon's, which also meant he had hair like Jesus, was handing out prayer cards and chanting, "God save our city." A middle-aged woman sold T-shirts that read THE PHANTOM IS A YANKEES FAN. Another young vendor plied shirts that simply said THE PHANTOM SUCKS. A twentysomething guy with dreadlocks sold those cheap plastic bracelets — these were black — that charities are always using now for fund-raising.

"Who benefits from these?" I asked him.

He looked at me carefully for a long moment, shrugged, and said, "I do."

Good answer. I bought one for two dollars and stuck it in my pocket, yet another contribution to the American Dream.

Speaking of which, by the time I hit the revolving front door, any dream I had of being anonymous in this unfolding story was quickly broken. There were, I don't know, maybe twenty, probably closer to thirty, reporters and assorted crew members waiting for me in the front lobby, most of them thrusting microphones in my face as they screamed an indecipherable stew of undoubtedly inane questions. I swear I heard someone yell, "Who was your favorite seventies rock band?" That caused me to wonder for a moment when it was that Air Supply hit it really big, but I think that was the eighties.

I kid, for godsakes. I kid.

But not about the two dozen reporters and various cameramen and sound people with the boom mikes so strong they could pick up the rapid beating of my famously oversize heart and beam it clear as day to any fans out there on the moon. The reporters, some of whom I recognized either as old friends or Washington colleagues from my time in the capitol, or from watching TV, quickly surrounded me.

"Have you met the Phantom?" one perfectly coiffed man yelled above the din.

Let's think about that for a second, perhaps on his behalf, because he obviously had not. Had I met the Phantom Fiend, wouldn't I have gotten around to reporting that fact in the pages of my beloved *Boston Record?* Wouldn't I have let people know on my own? Does he really believe I would have held back on my own employer and readers to first bestow such knowledge on the dozens of daytime viewers of FOX News?

Everyone fell completely silent and stared at me in hopeful expectation of a brilliant or newsworthy answer.

"I have not," I said, sorry to disappoint, though not really.

"Why not?" a woman shouted.

Okay, so the questions were going to grow increasingly stupid.

"Because he hasn't chosen to make himself available to me," I replied, trying not to be terse. "I think he has a pretty good idea that I'm always available to meet with him."

I started wondering if this was really what I did for a living, what these people were doing to me now, and I took instant pity on anyone I'd ever covered on the wrong side of the microphone and notepad. The necessary patience with the news media alone should qualify every public official for sainthood. Though maybe not.

One sweating cameraman was all but pressing up against me with the tools of his trade, so close that I thought he was going to bang my head on his camera. Another bespectacled scribe, obviously a print reporter, was carefully sizing me up from head to foot as he jotted notes on a legal pad. When I glanced upside down at his writing,

I thought I saw the word *pecs,* but maybe not.

There were more shouted questions — how many times have I heard from him, have I been fully cooperative with police, why do I think he picked me. To that last one I replied, "Because I'm the best reporter I know." I said this laughing. No one else in this circle jerk even cracked a smile. I made a mental note not to watch what would undoubtedly be the painful coverage on the midday news.

So I added, "I'm kidding. Guys, I'm not the story here, obviously. You know that already. I'm in this by happenstance. Could as easily be any one of you. And everything I know, you've already read in the *Record.* Anything I learn, you'll read that there as well." Not a bad little plug for my paper, I thought.

That's when one second-tier network reporter, a woman with skin so tight and tucked she could have been a spokeswoman for Saran Wrap, said above the noise, "Jack, the police are complaining in this morning's *Traveler* that they believe the *Record* is encouraging the Phantom to work through them, rather than directly with authorities. And by doing this you're stymieing the investigation. Do you have any comment?"

I hadn't read that, mostly because I hadn't read the *Traveler* yet, which was no great loss lately, given how much they were slashing the budget of that paper. They'd been left so far behind on this story, which should have been right in their wheelhouse, that they were rendered irrelevant. Still, I could feel my face flush, partly in anger that Hal Harrison or Mac Foley would level such a stupid accusation, and partly in embarrassment over my foolish negotiating antics with the Phantom himself, or at least with someone I thought was the Phantom. I reminded myself that the cops wouldn't have any idea of my attempts at negotiation. They were just trying to get me off the story, dead or alive, it seemed.

I said, "I haven't seen that, but it sounds exquisitely ridiculous." After I said this, I wondered, nearly aloud, why it was that I always have to throw in an extra adjective. Or is *exquisitely* an adverb? Either way, not the point. I continued, "Look, I'm just doing what you guys would all do, and that's report news. If someone sends you something in the mail or has a message delivered identifying where a murder victim might be, you contact authorities and you report this in your newspaper or on your network. Maybe you try to get a look yourself, to make sure the investigation is proceeding as it should. That's exactly what the *Record* has done in all three instances. I'm not sure why the police would have a problem with that."

A door to an auditorium behind the scrum opened, and a uniformed police officer announced, "Commissioner at the podium in two minutes." The reporters surged as one toward the opening, pushing their way inside, leaving me alone in the hallway. When they were all inside, I went in as well, notebook in hand, ready to do what I do best, which is report news rather than make it.

What a business, what a life, what a world.

Commissioner Hal Harrison, the man who would be mayor, strode to the podium as if he was about to attack it. He was in the hushed, carpeted media center, the place awash in the soft color blue — royal blue carpet, pale blue walls, men and women in navy blue uniforms, aging newspaper reporters in the frayed blue blazers that count as couture in the realm of words and news.

The gathered media had followed the universal, perhaps natural order of things. The better-dressed television reporters — the women in expensive suits, the men in

Brooks Brothers and ties — dominated the front of the room, with the occasional newspaper reporter who hadn't yet learned of his or her proper — or as is more often the case, improper — place. Behind them, the bulk of the disheveled print reporters in open collars or jean skirts sat with noticeably less practiced postures. Behind them still were the unshaven men in unintentionally low-riding jeans peering through the lenses of a couple of dozen television cameras, often flanked by similar-looking men wielding the aforementioned boom mikes. And behind them were the photographers, known in campaign parlance as the stills. The commissioner's many police advisers and campaign strategists sat in chairs along the two side walls of the room, their shoes as shiny as the bathroom mirrors at a Holiday Inn.

I took a position, standing, pen and legal pad in hand, in the back of the room, off to the side, with a clean vantage over the masses. The whole thing had the feel of something large, not least for the reason that as Harrison took center stage, a CNN reporter stood on camera in the middle of the room, announcing, "Boston Police Commissioner Hal Harrison is ready to address the issue of whether the Boston

Strangler, the most notorious serial killer in the history of the United States, has reappeared after a forty-plus-year absence; we're carrying this to you live."

"I'd just like to make a couple of brief comments and announcements, what have you, and then I'll take a few of your questions," the commissioner began.

"I'd like to start by saying this is a trying time in Boston, and certainly a challenging time in the Boston Police Department. We don't like to see one single innocent person killed, never mind three of them, all women. I would like to take a moment to assure the public, particularly women, that we have every available resource dedicated to solving these prior three murders and preventing any future ones, and we are confident on both fronts that that is exactly what will be the case. I would encourage women to exercise appropriate precautions until the perpetrator is identified and apprehended. But as long as people use basic common sense, the city is safe. I repeat: Boston is safe."

I've been to, what, a hundred police press conferences over the years? Maybe two hundred? Probably more. Never once have I heard a police official announce that they are addressing a problem halfheartedly, probably without enough manpower, and with no expectations of making any headway in the investigation anytime soon.

So, translated from police-speak to every-day English, what he'd just said was that he was totally screwed and completely pan-icked. If he was a woman, he'd stay inside, buy a pair of unneutered rottweilers, then nail plywood over all his windows. But look at the bright side: not dining out at expen-sive restaurants is probably a good way for the entire female population of Boston to save a few bucks and lose a little weight.

He said, "We have a team of the city's best and most experienced homicide detectives on the case, around the clock, augmented by detectives and uniformed officers in virtually every other division of this depart-ment. We are all pressing our informants for leads. We have additional officers on patrol, keeping their eyes on the city's neighbor-hoods. I have canceled official travel plans for the foreseeable future so I can remain in Boston overseeing the investigation."

Translated: I don't have the slightest semblance of a clue as to who is offing women at a stunning clip of one every other day, and nor do my tired old detectives in the homicide bureau. Of course, they're all going to soak me in overtime on this thing, so much so that I don't have the money left in my budget for the chiefs' convention at the four-star resort in Cancún.

Real life: "At this time, with acting mayor Mara Laird's approval, I would also like to offer an award of twenty-five thousand dollars for any information leading to the arrest of the killer of any of the three victims. Believe me, I'm fully aware what's at stake in this case."

Translated: The know-nothing acting mayor is so far up my ass on this thing that I can feel her hair tickle my lower intestine, not that she needs to be. My whole political career is at stake. So in utter, total desperation, we'll simply throw money at the problem in hopes that some street scum turns on some other street scum, alleviating the need for any good detective work.

The commissioner said, "In anticipation of your questions, I'd like to make a few important points. As you know, we discovered the body of Kimberly May in her apartment yesterday, based on a tip to the news media, presumably from the perpetrator of the crime. I encourage each and every journalist in this room and in this city, and probably in this country, if you've had any contact with anyone who identifies himself as the killer of these women, or provides information about other possible killings, to please contact us immediately. This is imperative. An investigation with multiple victims unfolding over a lengthy period of time is complicated enough. It becomes unnecessarily complex when the news media plays something less than a constructive role in the investigation. I would remind you that interfering in an active investigation is a prosecutable criminal offense."

Translated: It's driving us fucking crazy that we've even had to admit there's a serial murderer on the loose and that we have no idea who or where he is. The fucking media, meaning you, Jack Flynn, should stay the fuck out of our way. Or else.

"With the third victim murdered in similar fashion, we are now pursuing the theory of a single killer, even while we continue to keep all other options open and under investigation. Many of you have posed the question as to whether this could in any way be linked to the killings in the Boston Strangler spree from mid-1962 to early 1964, much as a serial killer in Wichita, Kansas, emerged after two decades of silence and criminal inactivity."

No translation necessary here. Ten minutes in, he was finally getting interesting, even making news. I hadn't taken a note yet, but marked my legal pad with the letters BTK — the acronym for "bind, torture, kill," the self-administered nickname for the Kansan killer who had reached out to the news media some twenty years after his last known slaying.

"That, obviously, is impossible here. The man who confessed to being the Boston Strangler, Albert DeSalvo, was killed in prison in 1973. I personally worked on that case in the early sixties. In the last couple of days, I have gone back and reread key parts of his confession from 1965. I am as convinced now as I was then that DeSalvo was, indeed, the perpetrator of those violent crimes, and what we have now is a copycat killer, seeking fame and press attention that he is receiving, and that consequently is fueling his desire to kill again."

Translated: Don't you dare question the good work from the sixties that propelled my rocket ride to the commissioner's office. And by the way, this whole thing is the news media's fault.

"We have already consulted with some of the most distinguished and accomplished criminal profilers in the country, who have compiled a psychological composite of the perpetrator of these crimes. As we review and refine it, we will make our findings public. In the meantime, I will say that any suspect is certainly a male, probably someone who lives alone, perhaps grew up in a single-parent household with a strong mother or maybe dominant older sisters, works in a largely unheralded job, craves attention that he doesn't get in his everyday life, and likely has a criminal record involving other violent crimes. We suspect he's in his thirties or forties, and for obvious reasons, we believe he has a keen interest in history."

My cell phone vibrated in my jacket pocket, and I pulled it out, assuming I'd see Peter Martin's number on the caller ID, Martin thinking I should already have half the story written before the press conference was actually over. But by the time I got the phone in hand, the vibrations had stopped. A notice appeared on the face of the phone informing me that I had a text message. How Modern Age, though not really.

I had a girlfriend for what seemed like the duration of a cup of coffee who used to text-message me every time she wanted sex, which, as it turned out, was quite often, which was good until the day it wasn't, but that's not really the point here. I pressed a few buttons and the message appeared on my screen: "The phantom fiend is the bos-ton strangler. i know. i am him. will contact you asap. pf."

I stared at it in disbelief, and not just because of my confusion over whether "I am him" was proper grammar. I had re-ceived two typed notes accompanying the driver's licenses of fresh murder victims that most assuredly came from the Phantom Fiend, as well as a DVD that could only have come from the Phantom Fiend. In ad-dition, I got the phone call from someone who claimed to be him, though I doubt it, given the result, which was almost my death but instead was that of an innocent by-stander. But this, a text message on my cell phone? Could a serial killer who had emerged from forty years of dormancy really be so technologically savvy? Or did a text message even count as technological savviness anymore?

I reread the note again, noticing for the first time that there was an origination number on the bottom of the text message, causing my heart to skip a beat. Maybe the Phantom Fiend wasn't as savvy as he thought he was. Maybe it was his phone number, easily traceable through cell phone records. Maybe this simple clue, this junior varsity mistake, would break the case, much in the same way Sam Berkowitz's parking ticket near a murder scene helped break open the Son of Sam spree in New York City.

I reread the message yet again. The commissioner prattled on with the requisite thanks for the widespread cooperation among departments and agencies, even though the Boston Police was constantly at war with the state police and the FBI. Translated: We're taking control of this thing and if any other agency tries sticking their incompetent and corrupt noses into our investigation, we'll pummel them senseless.

Fuck the commissioner, fuck his defensive by-the-numbers press conference, fuck his nonsensical blame-the-media strategy. Maybe I should give him exactly what he wanted, I thought: raise my hand and announce, "Sir, I have just received word from the Phantom Fiend that he is, in fact, the Boston Strangler, contrary to the theory that you are pursuing in your own investigation."

I decided against that. Instead, I stepped out of the room into the lobby, where I had been surrounded by my comrades-in-words twenty minutes earlier and dialed the number that was on the bottom of the message.

It rang three times before the recorded voice of a woman came on announcing that this line didn't take incoming calls, and to please check the number again and try redialing. I did as told, as I occasionally do, with the same result.

Before I could place the next call that I wanted to make, my phone vibrated again, this time with Peter Martin's number on the caller ID.

"Are you watching this bullshit?" I said, picking up the phone.

"I was," he said, his tone less calm than it had been the night before. "Right now I'm watching something else. I'm watching a video of Kimberly May's apartment on a blog site called Hubaloo.com — 'all the news the *Record* won't print.' They've got the entire clip, and they're showing her body unimpeded — just a dead girl on the web. I don't know how they got it — a police department leak, or whether your Phantom gave it to them. But right now the site has so many hits that it's already crashed twice on me while I'm watching."

"Clever name and slogan," I said. At the same time, I swore under my breath — stupid goddamned bloggers, freaks of nature who sit around their dingy apartments in ratty bathrobes and black socks posting total crap on the web and thinking it counts as hipster journalism, the next big thing.

"I'll tell you one thing," Martin said, his tone growing uncharacteristically angry now. "Seeing this makes me truly believe we did the right thing by not running it. The ad people could die because of the dollars we would have made, but not worth it."

Then he asked, "You on your way back here?" I thought so at the time, so I answered in the affirmative. We hung up and I placed an immediate call to Vinny Mongillo in the newsroom. I asked him to check with his phone company sources on the number that appeared at the bottom of the text message. He put me on hold, came back, and said, "That traces to one of those disposable cells. It was purchased with cash. There's no name on the account. You're out of luck."

"Could you check and see if they know what other calls were made from that phone? Maybe I can track down someone who was called by the owner."

"Already did, Fair Hair. No other calls to this point."

"You think they'd be willing to monitor it for future use?"

"They're already planning on it."

"Dinner tonight?" I asked.

"Well, now you owe me, so at a place of my choosing. You're on your way in here? We need to go over the Paul Vasco information. We should be able to pay a call on him at our earliest convenience."

"Which may well be today. I'll be in shortly."

The door to the media room flung open and the reporters and their cameramen poured out en masse. The press conference was over. Within minutes, CNN, FOX News, MSNBC, and, later, the three networks would authoritatively report that the serial killer was profiled by crime analysts as being a history buff in search of attention that he never got in his everyday life, careful and media-savvy, a new Boston Strangler for a new generation.

And that serial killer would soon be telling me things I wasn't ready to hear.

22

I quite literally jumped out of the Navigator as Toby glided to a stop at the front door of the *Boston Record.* I bounded up the few stairs and into the glassed-in front lobby, where Edgar Sullivan was there to greet me.

"They don't pay you enough, Edgar," I said, striding past him as he leaned on the reception desk.

He began walking alongside me, keeping pace, the two of us heading side by side toward the escalator. He replied in a confiding voice, "Are you kidding me? Most guys my age are sitting on folding chairs in the rec rooms of retirement communities all over this country. They'd give their left walnut to have just five minutes of the excitement I'm having trying to help you escape Father Fate."

I looked at him, at his neatly pressed blue blazer and tan pants that were in sharp contrast to his wrinkled face and hands, old but young, stern but happy. He was between wives, was his line, meaning he was between his fourth and fifth wives, assuming the next one would come along, which she undoubtedly would. I pictured him sitting in a neighborhood tavern after work beside a date twenty years his junior, explaining to her how he had pulled the paper's kiester out of the fire again that day as he single-handedly tried to make this city safe for its entire female population. Retirement my ass.

"You know you're doing one hell of a job on this, right?" I said this in all seriousness.

Edgar replied, "I'm just doing my job, Jack. It's you who's putting yourself at risk and writing this great stuff."

I shook my head. "I don't really have much of a choice. I've been put in the middle here. You — you could be off playing golf or throwing baseballs with the grandkids."

"Ah, my golf game is awful and my grandkids are brats." He hesitated, then added, "They're good kids, actually. They're just not into sports."

We were at the top of the escalator now, walking toward the newsroom, still shoulder-to-shoulder, moving fast. Edgar pulled a white envelope from inside his jacket pocket. He held it out in front of us and said, "Jack, this came for you via courier about twenty minutes ago. My guys were under orders to grab me before any courier left. They did. I questioned him and he said the account was paid in cash, and he has no name, and no return address. He picked up the package from a man who he said he couldn't identify, on a street corner in Downtown Crossing. I haven't opened it. Maybe it's nothing. But it's starting to fit a pattern, and I thought you'd want to see it right away."

He handed me the sealed envelope with my name typed on the front in small letters in a familiar font — familiar because it was the same size and font as the type on the envelope that contained Jill Dawson's driver's license four days before.

Four days. Seemed like four weeks, or four months, a veritable lifetime ago. *You're going to help me get the word out or other women will die. The Phantom Fiend.* That's what he wrote at the time, and I still wasn't sure what he meant. The only thing I was sure about was that other women had died, and more women were undoubtedly about to. As a matter of fact, I was probably holding either a death sentence or a perverted death certificate in my very hand. What the "word" was, how I was supposed to help get it out, whether I could help, these were the things I didn't know.

Until now.

We were walking into the newsroom, toward my desk. Edgar said, "Do you want me to stay with you while you open it?" He nodded toward the envelope as he spoke. "You know, could be anthrax or some other chemical."

"Not his style, if this is even from him," I answered. "Give me a moment with it." He peeled off. I made my way through the maze of desks in the busy newsroom at the start of another news cycle.

Once I settled in, Martin, of course, arrived in about three nanoseconds with a whirl of questions, expectations, and instructions. I asked him to give me a minute, perhaps not as politely as I might have. Oddly enough, without questioning me, he did, and walked away.

I carefully opened the envelope with a painfully familiar sense of dread. Another correspondence, another dead woman, whether it be Jill Dawson or Lauren Hutchens or Kimberly May. Maybe I should have been invigorated to be injected this far into the biggest unfolding story in the country, but what I really felt was a gloomy sense of futility, and the worst thing a reporter can feel is futile, even if we so often are. I heard about each of these women after they were no longer alive. My reporting only brought bad news. My published words could do nothing to help them. I could only carry the distant hope that I might be bringing a sense of caution to those who would — or perhaps wouldn't — be next.

I reached into the envelope and felt a single sheet of paper, but nothing else — meaning no disc that would show a dead woman's body splayed out in her apartment, no driver's license to lead us to the next victim. The sheet was folded over once. I opened it up and looked at it warily.

"Dear Mr. Flynn," it began, again in that same printed font. "It is well known that no one was ever charged or convicted of any of the killings attributed to the Boston Strangler. What is less well known, except among a small group of experts, is that the real Boston Strangler is alive, well, and killing again today. I am the Boston Strangler. The authorities have it as wrong now as they did in 1965. You should ask them why. The answer, should they choose to give it, will be of enormous public interest.

"I will kill again, soon. If you don't print

this note, verbatim, above the fold on the front page of tomorrow's newspaper, I will double the pace of my killing. Blood will be on your hands.

"The Phantom Fiend, also known as, The Boston Strangler."

Okay, a couple of things are worth noting here, the first, and perhaps most obvious, is that we had a grammatically correct killer on the loose in Boston. I mean, good God, I didn't write English as elegant as my cold-blooded correspondent, and I wrote for a living. It was as if he was writing a thank-you note to the queen.

That aside, three bodies later, he finally got around to answering the question of what he wanted from me: fame. He wanted to be on center stage in Boston, and he wanted my newspaper, the *Record*, to put him there. He wanted to intrigue the city with his words and hold it captive with his vicious actions. He wanted to play me. In turn, he wanted the newspaper to play its readership. He wanted me to be involved at the dead — pardon the pun — center of this story in a way reporters usually aren't. He wanted my newspaper to do things newspapers usually don't, in the name of a person who doesn't do what normal people do, which is kill multiple women.

This, in short, was not a good state of affairs.

I reread the note. One hand was shadowing my eyes, while my other hand held the single sheet of paper. That hand, I realized, was trembling. He was short, firm, to the point. Maybe he was like that in real life. Lines kept jumping off the page at me — *I am the Boston Strangler . . . You should ask them why . . . I will kill again, soon . . . I will double the pace of my killing . . . Blood will be on your hands.*

I had Bob Walters, the former Boston Police detective at the head of the old Strangler investigation, telling me that De-Salvo was the wrong guy. Unfortunately, he was very recently deceased. I had the current killer of three women — and counting — telling me DeSalvo was the wrong guy. Unfortunately, neither was available for questions, Walters never again, and my correspondent not for the moment.

On the other side of the ledger, it was starting to seem like all the lead people who had implicated DeSalvo in the Strangler case had benefited enormously from their actions in the investigation — most notably Hal Harrison, the detective who became police commissioner and was now vying to be mayor, and Stu Callaghan, the former

Massachusetts attorney general who went on to win a seat in the United States Senate.

The authorities have it as wrong now as they did in 1965. You should ask them why.

This implies that authorities knew they had it wrong some forty-plus years ago, and know they have it wrong again. My head hurt, not from too much information, but from a lack of it. What I needed were some answers from people who either weren't shooting straight or weren't around to speak.

"All right, long enough. What did it say? Is this going to carry the day for us tomorrow?"

That was Martin, reappearing at my desk, a bundle of nervousness and personality quirks. He was scratching at his forehead. He was tapping what looked like his Buster Brown shoes against the bottom drawer of my desk, and not in any particular rhythm. His right eye seemed to be twitching. Forget that Zen zone he would often enter. He looked like Nomar Garciaparra stepping up to the plate.

I merely shook my head in response and handed him the note to read himself, which he did, first fast, and then a second time slowly, all the while standing over me. What

I was coming to learn about Martin, perhaps later than I should have, was that it was never news that made him nervous, but the lack of it. News he can handle. News he can revel in, shape, edit, then publish. It's not having news, not having information, not having something that the competition doesn't that makes him near crazy. For this, he will always have my respect.

"What the fuck," he said, but he said it in a tone that betrayed an enjoyment of the decision that was to come, that decision being whether to publish the Phantom Fiend's words, verbatim. Then he added, "Any idea if he's sent this to any other media outlets?"

"My best read is that he's still dealing exclusively with us. He sent me a text message on my cell phone earlier this morning saying pretty much the same thing."

"I don't even know how to send a text message," Martin said. "Then again, I don't know how to strangle a woman, either."

With that, Martin said, "My office in twenty minutes." As he walked away, he shook the Strangler's note in his left hand and said, "I'm going to need this until then."

I was on the telephone with the Las Vegas Police Department, trying to ascertain the cause of death of Bob Walters, or at least their version of the cause, when I saw them walking along the outer edges of the newsroom.

They were two middle-aged guys in ill-fitting suits with bad haircuts, meaning they were cops — detectives, actually, maybe homicide. I could spot them a mile away. It's as if every cop over forty in the city went to the same barber, the one they had since childhood. For that matter, they all seemed to have the same tailor, the one who thought it better to keep their cuffed pants nice and short.

These two gentlemen were accompanied by one of Edgar Sullivan's minions, who led them in silence toward Peter Martin's office. I watched as they paused briefly outside Martin's office before being escorted in. At that point, I couldn't see them anymore — until, that is, they came walking back through the newsroom just a few minutes later. This time one of them was carrying an envelope in his hairy hand.

At that point, an e-mail flashed on my screen from Martin, asking to convene a meeting.

When I walked into Martin's office, Publisher Justine Steele was already there, sitting in one of half a dozen upholstered chairs that surrounded a perfectly forgettable coffee table. Martin sat in a chair facing her. Right behind me, Vinny Mongillo walked in carrying a brown bag with what smelled like cat excrement, but ended up being an Italian cold-cut sub slathered in various oils and spices.

As he unwrapped it on the coffee table, I think I saw Justine physically gag. Martin reflexively reached for a stash of paper napkins inside a desk drawer. I said, "Jesus Christ, Vinny, it's ten-thirty in the morning. What the hell are you doing with that crap?"

"Crap?" he replied, incredulous. "These are some of the finest cured meats that money can buy, shipped here straight from Genoa, Italy, by artisan chefs. The hell you talking about crap? And I've been up since five a.m., so this is like your late afternoon."

I can't argue with that. Actually, I probably could, but Martin interjected. "All right, we need to figure out fast how we're going to handle this letter. Let me bring you up to date on what we've already done."

I was tieless and jacketless. I don't know why I bring that up, except for I rolled up my sleeves and let my bare forearms rest against my knees, and as I did, a little piece of pickle came flying off Mongillo's sub and landed in the little hairs below my wrist. I flicked it on the carpet and stared at Martin.

"Jack, as soon as I got the copy of the letter from you, I, of course, flagged Justine." Martin nodded toward Justine as if none of us knew who she was. The two of them gave each other a funny look, though not funny in the ha-ha-that-Jack-Flynn-is-such-a-riot kind of way.

"Justine, in turn, felt it important to alert Mara Laird about the existence of this new correspondence. I agreed with her on that. We got pummeled pretty hard in the *Traveler* today, I believe unfairly so, about not being cooperative enough with police. We want to make sure we look like we're doing everything in our power to help them catch this killer."

At this point, Martin was slowly easing into that Zen-like tone that he gets, the one with the exaggerated sense of calm. Justine listened to him intently. Mongillo finished the first half of his submarine sandwich and lit into the rest. I sat in still silence, starting to get slowly pissed off, though why, I wasn't quite sure yet.

Martin continued, "Justine, do you want to fill us in on your conversation with the mayor?"

It all sounded rehearsed. Justine nodded,

looked from me to Mongillo and back to me again, and said, "She's not thrilled with this — or with us. The conversation was brief. She put me on a conference call with Hal Harrison, and the two of them said that if we publish that letter, as the writer of it wants us to do, we will push the city of Boston into a state of what they called 'unwarranted chaos.' "

As she said those last two words, she looked down at a sheet of notes she had in her hand.

She continued, again looking down. "They said we would be 'seriously impeding' their investigation — again, their words. They said they need another day or two to" — she gazed down again here — " 'fully develop some promising leads.' And in no uncertain terms, they said that if we go ahead and print that letter, we should never again expect to receive help on breaking stories from Boston PD, or, for that matter, from city hall."

Mongillo guffawed. Or maybe he was choking on his mortadella. Either way, he said, "How could you tell if Boston PD becomes unhelpful?"

A good question, or rather a point. Martin nodded; Justine said and did nothing. Martin broke a brief but strained silence and said, "Jack, give us your take."

So I did. I gave him exactly what he expected to get.

"I'll be honest with you," I began. "First, I understand that we had to turn that letter over to the cops; I just wish I had been consulted on it. Second, I didn't realize we were consulting with the acting mayor on editorial policy and decisions. From here on in, should I plan to run all my stories past Mayor Laird to make sure they meet with her approval?"

Steele frowned. Martin was about to interject, but I continued before he got the chance.

"Third, as the Phantom Fiend points out, that blood he's talking about will be on my hands, so I'll be up front by saying I'm in favor of getting this thing into print as soon as possible, tomorrow being barely soon enough. Maybe we ought to even consider putting it out on the website today, though he didn't ask us to do that, so that could screw things up.

"And fourth, there's already blood all over the floor — Bob Walters's blood, Kimberly May's blood, Jill Dawson's blood, Lauren Hutchens's blood, Joshua Carpenter's blood. This thing broke on a Monday. It's Friday now. Boston PD has had a week on this, with a stream of clues provided by us. You really think another twenty-four or forty-eight hours is going to change the scope and direction of their investigation? Or do you think they're just worried about the additional pressure?"

I paused and looked from Peter Martin to Justine Steele, then added, "And let's assume for a moment that it's the latter. Is it really our job to take pressure off the cops, or is it our job to put pressure on them?"

There was a moment of silence. Well, not entirely silence. Mongillo chomped on the last few potato chips, then noisily balled up the sandwich wrapper and let it sit on the table.

Finally, Steele asked, "Who's Bob Walters?"

I explained his former position, then I shared the details of my Las Vegas trip — his drunken wife, his theories on the Strangler, and then Bob Walters being carried out of his house in a black body bag that shone brightly in the desert sun.

I haven't even tried taking a step in a year.

Why on that one day would he have ever thought to have tried? The likely answer: he didn't.

Mongillo, fully nourished now, piped up. "I'm with Jack on this. Since when do we hold shit back? Since when do we climb in the sack with the cops, rather than serve as a check on them, and without even a promise of exclusive information if this thing pans out? Since when do we not warn the damned public about what we know, when we know it?"

He paused, seemingly getting more wound up, then added, "This shit is life and death. This isn't some journalism exercise about confirming a source. This is about letting women know they're in dire danger out there."

I added, "Hal Harrison doesn't want people to think there's danger because he's running for mayor. Mara Laird doesn't want people to think there's danger because she is the mayor. We don't get this letter into print, we're not doing our jobs."

Again, silence, until Martin asked, "You don't think that by printing this letter, verbatim, that we're turning over editorial control of the newspaper to a serial killer?"

A good point. But let's face it, like it or not, what the Phantom Fiend had to say — that the Boston Strangler lives, that they had it wrong before, that they're getting it wrong again — was news, blockbuster news, actually. And this was the same sort of journalistic issue that the editors of *The New*

York Times and *The Washington Post* wrestled with in 1995 before finally deciding to publish the Unabomber's manifesto, as he had requested. The publication led to his arrest.

I said all this, and Justine and Martin simply nodded in response, though Justine also noted that with the Unabomber case, federal officials were pushing the newspapers to publish because they had a paucity of other clues. In this case, Boston PD claimed to have other clues that needed to be pursued, and didn't want the published letter to get in its way.

This was getting frustrating. Martin was being deferential to his boss. And his boss, Steele, was being entirely too corporate, far more cautious than she typically was, or at least used to be when she was editor. Maybe it was the lawsuits that newspapers were losing around the country. Maybe it was the diving stock price. Maybe it was her friendship with Mara Lairdo. Maybe it was the barrage of accusations that the news media was growing irresponsible and increasingly cavalier about the truth. Hell, maybe she was losing her backbone. I glanced over at Mongillo and saw that he was gripping his balled-up sandwich wrapper so tight that the veins were popping through his wrist.

Martin said to both of us, "You've been very helpful."

Gee, thanks, Peter. With that, we got up and left. When we got out of earshot, Mongillo said, "I've got a suspected serial strangler we need to go see."

Hey, why not? We already seemed to be getting the life choked out of us.

23

At first — and I should probably be embarrassed to admit this — I almost didn't recognize her voice.

"Hey, Jack," she said. That was followed by a long pause. "I'm back in Boston," she continued. I was still somewhat confused at this point, sitting at my desk, listening to my messages before Vinny Mongillo and I headed out into this great city in a bold attempt to change its fate.

"I'm a little bit ashamed," she said.

That's when it struck: it was the elusive Maggie Kane — my fiancée, or again, maybe that's ex-fiancée, or perhaps it's simpler to just describe her as my would-be wife, the woman I had been planning to marry a week before, until the morning I wasn't. We were supposed to be splashing around in the Hawaiian surf right about now, sharing frozen strawberry daiquiris at a swim-up bar, relentlessly having sex in our overpriced room as a sea breeze drifted through the open French doors.

Her voice started to waver at this point. "I feel awful," she said. "I feel stupid. I feel so bad about what I've done. And Jack, I'm really lonely."

I squinted in confusion, through the haze of the Kimberly Mays and Jill Dawsons and Lauren Hutchenses that had so recently left this world, wondering what it was that Maggie had done. Okay, yes, she ran out on our wedding day, fled not only our relationship but the state, climbing aboard a jet that landed in Atlanta, leaving me figuratively and literally behind. Of course, I'd never gotten the chance to tell her that I fled as well; I just didn't make as big a physical spectacle of it as she did. I'd like to think I'm a reasonably subtle guy, was probably never more so than when I called off my wedding without actually telling anyone — the bride-to-be included.

"Is there any chance we can talk?" she asked. She was doing this thing that she always used to do, which was basically carrying on an entire conversation on my voice mail, asking questions that I wasn't on the line to answer, giving answers to questions that I wasn't on the line to ask. Like so much else in a relationship, when she first used to do this shortly after we met, I thought it was enormously adorable and often sexy. Now I just found it annoying, even if it was slightly comforting to hear the familiar sound of her voice.

"Jack, I know how furious you probably are. You completely have the right. I panicked. I did a shitty thing. I'm going to regret it for the rest of my life, for what I just did to the rest of my life, and more important, for what I did to you.

"But Jack, can you please, please let me talk to you for a little while, face-to-face." She began crying here — sobbing, actually. She fell quiet for a moment, apparently trying to compose herself. I heard her sniffle, and could all but see her wipe the back of her right hand across both her cheeks the way she used to do at the end of our occasional arguments. "Jack, please call me back."

Another long pause, another sniffle, then, softly, "I'm so, so sorry for all this."

And click.

"Maggie, it's okay, I wasn't planning on going through with it either." That was me, talking into the dead air on the phone where Maggie Kane's voice had just been. I wondered if I would ever tell her that. I wondered if we'd ever even get together. I supposed I should have wondered where and when and how it all went so wrong, but I didn't, and can't completely explain why not, not even to myself. So instead I pressed 3 and heard a woman's voice say, "Message erased, next new message."

The rather clipped voice of a middle-aged man came on, carrying something of a Western twang.

"This is Sergeant Wit Jackson of the Las Vegas Police Department public relations division, returning a call to Jack Flynn." He left his number, told me to have a good day, though it didn't sound like he particularly cared if I did, and hung up the phone.

I listened to a couple more messages from guys with names like Gray and Stone from television magazine and tabloid shows, and that was that.

I clicked off that line and onto another, the fresh dial tone filling my ear. Meantime, Vinny was standing at his desk, staring at me, making a twirling motion with his right index finger, his way of telling me that it was time to go. Subtle he was not.

I had time to return one call. Maggie Kane or Wit Jackson. Wit Jackson or Maggie Kane?

I called Wit Jackson. Don't ask me why, though if anyone had, I'd probably have answered that I didn't have the time I'd need to have the conversation with Maggie that I'd want to have. Or maybe I just liked the name Wit because it reminded me of myself. Good answers. But what's the real answer? I don't know the real answer.

Wit picked up the phone halfway through the second ring and we exchanged greetings. He asked, "What's a reporter from a hotshot Eastern newspaper want to know about our sandy little city?"

Sandy. Desert. Las Vegas. Get it? Wit was really living up to his name.

I laughed out of politesse, then turned my questioning toward Bob Walters's death, saying that I was trying to determine a cause of death and whether an investigation was under way. I could hear Wit typing into a computer, and then silence as he was undoubtedly reading something on the screen.

He said, "Cause of death determined to be head trauma from a fall down a flight of stairs at his house."

"Suspicious death?" I asked.

"Apparently not," he replied, then added, "Sometimes an accident is just an accident."

And sometimes not. But I didn't say that.

I asked, "Anything else of note from the death scene?"

For the first time, Wit sounded somewhat

suspicious. He asked, "What's your interest in some old retiree living out his years in the sun?"

"Former member of the Boston Police Department — a homicide detective, and a damned good one," I said. "I'm just making sure he's well tended to in death."

Wit seemed to appreciate that, as I suspected he would. He said, "Well, it looks like there was a pair of eyeglasses, broken, found near the body of the deceased at the bottom of the stairs." He fell quiet again, probably reading from the screen. I heard him press a button a couple of times, like he was scrolling down. Then he said, matter-of-factly, "And there was a single key on a small key ring retrieved from the bottom step. The assumption is that he was carrying it downstairs."

A key. His eyeglasses. An accident really may have been an accident. Bob Walters might have forced himself out of bed after I left, struggling down the stairs to get something that was locked away before I returned. And he fell. But what was it?

I asked, "Sergeant, off the record, can you share next of kin?"

"Well," Wit responded, "it'll be in tomorrow's obituary anyway. He leaves a wife, Patricia. And I've got here a Deirdre Walters

Hayes, a daughter who lives in the area."

"Number?"

And he gave it to me — Deirdre's telephone number. Boston PD should be so kind. I hung up with sincere thanks.

When I looked up, Vinny Mongillo was standing over me, a king-size box of Junior Mints in one of his oversize hands, a small reporter's notebook in the other. The box of candy, I noted for no particular reason, was larger than the pad.

"Let's go," he said. "And bring your A-game. This is no time for us to choke."

Choke. Strangler. Get it? Neither did I.

24

It was to the point where minutes, even seconds, felt like they mattered, not only to the women who would become victims to the Phantom Fiend but to the people whose help I was seeking. Everyone kept dying, naturally and unnaturally.

Which would explain why I was speeding through the city of Boston, taking a left on red, among other automotive transgressions. And it would furthermore explain why a Boston Police cruiser came racing up behind me, its overhead lights whipping blue and white, its headlights pulsating on and off. I had no idea that Boston cops bothered pulling anyone over for speeding anymore.

"Who the hell knew that Boston cops pulled anyone over for speeding?"

That was Vinny, taking a quick break from gabbing away in the passenger seat on his cell phone. Great minds, it seems, really do think alike — or at least one great one and a slightly above-average one. No need, I hope, for me to distinguish whose is whose.

An old Irish gray-haired cop walked up to the driver's window of my car after I pulled to the side of Cambridge Street near Government Center in downtown Boston.

"Quite the hurry, aren't you?" he asked.

This was a good thing. It was a good thing because when a cop engages you in any way during a traffic stop, it gives you the opportunity to squirm your way out of the citation. It's the cops, almost always younger cops, who act robotic and make no conversation as they issue you a ticket, who are a lost cause.

"Just trying to save the city, until you got in my way," I said.

Actually, I didn't. What I said was, "Too much of one, sir. I shouldn't have been going as fast as I was."

He nodded. I handed him my license and registration without him having to ask — another gesture that I think they like. Vinny continued to chirp on the phone, talking at that point about the prior night's Celtics game.

"Any special reason?"

With that, I was reasonably certain I was off the hook.

"There is, sir, but it doesn't change the

fact that I was speeding, so I won't bore you with it."

I mean, shit, someone should write this stuff down and put it in a manual for how to avoid traffic fines, or, for that matter, maybe any other prosecution.

"No, go ahead. I want to hear."

Vinny was yelling that Paul Pierce doesn't play any defense. I noticed half of humanity slowing down on their way by to get a glimpse of the poor bastard who had been yanked to the side of the road. The officer's radio cackled like a dying chicken, though I'm not sure what a chicken actually sounds like when it's about to take leave, so that may be inaccurate.

I sighed, not at the cop but at life, and said, "Sir, I'm a reporter for the *Record*. I'm writing about the serial murderer. I'm on my way to an important interview and didn't want to be late. That's the reason why I was speeding, but I by no means offer it as an excuse."

I was lighting it up here, and Vinny wasn't giving me a second thought, let alone a first one. At least the cop was. He looked intently at my driver's license, hunched down toward the window, and said, "You're the guy who's been getting the letters from the killer?" He said this softly, casually, his voice a little hoarse. When you're a cop, even a street cop, maybe especially a street cop, you've seen a lot of the world, some of the good, but more of the bad. You know how easily people slip into the abyss, breaking through the flimsy little barriers that separate normalcy from desperation. And you begin, in some odd way, to understand, and understanding more often than not leads to empathy.

I nodded and said simply, "I am." I didn't know the reaction I was about to get. Maybe it wouldn't be a reaction at all but a ticket, which I suppose was a reaction as well.

He handed me my license and registration and said, "Keep at it, young man. Tell the truth. Because in this matter, too many people aren't." And just like that, he walked back to his cruiser, leaving me to go on my way.

Even Vinny looked at me with the phone still pasted to his fat ear and said, "Wow."

The neighborhood of Charlestown is, among other things, home of the Bunker Hill Monument, the occasionally contentious host of the nouveau Olives restaurant, and creator of the infamous code of silence that let so many murders go unsolved in the 1980s. But it is arguably best known for producing more bank robbers per capita than any other neighborhood in the country. It's as if "Safecracking" and "Demand Notes" are curriculum requirements at Charlestown High.

I bring this up only to point out that the halfway house that Vinny and I had just pulled up to was something of a rite of passage for what seemed like half of Charlestown's native male population. These men are known as townies, though they don't live in "the Town." No, "the Town" is South Boston, also known as Southie. But natives there are called, well, residents, I guess. Yet another little point of confusion about my little hamlet of Boston.

But more to the point, I pulled the car to the curb across the street from the state-operated halfway house where Paul Vasco was supposed to be in temporary residence. It was a big, gray, nondescript wood-shingled house, four stories high, butting right up against the sidewalk, sitting on the side of Charlestown that had not yet been transformed by wealthy young professionals who, depending on your point of view, either cleaned up and added value to city neighborhoods, or sucked the spirit and history right out of them.

On this particular house, the paint was

chipping. Old coffee cups, candy wrappers, beer cans, and corroded newspapers had gathered in the wells around the basement windows. Hinges that were supposed to hold shutters held nothing at all but rust. The mismatched front door looked like it was made of untreated plywood. I suspect it had been kicked in a few times.

"Remind me never to cheat on my expense account ever again," Vinny said, gazing upward at the structure from the passenger seat of the car.

He reached into his coat pocket, pulled out a rumpled sheet of paper, and unfolded it.

"Paul Vasco," he said, his voice now taking on an official tone. "Age: sixty-two. Occupation: former handyman. More recently, convict. Most recently, ex-convict. Residence: 652 Bulham Avenue, also known as the Bunker Hill prerelease facility. Criminal record includes convictions on rape and first-degree murder. Notable characteristics: known to have an IQ that exceeds the level of genius."

I said, "Well, the two of us will have something in common."

"You're a handyman, too?"

As he said this, Vinny shoved the paper back into his coat pocket. He added, "And now, ladies and gentlemen, he may be killing all over again. It's on Jack and Vinny, Vinny and Jack, to stop him."

Obviously, some of this stuff I had heard already. The handyman part I hadn't. So he's adept with his hands as well as his mind. I asked, "Our strategy?"

"First we have to get to him. My sources at the Department of Correction tell me it's pretty easy access — hit or miss whether there'll be an unarmed security guard around the house. They suggested that he was assigned to a room on the second floor, facing the rear, number twenty-seven, but couldn't guarantee me that he hadn't switched with someone, which they say is reasonably common."

"Carlton Fisk," I said.

"Huh?"

"Twenty-seven. That was Carlton Fisk's number. He hit the most famous home run in Red Sox history" — to win the sixth game of the 1975 World Series against the Cincinnati Reds — "which maybe is a sign that we're about to hit a home run."

It should have been obvious to him. You're in Boston, these numbers mean everything — 33 is Larry Bird, 86 is the year the Red Sox lost the World Series to the New York Mets, 4 is Bobby Orr, 9 is Ted Williams, 12

Tom Brady, 16 the number of Boston Celtic championships — a figure, by the way, that seems to be stuck in time. I could go on, but I won't.

Vinny looked at me funny. "Right," he said. Then, "He has supposedly been assigned to a job with the state highway department, picking up trash on median strips and the like, but it doesn't start until tomorrow. He's wearing an electronic bracelet that requires him to be home when he's not either at work or commuting to and from work. My guy over at DoC said he was home this morning."

I can't say it enough, you've got to love Vinny Mongillo. If I ever become a good reporter, I want to be just like him.

I said, "Well, let's go see if we can make hay of a diabolical murderer."

"It's about time."

Interested parties, by the way, might notice that we had no interview strategy, Vinny and I — or maybe that's Vinny and me. There was no discussion of the good cop and the bad cop. We didn't review possible questions and the most probing follow-ups. We didn't set a sequence. We didn't plot out our tone. No, Vinny and I are from what would best be described as the wing-it school of American journalism, raised with the belief that reporters have to adapt to the situation, and not try to dictate it in any sort of preordained or formulaic way. Nothing drives me crazier than watching a blow-dried television interviewer sit and read a bunch of questions off a pad of paper that one of his or her producers had already sketched out. No conversation, no flow, just one preordained question following the next.

The aforementioned front door was unlocked, which was our first bit of good fortune on this mission, though maybe it wouldn't prove to be so fortunate. It opened into a dark, bland hallway characterized by a threadbare carpet and peeling floral wallpaper illuminated by a single bare low-wattage lightbulb. The Department of Correction might seriously think about hiring a new interior designer for their interim housing. I'm a criminal spending more than an hour in a shithole like this and I'm doing everything in my power to get myself back into prison, including committing new crimes. At least the jailhouse color scheme — gray — is pretty uniform.

We were both silent and tiptoeing, though I'm not entirely sure why, and Vinny tiptoeing is like anyone else walking — with a sack of cement on their shoulders. Vinny motioned upward and we both began ascending the steep, creaky wooden staircase, which sounded very much like it might collapse before we got to where we were hoping to go.

The second-floor landing was neither better nor brighter. Think of a men's room in a highway rest area, only this place smelled worse — a roundish, biting, aggressive odor that seemed to reach right into your nostrils and hit the back of your eyes. If hopelessness had a smell, this was it.

The hallway was longer than I thought it would be. If there had ever been carpet laid down, it wasn't there now. Instead, the floors appeared to be made of scratched and grooved particleboard, stained in various shapes and sizes and colors. The dingy walls hadn't been painted since the Republicans and Democrats in Washington all got along. I could hear the tinny sound of cheap televisions and radios, and was picking up the fumes of cigarettes. All in all, not a pleasant place.

"This feels like my old college frat house," Vinny whispered to me.

"I had no idea you went to college," I whispered back.

He ignored that and motioned for me to follow him toward the rear of the house. We passed several dark, old-fashioned doors, some with numbers on them, others not. The floors creaked, the air reeked, and it kept getting darker the farther back we walked.

Mongillo stopped in front of the last door on the right. It had the metal number 7 on it, and you could see the outlines of where the 2 used to be but wasn't anymore.

I put my fist next to the door, waited for Mongillo to nod, and I knocked, twice softly, then three times firmly. We both stood and listened intently in the dark.

Nothing.

Well, at least nothing from behind this particular door. Down the hall, we heard a bolt get pushed into a lock. We heard a television set get turned down. We heard someone urgently dragging an unknown object across an unseen floor. And then we heard nothing at all.

I looked at Mongillo. He nodded back at me. I knocked, even louder this time, four firm raps with the side of my right fist.

Another lock turned down the hallway. Someone somewhere fell into a coughing, wheezing, hacking fit. A fly buzzed between our two heads.

But again, nothing from this unseen room.

I said, loud enough to be heard inside,

"Mr. Vasco. Are you there? Mr. Vasco?"

The sound of my voice bounced off the bare hallway walls and melted into the hazy darkness. If Mr. Paul Vasco was indeed inside, as he was supposed to be, then he was either an incredibly sound sleeper, or he had no designs on entertaining visitors right about now.

I put my hand on the knob and began to turn it slowly. Mongillo squinted at me like I was some sort of maniacal nut, but did nothing to stop me. The knob, to my surprise, kept turning, turning, sliding all the way to the right. Just as it got to the end and I was about to slowly push it open, a latch opened across the hall and the door matter-of-factly swung open.

Vinny and I whirled around simultaneously. I half expected to be shot right between the eyes, gunned down in my own cold blood in a dingy halfway house on the fringes of Charlestown while I was in hot pursuit of the most befuddling story of my otherwise stellar career.

There was no gunfire, though, not even the flick of a knife. Instead, a voice from inside the darkened room called out, "You looking for me?"

It was a voice that was at once gravelly yet pointed, weary yet strong — the voice of someone who was energized by his new-found freedom, yet at some deeper level not quite sure, after all these years in prison, how to handle it all.

I asked, "Are you Paul Vasco?"

Still the person didn't appear. Vinny and I were staring at the darkened, open doorway the way Dorothy looked at the stage that supposedly held Oz.

"Who the fuck are you?"

That was the voice, not Dorothy.

I replied, "Sir, may we talk to you in private?"

That inquiry was followed by a spate of silence, which was followed by the sounds of footsteps and the movement of a shadow; suddenly a silhouette appeared in the doorway.

I strained to see him, and what I saw through the gloom was this: a wiry man, about five feet ten inches tall, one of those guys who you suspect is probably about ten times stronger than he first appears. His head was shaved, and his eyes were so dark that I think they might be black. He had about a week's worth of salt-and-pepper growth on his face. He wore a pair of tattered old jeans and a T-shirt with the sleeves haphazardly scissored off, exposing arms that seemed disproportionately large for his

frame. He had beads of sweat on his forehead — odd, because it was by no means
hot. He looked nowhere near his age, which
made me wonder about how much we're
spending on prison health care.

"You may tell me who the fuck you are."
He said this in a tone that was in no small
way mocking.

I replied, "I'm Jack Flynn, a reporter with
the *Boston Record*." As I said this, I stared
into his eyes, probing for any sort of flash of
recognition. I didn't see any. "And this is
my colleague, Vinny Mongillo. We were hoping to get a little bit of help from you if you
had a few minutes."

He smiled at this, a diabolical little smile,
exposing graying, yellowish, misshapen
teeth. Perhaps we were saving money on
dental care.

"You want to talk about dead women,
don't you," he said, his tone one of sudden
amusement.

"We do," I answered.

He asked, "Then or now?"

Without missing a beat, I replied, "Both."

"You scum-sucking assholes can never
leave it alone, can you? You can never admit
you were wrong. Never leave a guy to live in
peace."

That's just great, by the way, being called

335

a scum-sucking asshole by a convicted rapist and murderer. Funny part is, if he called us this on one of those cable-television shoutfests, say *The O'Reilly Factor,* the audience would probably cheer, and O'Reilly would tell him he's spot-on in his fight for freedom and truth against the elite liberal news media.

Since this was real life, not cable, I answered, "Not when we're trying to get to the bottom of a serial-murder spree and we think that you might have a little information that would help get us there. We just need a few moments, Mr. Vasco, and you'll never have to deal with us again."

"I don't have to deal with you now."

He was right, actually, but at this point, I already knew he would. Maybe it was the way he held himself as he continued to lean casually in the doorway, his sizable arms folded against his chest. Maybe it was the look on his face, the one that betrayed how much control he felt over the situation, and the smug satisfaction he seemed to get from this impromptu give-and-take. I don't imagine the discourse in the Cedar Junction state prison rec room was particularly highbrow or challenging.

Vinny must have sensed the exact same thing I did, because he finally opened his mouth and said, "You're absolutely right, Paul. But what else do you have going at the moment? Why don't you let a couple of guys troll for a little bit of information, and see if it might be there?"

He looked at Vinny as if he had just noticed him for the first time. He said, "Those murders are ancient history."

Interesting choice of words. Not "I didn't kill anyone." Not "You're wasting your time, I don't know anything." Not "The Boston Strangler is long-ago dead and buried." But rather, those murders we wanted to ask him if he committed are so old that they're not worth anyone's time.

"Not anymore," I replied. "Not if the killer is at it again, or even if someone's just trying to copy him." I paused here, a new thought clanking around in that broad expanse of my head: If this was a copycat, maybe the real Boston Strangler, Paul Vasco, would be irritated enough by it to guide us. So I added, "We need your help."

With this, we stared back and forth for a long moment, stared until his eyes finally fell to the floor before they rose up to Vinny. He shook his head as if he had been egregiously burdened with some enormous misfortune, and said, "Then come in."

He turned and walked into the room.

Vinny and I followed, single file, Vinny first. I shut the door behind us.

We hadn't walked five feet when we both stopped short in a clichéd mix of shock and horror as we stared around the dimly lit room at what was hanging on virtually every free inch of his walls.

"Let me explain," Vasco said calmly, even amusingly.

"That would be good," I replied.

The follow-up comment that I didn't make was that it better be good enough.

25

The room had a bare mattress on a single bed covered by a rumpled blue blanket so old that the fabric was almost transparent, but for the hairs and pieces of food stuck in the little balled-up pieces of wool. There was a straight-back wooden chair, the type of furniture you'd expect an old grammar school teacher would have used in centuries gone by.

The whole room was maybe a hundred square feet, no bigger than a walk-in closet to the privileged denizens of an upscale town like Weston or Wellesley. By the door, there was an old porcelain sink with those old-fashioned turn handles for hot and cold water that you don't see much of anymore. Water dripped from the faucet.

At the far end of the room, though the term *far end* was something of a misnomer in this room, was a single narrow window covered by a torn, drawn shade. Daylight poked through a few of the holes, casting an odd glow across the filthy wood floor.

And then there were the walls — yes, the walls, a different story altogether. The walls were covered with pornographic pictures torn out of magazines. We're not talking soft porn either, like a bare-breasted woman sprawled across a chaise lounge with a caption that identifies her as someone named Angelica who enjoys baking cookies in the nude and loves riding horses. No, we're talking about the hardest of hard-core porn, the raunchiest possible raunch — women with animals, women on women, multiple women with men, multiple men with women with prosthetics, women being beaten, dead women, all of them displayed one picture after the next all over the room. There was even the requisite horse, but believe me when I say the woman wasn't riding him, at least not in the traditional sense.

I was looking at the pictures out of the corner of my eye, shell-shocked. Mongillo saw no need for subtlety. He stared at them for many long moments, his eyes drifting from one to the other, from one wall to the next, until he finally turned to Paul Vasco, who was sitting on the edge of his bed, and said, "That's quite an elaborate collection you have there."

Vasco didn't even hint at a smile. Instead, in a dead-toned voice, he said, "Forty-two years and twenty-one days I was in prison. You have any idea what it's like to spend even one fucking day in there? You have any idea what it's like to lose all your liberty, all your dignity, all your pride? My first week in, I was raped in the communal shower while two prison guards watched and laughed. I was still bleeding a week later, but nobody gave a fuck. I ate crap. I was given thirty minutes to exercise a day. I read not what I wanted, but what they gave me. I had cockroaches running across my face as I tried to sleep. We were treated like animals, so we acted like animals."

He paused, looking down at the floor beyond his feet. Mongillo took a seat on the one chair. I leaned on the sink. Vasco said, "When they cut my hair, they had me in handcuffs and leg chains. They put a muzzle over my face. A fucking muzzle, like I was a fucking wild dog."

He shook his head incredulously. It occurred to me that it would be perfectly reasonable to point out that he was in prison for rape and murder, and what he faced were mere consequences of his incredibly heinous acts. It would be reasonable, but not particularly productive, so I kept my trap shut and continued to listen to him vent. I didn't get this far in this business because of my moralistic tone.

He looked up, nodded his head around the room, and said, "What you see here is me letting one of my pent-up obsessions run its course." Another pause, and then: "Not that I owe the two of you any explanation for anything I do."

"No, you don't," I said. "You don't owe us anything. So we appreciate you taking a moment. You might have some information that we need, and we're hoping you might see your way to helping us out."

Something was bothering me about these pictures, nagging me, something unsettling that was hitting at my subconscious, throwing me a little bit off my game. And no, it wasn't the dead woman being violated by a guy with a whip in his hand, or the two women simultaneously pleasuring the dwarf in the police uniform. It was something else, something I couldn't put my finger — or my eyes — on.

Vasco reached under the blanket, and the thought struck me that he might pull out a gun. Instead, he held a pack of cigarettes in his hand. He put one in his mouth, struck a match, and lit it. The smoke instantly filled the tiny room without so much as a vent to seep into.

He said, his tone softer now, "So you, like everyone else, think I'm the Boston Strangler." I swear he almost let loose with a smile.

Mongillo quickly replied, "Not everyone else. There were some very influential people back then who were very eager to pin everything on Albert DeSalvo, even though a lot of other people didn't think DeSalvo did it."

My gaze floated around the room, across the disgusting pictures, looking for something that was scratching at my psyche.

"Tell me your name." That was Vasco, addressing Mongillo.

"Vinny Mongillo," he replied.

"Well, Mr. Mongillo, and you, Mr. Flynn, do you have any idea what it takes to kill another person? Do you have any idea what it takes to shed centuries of civility, to cast off all of society's norms, to disregard the repercussions, and thus to return to our more primitive roots?

"Do you have any idea what it's like to wrap your hands around a weaker person's neck and squeeze until there's blood coming out of their ears and life oozing from their eyes, until their desperation turns to

343

dormancy and you know that the last lucid thought they had was of you taking away every single pathetic thing they ever had?

"Do you?"

Neither of us responded to his trancelike recitation. The room fell so quiet that I could hear Mongillo's telephone vibrating in his back pocket with yet another call. The white smoke continued to float from the end of Vasco's cigarette toward the low ceiling.

"Well, then, I'll tell you what it's like. It's power unlike anything else you've ever felt in your life. It's ego. It's the ability to end that which wasn't ready to be over. It's total dominance. It's telling the rest of society to fuck off. It's sexual."

He paused for emphasis, then added, "It's addictive." He smiled here, an unashamed, no-holds-barred smile, his gnarly yellow teeth clutching the fading cigarette butt between them. "It takes a strong man to kill. It takes a stronger man to kill just once."

He blew smoke into the air and asked, "How strong do you think I am?"

Mongillo looked at me. I looked at Mongillo. I was pretty happy at this particular moment that I wasn't interviewing this guy in this room alone.

Vasco asked, "Do you think I'm the one who shoved a shard of glass in Dottie

Trevorski's right eye because she blinked once after she was already supposed to be dead?"

I knew from my reading that Dorothy Trevorski of Chelsea was the fifth victim of the Boston Strangler, when he was still in his elderly victim phase. She was a spinster who was found by her sister sprawled across the living room couch with a pair of stockings formed into one of the Strangler's trademark looping bows tied around her neck. She had been raped, possibly after she was dead. I don't recall ever seeing anything about a piece of glass having been shoved in her right eye.

"That's what you think, that I have no control, even while I have all the control?"

This could well have been a confession, though I wasn't sure yet, because as I said, I wasn't sure of the glass in the eye. Maybe it was concocted. If true, maybe it was something he had read in the papers that I had missed. Maybe it was something he learned right from DeSalvo's lips in their many jailhouse conversations. Or maybe he was trying to tell us something that we needed to know.

He said, "Do you think it was me who couldn't help but jack off on the floor beside so many of those corpses? Do you think I

345

had absolutely no control, that I'd risk having someone walk into the room?"

I asked, "Were you the Strangler?"

He laughed. It wasn't a soft laugh, or a subtle laugh, or a fun laugh. No, it was a howl, equal parts indignation and pride. For all his protestations, he liked to be asked, to be considered in the game, capable of such heinous acts, smart enough to have had his secret sprawl across four decades, constantly probed but never penetrated.

He wasn't answering, so I said, "Well, I'll put it to you again: Were you the Boston Strangler?"

He rubbed his hands across the top of his smooth head, looked up at me with those funereal eyes, and said, "What difference does any of this make? What fucking difference? People live, people die, or as Plato said, 'Must not all things be swallowed up in death?' "

"In time, yes. In time," I said. "But must not nature be allowed to work its course?"

"Death is better, a milder fate than tyranny," Vasco replied. "That's Aeschylus, the father of Greek tragedy."

"But isn't it a tyrant who takes a person's life?"

Look, I don't know where I was getting this stuff from, and I certainly don't know how Paul Vasco was pulling these quotes from Greek writers and philosophers out of thin air — or maybe it was his ass he was pulling them from. Either that or he really was that smart, or at least well read.

The bottom line — as I looked at him, squirrel-faced, his black eyes darting about the room as he puffed on his stupid cigarette — was I wanted to grab his neck and squeeze it to show him what it felt like to be on the other side of the situation. I wanted to shake him, to beat a confession out of him that he had already seemed to start, and to know there wouldn't be any more young women's driver's licenses arriving in my mail. Normally I like being at the center of a story, breaking news, but this one, no, and even less so with every passing moment.

I asked, "Mr. Vasco, have you been writing me notes? Have you been sending me the driver's licenses of your victims?"

He looked at me with that something that leaned toward a smirk, a matter-of-fact, shoulder shrug of a look that pretty much said the victims were worthless and the efforts to solve their murders would be entirely fruitless.

He stared into my eyes and said, "You fancy yourself a writer, Mr. Flynn. You ever read the work of Robert Heinlein, the greatest science fiction author who ever lived?"

I couldn't say I had, so I didn't.

Vasco held my gaze and said, "Mr. Heinlein once famously said, and I think this is an exact quote, but please don't think less of me if I'm wrong, 'Writing is not necessarily something to be ashamed of, but do it in private and wash your hands afterwards.' "

He paused and added, confidingly now, "I've been writing for a long time. I follow Mr. Heinlein's sage counsel. I do it in private."

Mongillo, growing impatient with the upscale discourse, said angrily, "Mr. Vasco, let's cut through the crap. Did you kill women then? Are you killing women now?"

He didn't answer. Instead, he flicked his cigarette butt the few feet across the room, toward a squat metal pail filled with other butts and an old Jim Beam bottle. Problem was, he missed, and the cigarette landed on the decrepit wood floor, the plume of smoke rising up the wall toward the low ceiling. I followed the smoke for reasons I can't explain, followed the little cloud until it rose past my waist, then my head, and that's when I realized what it was that I saw.

Set amid the glossy, raunchy pornography

was something a world apart: three photographs, one each of Jill Dawson, Lauren Hutchens, and Kimberly May. The pictures were carefully cut out of the *Record,* then meticulously adhered to identical cardboard mats, hung side by side. Above them was a much larger photograph of two bare-chested blondes, a garden hose, and — well, never mind what was above them. But suffice it to say that it was enough to get my blood boiling, and I don't mean that in any sexual sort of way.

Vasco was quoting Cicero while trying to explain to Vinny that he was missing the point, but I couldn't concentrate on what he was saying, I was so riveted by these photographs. Actually, it wasn't so much the photographs but their juxtaposition with the overwhelming filth in this room. All over the walls were pictures of abnormally buxom women performing unmentionable acts. In real life, I imagine these photographs were born of desperation, filled with women willing to do just about anything to make a buck. They were probably abused as girls, never infused with a sense of right and wrong, normal and abnormal, respect and disrespect. Here they were, doing anything that the photographer wanted done for as much money as they could possibly get.

And in their midst were three remarkably different women — women, I would dare guess, of some ambition, women with culture, women with style and urbanity, women of emotional means. They didn't belong. They didn't fit. And yet, in Paul Vasco's eyes, they somehow did, because here they were on this wall of shame, mixed in with the rest of the raunch.

I looked at him, still prattling on to Vinny, now about the quote-unquote right questions he should be asking as a reporter, and I wanted to give him a roundhouse punch to his pointed nose. I wanted to see blood gushing down his smug face. I wanted to see his eyes blacken. I wanted to watch as he writhed in pain like all those women I was becoming convinced he had killed.

Instead, I intentionally kept my eyes from the photos of the three dead women, hard as I was finding that to be. I walked over and stamped on the cigarette butt before the whole decrepit place burned down. Still standing, towering over Vasco as he sat on the bed, I said sharply, "Game's up, Paul. You killed these women. You killed them then, you killed them now. Tell us why. Why'd you start all over again after all those years?"

He whirled from Mongillo to me, craning

his neck to look up, and for half a fraction of a fleeting second, I thought I saw fear in his eyes, the kind of fear that liars betray when their lies are up, or that adulterers show when their mates walk in on them in the lurid act. But as fast as that look flashed across his face, it fled, and I was left with him inexplicably smiling at me, his teeth protruding like those of a hamster.

"The truth is rarely pure and never simple," he said. He paused for effect, then added, "Oscar Wilde."

I said, "I'm going to nail you so cold on these killings that the jury's going to cheer when they send you back to Walpole." I paused for effect, then added, "Jack Flynn."

Then I slammed the side of my fist against the wall, just below the pictures of Jill Dawson, Lauren Hutchens, and Kimberly May, and I said, "Did you kill these women?"

Mongillo walked over and got a closer look at what I was talking about.

"Did you kill these women?" My voice was so taut that the words shot out of my mouth like arrows flung from a bow.

No response, though he flashed a smile — *this evil fucking smile,* as Bob Walters had described it to me before he died.

"Let's go." That was Mongillo, grabbing me by the shoulder and prodding me toward the door.

I said, "Why have you put me in the middle of a story that I can't do anything to change? Why are you doing this?"

He stood, finally, and asked, "Would you rather not be part of the story?"

He had me. He had me cold. He was as smart as he seemed.

Vinny continued to pull me away, and I began to follow his lead. Before I got to the door, though, I turned around and seethed, "I swear to God, Vasco, when I prove you killed these women, and I *will* prove you killed these women, I'm going to fucking kill you myself, and it's going to be slow, and it's going to hurt like fucking hell."

He said, "All truths are easier to understand once they are discovered. The point is to discover them. Galileo."

I was about to lunge. I kept thinking of the driver's licenses arriving in the mail, the video of the death scene, the guy who needlessly died in the Public Garden, Bob Walters falling down his own stairs seeking something that I didn't know. Every thought was a jolt, a call to physical action like I've never felt before, because of a guy who was screwing with the city and simultaneously messing with my mind. But before I could do anything, before I could say anything,

Mongillo flipped open the door to that dismal little room and pulled me into the hallway.

The two of us walked down the stairs in silence and out into the midday sun.

Mongillo grabbed the keys when I pulled them out and said, "I'm driving. You're out of control." I didn't argue. Inside the car, he said, "I'm trying to be like the reporters in *All the President's Men*. My partner here thinks he's the star of *Rocky*."

He started the car and pulled out. I could feel the tension seeping out of my pores, not all of it, but enough for me to take a deep breath and say, "Sorry about that. I don't know what just happened. This thing's getting to me."

"Don't worry about it," he said, in a tone far more distant and aloof than his norm, staring straight ahead at the road. Then he added, "It's getting to me, too. We're going to have to do something about it."

I had no idea what he was talking about, but wasn't of the mind to ask.

We both sat in silence for a while. We were crossing the bridge back into Boston when he said, "Until then, rather than try to kick the shit out of everyone, I think I've got another plan."

26

There were definitely days in my life that had gone better. Off the top of my head, I can't think of many, outside of the obvious, that had gone any worse.

It had started out with another communication from the Phantom Fiend, in this case, an order to publish a letter to the people of Boston on the front page of the *Record.* That was quickly followed by a decision by the *Record* publisher not to publish the letter because said publisher, hitherto a respected newswoman, didn't want to tick off the acting mayor and the commissioner of police. This failure would mean that the Phantom would ratchet up his killing spree because I couldn't convince my paper to take action. On top of this, I lose my temper with the guy who probably was and probably still is the Boston Strangler or Phantom Fiend or whatever he should be called.

And all this followed the death of Bob

Walters — a death that occurred before he could get me the information he said he had. And that, of course, followed the death of Joshua Carpenter, the innocent guy in the Public Garden. And of course, there were the stranglings of three young women in various parts of town.

I bring this up to explain why I was in the gymnasium of the University Club at four in the afternoon on what could have and should have been a critical day of reporting and writing at the *Boston Record*. Mongillo, in his inimitable way, told me, and I quote, "Go get some sleep, some sex, or some exercise, before you ruin this entire story."

The first presented option, I was too antsy for. The second, I had few possibilities and even less desire. The third, well, I could use a tour through the gym, so that's where I went.

The place was barren, given the hour. The lunch crowd was long gone, and the evening crowd wouldn't arrive for another hour, so I sat on an exercise ball and knocked out seventy-five crunches, feeling my abdominal muscles tighten more with each successive one. I worked the lat machine and the bench press, and did some flies. I skipped a little rope. I did more abdominals. I struggled through the shoulder press.

The work felt good. The sweat that opened up on my forehead and flowed down my face felt even better. The stereo system was turned down, and the only sounds in the gym were the plates of weight clinking against one another and my own labored breathing, all of which gave me a little time to think.

I thought of the call I had yet to return to Maggie Kane. I decided we weren't engaged anymore; that designation expired one way or another with the passage of a wedding day.

I thought of the call I had just received from Peter Martin, telling me that the publisher wasn't yet ready to run the Phantom's letter, and maybe never would be. He basically told me to be on high alert the next morning, in expectation that we or someone else would face the Phantom's wrath.

I tell you, newspapers will break your heart just about every time.

I did one last set of leg lifts, then sprawled across a hard blue mat and felt the energy flow from my torso, down my limbs, and right out of my fingers and toes. After a few minutes of nothingness, I collected myself, wandered downstairs into the locker room, stripped down, and headed for the steam room.

The place was still empty, which was nice, because I could sprawl across the tile bench without the fear that one of the older members would toddle into the room, not see me through the steam, and park his flabby ass somewhere on top of me. Granted, it's not a normal fear, but it's there nonetheless.

With the whoosh of steam blowing into the room, I thought again of Maggie Kane, and one more time thought it a shame that something that starts so good inevitably has to end so bad. Or maybe this wasn't really that bad. Maybe we rushed toward matrimony because of how it all looked on paper, when in real life we didn't really know. Maybe the fact that both parties put a halt to it in the final hours made it obvious that it wasn't meant to be — no marriage, no harm, no foul.

But here she was on the phone talking about being lonely and wanting to get together, and the only emotion that kept flowing over me was complete and total detachment, which may not be an emotion at all. If ever I should have missed Maggie Kane, it should have been now, when my professional world seemed to be falling in on me. And yet I barely felt a thing.

Elizabeth Riggs.

The steam kept blowing all around me, the temperature rising, and there she was, in my head, mostly because she never actually left it. She was beautiful that night in the waiting lounge of San Francisco International Airport — composed, elegant, sexy, relaxed — just as she was beautiful in Logan International Airport that day she left for California and I did nothing to stop her. She wanted me to yell out, to grab her shoulder, to block the door, to do something, anything, and instead I simply watched her leave, because I figured that's what people do in life — they leave. And nobody, not even Maggie Kane, has yet to prove me wrong.

The power of hindsight is sometimes a heady thing. It's showed me these last couple of years that Elizabeth didn't so much leave of her own volition as she was guided to the door by yours truly and encouraged in every implicit way to go. Maybe I never outright told her to get out, but my aloofness, born of my own past, manifested in my hesitance to allow anyone else to get too close, and proved impossible to take. God knows, Elizabeth Riggs tried. She really did.

Outside the glass door, one of the locker-room attendants, either Mike or Angel, flung open a nearby supply closet, the sound jarring me out of my heat-and-exhaustion-induced reverie. I could hear him fiddling with some equipment. He knocked absently against the door, and he was off.

Inside, the steam started surging full bore again out of a pipe on the floor, and the room was approaching the point of being unbearable, which was just the way I liked my steam rooms, if not my women. The thermometer on the wall read 117 degrees, and I told myself I'd gut it out until this round of steam stopped and then I'd go take a cool shower.

Another minute passed, and the steam was still flowing with abandon. The thermometer read 119 degrees. I lifted myself up from a lying position and began counting to twenty, waiting for the steam to shut off. It didn't.

So I started thinking like Ernest Hemingway might write, though I can't explain why. The room was hot. The man was sweaty. He wanted a cool shower. He would get a cold glass of beer. The beef he'd have for dinner would be charred and juicy.

Another minute later, it was showing no signs of abating — the steam, not the Hemingway impersonation. The temperature had risen to a heady 121 degrees, and the room had grown so thick I was about to lose sight of the thermometer. I wasn't a science or home economics major, but at 121 degrees, can't you boil sheep's milk?

So I gave up. In fact, I got up, staggered toward the door, opened it, and proceeded to take the most delightfully reinvigorating cool shower that anyone could ever possibly imagine, the memory of which would hang with me for a lifetime.

That was the plan anyway, but I ran into a problem, that problem being the door. It didn't budge. So I pushed against it again. Again, it didn't move. I shoved my shoulder into it. Still nothing.

Meantime, the steam was roaring out of the small pipe as hard as ever, and that pipe happened to be near the door, which meant that my feet were about to be scalded off.

I stepped back and gave myself a little bit of a running start, figuring that the door must have swelled in the heat and was stuck on the frame. I took two long, fast steps and hit it hard with the sole of my foot. I might as well have been pushing against the side of a Greyhound bus, though I'm not sure why I'd ever do such a thing. The door wasn't going anywhere, and its sheer physical obstinateness knocked me to the hard, hot floor.

I scrambled up. Steam everywhere. I took a different approach now, trying to jigger the door around, maybe loosen it from whatever had it stuck. But again, it wouldn't move.

The gushing sound was all-consuming. The heat was raging. The thought struck me that I could die in the steam room of my private club, and I wondered how that would look in my obituary. How long before my fellow club members began using the room again? A day? Probably more like an hour. The coroner wouldn't even be halfway down the street. How odd it would be to have my boiling body shoved in the back of a refrigerated van.

I yelled. I had no choice. "Help!" I called out. Granted, it wasn't particularly original, but my brains were melting down into my neck.

Nothing but the gush of steam in response. I hollered, "Please open the steam room door! Help! The door is stuck. Help!"

I fully understood that one of my fellow members was going to casually happen along, open the door, and subject me to club-wide ridicule for the next five years. I was willing to accept that fate at this point.

But again, nothing. I slammed my fist against the door and tried to shake it open, to no avail. Any moment now, the after-work crowd should be arriving. They'd get dressed at their lockers and maybe hear my cries for help. Any moment now, Mike or Angel, the attendants, should come back to the supply closet and see that I was stuck. Problem was, any moment now I could be dead of heat stroke, if you can die of such a thing, though I wasn't sure. It certainly felt like it.

I yelled again, then retreated from the scorching pipe to the bench on the other side of the small room. It felt as if half my body had already sweated out of my pores and dripped down to the floor. It felt as if I'd never be cool again.

"Help!"

Nothing.

My mind began to drift in a way that probably wasn't too good. I was pushing a blond-haired, pigtailed six-year-old girl who was sitting on a swing set wearing a little denim skirt and a Red Sox T-shirt with Bill Mueller's last name spelled out across the back. I mean, no one wears a Billy Mueller T-shirt, but this girl always needed to be different, so she did.

She was laughing, calling me dad, telling

me to push her higher into the clear blue horizon of a gorgeous weekend afternoon. We were at a neighborhood park. My Audi was within eyeshot, which was interesting, because I've never driven an Audi. We were meeting my wife, the girl's mother, for dinner at a local clam shack in a little while, but we stopped at the field to play along the way. And the girl kept laughing, and I felt this emotion in my chest, tranquility, or maybe it was security, or some combination of the above. Regardless, it was a feeling I hadn't had in years.

The girl got off the swing set, gripped my hand, and out of nowhere asked, "Daddy, why do people have to die?"

"It's a natural part of life," I replied. "It's what happens after you've done everything you wanted to do in life."

She looked up at me as she walked along, her big blue eyes boring into mine, and she asked, "But what happens if you didn't get the chance to do everything you wanted to do?"

I thought about that for a moment as we arrived at my car and I buckled her into the backseat with a kiss on her temple. I said, "It's why you should live your life as hard and as well as you can, every single day. Everybody has to die sometime. It's completely natural. But you want to make sure you did everything you wanted to do first."

At that moment, I felt someone's hand on the back of my neck. A voice called out, "It's Jack Flynn. He's unconscious. Hold the door. We've got to get him out of here."

I was boiling hot and limp as a leaf of lettuce at a Texas barbecue. I mumbled something that no one heard. I suddenly felt myself being moved in someone's arms, carried, then another voice called out, "I'm a doctor. Get him under some cool water."

And then I felt the chilling spray of a shower. As I gained my bearings, I saw three guys looming over me, and one guy in a suit kneeling down in the shower beside me, taking my pulse, getting soaked in the process.

"I'm Bill Dennis. I'm an MD," he said. "You're going to be fine. You just had a little scare in there."

I half recognized him around the gym as another member, but never knew him well enough to say anything beyond a hello. I mumbled, "I thought you were a plumber."

"That's my wealthier brother, Bob," he said.

I was regaining more and more of my faculties, enough, anyway, to realize that the tranquil feeling in my chest was a figment of my imagination, or the stuff of a very good dream.

Dr. Dennis asked, "Did you black out in there?"

I said, "The door was stuck."

Another member, standing off to the side in a sweat suit, said, "I found a mop wedged against the door, so it couldn't be opened from inside. When I looked in, I found you there."

I said, "I think Mike or Angel might have dropped it there by mistake."

Mike, who was in the background, said, "I've been on break for the last half hour. Angel's not in yet. None of us put that mop there."

I asked, "Why didn't the steam valve shut off?" The thing is supposed to go off automatically when the temperature in the room goes above 116 degrees.

Mike walked over to the wall where the On/Off button is for the bath. He called out, "This is weird. It looks like there's a glob of glue or something holding the button in."

I stood up and leaned against the tile wall. I knew then precisely what had happened, but it wouldn't do any good for anyone else to know — not that they'd believe it, anyway. Sure, Jack, someone tried roasting you to death, like you're a fucking hot dog, a Fenway frank. Good one.

Dennis said, "Listen, you'll be back to normal by morning. Take some aspirin. Prepare yourself for a headache. Get to bed early. And most important, drink lots of fluids tonight to rehydrate."

"Does beer count?"

"Ah, no."

Dennis walked away, as did everyone else, leaving me in the privacy of a cooling shower.

"Yes, little girl," I whispered, mostly to myself, "it's pretty bad when you die before you're ready to go."

I had just gotten my clothes on and downed a second two-liter bottle of water when a faint buzzing sound made its way up the back staircase and into the locker room. When I first heard it, I didn't think I heard anything at all; I told myself it was in my head. But then I saw Mike, the attendant, grab for the phone, and I yelled over to him, "What's that?"

"Sounds like someone went out the emergency exit in the back," he said.

I bolted. I descended the back staircase three at a time, my hand on the railing to balance me. I shot across the short first-floor landing and crashed against the bar that would open the fire exit, finding myself in the small rear parking lot of the club.

A Latino kitchen worker sat on a milk crate with his back against the brick building. "Did someone just come out of here?" I asked.

He nodded.

"Which way?" I said, trying to control my excitement.

He pointed out across Clarendon Street, heading toward the South End. I took off in a sprint. It was the early side of rush hour, and as such, the sidewalks were growing crowded with pedestrians on their way out of work, a fact that might have impeded my chase.

I say might have, because it didn't. The workers were mostly attired in suits and ties, walking purposefully, but by no means urgently. Across the street, I spied a guy in a windbreaker running wildly on the sidewalk as he looked back over his shoulder. So I stormed across the street in pursuit. I mean, I've heard of chasing down a story, but this was taking it to ridiculous extremes. He was about forty paces ahead of me, the two of us weaving in and out of other pedestrians as we headed toward Columbus Avenue, when it happened: a cramp in my thigh so immense and intense that I immediately fell to the ground in restrained agony. Truth be told, I thought my leg would need to be amputated. What I really needed was more fluids.

From my vantage on the sidewalk, I saw my would-be killer slow down to a fast jog as he approached the next intersection. I saw a blue van pull to the curb, and the side doors seemed to pop open at just the right time. I saw my assailant jump inside the van. I saw said van melt away into the rest of this big city.

I was in desperate need of a break on this story. What I felt like I had was a broken leg.

27

A guy walks into a bar with a weight on his shoulders.

All right, the guy was me. The bar was the always luxurious Max Stein's in the wealthy suburban town of Lexington. The weight was of the whole world — or at least it felt like it at the moment.

Max Stein's, though, represented something of a respite, a place to gather with legendary *Record* reporter Vinny Mongillo during what felt like an uneasy calm before a particularly nasty storm. Or maybe it was the eye of the hurricane. I'm trying to think of other suitable weather-related clichés, but none come immediately to mind, except maybe that it was raining trouble, so with sincere apologies, we'll leave it there.

As I walked through the double doors, the appropriately named Richard Steer, the ever hospitable general manager who I'd known since what felt like the beginning of time, gave me a long, two-fisted handshake. "I'm betting this one's driving you crazy," he said. I only needed to nod for him to know that he was as on-point as usual.

Vinny was already at the bar, two glasses of red wine in front of him and one in his hand, which he happened to be holding nearly sideways, peering through the glass, saying to my favorite bartender, Nam, "It's got terrific legs."

Who knew wine had legs? Vinny and Nam, that's who. And probably all the good waiters who were walking through the room carrying groaning plates of dry-aged sirloins and cottage fries and sautéed spinach. I was amazed that Vinny could keep his attention away from it, but he did.

"Hey, Mike Tyson," he said as I sidled up to the bar. Nam gave me his characteristically cheery hello and my characteristic Sam Adams, icy cold from the back of the chest.

I poured my beer slowly into a glass and said, "Great legs." But I was looking at a woman down at the far end of the bar.

Well, all right, that really didn't happen, that last part, but Mickey Spillane would have been proud if it did.

"You doing any better?" Mongillo asked me, meeting me square in the eye.

"I was never doing bad," I replied, not

370

meaning to sound quite as clipped as I probably had. "I just don't like being played by a murderer, that's all."

Vinny looked at me funny, eyeing my face and then my hands, almost analyzing me. He said, "Wait a minute. You look funny. Like a prune."

"Long story," I said. "One that I'd just as soon forget about."

Vinny did. He took a long sip of wine, and I gulped my Sam. Nam came back over and asked Vinny about the "Russian Valley cab."

"There's a taxi here already?" I asked. They ignored me.

"Big nose, very broad, and a little bit acidic," Mongillo said to Nam.

"You just described my aunt Toni," I said.

He ignored me again. So did Nam, who was pouring yet another glass of wine. He handed it to Mongillo with a look of concern and said, "Tell me if you think this is too buttery."

Enough already, so I used the one trump card I hoped I still had with Mongillo and said, "You want to eat?"

He looked at me almost surprised, as if he had forgotten that's why we were there, though I'm reasonably sure he hadn't, and said, "Great idea."

My first one in a long while, actually.

371

Nam sent a waiter with a tray to ferry Mongillo's wines to the table, though I'm not sure wine can be made plural like that. I carried my own beer and drank it along the way.

Once we were settled into a booth, Mongillo met my gaze and simply said, "Paul Vasco was the Boston Strangler."

I wasn't sure whether to say "No shit," or ask "How do you know?" So instead I told him, "Go on."

"Because Dorothy Trevorski really did have a shard of glass shoved into her eye," he said, his gaze staying on mine. "It was never reported by any newspaper at the time. It was never revealed by the cops. It was one of those bits of info they held back so they'd know whether they had a professional confessor on their hands or the real thing."

I said, "Well, if that's the case, then wouldn't they have known that DeSalvo wasn't the real thing?"

"Maybe," Mongillo said. "Or maybe Vasco told DeSalvo about this detail in one of their many prison walks, and he parroted it to the interrogators."

I said, "Or maybe DeSalvo told Vasco."

Mongillo thought about that for a long moment. Either that or he was just looking for an excuse to take a drink of wine from the glass he had been swirling.

"I suppose," he finally said. "But there's something else, too. Seven of the murder scenes had sperm on the floor several feet from the bodies. Vasco just about admitted pleasuring himself over the corpses. I don't know if that's something two guys would have talked about in prison, you know?"

I thought about that myself, and used my thinking time to drain my beer. Before I even put it down, a waiter named Jack, God bless him, appeared with another.

We ordered. I got grilled swordfish with cottage fries. Mongillo basically got the right side of the menu — or at least it sounded that way. Then he asked for the wine list back. I could all but hear Peter Martin's lines when he looked over the expense account: "Is there a deposit on this dinner that we're going to get back?"

Once the waiter retreated to the kitchen to inform the chef that there appeared to be a patron at Table 23 in pursuit of the world's beef-eating record, Mongillo leaned toward me and said, "The most important thing that happened during that session with Vasco, I don't think you even saw."

"The fact that you picked up his cigarette butt, which contains his DNA?"

He furrowed his brow and squinted at me. "You saw that?"

"I think Ray Charles would have seen that." I paused and added, "I was going to do it myself, but you beat me to the punch. Good move."

Vinny asked, "Do you think Vasco saw it?"

I shook my head. "I don't know what that guy sees, besides torture and necrophilia."

We both fell quiet for a moment, maybe thinking of the women he tortured and the corpses he violated. Or perhaps Vinny was merely regarding his wine. Either way, I said, "You have someone in the BPD crime lab who will run it?"

He nodded his head knowingly. Of course he did.

I said, "It's too bad we can't get some of DeSalvo's DNA. Then we'd have all bases covered — the ability to prove and disprove."

Mongillo shot me an odd look and said, "We may get lucky on that count. Stay tuned, and don't ask."

So I didn't, which runs entirely antithetical to every cell of my being, but it was that look on his face that gave me pause.

In the gulf of silence, a veritable team of waiters arrived at our table en masse — one of them carrying the seafood platter Vinny had ordered to kick things off, another a plate of fried calamari, and still another a Caesar salad and the wine list. Fortunately, the table was sturdy enough to withstand all the added weight on Vinny's side.

Vinny asked Jack (the waiter, not the handsome but momentarily frustrated scribe), "Do you have an unoaked Chardonnay muscular enough to withstand shellfish?"

Somehow, Jack the waiter understood. As Mongillo dressed an oyster, I said, "Can I ask you something?"

He nodded.

"How is it that you know so much about DeSalvo, Vasco, and the Boston stranglings? You weren't even old enough to talk then."

A pretty good thought, by the way: Mongillo unable to speak.

He sucked down the oyster. Jack the waiter arrived with the wine and the two of them went into their whole overdone uncorking and tasting routine. Finally, that over, Mongillo said to me, "When I was eight, nine, ten, even older, all the kids in the neighborhood, my own brothers, used to go down to the park at the end of the street and play baseball. They'd play for hours, until it got so dark that you couldn't see the ball, and then they'd come to our house or one of the others and eat Popsicles and talk about how they just played."

He sipped his wine appreciatively.

"I'd go down to the park and they'd make fun of me. 'Fat Vinny.' 'Tubby.' 'Lard ass.' And a whole lot worse. They wouldn't let me play. So after a while, why bother trying. The kids were all out playing baseball or kick the can or whatever else, I was inside reading everything I could get my hands on about old Boston crimes. Ask me anything about the Brinks robbery or Sacco and Vanzetti. The Boston Strangler, it's like I needed to know as much as I could about that one."

By now, Mongillo's plates had been cleared without him ever so much as offering me a leaf of romaine lettuce. The entrées arrived and it looked like he had ordered his food by the pound.

I told him about the steam-room incident of a couple of hours before. He immediately snapped up his cell phone and relayed the information to Edgar Sullivan.

When he hung up he said, "You should drink a lot more beer to rehydrate."

It was touching, this concern, but I said, "It doesn't work that way." He didn't seem to hear.

Idle conversation now. I told him about Maggie Kane and me not calling her back.

"That thing was never meant to be," he said.

I told him about running into Elizabeth Riggs in the San Francisco Airport.

"Now, there's a woman who loved you more than anyone you'll ever meet."

I paused mid-chew and stared at him. He looked at me defensively, shrugged, and said, "What do you want me to say? She did."

I asked, "How do you know that?"

"Fair Hair, how do I know anything? Intuition. My own personal radar. She didn't make it too tough, either, the way she looked at you, the way she talked to you, about you. A good woman. And good-looking, to say the least. That weird to see her?"

Suddenly, my swordfish didn't have a whole lot of taste and the cottage fries seemed limp, though maybe that was just me.

I mumbled, "Yeah, it was pretty strange."

Vinny chewed on his steak, took a sip from a glass of ruby-red wine that Jack had brought over, and said, "Yeah, I bet it was bizarre, huh? She still look great? Those big eyes? That flat stomach? God, that hair that frames both sides of her face?"

"All right, never mind. Forget I brought

her up." I pushed my dinner plate a couple of inches away from me, almost reflexively.

Mongillo said, "Oh-oh. Someone's got a little case of the regrets. Or maybe they've come down with love sickness."

I wanted to tell him she was pregnant. I wanted to tell someone, anyone. But then I didn't want to have the inane conversation that would inevitably follow, so I said sharply, "Drop it, Vin, okay? Not the time."

For a moment, he actually looked hurt. That moment passed quickly when Jack returned with dessert menus. He said, offhandedly, "Well, go get her all over again, and this time don't be such a fuckup."

Ah, if life really was that easy: me being able to get her all over again, me not being such a fuckup.

28

I left Mongillo and Nam at the bar mulling various dessert wines — Moscatos and Brachettos and other types I pretended to know even though I didn't have a clue. And I headed out the door in hopes of finally putting this long, absurd, and occasionally dangerous day behind me.

My car was already parked right out front, so I fidgeted in my pocket for a ten-dollar bill and asked the valet for the keys.

"I don't have them," the kid said.

Great.

"Who does?" I mean, it's a perfectly legitimate question to ask a professional valet about the keys to my own car.

"He does," he said, and as he said it, he pointed to someone or something behind me. I turned suspiciously around and found myself face-to-face with none other than Edgar Sullivan.

"Hello, Edgar," I said. "You're my designated driver?"

"I'm your guardian angel," he replied.

He was sitting on a bench tucked amid some shrubbery and surrounded by two ornate buckets that were nothing more than glorified ashtrays. Massachusetts forbids smoking in all public places, and this bench was obviously put here as a little haven for the nicotine addicted. It's one bad habit I never took up, though perhaps I still had time.

Edgar stood up slowly, the way old men always seem to do, his knee audibly cracking as he breathed a tiny sigh. He smoothed out his pants and walked stiffly toward me, thrusting out his right hand and saying, "I heard you almost melted to death today. I'm you, I'd be really steamed."

"Didn't I see you on Comedy Central last week?"

He smiled, not quite embarrassedly, but almost. "You sound like my second wife," he said.

"Was that the really young one?" I asked.

"No, she was twenty-eight," he replied.

I left the obvious question unstated.

A few stragglers were leaving the restaurant and handing their stubs to the valets. Others waited patiently and impatiently in the cool night air for their various BMWs,

Audis, and Mercedes to be wheeled around. Edgar jingled my keys and said, "Come on, I'll get you home safely."

Truer words had never been spoken, but in retrospect, the cost was almost too much to bear.

We were floating down the wonderful riverside highway known as Storrow Drive, talking about nothing and everything at the same time. Ends up, I was learning, the young wife, the third one, was twenty-three years old. The first one was thirty. The fourth was an age-appropriate fifty-four.

"The next meaningful relationship I have is going to be completely platonic — with a dog," Edgar said. He shook his head and added, "Sounds good when I say it, but don't bet on it. I can't help myself. I love wedding days. The celebrations, the well-wishers, the high expectations. It's the marriages that don't turn out so well."

The Charles River was on our left, with Cambridge beyond it. The Back Bay of Boston — a neighborhood, not a body of water — was on our right. We were rolling toward the waterfront when I checked the clock on the car and said to Edgar, "Do you mind pulling off on Beacon Hill for a minute? I want to grab tomorrow's paper."

And he did. I wanted to see what the Phantom Fiend would see when he opened the *Boston Record* in a few hours — or more to the point, what he wouldn't see, which was his miniature manifesto, if a manifesto can be done in miniature, which I don't think it can. I wanted to know what he'd be reading instead of his own words, to get some empathic sense of what might set him off, and how.

I requested Beacon Hill because for whatever reason, the *Record* delivers the third batch of papers fresh off the press to a twenty-four-hour drugstore on the back slope of Beacon Hill. The first batch, by the way, goes directly into the newsroom, and keeping with tradition, the second batch always gets hand-delivered to the newsroom of the *Boston Traveler,* our main competition. They, in turn, send a stack from their early run over to us.

Edgar pulled off onto Cambridge Street, which isn't in Cambridge, but go figure. I don't know if Cambridge has a Boston Street, but I kind of doubt it. He glided up in front of the all-night CVS, stuck the car in a no-parking zone, and turned off the ignition.

"I'm going to run in," I said.

He opened the driver's door and said,

"Not without me you're not."

The navy blue *Record* delivery truck was just pulling away as we stepped through the front door of the CVS. I can't vow that this was the most upbeat place in the world at five after midnight. An Arab-looking clerk stood behind the counter reading that month's *Cosmopolitan* — the one with the "Seven Sexual Secrets That Men Want to Tell" on the cover. And yes, he was a man, undoubtedly with secrets of his own. There was an elderly woman with a kerchief in her hair checking the use-by dates on every six-pack of Pepsi at a display near the front of the store. Otherwise, the place looked barren.

The *Record*s were still in a stack near the door, bound by plastic wire. As I leaned down and pulled the plastic apart, Edgar said, "You know what I want? A Hershey's bar with almonds."

I replied, "You know what I want? I want to catch the Boston Strangler, I want to save any number of women from their miserable deaths, and then I want to win the Pulitzer Prize."

Actually, that's not what I said. What I said was, "Shit, you know what else I need? Some aspirin."

A more inane conversation had never

taken place among two people not married to each other.

Edgar lumbered up to the candy counter in search of his chosen bar. I grabbed a paper and scanned the front page on the very off chance that Justine Steele had changed her mind or that Peter Martin had grown a set of brass balls. Neither appeared to have happened. So I wandered the aisle where the sign said FIRST AID AND PAIN-KILLERS for something to quell the headache that their inaction, among other things, had caused.

That's where I was when the killer came into the store, in Aisle 2b, looking for a god-damned bottle of extra-strength Excedrin.

I didn't hear the door open. I didn't see what the security camera would later show, which is that once inside the store, he pulled a ski mask over his head. I didn't see him pull the gun out from the shin-length black trench coat he was wearing. I didn't see it because I was shopping for a bottle of Ex-cedrin. If so much of being a great reporter is just making sure you're at the right place at the right time, then I failed miserably here. Or maybe I didn't, because I'm at least alive to tell about it; it's all a matter of perspective.

The first inkling of trouble I got was the

loud voice calling out, "Don't do nothin' stupid."

I looked up from the aforementioned Aisle 2b and saw the similarly aforementioned man in the black trench coat waving what looked like a semiautomatic pistol. He was talking to the counter clerk. Edgar was standing near a magazine rack off to the side, watching the situation unfold and remaining very calm.

If it was a robbery, I was perfectly willing to let it happen, and I suspect Edgar Sullivan was as well. Let the guy get his $280 or whatever from the till, make off into the night, and buy another week's worth of heroin to make his miserable life remotely bearable.

But oddly enough, rather than tell the clerk to give him all his cash, he scanned the store, his gaze seeming to pass over Edgar and the older woman in the kerchief, and settling on me, still standing, appropriately enough, in the painkiller section.

"Everyone up here," he barked. "I need people up here — now."

His voice was shallower than a robber's should probably be, and his build was slighter than he probably would have preferred — though his gun was undoubtedly every bit as powerful as the next one.

I didn't move, or at least not quickly enough. He hollered, "Get up here, now."

I began moving slowly up the aisle toward the front of the store, sans the Excedrin I came in for. I figured my headache was the least of my problems right now.

As I walked up, I noticed Edgar drifting farther off to the side, away from the cash registers. I saw out of the corner of my eyes the older woman slipping toward the door, and then out. The assailant heard the door open, whirled around, saw her leave, and did nothing but say "Shit" just barely loud enough for anyone to hear.

"Faster!"

I was staring into the distant barrel of the pistol. I don't think the president of Smith & Wesson had seen as many guns as I had in the last few days. I picked up the pace a bit, but I wasn't exactly setting a land-speed record. Time, I figured, bought opportunity. I just wasn't clear what that opportunity was yet, though I had reasonable hopes that Edgar Sullivan might figure it out.

I'd be remiss in not noting that as I walked to the front, my mind flashed over the Starbucks massacre of 1997 in Washington, D.C. — three employees executed in an apparent robbery — and the Blackfriars Pub massacre of 1978 in Boston — five people executed for unknown reasons. Is this what we were destined for tonight?

I kept walking, Edgar kept drifting farther away, the clerk kept standing near the register, being no apparent help whatsoever. When I got to the front, maybe ten feet from the masked assailant, he said, "Get on the floor, facedown."

This didn't bode well. I thought about charging him, ramming his midsection, maybe giving him a kung-fu kick to the family jewels. I thought about grabbing one of the oversize bottles of Tide on a shelf within arm's length and flinging it at his face. Instead, very slowly, still buying time, I descended to my knees, and even more slowly spread out on the grime of the cheap commercial carpet at the front of the Beacon Hill CVS.

I thought it extremely curious that of the four people in the store at the time of his arrival, I was the one to be singled out. But I didn't think I was in much of a position — meaning facedown on the floor with a gun pointed at the back of my head by a masked assailant — to question why.

I saw him take a few steps toward me, saw his black trench coat swish against his jeans, until I could smell the leather of his dirty tennis sneakers. I heard his gun cock. And I heard a voice — Edgar Sullivan's voice — shout out, "Drop it. Police officer. I'm armed and I'll shoot."

I don't know if you can feel a gun's aim leave you, but I'm pretty sure I did. I shifted my face to the other side and saw Edgar, pointing a pistol of his own at the guy who had been pointing a pistol at me.

Edgar repeated, "I said drop it. I'll shoot you in the balls right now."

There was a long moment of agonizing silence, during which I poised my body, and without warning shot upward, slamming the masked man in the bottom of the chin with the full force of both my forearms. It was probably stupid, but the alternative, which was nothing, seemed even more so.

He reeled back and toppled over from the shock and the force. The gun dropped aimlessly onto the carpet several feet from his grasp. Edgar pounced on it as if he was twenty-five years old, scooped it up, and put it into the outer pocket of his blue blazer. I jumped on top of our attacker and delivered one ferocious roundhouse punch to the vicinity of his nose, feeling flesh and bone crack on impact. I hoped it was his flesh and bone, not mine.

He groaned and I furiously yanked the

mask from his head, revealing a panicked-looking fortysomething guy with a bad haircut and blood gushing from his oversize nose, across his upper lip, and down his chin.

Edgar yelled, "Step back, Jack." So I did.

Edgar turned to the cashier and shouted, "Call the damned police."

The clerk, who looked like he had gone into complete shock, turned around and began fumbling with a phone on the back wall.

And that's when it happened. Edgar Sullivan's arm was slack at his side, the gun in his hand pointing downward at the floor. The clerk was finally summoning the police. The assailant was still writhing in pain on the ground. I was collecting my breath and my wits. All of us just standing or lying there, playing our respective roles.

In a flash, the bloody intruder reached into his coat, yanked out a second pistol, and fired it. He fired it at Edgar Sullivan, once, twice, three times. The thing is, I remember hearing four shots, and quickly realized why: somewhere in the mix, Edgar returned fire.

His shot hit the perpetrator on the wrist of his shooting hand, causing him to drop the gun in screaming agony. The perp's blood gushed out of him with such force that it splattered on my cheek.

I looked over at Edgar, who was lying on his side, bleeding from his face, his stomach, and his leg, and raced toward him. As I did, the shooter bolted for the door, screaming all the way out onto the street, his gun still on the floor inside.

"Edgar, we're getting help," I cried out. "Help is on the way."

His eyes were glazed over, fading from life to death. I turned toward the clerk and yelled, louder than I intended, "Did you get hold of the cops?"

He looked at me, panicked, but said nothing.

"Call them again and tell them a man's been shot!"

He picked up the receiver again and dialed 911.

I got on the floor and cradled Edgar's bloody head in my lap. I peeled off my sweater and pressed it against the wound near his temple, hoping to stem the flow of blood.

"Help is on the way, pal. Just stay with us, okay? Edgar, just stay with us."

I tried to sound reassuring, but I probably sounded anything but. My thoughts drifted back to the time *Record* colleague Steve

Havlicek was wounded in a bomb attack on my car, and I sat with him on a George-town street waiting too long for an ambulance to arrive. He died a few hours later.

In the distance, I could hear the faint sound of a siren, and announced to Edgar, "Here they are, pal. They're on the way. They'll be here in a second."

No response.

The siren got louder, closer, too slowly.

"Just stay awake for me, Edgar. Don't go anywhere on me. I want to be toasting you at your next wedding."

Still no response. His eyes were closed now. I placed a finger under his nostrils and barely felt a breath.

His head was heavy to the point of being — and I don't like using the expression here — dead weight, his neck slack. His blood was flowing right through my shirt and spilling down my legs.

"Edgar, we've got way too much left to do on this story for you to go anywhere, so don't even think about it."

The siren was now blaring outside. I could see the flash of blue lights reflected in the front window — a police car, not an ambulance. The doors to the store jolted open as I screamed at the clerk, "Call a fucking ambulance — now!"

In a second, there were two cops flanking me, both of them down on their knees. One of them asked what had happened.

I said, "He was shot three times by a guy who fled out the door about three minutes ago. Bullet wounds in the head, the stomach, and his leg. He's losing blood. He's unconscious. He's barely hanging on."

Another siren outside, and then another one after that, and still more in the distance. I could see blue lights reflecting in the window, and then red ones, meaning an ambulance was pulling up, thank God.

One of the cops stood up and barked into his radio, "APB for a suspected gunman who fled from the CVS on Charles and Cambridge Streets within the past five minutes."

He looked down at me and asked, "What'd he look like?"

I still held Edgar's head in my arms. His face had gone from pained to peaceful, which should have been nice, but instead scared the hell out of me.

"White guy, forties, black trench coat, bloody nose. That's all I know."

The cop repeated that into his radio. A whole cadre of police and EMTs burst through the front door. I heard someone drop a stretcher beside me. A guy in a brown uniform knelt down next to me and edged me slowly away from Edgar, saying, "Let me take over from here." I stood up, and Edgar was surrounded by rescue workers.

The cop who was the first on the scene put his hand on my elbow and asked, "Can I get a word with you?"

We walked a few feet down an aisle that held deodorants and razors on the well-stocked shelves. Don't ask me why I noticed this; I just did.

"Can you give me a brief account of what just happened?"

That was the cop, doing his job, though at the wrong time. My eyes and my thoughts remained on Edgar. The EMTs had spread him flat on the floor, on his back. One was ripping off his clothing and tending to his wounds. Another was pumping his heart, pushing his forearms down almost violently into Edgar's chest. A third, a young woman, cupped her hands around Edgar's mouth and administered mouth-to-mouth resuscitation, that last word appearing to be a misnomer here. Edgar would like that part of the life-saving exercise very, very much. I hoped to hell he realized what was happening.

The EMTs were pumping and breathing

feverishly, synchronizing their moves, talking to one another in increasingly loud voices. They did this until they didn't, until the man pumping his chest placed his ear against Edgar's heart, lifted his head, and announced to the others, "We've lost him. There's nothing there."

I pushed past the cop, plaintively yelling, "No! No! Keep trying!"

The three EMTs looked up at me simultaneously. The one on Edgar's chest climbed off, stood up, and said to me, "I'm sorry. All his vitals have disappeared for too long. He's gone. There's nothing we can do."

I looked down at Edgar Sullivan, sprawled on the floor of a Boston CVS, his clothing haphazardly torn away from his body, and tears immediately began flowing down my face. I thought of the help he had given me in a series of stories I wrote bringing down the mayor. I thought of his various ex-wives, his love of life, the extraordinary wisdom and wherewithal that he brought to his job. I knelt down and kissed his forehead, still warm, and whispered, "Thank you, Edgar. Thank you for everything you did."

As I got up, the same uniformed officer who had tried questioning me shouted out, "This is a homicide scene. I need to ask everyone to step back and leave the body exactly as it is."

I stepped away, toward the front counter. The cop walked over and asked the clerk, who had been standing there all this time, what had happened.

"It was a robbery," the clerk said in a thick accent. "A man in a mask came in and tried robbing the store."

The cop had a little notebook in his hand, jotting things down in a way not unlike I might have done if I was covering the story — which I wasn't, but maybe I should have been. He looked at me and asked, "A robbery?"

I thought about that for a long moment. No, in fact, it wasn't. A robbery would have involved the masked man trying to take money from the cash register. A robbery would have involved the gunman paying closer attention to the store clerk. That never happened. Instead, the assailant seemed hell-bent on executing me.

But was this the kind of information I wanted to share with the police? If I did, it would mean that I'd be thrust even further into the center of a story I was trying to unravel. It might also render me useless, because suddenly I'd be bogged down with detectives, answering questions rather than doing my job and asking them.

So I nodded my head. "Apparently," I said.

Please note the Bill Clinton–esque answer. In a court of law, it would allow me to worm my way out, even if in the court of common sense, it would still be known as a lie.

Before he pinned me down any further, I changed the subject, saying, "The guy you're looking for is going to have a gunshot wound to his wrist." Then I added, "I need some air. I'm just going to step outside for a moment."

I walked past Edgar Sullivan's body, my eyes never for a moment leaving his. Another cop held the front door for me. The sidewalk around the store was cordoned off by yellow crime-scene tape and protected by a phalanx of uniformed officers. Police lights still cut through the air, though the ambulance had already left. I leaned against the front of the building and sucked in the cool night air as hard and as fast as I could.

Edgar Sullivan was dead. He died protecting me. And someone was going to pay long and hard for what he had just done.

29

The first nonstop flight from Boston to Las Vegas leaves at 7:10 in the morning, and the passenger list isn't exactly a roster of Boston's social register. There were guys in tank tops, women with fanny packs, kids with two days' worth of snot hardened around their noses. And this was first class, which cost me just enough of the *Record*'s money that Martin would undoubtedly ask if we now owned a percentage of the plane.

I felt a tinge of relief, a lot of trepidation, and overwhelming sadness as we ascended from the runway at Logan International Airport and banked over South Boston — the emotions having nothing to do with the physical act of aviation.

Rather, it felt somewhat good to get the hell out of Dodge, even for a day. Dodge was about the death of someone I loved and truly respected, Edgar Sullivan. Dodge was about another death of a man I never even knew in a place — the Public Garden — where I was supposed to be. Dodge was about the murders of young women whose licenses and videos I received shortly after they died.

I was feeling guilt. I was feeling helpless. And I'll admit, I was feeling a little more than a little bit of fear. Someone wanted me vacated from this good earth, and, even if incompetent in their execution (pun partially intended), they were going to clever extremes to mask their efforts — a possible drowning, a daytime robbery, a faulty steam-bath door, a store holdup.

A few things happened before my flight that are worth noting, first and foremost being the conversation I had with Deirdre Walters Hayes, daughter of the late Bob Walters, retired detective with Boston PD.

She had known I had been at the house, known I was there because, she said, her mother had a vague recollection, and she found my business card on her father's dresser. She didn't seem particularly angry at me, which was a good thing, maybe even a great thing.

After my condolences, I cut to the quick. "Las Vegas Police said they found a key on the stairs above your father's body," I said. "Any idea what it unlocked?"

She didn't hesitate. "An old footlocker that my dad kept in the garage," she said.

My breath quickened. I asked, "Any idea what's in it?"

"His life. His career. Things he cherished from his old days in Boston, and things from some old cases that haunted him right to the end. After you left, he must have gotten it in his head that he needed to see some of these things again."

She hesitated, then said, her voice starting to crack, "But he didn't have the strength. He should have known that."

I knew what I needed, and what I needed was to see what was in that box. I also knew that Bob Walters wanted me to see what was in that box, which is why he was trying to get to it before I returned to his house. But I didn't want to look overeager. So I said to Deirdre, "Listen, I came out there to ask your father some questions about the old Boston Strangler case, and he was phenomenal about answering them. Would you mind if I came back out and took a look to see if there's anything that might be helpful in that locker?"

"Come on out," she said. And that was that.

It's also important to mention the story I filed for that morning's *Record* about the murder of Edgar Sullivan. Maybe I shouldn't have written it, but more probably I should have. Edgar was a lifelong employee of the *Record,* forty-three years running the newspaper's security operation, and I think he would have gotten something of a kick being memorialized on his paper's front page on his way out the door.

It's one thing to be evasive with cops, quite another to be that way with readers, so in a first-person account, I provided many more details in my story than I let on to detectives at the scene of the crime the night before. That's not to say I wrote everything. Rather, I described how the older woman was allowed to escape from the store. I indicated that the gunman seemed more concerned with the people in the store than he was with the money in the register. And I went into more graphic detail about the gunfight, portraying Edgar Sullivan to be exactly what he was: a hero who saved the life of a colleague, that colleague being me.

That particular story, written in an hour on deadline, inspired a 6:00 a.m. voice mail from Police Commissioner Hal Harrison to my cell phone, during which he said, and I quote, "I'll slap you so hard with a subpoena that you won't be able to spell the words

Boston Record."

Fuck him. Anyway, he'd have to have a Nevada sheriff serve it, and I doubt that was going to happen, mostly because he wouldn't have any idea where I was — at least that was a key part of the plan.

Speaking of which, the plan called for me to parachute into Las Vegas, though not literally, drive immediately to the home of the newly late Bob Walters, meet his daughter, Deirdre, analyze and possibly retrieve whatever it was that was in that locker, and catch a four o'clock flight that would get me back to Boston by half past midnight. One added benefit of this trip was that it would get me out of the firing range that Boston had become, at least for a few hours.

Of course, I can't remember the last time anything in my life went according to plan, so why should this day have been any different.

The last time I had pulled up to Bob Walters's house on Rodeo Road, the county coroner was parked out front and Bob was already zipped up in a shiny black body bag and getting wheeled out the front door. That was not a good day, but then again, not many of them had been lately.

This time, no coroner, no body bags, no

police cars, all of which was good news. Just desert serenity, with chirping birds, the distant sound of a gurgling fountain, and the dry, superheated air. I strode up the Walterses' walkway and knocked on the front door.

I wasn't exactly prepared for what happened next, but then again, preparation had hardly been my calling card of late. A woman answered, I don't know, somewhere in her thirties, maybe about five feet six, 110 pounds, dressed in a miniskirt and a skintight white tank top that could just about make a man — especially this man — buckle at the knees.

Beyond that, she wore heavy eyeliner and bright lipstick, and her wavy auburn hair was bunched back in a ponytail. She said, "You must be Jack. I'm Deirdre Hayes."

Now, Deirdre is one of those names I associate with navy blue pantsuits and white silk shirts that button to the neck — a conservative name for a conservative woman who, because of that, has probably achieved some modicum of financial success. It's like Alice or Patricia or Ruth. You don't expect to see a Deirdre dressed like this.

On the flip side, throw the name Tiffany around and that's a woman I want to meet, or for that matter Alex or Andi or Jen. Kate can go either way, as can Liz or Anne.

Back to Deirdre. She must have sensed my, um, surprise, because she said, "Forgive my appearance; I'm just getting off the overnight shift. I'm a waitress on the Strip."

I said, "I'd like to spend a few hours with my good friend Jimmy Beam in that bar."

Just kidding. What I really said was, "I'm so sorry to intrude like this. Things are crazy back in Boston, and the sooner we did this, the better."

"No apology necessary."

She invited me inside. The place smelled strongly of cleaning fluids, which, given what had gone on in there over so many years, was probably a good thing. All the blinds and drapes were pulled open, allowing sunshine to flow inside. Classical music poured through a central speaker system — Mozart's Piano Concerto Number 19 in F, if I'm not mistaken. All right, I'm bluffing here, but someone was tickling the ivories, and it sounded pretty damned good, even if it didn't seem to go with the woman before me.

Deirdre led me back into the big kitchen and offered me a cup of coffee, which I declined, and then a bottle of water, which I gladly accepted. Last time I was in this room, her mother was flinging a glass against a wall and killing herself slowly with booze. This time, there was no hint of her, so I asked, "Is Mrs. Walters home?"

"My mom's in rehab," Deirdre replied, leaning back on a countertop, holding a mug of coffee in both her hands. She paused, then added, "And not by her choice. You saw her. She was a mess. Her whole life had fallen apart. I had to get an appointment by the court to be her guardian, and the first thing I did was send her into a clinic to dry out. She needs the kind of help that I can't give her."

Deirdre Hayes said this matter-of-factly, though I was pretty certain the facts of her life had to hurt.

I said, "You're a good daughter."

She replied, "Thank you, but for chrissakes, look at me. Hardly good enough, hardly what my old man wanted me to be. My mother's had a tough life. I'm intensely proud of my father. He was a great detective, and he helped a lot of people over the years — hundreds and hundreds of them. But he was never the same after the Boston Strangler case, and he never made it easy on my mom."

I nodded. "I think that Strangler case ruined a lot of people's lives." Not to mention ended; Edgar Sullivan's corpse flashed in my mind like a slide in a PowerPoint presentation, but of course I didn't mention it. What I said was, "I know it's not exactly making mine a pony ride at the moment."

Now she nodded knowingly, with a smile, though I wasn't sure what she actually knew. She said, "Good Lord, he was tough to get along with. My mother's an alcoholic. I ended up spending my twenties shoving heroin into my arms and up my nose. I lost everything I had. My husband, my child, my job. I'm not blaming my old man, I'm really not. You create your own problems in life. But man, he didn't make it easy to get out. He was a miserable old guy, right to the end. Maybe the Strangler case was the cause, or maybe it was an excuse. I was never sure."

I said, "I'm sorry."

Deirdre Hayes shrugged. "My mother has alcoholism in her family, but my dad brought it all to the fore. If I was her, I can't tell you I would have done it any differently, except maybe divorcing him and living my own life on my own terms."

We talked a little bit about my meeting with her father the day that he died. I mentioned how surprising it was that he fell down the stairs that day.

She said, "You triggered something in

him. He never got out of bed, but after you left, there was something he had to see."

I said, "He was trying to tell me something before I left, but he couldn't get the words out. Then his health worker showed up and kicked me out."

She nodded. I was beginning to hear the clock ticking toward my return flight, so I said, "I don't mean to be rude, but I'm on a tight schedule, and the truth is, I'm really eager to see what it is that your old man has."

"Let's go."

She led me from the kitchen down a short hall and out a metal door into an obsessively neat two-car garage, where the floor still looked like it was brand-new. There were no vehicles in the garage, giving it a cavernous feel. It was also un-air-conditioned, making it feel hotter than a day in hell, which perhaps this was and someone forgot to tell me.

Deirdre said, "The day after my father died, I was really sad for all that had happened, not just his death, but what became of his life, and my mother's life, and my life. I wanted to relive some of it, reach back to the better times and try to figure out what went wrong. I took a peek through his stuff myself. There's some interesting stuff.

Maybe it explains all this — his misery, the way he died. You know?"

I didn't know. Not yet, anyway. As she said this, she led me to the far rear corner of the garage, where an old footlocker — a chest, really — sat on the floor. The key was already in the hole. She turned it and opened the locker upward, revealing four old boxes in pretty good shape sitting side by side inside.

She opened the top of the second one and pulled out a notebook from inside. She slowly flipped through it to a section in the back that she had tabbed with a Post-it note, and she began reading to herself, getting lost in the words and her own thoughts. Finally, she looked up at me and said, "My father always said he had another prime suspect in the stranglings, but he would never tell anyone who it was. Here it is, in black and white, in his own words."

With that, she handed me the notebook. As I received it, I could already feel my heart falling. I read through the notes, which were of the exact interview he had already described to me in his bedroom on the morning that he died, the one with Paul Vasco. The session was held in an anteroom in Bridgewater at the prison for the sexually dangerous. Bob Walters was alone with nothing more than his badge and his gun and his total indignation that the state attorney general and some of his cohorts in homicide had fingered the wrong guy. There was no reason for him to be there. Vasco could have offered him a confession, and the other higher-ups would have told him it was all a lie. He was there only because he couldn't let it go.

The notes showed that he asked the exact question he told me he'd asked in the exact way he described it: "Hey, Paul, DeSalvo's gone. The case is off the books. But we had the wrong guy, didn't we?"

Beneath the question, he wrote, "PV remained silent. Didn't say a word. But he smiled like the devil, making sure I understood exactly what he meant. And I did." The word *devil* was underlined three times.

And beneath that he wrote, "Paul Vasco is the Boston Strangler."

I looked up at Deirdre Hayes, who was looking intently at me as I read the notes. I said, "Do you mind if I take this with me?"

She hesitated for a long moment, anxiously rubbing her hands together at her waist, looking more innocent than she probably should have in that particular outfit.

Finally she said, "I've never dealt with

408

reporters before. How do you handle payment?"

Terrific. I fly across a continent and am met by a woman who wants to turn a profit on her old man's death. Though hell, she probably had it coming to her, given the misery that the guy had caused.

I said, "We don't." I said this softly, attempting a tone of understanding, perhaps even empathy. "I'm not allowed to pay for information. Newspapers like mine, reputable news organizations, won't do it."

She looked surprised. "So these notebooks aren't worth anything?"

I said, "They're worth a lot. This information might someday soon be invaluable to the hundreds and thousands of other people who have been affected by the Strangler case, people not all that much different than you. It may give them some sense of closure, some little bit of freedom from the past. But I'm not allowed to pay for it."

She stood there in the garage, this beautiful woman dressed like a harlot, exhausted from pushing drinks to obnoxious, leering guys on the overnight shift at a casino bar on the Las Vegas Strip. She probably thought this notebook was about to rescue her from massive credit-card debt, or maybe was an opportunity to buy a nice used car. Instead, some schmuck from the East Coast was explaining to her that once again, she was screwed, just like she'd always been.

So I said, "I'd hate to think that you'd do this, but I feel like I should tell you anyway. A place like *The National Enquirer* might pay you good money for this." I could picture the headline, "Good Cop Fingers Real Boston Strangler From the Grave." The reason I mentioned it to her, aside from the fact that I felt legitimately bad, was that I already had the information from Walters himself.

She looked at the immaculate floor for a long, agonizing moment, and then up at me, and said, "No, I'd rather you had it. My father might have been a bastard, but he meant well most of the time. You'll do the right thing with it."

I said, "If you don't mind, I'd like to get a look at what else is in these boxes."

She nodded again. Then her brow suddenly furrowed and she said, "I always thought there was another box. For some reason, I always remembered seeing five of them. You know how you have that picture in your mind that just stays there? In this case, five boxes, stacked three and two."

She shrugged and said, "But I must be

wrong. I looked all over, and this is all there is."

And with that, she walked into the kitchen.

The first box contained a lot of physical paraphernalia, pieces of clothing and various trinkets from every one of the murder scenes that occurred within Boston proper, which was six of them. It was odd, holding a kerchief from one dead woman, a bracelet from another, an ashtray from someone else's apartment — but no odder than handling the driver's licenses of recently slain women.

The second box was filled with newspaper clippings on every one of the eleven murders, all of them yellowed, some of them crumbling, each one more fascinating than the last. I love reading old papers, partly for the simplistically done ads for products that probably no longer exist, partly for the more formal writing tone that reporters used to take. I had to convince myself not to get lost in the stories or I'd end up spending the night in Vegas, which may or may not have been a bad idea. Edgar Sullivan would have probably advised me to stay.

The third box was a collection of official-looking police reports, transcripts of interviews with witnesses and perhaps suspects, and minutes of various meetings convened by the state attorney general and a group of police and prosecutors dubbed the Boston Strangler Commission. I gave it a quick scan, but had neither the time nor the patience to give it a thorough review.

Should this stuff have been walked out the police department doors — read: stolen — and be hidden away for years in some anonymous garage in the middle of a sun-baked housing development? Absolutely not. But was it a common occurrence for police to grab documents and other various trinkets from cases that were dear to their hearts? It happened every day, and Bob Walters appeared no different than anyone else.

The last box contained many of Walters's personal mementos and correspondence that he undoubtedly pulled from his desk when he walked out of the homicide bureau that final time, at the end a bitter man. There were plaques from various victims' groups, awards from civic associations, framed letters of commendation from the commissioner. I was about to pack them all away, call it a day, and head for the airport, when a leather-bound scrapbook in a corner of the locker caught my eye, and I flipped it open.

In it were various notes and letters. The first was from Hal Harrison, then a homicide detective, urging Bob Walters to take some time off in the midst of the Boston Strangler case. Right after it was a hand-scrawled note from a detective by the name of Mac Foley — yes, I believed, the same Mac Foley — telling Walters he was absolutely right about DeSalvo and to keep pounding away on the issue. It didn't elaborate.

I flipped through page after page of what seemed to be meaningless material until I arrived at a handwritten note that gave me pause for reasons I can't fully explain. Maybe it was the penmanship, which seemed vaguely, oddly familiar, or maybe it was something else. I honestly don't know.

Regardless, the letter, dated November 1976, began, "Dear Detective Walters, I agree with you completely that Albert DeSalvo did not kill my mother. Thank you for telling me what you know, and for being honest about what you don't. My dying grandfather, though, needs to believe that my mother's killer has been caught and killed. He's been very sick with cancer, and as he tries to cope with his pain, it helps him to think that DeSalvo was the murderer. That's why your package was so helpful to him. Thank you for sending it. Me and my family truly appreciate all that you have done. Sincerely yours."

I had to read the signature twice, and then a third time, to make sure my eyes or my brain weren't playing tricks on me. It was jarring to see it there, like seeing an apparition, only this was the opposite: a living person so closely, unexpectedly associated with the dead.

I read it yet again, following the curve of the many letters with my eyes, picturing how old he must have been when he wrote his name across the bottom. And then I said it out loud, just to hear it, to put it in the public realm.

"Vincent Mongillo."

My colleague, my friend, a victim of the Boston Strangler, and he kept it secret all these years and, as important, all these crucial days. I reread the letter, which had to have been written when he was about fifteen years old.

I recalled being surprised at his breadth and width of knowledge on the Strangler case, and I recalled asking him why he knew what he knew. That's when he gave me the never-picked-in-the-neighborhood-baseball-games thing, that whole explanation of spending all that time sitting at home reading about old Boston crimes. Why hadn't he wanted me to know?

I looked over at the door to the house, which was ajar. I pulled the letter from the scrapbook and placed it in my coat pocket, separate from the pile of materials I was going to take back to Boston.

Quickly, I reloaded the boxes back into the locker and pushed it back into the corner. I headed into the house and told Deirdre I needed to get back to the airport. She had changed from her tank top and miniskirt into a loosely fitting T-shirt and a pair of short shorts — and still looked great, albeit exhausted.

She kissed me on the left cheek and hung on what felt like a moment longer than I had expected. I kissed her cheek in return and again told her how sorry I was about what had happened, and how appreciative I was about her help.

On my way toward the front hall, I felt in my pocket for the small roll of hundred-dollar bills I had brought on the trip. I placed it next to a stack of unopened mail atop an entry table by the door.

I could probably be fired for doing that, but no one would ever know, no one but me and Deirdre Hayes. It seemed like the right thing to do.

I got in the rental car and pulled down Rodeo Road for what I expected would be the final time in my threatened life and had no complaint about this fact. As I turned the corner, my cell phone vibrated in my back pocket. If I thought for a moment that Mongillo's name would be the biggest surprise of the day, I was about to be proven woefully, frighteningly wrong.

30

Trust.

It's an interesting concept when you really stop and think about it. In huge swaths of America, it's the way of the day, ingrained into the culture, the default attitude toward the people and institutions that make up civic life. On the sprawling farms of the heartland, in the village centers where ice cream sodas are still served at lunch counters in the local Rexall, people trust one another. They firmly believe that their neighbors, their friends, their colleagues, their business associates won't try to slip a curveball past them.

Shopkeepers allow customers to run monthly accounts, rightfully expecting that they'll always make good. Business deals are sealed on the power of a handshake. Families leave their doors unlocked at night. Little kids ride their bikes alone to the local park.

Of course, there are other huge areas of the country where trust is little more than a relic from a simpler, curious past. Here, people have double locks and police bars. They buy guns not to hunt but to protect. They hire $350-an-hour lawyers to comb through almost every single document that dictates their distrustful lives. Even Ronald Reagan's famous "Trust but verify" philosophy seems antiquated, because to these people, there shouldn't be any trust at all.

I'd like to think that my instincts belong with the former group, but my circumstances have thrust me toward the latter. I'd like to think that at my core, in my heart, I'm a trusting person, wanting to believe the words and respect the actions of those around me. But in my more self-aware moments, I know this not to be true. I didn't get into this bizarre profession of words and news to write day after day that government is basically good, that businesses will always do what's right, that people, left to their own devices, will always take proper care of one another.

No, in my advancing age, I'm as distrustful at anyone else — which is not to be confused with being untrustworthy. But who knows, maybe I've become that as well.

But never do I remember being more

distrustful in my entire wary life than I was at that exact moment, driving through the Nevada desert in the direction of McCarran International Airport and a US Airways Boeing 757 that would return me to a place I may not have been ready to go.

I didn't trust the Boston Police and other various government officials who said that Albert DeSalvo, long ago dead, was the Boston Strangler, responsible for the deaths of eleven women more than forty years ago who were identified as part of the Strangler spree, in addition to two other murders that he confessed to as well. I didn't trust the same police who were telling me that this recent string of deaths was the result of a fame-seeking copycat killer.

I didn't trust the sitting senior senator from Massachusetts, who built his career on his success in "solving" the Strangler case so long ago. I didn't trust the current police commissioner for the same reason.

I didn't trust the people I usually trust, and that may have hurt the most. I didn't trust women, mostly in the form of Maggie Kane, who walked out on a marriage before it ever began. Of course, I was about to do the same, but that somehow seems beside the point.

I didn't trust Peter Martin and publisher

419

Justine Steele to do the right thing — not after they were browbeaten by city officials into not running the Phantom Fiend's written assertion that the new strangler was the same as the old strangler.

I didn't trust Vinny Mongillo. I didn't think I'd ever say those words, except maybe in regard to leaving him alone with some really expensive food. But why on God's good earth had he not told me that his mother was a strangling victim all those years ago?

And I wasn't so sure I trusted myself anymore. The great Edgar Sullivan was dead because of me. So was some guy on the Public Garden who I never even knew. And here I was, ambling along, herking and jerking my way through a story that had no clear end. Was the Boston Strangler ultimately planning on confessing to me? Did he intend to kill another ten women, bringing his total this time around to what it had been before? How was this thing going to be resolved, and what role could I play in hastening a resolution?

And I certainly didn't trust that anything good was about to happen, not as I listened on my cell phone to the aforementioned Peter Martin explain to me that the Phantom Fiend had reached out to me again in his most foreboding note yet, this one in the form of an e-mail to my *Boston Record* account. In the hours after Edgar's death, Martin was wise enough to hire a security consultant, which had people monitoring my e-mail account, my U.S. mail, my house, and the newsroom. Thank God I didn't live a life of secret fetishes, constantly communicating online with big-breasted blond amputees, because I would suddenly have a lot of explaining to do.

That consultant, in turn, read the e-mail and forwarded it on to Martin, who, in turn, read it to me, and it went exactly like this: "Mr. Flynn, you didn't honor the one, simple request I made of you, to publish my words in the way I asked you to. I thought you were better than this. For that, there will be swift and severe consequences. People will suffer for your gutlessness. You will suffer with them. You may personally pick up a package at six o'clock tonight at the corner of Winter Street and Winter Place. The Phantom Fiend."

I swallowed hard as I listened to every dreadful word. The Phantom didn't seem to be a killer prone to hyperbole — i.e., see the word *killer.* Once he's willing to kill beautiful young women, there's not a whole lot that's really worth exaggerating about.

And now he was informing me that I, along with some nameless people, presumably other young women, would suffer from my gutlessness. I was half tempted to buy an advertisement in my cowardly little paper to let him know that I desperately wanted to run his words exactly in the way he had written them. Gutless my ass.

I said to Martin, "This doesn't bode well on pretty much any level." It was really all I had to say. There was no "I told you so" necessary. It wouldn't get me anywhere different than I already was, and I knew that immediately.

Martin was so upset that his voice was on the brink of quavering when he said, "Maybe it's not really him. Maybe this is the other side of the equation, the side that wants to see you dead."

I replied, "That doesn't add up." I didn't really intend to keep this mathematical metaphor going, but I did nonetheless. "I don't think the other side would know that we didn't print something from the Phantom that we were asked to print. That is, unless you and Justine spread the word around a little too far."

No, I was just about certain that, unlike that deadly debacle on the Boston Public Garden, this was the real thing.

Silence. It was rare for Peter Martin to offer a flawed analysis like that, rarer still for him to be at a loss for words. Maybe this thing was taking a harder toll on him than I realized.

So I said, trying to present at least the veneer of calm, "This presents us with a bunch of problems, most that we don't know about yet, but some that we do. First and foremost is that I'm not going to be back in Boston in time for that six o'clock pickup." The clock on the rental car dashboard read 2:06, which meant 5:06 p.m. in Boston. I don't know if I could have gotten there on the space shuttle, not that I'd be willing to fly on that thing anyway.

Martin said, "I've directed the security consultant to reply to the sender from your account, in your name, that you're out of town until later tonight and you won't be able to make the six o'clock rendezvous. He's doing that as we speak."

Okay, this was reassuring now, to hear Martin talk again like a man in control of a situation, like he usually is. I heard a muffled sound, as if he put his palm over the phone, then he got back on the line and said, "Buck, our new security guy, wants to know what time you're back on the ground."

I wondered if Buck would have put his

life on the line for me like Edgar Sullivan did, and quickly decided he would not. Maybe it was irrational for me to dislike him, even disdain him, without yet knowing him, but I did. I mean, give me a break on the name: What the fuck is Buck?

"Twelve-thirty. What's the e-mail address the Phantom's using?"

More muffled sounds, then, "PFBoston@yahoo.com."

I asked, "Any chance the origin can be chased and linked to a computer somewhere?"

Martin answered, "Highly unlikely, but Buck's working on it."

I was about to ask for funeral arrangements for Edgar when Martin shot out, "Hold on, here, Buck says we have a response. I'm going to make this easier and put you on speakerphone, Jack."

He pressed a button, because suddenly I could hear a low humming sound, like when you place a shell against your ear at the beach. Martin said, "Jack, I've got Buck here. Buck, this is Jack on the phone."

What followed was the typically awkward start of a speakerphone call. Buck called out, "How are you, Jack? Nice to meet you."

I wanted to point out that we hadn't actually met yet, and that it wasn't bound to be all that nice when we did. Instead I said, "Good, Buck. Where are we with the Phantom?"

Buck said, "He's just come back and essentially said he wants to meet in Downtown Crossing at one this morning."

I gritted my teeth. By the way, the Nevada desert was giving way to development, which was leading to the airport, which meant that I was getting close to being wheels up and flying home. I said, "Buck, I don't want to know what he *essentially* said. Tell me *exactly* what he said."

"Why don't I just read it . . ."

"Good idea, Buck."

"Sure. He wrote, 'Dear Mr. Flynn, then please appear at the corner of Winter Street and Winter Place at one a.m. Come alone. Do not alert authorities. Do not send anyone in advance. If you violate these conditions, you will suffer even greater consequences, and so will many more women. I will contact you at the appropriate hour and location. PF.' "

Buck added in a confiding tone, "I think the PF stands for Phantom Fiend."

"Thanks, Buck." I added, "Peter, can I talk to you for a moment?"

The line clicked and became clearer, and then Martin said into the phone, "I don't like the feel of it."

He didn't like the feel of it because he's the one who put us — namely, me — into this situation by not standing up to Justine Steele's bullshit.

I said, "But you're not going to do anything about it. You're not going to the police. You're not going to Justine. You're not going to flag the mayor. Every time we include authority figures in our thinking, we get screwed, Peter. Let's just do what we do best and report this story out."

I liked the simple sound of all that, apparently more than Peter did. He said, "You could get arrested for interfering with an investigation. And maybe so could I."

I replied, "Hey, jail's probably a hell of a lot safer than where I'm at now."

He didn't have a comeback to this one, least of all because he undoubtedly knew it was true. He said, "All right, against my better judgment, go. But I'm going to have Buck meet you at the airport when you arrive."

I said, "I don't think Buck can find the airport, but go ahead and let him try."

And then I heard another little click. Peter Martin had just hung up the phone on my ear.

Before I could even put the phone down,

426

it chimed anew. I thought it was going to be Martin calling me back to apologize for the abrupt cessation of our conversation. Instead, it was the serious voice of a self-important young woman telling me — not asking me, but telling me — in her words, to "please hold the line for Commissioner Harrison."

"I don't want to hold the line for Commissioner Harrison." That was me, replying, but there was no one on the other end to hear, no one except some Muzak version of the Rolling Stones' "(I Can't Get No) Satisfaction." Believe me, I know how you guys feel.

A good two minutes passed, and by then I was pulling into the Avis return lot, some guy in a brown shirt walking briskly toward me with one of those handheld checkout devices as jet airplanes roared overhead. Still no sign of Harrison on the phone.

It's an unvarnished power trip, this whole "hold the line for" stuff, a blunt declaration that my time is more important than yours, and you should be thrilled to wait while I finish up whatever else I may have been doing to get on the line and grace you with a few moments of my busy day. Another two minutes passed. "Satisfaction" morphed into "Rhinestone Cowboy," a song I've always liked, and that played to the end. By that point, I was curious as to just how long Boston Police Commissioner Hal Harrison was going to leave me waiting on the phone for a call I had neither made nor necessarily wanted to have. But I wasn't quite curious enough, so I hung up.

Ten minutes later, as I was walking through the airport terminal, my cell phone rang. This time when I picked it up, it was Harrison acting as if that whole prior incident had never occurred. Or maybe he just didn't know about it.

"Jack? Hal Harrison here." He said this in an abnormally loud voice, as if he were giving a speech at the morning roll call.

"Hello, Commissioner," I said.

"Jack, it's been too long since you and I got together and chatted about things. And that conversation the other day didn't exactly go the way I had hoped or planned. You know what I mean?"

I didn't, but I didn't say that.

Instead I said, "What do you have in mind, Commissioner?"

"Well, nice of you to ask. You're under a lot of pressure at the *Record* with these murders. I think I'm in a position now to share a little perspective on this whole thing with you, seeing as I was one of the lead detectives back in the sixties on the successful Strangler investigation. Mind you, I'm not looking for any publicity on this thing. God knows, we're getting too much of that as it is. I just think I might be in a position to give you a little help."

"When do you have in mind, Commissioner?"

"Any chance you might find your way to my office tomorrow morning, say, ten a.m.? I'll have coffee for us. I think I can make it worth your while."

"Count me in," I said. And with that, I secured another first-class upgrade and boarded the plane bound for Boston. If there were air-traffic controllers who had any idea of the metaphorical storm I was about to fly into, they never would have let the flight leave the ground.

31

As predicted, Buck wasn't awaiting my arrival at Logan International Airport when my flight landed at twelve-thirty. Or if he was, he was pretty effectively undercover.

Didn't matter. My man Hank Sweeney, attired in a blue blazer and a freshly pressed pair of khaki pants, stood at the airport end of the jetway, casually sipping on a cup of Dunkin' Donuts coffee, as I got off the plane.

"You strike it rich out there?" he asked, his voice the damnedest combination of silkiness and raspiness that I'd ever heard.

"So to speak," I replied, and the two of us immediately began walking with the flow toward the baggage claim and the parking lot.

I hadn't seen Hank since that Tuesday dinner we had at Locke-Ober, four days before, when he tipped me off as to the importance of the knife and the potential help of his former colleague Bob Walters. I was no closer to finding the knife, and Detective Walters was dead. All in all, things still weren't going as hoped or as planned.

He expressed condolences about Edgar's death. I thanked him, and we walked for a stretch in silence.

Finally, I said, "Your advice on Bob Walters was good. The big problem is, he died the day I spoke to him."

Hank nodded as if he knew this already, but didn't say whether he did or he didn't.

So I said, "And obviously Edgar was killed last night in a supposed robbery that I don't think was a robbery at all. I remind you of this because I'm going to head into this men's room here. While I'm in there, you might be smart to just keep walking down this corridor, get in your car, head home, and watch *Wedding Crashers* on pay-per-view. People around me have a way of dying lately, and I really don't want that to happen to you, Hank."

Cutting through my minidrama, Hank asked, "Then why'd you call me?"

It's true, I had. I'd called him just before I got on the plane in Vegas, explaining some of my predicament, laying out the dangers, and asking for his help. I needed an able-bodied, street-smart guardian angel — to use Edgar's term — over the next day or so, and so what if he happened to be about seventy years old.

"I might have been too rash. I've been thinking more about it on the airplane. I don't want to see more people dead because of me. I really don't."

"Go use the men's room."

I did, looking around suspiciously at the other men in there, not alone because of how few of them took the time to wash their hands on their way out the door. I was starting to wonder who was following me, monitoring my moves, waiting constantly for the opportunity to strike.

When I got back outside, Hank was still standing there, virtually in the same place and position as he was when I went inside. "There," he said, "now that we've got that little episode out of your system, maybe we can go find ourselves a strangler."

And we were off.

Hank had a black Ford four-door idling at the curb with a state police trooper watching guard. Normally these troopers are hassling harried travelers to get their cars out of the no-parking zones, not necessarily in the nicest or politest way. This trooper said to Hank, "That was fast."

"Life is fast," Hank replied, opening the

driver's-side door. "Look at me. I feel like I've just begun, but I probably only have one bullet left in my gun — and I was never that good a shot to begin with."

The trooper nodded and laughed. He looked over at me and said, "Good luck with the story."

I thanked him, and Hank called out, "Trust me, Teddy, the whole damned thing just flies by."

On the ride into the city, we went over a quick plan, which was barely a plan at all — basically what Hank described as a "lurk and listen strategy." He was going to drop me off a block away from my meeting destination. He gave me a cellular phone with a two-way radio, which he had programmed to remain on at all times. He would be ready to descend on the scene if needed, but would stand down otherwise.

Me, I had an odd sense of faith in this situation, don't ask me why. The Phantom Fiend was trying to get me information, lurid as that information inevitably ended up being. He didn't want me dead, because then his conduit to the public at-large no longer existed. No, it was someone else who wanted me dead, but on this night, given that the e-mailer had known about the manifesto, I had faith that it was indeed the

Phantom Fiend. Of course, I've been wrong about less important things in my life, which might explain why my extremities felt like they were going numb.

My phone rang — my real phone, not the Hank-issued one — and I almost jumped through the moonroof. And the moonroof, by the way, was closed.

"Easy there, tabby cat," Hank said.

When I answered the call, it was Peter Martin, making sure I was safe and sound and in the company of the security agent named Buck. I explained that I was the former, but not the latter, and that Hank Sweeney was my chaperone and chauffeur.

"Hold on," he said. I heard him pick up another line and say, "Hey, Buck, why aren't you with Jack?"

Pause.

"You're waiting for his flight? Where? Hold on." Then, to me, "What airline did you come in on?"

I told him.

To Buck, "That's US Airways, not United." Pause. "No, it's Las Vegas, not Los Angeles." Pause. "No, he's off property. Never mind, just come back here."

"Why don't you put him on the copy desk," I said to Peter. "He'd probably fit right in."

He didn't appreciate that. Instead he told me, "Be careful. Next time I see you, I don't want to be paying my final respects."

At one o'clock on a Sunday morning, the Downtown Crossing side of Boston Common isn't a place most normal people want to be. Abnormal people, yes, which probably explains all the punked-up Mohawks, the various body piercings, and the bizarre Gothic fashion sported by the dozens of early twentysomethings who gathered in formless clusters near the corner of Tremont and Park Streets, where I stepped out of Hank's car. I'm not sure what they were waiting for, but I had a feeling it wasn't coming anytime soon.

"Be calm, be cool, remember I'm armed, we'll get out of this just fine." That was Hank's last bit of advice to me as I shut the door and walked toward the meeting site.

I didn't take the time to tell him that Edgar Sullivan was armed as well.

Once off Tremont, Winter Street was dead, and again, I don't use that word loosely anymore. The doors and front windows of the various discount stores were sheathed in steel grating — dark, hulking structures that repelled the vague light from the streetlamps. Even on a gorgeous June afternoon, Downtown Crossing isn't exactly Piazza Navona, if you know what I mean. In the post-midnight hush of an early spring night, it took on the look of a stage set from the type of horror movie I'd never bother to see.

Winter Place was little more than a dead-end alley halfway down the block, known only because it is the home of the Locke-Ober, where Hank and I recently dined on that dreamy bisque and those delicious steaks. When I pulled up to the corner, there wasn't another person around, or at least not within my view. I had a moment where fear dripped into awkwardness because I didn't know what to do. What I really wanted was a shot of whiskey from the Locke-Ober bar, and I don't even drink whiskey. But the place was dark for the night, so that wasn't really an option.

Instead, I stood in the middle of the street, away from any buildings where a predator might emerge from the shadowy entrances without me having time enough to fight back. Mrs. Flynn of South Boston didn't raise any fool. I put my hands in my pockets. I took them out. I shuffled my feet. I stood completely still. It felt like an hour; it was really about five minutes. And that's when my cell phone rang.

It was as quiet as the country out there, and by country I don't mean Prague or Helsinki, though I'm not sure those are even countries. Regardless, I mean the American country, like the middle of the country, a wheat farm in Nebraska, where the only sounds in the distant fields are the crops whistling in a summery breeze.

Which is a long way of saying the chime of my phone sounded not unlike a car crash for the noise it made. I all but leapt off the ground as I yanked it from my pocket. The caller ID said "Unavailable." I flipped it open and said, "Jack Flynn here."

"Pick up the envelope halfway down the walkway at the end of Winter Place."

That was followed by a click, which was followed by silence.

"Who is this?" I asked, a question that admittedly lacked even a hint of originality. But as I suspected, there was no one on the line to respond. So thinking quickly, as I rarely do anymore, I said, "Okay, the walkway at the end of Winter Place." I said this for Hank Sweeney's benefit, and ultimately mine as well.

That one spare directive had been delivered in a monotone, emphasizing neither words nor syllables. It was a man's voice, gravelly yet pointed, indiscernible in age.

437

He could have been thirty, he could have been sixty. I truly had no idea, though for some reason I pictured a guy with two days' of growth on his cheeks and an old ball cap on his head speaking into a pay phone somewhere nearby.

It was the pickup spot that bothered me more than the voice. The walkway at the end of Winter Place is a long, narrow passage that links on the other side to a short side street called Temple Place. The walkway is effectively a single-file space that exists between two old buildings, another only-in-Boston kind of place. A person walking within it is essentially sitting prey, and no one in their right mind uses it as a shortcut anytime after dark, Arnold Schwarzenegger aside, though I'm not sure he fits into the category of right-minded people.

With no great enthusiasm, I turned toward Winter Place, which is about forty yards long, and looked suspiciously toward the end. I could disappear within that passageway and never be seen alive again, bound for that celestial place where Bob Walters and Edgar Sullivan were already holding court, not to mention a collection of young women formerly of Boston. I wondered if they'd appreciate my meager efforts on their behalf.

I reminded myself of my belief that the Phantom didn't want me dead. Problem was, I was also reminded of the fact that the last time I showed up at a meeting supposedly created by the Phantom, someone ended up dead on the Public Garden. I put that out of my mind, perhaps out of desperation, maybe ignorance, probably both.

And I began walking, slowly, buying time, but for what I wasn't sure. Probably for Hank Sweeney to get himself in better position. I walked past the door to an office building on my right, then the darkened entrance to Locke-Ober on my left. Inexplicably, the thought occurred to me that thousands of patrons of that restaurant, given its two-century tenure, had left this material world, and I wondered if I was about to join them. My thoughts, my mood, my expectations were of little more than death.

Or were they? One more time, I reminded myself that the Phantom wanted me alive. Very, very much alive. I was his mouthpiece for a message he hadn't yet gotten out, and I don't think he was about to kill me out of spite. Maybe somebody else was, but not the Phantom.

I arrived at the passageway, every bit as long and narrow as I had envisioned, and even darker than I had imagined. There wasn't a single light along the way, which was a metaphor for something in my life, but damned if I could conjure up what.

This was really stupid, I realized, arguably the stupidest thing I had ever done, not just putting myself in harm's way but voluntarily walking, unarmed and barely protected, into the most vulnerable crevice in all of Boston.

And yet I took that first step. And then another. And another yet.

They were slow steps, cautious and methodical. Pretty soon, it was as dark behind me as it was ahead — so dark that I couldn't see my hand in front of my face. I heard a dull squeak, and felt a swoosh along the pant leg at my shin. A rat, though, was the least of my worries. The passage was so narrow that I kept brushing against one of the cement sides with my shoulders.

After each step, I paused, looking for something that I couldn't see, trying to hear something that perhaps wasn't there, feeling for something that didn't exist. I didn't know. I only knew what my gut told me to do. There are thousands of newspaper reporters in this great country of mine, good reporters and bad, curious and incurious, ambitious and lazy, and I was the one, the single one, who was a big enough jackass to be meeting a killer in a tiny, blackened, concrete-enclosed sliver of downtown Boston tonight.

I got what I estimated was about 40 percent of the way through the walkway when I thought I heard a noise emanating from the other end. It was a vague scraping, shuffling noise, and I stopped, held my breath to stifle my own sounds, and strained to figure out what it was.

Scrape, scrape.

"Who's there?" I called out.

My voice ricocheted off the walls, magnifying along the way, then echoing mournfully toward the end.

Silence.

But only for a moment. Then the scraping resumed, and the scraping was accompanied by hard breathing. I had a terrible picture in my mind of one of the Phantom Fiend's victims lying on the passageway floor, not quite dead but barely alive, searching for help that maybe I was there to give.

So, frantically, I shouted again. "Who's there? Say something! Who's there?"

A panting noise now, and more scratching. I surged forward, perhaps in vain, maybe in stupidity. With each step, I poked ahead with my foot and pushed at the air with my outstretched arms. I took maybe four steps this way, looking not dissimilar to the way Frankenstein looked when he lurched across wherever it was that he lurched.

And that's when the collision occurred.

Whatever it was, it was low to the ground, where I pictured the injured woman to be. I hit it with my knee and my foot at the same time. It was solid and resilient, very much alive. As I pushed against it, I heard a guttural noise, and whatever it was pushed back against me, knocking me off balance, toppling me against the side wall, and then to the ground.

I thrashed on the pavement, making contact with whatever it was, pushing against it while it pushed back at me.

"Who is it?" I yelled, my voice reverberating off the two walls. Again I got no answer, but I didn't think I would; part of the reason for yelling was so Hank Sweeney could hear me out on the street.

I rose into a crouching position and felt around my knees — carefully. But just as I made contact with my hands, whoever it was, whatever it was, lunged at me, driving into my waist and chest, trying to take me down onto the undoubtedly urine-stained floor of this ancient passageway yet again.

I retaliated hard, quite literally fighting for my life. I grabbed he/she/it, forcing it off me, and then pinning it to the ground as I climbed on top of it, my face grazing one of the side walls. But still it wouldn't give up, thrashing as it was. It felt solid. It felt muscular.

It felt, um, furry.

So I cupped my hands, ran them across the squirming figure, up and down in unison, until I felt an unmistakable shape I've felt thousands of times before: a dog's head.

I felt its forehead. I felt its muzzle. I felt its floppy ears. I was relieved until the second I wasn't, which was when it occurred to me that it could be a vicious pit bull or an aggressive rottweiler, sent into this enclosed space to tear me apart like the lions used to kill Roman peasants.

I grabbed whatever it was by the muzzle and held it closed with one hand, hearing a soft whimper in response. I patted around the animal's neck with my other hand until I felt a collar, and I slipped my fingers inside. I struggled awkwardly to my feet, with both my hands otherwise involved in this creature, and began yanking him toward the direction from whence I came.

He or she was a willing prisoner, and

reasonably polite, given the circumstances, passing along with me as I backed toward the entrance. My shoulders kept colliding with the walls, sending me staggering, but I never lost my grip on his nose or his neck.

And finally, I felt a little breeze on my neck and the sides of my face. The air became softer, less pungent, and a streetlight glowed from above. My eyes readjusted for a long moment, and I looked down at my hands to see a singularly frightened but particularly handsome black Labrador retriever staring at me with his enormous brown eyes. I let go of his muzzle, but not his collar.

Immediately, he hung his jaw open, gulping at air, panting hard. I knew how he felt. Then he voluntarily went into a sitting position in front of me, his eyes never leaving mine.

"What the hell were you doing in there?" I asked him.

He didn't respond.

Well, actually, that's not entirely true. He banged his tail hard on the pavement about half a dozen times, still staring at me staring at him.

For Hank Sweeney's benefit, I said, "What's a good dog like you doing in a dark alley like that?"

More tail thumping. I let go of his collar and he didn't move away from me. Instead, he scratched at my leg with his left paw.

I crouched back down, this time in a show of peace. He licked me hard across my face, his grainy tongue seeming to pause on my cheek before it swept against my nose. I laughed, which was no small feat on this night, and memories, nice memories, wonderful memories, of my own golden retriever, Baker, dead a year now, washed through my head. So I pressed my face against his and rubbed the soft underside of his chin.

Which is when I felt it, an object jutting out of the bottom of his collar, much like a cask a Saint Bernard would carry. I maneuvered his collar around until the object was illuminated by the streetlamp. It was an envelope, business-size, folded over, fastened by a pin. I pulled it off delicately so as to not prick my new friend. Through the dark haze, I saw that the envelope bore the name Jack Flynn. I think I've heard of the guy. Tall. Handsome. Brave.

I was getting punchy, obviously, or maybe just relieved that I got out of that passageway alive. I pulled the dog by the collar down to the near end of Winter Place, out onto Winter Street, and toward Boston

Common. I didn't want to let go, because I didn't want him to get hit by a car. He walked agreeably, nearly appreciatively, beside me.

Out on the main intersection, where the passing traffic gave me the feeling of safety, I pulled him into a Bank of America storefront that contained an ATM. It was relatively clean, and bright, and enclosed, all good things at the moment. We were alone in there, so I let go of his collar. He sprawled out on the floor with a short groan, followed by a long sigh, as I opened the envelope. I tried to be careful in tearing the paper in case there was any forensic evidence involved.

Inside, I felt a heavy laminated card, and my heart immediately sank into my stomach: a driver's license, another dead woman, killed on my watch, as I did too little to stop it. I held the license in my hand for what felt like a long minute without looking at it, frustration and helplessness seeping through every pore of my exhausted body. My prior relief devolved into contained fury. The dog sprawled on the floor with his eyes at half-mast. A car honked its horn out on Tremont Street. A group of teenagers laughed as they strode past on the sidewalk.

I slowly lifted the license to my eyes. I

wasn't in any rush to see the next victim, because it didn't really do me — or her — any good to know. My only job here, courtesy of the Phantom, wasn't to help or to stop or to investigate, but merely to convey. Another day, another license, another dead woman somewhere in Boston. How many more women would die before this story came to an end?

I flicked the license over and stared at it, but what I saw didn't fully, immediately register. The face, it was familiar, the way her hair was pulled back in a ponytail. Her eyes were piercing, and she was giving this look as if she was about to call out my name, not in any sort of plea, but casually, like she had a million times before. *Where do you want to eat. What movie do you want to see. Let's go grab a drink after work.*

I melted at her image, almost as if I hadn't realized yet why I was seeing it.

And then I did, and I screamed, except nothing would come out. Finally, with blurred vision and with trembling hands, I read her name, just to be sure I hadn't lost my mind, that my eyes weren't playing tricks on my brain. But it was there in black and white, the newest victim of the Phantom Fiend.

Elizabeth Riggs.

32

Next thing I knew, the door of the ATM storefront blasted open, and I looked up to see Hank Sweeney, sweating and panting, lunging toward me. Much later, I'd ask him why he didn't simply buzz the door open with his bank card rather than kick it down with his foot. And at that time, he'd explain to me that he didn't carry a card because he didn't trust what he called those "fancy-schmancy financial gimmicks," adding, "I'm a cash-and-carry kind of guy."

On his end of the two-way radio connection, he thought I was a man in distress. And I was, just not in the way he expected. I was hunched over the counter with the ATM deposit envelopes and the pens chained to the faux-wood top. I showed him the license in my hand and he said, "Oh God. That son of a fucking bitch."

By the way, alarms were sounding, courtesy of Hank and the broken door. I have virtually no doubt that our images were clearly captured on the two surveillance cameras inside, and soon enough, our faces would be hanging on bulletin boards in post offices as far away as Nebraska and Wyoming.

He grabbed me by the arm and the two of us bolted out the door and across Tremont Street toward his parked car. When I put my fingers on the door handle, a synapse fired in my brain and I exclaimed, "Fuck!" I looked across the roof of the car at Hank and said, "I'll be right back." And I bolted across the street from whence I came, weaving amid the late-night traffic.

When I got to the ATM, the dog was still inside — sitting by the glass door, which was broken but shut, just staring out into the dark street. When he saw me approach, he stood up and began to pace, his tail furiously wagging. When I stepped inside, he was crying with joy.

I scooped him up in my arms, all seventy or so pounds of him, and scampered back across the street, carrying him all the way to Hank's car, his head resting placidly on my shoulder, his wet muzzle pushing against my ear. When I pushed him into the backseat, Hank flatly said, "You're going to put that beast in my nice clean car?"

I gave him a look.

Hank asked, "How do we know he doesn't bite?"

I looked back at the dog, who had already spread himself out across the seat, panting softly, staring straight ahead in contentment. I said, "Hank, he's wondering the exact same thing about you. Shut up and drive."

So he threw the car into drive — Hank, not the dog, though where we were heading, I neither knew nor particularly cared. I pulled my cell phone out, located Elizabeth Riggs's cell phone number on my speed dial, and pressed Call.

It took an agonizing moment to connect, and finally I heard a ring. Then another. And another — five times in all. Her recorded voice came on the line and said, "You've reached Elizabeth. You don't need me to explain what to do." And then a beep. The futility of this exercise was starting to overtake me, yet I left a message anyway. You don't have anything when you don't have hope.

"Elizabeth, Jack. This is an emergency. Call me immediately. Immediately. Please." And I hung up.

I located her home number on my speed dial and pressed Call. Same drill — another agonizing moment, then a ring, followed by several more, followed by her voice saying, "Sorry I'm not around. Let me know who it is, and we'll talk soon."

"Elizabeth, Jack. Sorry for the hour, but this is really, really important. Call me ASAP on my cell."

I stared at my cell, willing it to ring. In the meantime, I punched out 411 and asked an operator to connect me to San Francisco Police. I thought of that night at the San Francisco Airport, her sidling up to me, the casual banter, the look she gave me after I kissed her on the cheek, her bombshell announcement that she was pregnant.

And then it struck me like a lightning bolt that someone had followed me out to Las Vegas, and had seen me in the waiting lounge with Elizabeth. He undoubtedly assumed we were lovers, and that's why he targeted her now.

"Hold the line, please, for the San Francisco Police Department." That was the woman from directory assistance, patching me through.

Another woman answered the phone and informed me that this call was being recorded. I told her that someone in her city might be in trouble. She asked, skeptically, what I meant. Good question. I told her I

451

had received an ominous threat. She asked the address. I gave it to her. Then I gave her my number.

That call ended, I looked at Hank and said, "Where are we headed?"

"The newsroom. It's where you do your best thinking." And then he added, "You need to call Boston PD."

I did. He was right. But something was holding me back, that something known as distrust. Still, his first simple answer — "the newsroom" — jarred something in my head, and I pulled my phone open again, dialed 411, and asked for the number for *The New York Times*.

After an infuriating five-minute session with the newspaper's automatic telephone system, a real live human being finally picked up a phone, announcing in a bored voice, "National Desk." It was now 1:45 a.m. I suspected they were just past deadline for their final edition.

I said, "This is Jack Flynn. I'm a reporter for the *Boston Record*. Is the national editor on duty around?"

"You're talking to him." No name, no nothing. His voice remained every bit as bored and almost painstakingly unimpressed by the announcement of my identity. I mean, I assumed everyone at *The Times* knew who I was, dating back to that botched presidential assassination deal a few years back when I kicked the shit out of them for a month straight on the biggest story in the world. And here I was at the heart of another story that was increasingly national in scope.

I said, "Sir, this is something of a life-and-death emergency. I'm the *Record*'s reporter on the Phantom Fiend/Boston Strangler story. I desperately need to contact your San Francisco reporter, Elizabeth Riggs, but she's not answering her home or cell phone number. Do you know if she's on the road? Have you talked to her recently?"

"Tell me your name again."

Good Christ. Your name would have to be Bartleby Hornsby III to have any impact on these clowns, and then the most he'd probably ask is if I had a brother who went to Deerfield or Exeter.

"Jack Flynn," I said, gritting my teeth.

Hank was steering through the Theater District now, such as it is in Boston, heading toward the highway for the short jaunt to the *Record*.

"And why do you need her?" Bored as ever, the words coming out of his mouth like marshmallows.

I said, "She may be in grave danger. Look,

453

I'm a *Record* reporter. I'm covering this story. If it helps at all, *The Times* has twice offered me a job."

Working in the company cafeteria.

I fell silent. I could hear him pecking around a keyboard, presumably with his fingers. And then he said, sleepily, "Our file shows she's in Boston on assignment."

My heart fell even further, if that's possible, and I didn't think it was. One more bit of bad news and the thing would be beating in the soles of my feet — or not beating at all.

I said, "When did she get here and where is she staying?"

More silence, though I could again hear the pecking in the near background.

He cleared his throat. "Tell me your name again," he said.

I did. Then he said, "The Fairmont Copley Plaza hotel. I have her down in Room 533. She was supposed to have arrived yesterday."

I hung up without saying good-bye, and all but screamed at Hank to point the car toward Copley Square, which he did.

On the way crosstown, on the virtually empty streets, I punched out 411 again and asked for the hotel number. It rang through and a man in an unfamiliar accent — prob-

454

ably best known as hotelier — answered the phone. When I asked for Elizabeth Riggs's room, he hesitated for what felt like forever, asked me to spell it, put me on hold, and then got back on the line.

"I'll put you right through, sir," he said. And he did.

The phone rang once, twice, three times, then four, before it kicked over to an automated voice system with a generic woman's voice.

"Elizabeth, Jack. Call me," I pleaded.

I hung up. We were about a minute out, zipping through the South End, Hank intent behind the wheel, the dog stretched out and sound asleep already in the back, and me just about climbing onto the roof of the car.

About thirty seconds out, and my cell phone rang. Hank whispered, "Thank God." The dog raised his head. I waited until the second ring, saw that the caller ID said "Unavailable," which could well be the designation for a big hotel, and answered the phone with high hopes.

"Jack here."

Silence.

Well, not exactly silence, but a muffled noise, which could have been a woman fighting off an attacker, fighting for her life in a hotel room that might be the last place she'd ever see.

I just about shouted, "Who's there?"

More muffled sounds, as if someone's hand was cupped over the phone to mask the commotion in the background. And then I heard a vaguely familiar male voice say to me, "Jack, I'm in some trouble. I need your help."

Vinny Mongillo.

But the thing was, it sounded nothing like the Vinny that I knew so well. This Vinny was seriously distressed and somewhat embarrassed. He sounded exhausted, and scared.

I said, "Vin, I'm in the middle of a world of trouble right now. Tell me fast."

And unlike the typical Vinny Mongillo, who would have imparted some sort of sarcastic or even caustic comment here, he did.

"I've been taken into custody by the Boston Police. They're about to charge me with something in relation to the Boston Strangler case. It's not what you think. It's not what they think either."

Hank was wheeling around the hotel, pulling up to the side entrance. My mind flashed to Vinny's letter in the garage on Rodeo Road — a letter that was still in my pocket at that moment. Was I missing something? Was there a link I hadn't made, a connection I couldn't grasp? Was Vinny capable of doing something that I couldn't even imagine?

He continued, "I'm going to need a lawyer and some bail. I'm in headquarters. This is the only call they're giving me. And you and I desperately need to speak. Can you get here as soon as possible?"

This was a lot to process. By now the car was stopped. Hank was out his door. I said, "Vinny, soon as I can. I have something else I'm taking care of right now, but soon as I can."

And I leapt out. Hank and I dashed side by side through the door. Inside, I slammed my hand against the elevator call button. A bell dinged, the doors opened, and we were in business. The ride up felt like we were climbing Mount Everest. When we hit the top, we ran left, then right, then right again, and there we were, the two of us, Hank and me, standing directly outside of Room 533. He glanced at me and I glanced at him. That's when I reached out and firmly knocked.

33

Some of the best hotel nights in my life have been spent in the stately rooms of the landmark building that is Boston's Fairmont Copley Plaza hotel. I spent my wedding night in the presidential suite. I used to stay there when I was a Washington reporter for the *Boston Record* during my frequent trips home. My own mother would visit me and look around at the valets and the concierge and the turndown service, and she'd smile that smile of hers and say to me, "You think you're such a big shot." Maybe I did.

I'd spent many a night in the Oak Bar with Elizabeth Riggs, listening to great jazz musicians beneath the frescoed thirty-foot ceilings, sipping cocktails served by waitresses and bartenders who counted their tenure not by years but by decades. I once gleaned invaluable information from an old friend named Gus in a corner suite at the hotel as I reported one devastating story after another about the mysterious background of the president of the United States.

All these good feelings and good memories, along with so much more, were about to come crashing to an end on this night, because when you really think about it, that's what happens in life — things end.

No one answered my knock. There wasn't so much as a whisper of a sound from inside the room, at least as far as we could hear, and Hank should have been able to with his ear pressed up against the door. I turned the knob and it was locked. Hank pulled back a step, looked at me, and asked, "Do you want the manager to open the door, or do you want me to do it?"

I hated the idea of some nervous hotel manager arguing with me about disturbing guests, possibly summoning police to join us in this search, and then ending with six or eight people walking in on Elizabeth Riggs's body all at once. I wanted to see her alone, or at least only with Hank, as macabre as that might seem.

So I pointed to Hank. Before I could even drop my arm, his foot slammed against the door at its most vulnerable point. The door, in turn, flew open, bounced off a door stop, and started closing again. But by the time it had come back, Hank's foot was already inside. He had a gun drawn. And he stepped into the room, firmly reciting the words "Law enforcement. Hands up. We've got a whole crew here."

He stood in the shadowy entryway, illuminated only by the dim hall sconces behind us, as I forged past him. The lights were off, and I ran my hand up and down a nearby wall, looking for a switch. When I found one, I said to Hank, "I'm turning them on."

And I did.

I was expecting the absolute worst, and why shouldn't I have been? Every time I received a driver's license from the Phantom Fiend, or a video, a pretty young woman was dead, the body left in some gruesome manner by a publicity-seeking killer who immediately reported his misdeeds to me.

My eyes first settled on the bed, assuming that's where he'd probably leave her. And so I was shocked to see that the bed, apparently turned down by the maids that evening, was completely empty — just a comforter wrapped in a white duvet cover stretched tight across the wide expanse.

Hank repeated himself: "Law enforcement. Get your hands up before we shoot."

As he said it, he was holding his gun out like he was Don Johnson on *Miami Vice*.

The room, by the way, was a big, elegant affair, what some lesser hotels might describe as a junior suite. The carpet was royal blue, the walls were a pale yellow, and the furniture, every piece substantial in size, was tasteful in an Old World kind of way. The entire room flowed toward a sitting area tucked inside a bow window that overlooked the grassy park at the center of Copley Square.

And right now, it appeared entirely empty.

Well, not entirely. As I slowly walked through it, I could see the signs that we were, in fact, in the right place — Elizabeth's computer case, an overnight bag that I remember loading in the trunk of the car so many times, a barn jacket that I had bought her tossed across an upholstered chair. Another telltale sign: an empty bottle of Tab on her dresser. Who else in this life still drinks Tab?

As I walked toward the windows, which were near the bathroom entrance, Hank held his big, bearlike hand up to me, the one without the gun. I stopped. He looked under the bed. Then he began slowly walking toward the bathroom door, the gun poised at his side.

461

"You've got two seconds to come out," he said.

No reaction. He arrived at the door, which was slightly ajar, and pushed it slowly with his foot, the door swinging into the dark bathroom. I squinted, remembering full well that at least one of the Boston Strangler's victims back in the sixties was found in a bathtub. Hank reached his hand inside the door, flicked on the overhead light, and scanned the small space with his gun.

Again, nothing.

He looked at me and said in that easy voice of his, "Well, son, at this point, anything that's not bad is good." And don't ask me how, but that made all the sense in the world.

Now, suddenly, I felt like an intruder, a feeling that was reinforced when two beefy gentlemen in ill-fitting button-down shirts, apparently security guards, showed up at the broken doorway, saying, "If you move another inch you'll regret it."

Hank doesn't seem to know regret, which is one of the many things I love about the guy, so he walked calmly and casually toward them, gun at his side. One of the guards barked at him, "Hey, Gramps, stop where you are and put the gun on the bed."

Hank said, "My only son was killed before he ever had any children, so nice as it sounds, my name isn't Gramps."

The security guard didn't particularly seem to care, poignant as Hank's declaration was. He said, "One more step and I will break your fucking face."

So then I started walking toward them. No one talks to Hank like that, not when he's protecting me. Did I mention, by the way, that they were unarmed?

The two security guards were inside the room now, one of them chest to chest with me. I had no idea what was about to happen, but I know what did. A uniformed police officer appeared in the doorway and exclaimed, "Lookie here, Hank Sweeney, the man behind the myth."

Hank beamed. The security detail looked confused. I still considered all this a colossal waste of time, given that Elizabeth Riggs was still either dead or in imminent danger of becoming that way.

Hank and the cop, a guy introduced to me as Tommy Reilly, made small talk. Another cop showed up, and the first cop introduced the two of them. Then Reilly said to Hank, "I don't know what the hell you're doing breaking into a hotel room, but I assume you have good reason. Anything you need us to do?"

Hank started answering, started explaining about a woman being in extreme danger, when Tommy Reilly pulled his radio from his belt, contacted headquarters, and ordered whoever it was on the other end of the line to put out an immediate all-points bulletin for an Elizabeth Riggs. He stifled the radio for a moment, asked me for her date of birth and a physical description, which I gave him, and he relayed that information as well.

Reilly said to me, as well as Hank, "Technically, I should take you down to headquarters for some more information, especially since you have information in what might be a — well, might be something that's pretty dire."

Hank replied, "Technically, yeah, but the thing is, we slipped out before you had a chance to ask us."

The cop nodded. Hank grabbed my elbow and said in his easy, matter-of-fact voice, "We're out of here." And we were, leaving the broken door and the empty room behind, but carrying my deepest fears along the way.

Down in the lobby, another pair of uniformed cops were rushing into the elevator and up to the fifth floor. A couple — the man in a tuxedo, the woman in an evening gown — were bickering over something that was undoubtedly profoundly unimportant, but ruinous nonetheless to what was supposed to have been a grand night.

Hank and I faced each other, standing amid the gold-gilded environs of the Copley Plaza, unsure what to do and where to go. I should have been exhausted, but I wasn't. Rather, I was so frustrated by the events, by the complexities, by my helplessness, by the police higher-ups, by my own newspaper, by Paul Vasco's bravado, by Vinny Mongillo's secrets, that I thought I was going to explode.

It was either this or be sitting on a volcanic beach at one of the best resorts in Hawaii.

Wearily, I said to Hank, "In the absence of any better idea, we should get over to police headquarters to see what the hell is going on with Vinny."

Hank replied, "The better idea might be to have a quick word with Elizabeth before we go."

I shot him an incredulous look, as in what the hell was he talking about. He nodded calmly and casually down the long, carpeted hallway toward the front door of the hotel. I looked in that direction, and in the distance, Elizabeth Riggs was walking toward us, accompanied by Boston Police Detective Mac Foley.

"Wait for them here," Hank said softly, not even turning to face me. So I did.

She was wearing a sweater and a pair of jeans, carrying a notebook in her right hand, her hips swiveling in that way they do, her hair framing both sides of her face. My body nearly went limp at the sight of her — limp with joy, with relief. It was as if the only emotion that had been propping me up was that of utter fear.

At the same time, the sight of Mac Foley with Elizabeth gnawed at some nugget of suspicion buried deep within my brain — or maybe it was buried inside my gut. It was nothing overt, but I felt a latent sense of unease for which I wasn't yet able to provide words or thoughts.

The two of them were walking and talking. Elizabeth wasn't wearing or carrying a coat, indicating that they had been in the Oak Bar, which was just closing for the night. They would have walked right by us without noticing, except I said, "Hello there, Elizabeth Riggs."

She stopped, looked, and allowed a big smile to spread across her face. "Hello there, Jack Flynn."

At the same time, Mac Foley exclaimed,

"I don't believe it, the legendary Hank Sweeney, in the flesh. Look at you, you look like you could step back into roll call tomorrow."

Hank smiled. Elizabeth said to me, "What are you doing here?"

"I was about to ask you the same question."

"*The Times* has me nipping at your heels on the Phantom Fiend story. Jack, this is really terrifying."

She was about to find out just how terrifying.

I asked, "Did you lose your driver's license?"

Hank and Foley began chatting amiably about the old days and the new ones. More stragglers from the Oak Bar wandered past us. Elizabeth gave me a surprised look and said, "Yeah, someone swiped my wallet when I got into Boston this morning. How'd you know?"

"Because I have it," I said. "I hate to tell you this, though you have no idea how happy I am to be given the chance. It was sent to me by someone claiming to be the Phantom. There was no note, no nothing. The way I took it, the Phantom was telling me that you were his next victim. I'm so thrilled to find you alive that I almost can't speak."

She stood in uncharacteristic shock for a long moment, her eyes staring into mine, trying to process what I had just said. Foley glanced over and said, "Hey there, Jack." Then, to Elizabeth, "Everything all right?"

She didn't answer. Instead she looked at me, her laudable first instinct always to protect a reporter's information, rather than share with authorities. I said to Foley, "Just some more dramatics in the case. Your colleagues up on the fifth floor can fill you in."

Hank spoke up for the first time, saying to Elizabeth, "You're one hell of a pretty sight for a lot of reasons."

Elizabeth gave him an exaggerated wide-eyed look, then a kiss on the cheek.

I said to her, "Let me grab you for a second over here." Not literally. But I pulled her aside as Mac Foley watched us walk a few paces away.

"Listen, the cops are going to offer you protection. I'd just as soon have Hank watch over you. There are too many moving parts, and I can be sure he's not one of them."

Truth is, I was so relieved as to be almost euphoric, but at the same time so exhausted as to be a zombie. And yet something, some distant feeling, a little emotional tic, kept tapping at my gut.

She stared me straight in the eyes, her look a cross of confusion and vulnerability, and she said, "I'll do what you think is best."

I let my guard down a bit and told her, "I'm just glad you're okay. This isn't what I expected to find: you alive, talking to me, the two of us figuring out a plan. This isn't what I expected to find at all. Thank God I did."

Elizabeth took a step toward me, maybe cutting in half the distance between us. If I took a step forward as well, there wouldn't be any distance between us, and maybe that's what I was supposed to do. But I didn't. Didn't matter. She said, "Why don't you stay here tonight. You love hotels."

I did, and the invitation was an extraordinary one, the type of offer that could boost your spirits for hours or weeks or maybe longer.

I had been up the entire night before, after Edgar Sullivan was killed. I had flown to Vegas early that morning, hunted through the boxes in the desert heat, jetted back here, met my friend Rover in the darkest sliver of Boston, learned that my ex-girlfriend might be dead, burst into her hotel room, found her alive in the lobby, and now I'd just received an invitation to stay with her.

I was about to answer in the affirmative when the vision of Vinny Mongillo popped into my mind. This isn't a good thing to have happen at any time of any day, but it's especially bad when it happens at two-thirty in the morning and essentially means you've got to take a rain check on any extracurriculars with a woman you once loved and perhaps still love.

I said, "I'd love to, but believe it or not, this day's not over."

She replied, "You're about to kick the shit out of us on this story, aren't you?"

She was designated as a Phantom victim. And she's worried about getting beat in the next day's paper. No wonder why I feel the way I do about her.

"I hope so," I said.

With that, I kissed her on the cheek. I told Hank his new assignment was to make sure she stayed alive. Then I gave Mac Foley a long look before I walked out the hotel door.

On the street, I opened up Hank's back door and beckoned the black Labrador to come with me. I hailed a cab, and the two of us settled into the backseat, sitting side by side.

That little tic was turning into a hard rap,

and I was beginning to get a better handle on why.

34

The aging desk sergeant at Boston Police headquarters at Schroeder Plaza barely looked up when he asked, "What do you need?"

What did I need? Where to begin. How about starting with a fresh lead on the Phantom Fiend, a way to tie the murders to the person I believed was in all probability committing them: Paul Vasco.

Then how about giving my dear colleague Edgar Sullivan the final years he deserved in peace?

How about giving me the real Peter Martin back, the one who would never tolerate the publisher checking in with city officials before deciding what to print — or, more relevant in this case, what not to print? How about letting me be just an everyday excellent reporter, and not some mouthpiece for a crazed serial murderer who seems to have emerged some forty years later?

I didn't think this particular officer of the law was of the mind or place to give me any of this, so instead what I requested was directions to the visiting room in the station lockup. This prompted him to look up at me for the first time in our brief exchange, a weary look on his face. He said in a tone that dripped contempt, "Who wants to know?"

"My name is Jack Flynn. I'm a reporter for the *Boston Record*."

He looked at me for a long moment, his eyes wandering across my face. His expression changed as he pulled his glasses off his face and rubbed his eyes. He said to me in a voice that reached toward politeness, "Take that elevator over there down one floor. I'll call ahead and have an officer on duty meet you there and take you to where you're supposed to be."

It was three o'clock now, and as I walked across the hard floor of the wide expanse of the lobby, the sergeant called out to me, "Good luck, kid. You're doing important work."

I wish I could have captured that on tape, because trust me when I say that cops don't ordinarily talk to ink-stained scribes like that.

Downstairs, a similarly aging — and

respectful — sergeant met me at the elevator bank and escorted me into a windowless room furnished with only a pair of wooden benches and a row of four plastic chairs bolted to the tile floor. At the far end of the room was a pair of thick Plexiglas windows with a wall phone next to each one, just like you see on TV. I couldn't believe that in a moment I'd be sitting there talking to Vinny Mongillo through a bulletproof partition.

Fortunately, I never did. Just as I sat down on one of the benches, without so much as a dated *People* magazine to pass the time, a heavy steel door opened in the far corner, and in walked Vinny Mongillo, shaking a fistful of peanut M&M's out of the familiar bright yellow bag. He turned around and said to the uniformed cop walking behind him, "Thanks a million, Ralphie. And make sure you tell Jane I said she's all wet on the mother-in-law issue."

Ralphie said to both of us, "I'll leave you boys to yourselves. Knock on the window when you're done." He laughed and added, "Nothing conjugal." My skin crawled, but that's okay. It was good to see Vinny, even behind bars.

Vinny raised his eyebrows at me, then sat down on a facing bench, about five feet apart from me. He finished off the last of his M&M's without offering me any, which I guess was okay, seeing as I could buy some on the way home, and maybe he wouldn't be going home, not tonight, anyway. He seemed infinitely more relaxed than he sounded on the phone, far more himself.

Amid his crunching I said, "Um, do you want to explain all this?"

He nodded, but as he did, he looked at the floor between us rather than at me. He crinkled up his bag and stuck it in the side pocket of his heavy khakis, his gaze never looking up. It was quiet in the room, the buzz of the overhead fluorescent lights creating the only sounds.

Finally, he said to me, "My mother was one of the Boston Strangler victims — she went back to her maiden name, and I thought I could keep it secret." When he said this, his eyes never left the grimy patch of floor just beyond his feet.

"I know," I replied. "And I'm sorry about that. I really am. I wish you had told me earlier."

His head jerked up, and he looked at me for the first time since he entered the room. "How long have you known?" he asked. His eyes betrayed a sadness that I could all too well understand. Sadness, and resignation.

Before I could respond to his first question, he asked another: "Why didn't you say anything?"

"I just found out yesterday, and I had to fly all the way to Las Vegas to learn about it. That retired BPD detective, Bob Walters, left a bunch of old files and other pilfered evidence in his garage. Your name was in there."

Vinny nodded. "A good man," he said. "He tried his best, just like a lot of others. Their best just wasn't good enough.

"And you," he added, "you're no Vinny Mongillo, but you're still pretty good. I figured you were going to find this out. It was just a matter of how and when."

I wanted to talk more about Bob Walters, wanted to know what exactly he meant. But I also wanted to know why Vinny Mongillo, my Vinny Mongillo, was sitting in a Boston Police Department holding cell in connection to perhaps the most storied serial murders in the nation's history. So for lack of a better way to put it, I asked, "Vinny, what the hell are you doing in here?"

He nodded, pursing his lips as he did, and he fell silent, his gaze again dropping to the floor. I felt a sense of dread roll down my spine. Could Vinny be charged in his own mother's slaying? Impossible, I quickly concluded; he would have been far too young. Could he have some role in the new murders? That I wasn't quite so certain about, even if I was.

I said, "Vinny?" The word came out more pointed than I had intended, but it seemed to snap him back to the present.

He said, "They want to charge me with receiving stolen property. The head of homicide, a guy I don't know well, is saying that's the minimum charge I'm going to face. He said they plan to look into what else I might have done."

He paused, his eyes meeting mine again, and he added, "I'm a little worried about some of these bastards framing me on something."

I swallowed hard, trying to process the little I had just learned. Questions filled my head, so I began releasing them.

"What's the stolen property?" I asked.

He stared me square in the face and said, "The knife used to kill Albert DeSalvo."

The knife. The infamous missing knife. The knife that held DNA evidence that could determine whether Albert DeSalvo was indeed the Boston Strangler. The knife that Hank Sweeney told me I needed to find was right under my nose all along. It could have been sitting in a Ziploc bag in the bottom drawer of a colleague's desk, for chrissakes.

I asked, "You have the knife, as in, *the* knife?"

I'm not sure why I felt the need to ask again. In response, he nodded.

"How did you get it?"

"Detective Bob Walters gave it to me."

Immediately, my mind clicked to my bedside interview with Walters, the grungy room, the sallow look on his face, his determination to have some things known.

I had the knife. I gave it away.

He had said that so matter-of-factly.

I gave it to the family of one of the victims.

It gave them closure. That's a fancy word that all the victim advocates use for helping them get over the fact that the human race sucks. That knife wasn't doing me a damned bit of good.

And then that thank-you note from Vinny to Bob Walters.

My dying grandfather, though, needs to believe that my mother's killer has been caught and killed. He's been very sick with cancer, and as he tries to cope with his pain, it helps him to think that DeSalvo was the murderer. That's why your package was so helpful to him.

I finally said, "It was you who Bob Walters

gave the knife to all those years ago?"

Vinny looked at me quizzically, but the look quickly faded to his prior despondence. "The problem," he said, "is proving it. It's not the kind of thing you get a receipt for."

Don't be so sure. But before I explained what I had, I asked, "How did the cops find out you had the knife?"

He shook his head and said, "Because I gave it to them. I'd been holding it all these years, preserving it, because it held all these wonderful, scientific clues in regard to DNA. I gave it to a source of mine over at the police lab because they had pulled out some evidence from the original stranglings. This source said he'd do some tests on the sly. But someone else in the lab got wind, and next thing you know, I've got Boston's finest pulling me off the treadmill to take me downtown. One asshole even tried putting me in cuffs before a cop friend cut in. Evidence tampering, receiving stolen goods. All that crap."

I said, "Bob Walters might be helping you again — from the grave."

This prompted him to give me a look that wasn't so much curious as annoyed. "The fuck you talking about, Fair Hair? Come on, I could find myself in some real shit here, and the last thing this paper needs right now as we get this story shoved down our throats is for one of our lead reporters on it to be carted off to prison for possible involvement in the case. I mean, the *Traveler*'s going to have a fucking field day with this."

That they would, and for good reason. I said, "You think the higher-ups here are hassling us to quash the story?"

He nodded hard. He was the old Vinny again, animated to the point of being emotional. "They absolutely are. They hate this story, because all it can do is hurt the guys who used to be in charge — Hal Harrison and Stu Callaghan. There's nothing good in this for them. They know it's not going away, because these murders aren't going away. But they don't want the *Record* to be on a crusade. If they weaken us, we can't be."

He was telling me what I already knew, but it was good to hear nonetheless, reaffirming in a world that was suddenly spinning beyond control.

I said, "So they charge you with receiving stolen merchandise. They ominously say that the investigation is 'continuing.' Maybe they bring some witnesses before a grand jury and leak a few tidbits to the opposition. And suddenly, the focus isn't on them, it isn't on the Phantom Fiend, but on the *Record*'s coverage of the Phantom Fiend."

Vinny nodded again. "And I'm stuck in the middle."

"Maybe not."

He gave me that annoyed look again.

I reached into my coat pocket, pulled out the sheet of paper, and unfolded it. I began to read to him the particularly pertinent parts, concluding with, "That's why your package was so helpful to him."

I thought Vinny might start to cry, and I knew if he did, it wouldn't be because I had just saved his sorry and substantial ass, but because of the paper, which is just another reason why I love him so, even if I'd never want a conjugal visit.

"I have my receipt," he said, nearly in disbelief. "Holy shit, I have my goddamned receipt."

He simply stared at me in wonderment, the way a dog might stare at the master that just gave him a particularly meaty bone. Then he said, "Next time I'm about to think something negative about you, which will probably be within the next thirty minutes, I'll think of how you got this letter."

"Good policy," I replied.

He said, "Now, in case they charge me, did you bring bail?"

I reached deep into my pants pocket and pulled out three single dollar bills and thirty-nine cents, holding it all out to him. "You think this will cover it?"

"Forget what I said," he replied. "You really are still a horse's ass."

I ignored that, which is my right, and instead gave him the *Reader's Digest* version of the Elizabeth Riggs saga. He shook his head in disbelief and said, "This thing's out of control."

I changed my tone and said, "Vinny, think back for a second to this past Tuesday, to Lauren Hutchens's place on Park Drive. When you went down to meet the cops, you never even made it to the elevator, right?"

He replied, "Right. They were just getting off."

I asked, "Had you pressed the call button yet?"

"No."

I stayed quiet for a moment. He was looking at me suspiciously, squinting, the wheels turning inside his head just as they were already turning inside of mine.

I said, "I never told Foley on the phone what apartment Lauren Hutchens lived in. It wasn't on the mailbox. It wasn't in the phone directory. It wasn't in any information I could find online."

I paused, looking at Mongillo sitting there looking at me in the locked confines of a Boston Police visitation room. I asked, "How did they know to come to the fourth floor?"

Mongillo said nothing. He said nothing for many long moments until he asked, "You're sure you didn't tell Foley?"

I nodded. "Positive. Something's been bothering me for a while on this, and I couldn't figure it out. It came together when I saw Foley walking with Elizabeth toward her room tonight — at the same time I got the driver's license saying she was a Phantom victim."

I paused, thinking of the absurdity of it all: the detective as a serial killer, then and now. Then I said, "I never told the cops, but they knew exactly where to go. How?"

Mongillo looked at me hard and said, "Fair Hair, this is a pretty fucking extraordinary allegation you're bantering about here —"

"Let me check something," I said, cutting him off. I pulled out my cell phone, snapped it open, and called Elizabeth Riggs. It was three in the morning, but I was pretty certain she wouldn't be asleep yet. Hell, she and Hank were probably replaying their favorite Jack Flynn moments — or at least that's what I wanted to think.

Elizabeth picked up on the second ring, sounding not like I woke her up.

"Jack here," I said, all business now. "Let me ask you something. Were you supposed to meet Mac Foley earlier today instead of tonight?"

Hesitation, then she said, "Yeah. I did. Early this afternoon. We met for an interview in the hotel. But I got a call from the national desk and had to run out on something else just as it began. So he agreed to come back later."

She paused, then asked, "Why?"

"I'll explain later," I said. "Is Hank right there?"

"Yeah, we were just talking about you."

See?

Hank got on the phone and I said, "I'll explain this later, but don't let her out of your sight, and don't let Mac Foley within it."

He replied in his easy voice, "I'll be waiting to hear this one."

When I hung up, I said to Mongillo, "There was a cop at the scene of the Lauren Hutchens murder who you seemed to know pretty well — Woody, if I remember right. I need you to ask him how he knew the apartment number."

"Woody Garner," Vinny replied. He looked at the clock on the wall, which said 3:05, and asked, "Now?"

"As soon as you can."

He got up, walked over to the Plexiglas, and rapped on the window. The same cop as before came to the door, and Vinny said, "Hey, Ralphie, any chance you could check when Woody Garner's on the clock again? Knowing him, it's probably sometime next month."

Ralphie laughed as if this was funny, then disappeared. He came back two minutes later and said, "Computer shows he's doing an overnight detail for the gas company as we speak."

Vinny, sitting across from me again, asked for his cell number.

"Always needing something else," Ralphie responded. Then he gave it to him and disappeared again.

I offered Vinny my phone, but he reached into his back pocket and pulled out his own.

"They let a prisoner keep a cell phone?" I asked.

"Hey, it's one thing to take away my liberty. It would be cruel and unusual punishment to take away my cell phone. Ralphie understands that."

A moment later he said into the phone,

"Woody, baby, Vinny Mong here. You never call, you never write."

Silence.

"You kidding me?" he said. "It works like a dream. I've lost two pounds already. I've got to hook you up with this guru I have. You'll love her."

Silence.

"Listen, I've got an odd question."

Silence.

"Yeah, I'm an insomniac. At least you're making money for not sleeping. Anyway, like I said, odd question. When you were courageously and heroically the first one to arrive at that murder scene Tuesday, how'd you know what apartment that dead girl was in?"

Silence.

"You're sure?"

Silence.

"Hundred percent?"

Silence.

"Thanks, Woody. Cut down on the fruits. That's the whole key. I know you have this thing for applesauce. No more applesauce, okay? We'll get together and play a little handball."

He hung up and said to me, "Woody says the order came down from Mac Foley with the street address and apartment number.

He's sure."

I shook my head, got up, and rapped on the Plexiglas, at once incredulous at what I was thinking, exhilarated that I was finally seeing little cracks of light, and nervous over what was to come.

Ralphie appeared again and I said, "I'm ready to go, sir."

Mongillo called out, "What the fuck? What about me?"

Good question. "When they're ready to let you out, call."

I got outside, climbed into the awaiting cab next to a snoring dog, and promptly fell asleep before I ever got home. The day that wouldn't end was finally over.

Well, almost.

35

I staggered through the door to my condominium at three-thirty in the company of a guard dog newly named Huck — a combination of Hank and Buck, the two bodyguards who were no longer at my side.

The two of us stumbled into the kitchen and both had a long drink of water — Huck from one of Baker's old bowls that I could never bring myself to throw away, me from a bottle of Poland Spring that represented the only food in my refrigerator. My excuse could be that I had been planning on being on my honeymoon for two weeks, but in truth I never had anything in my refrigerator. Maybe that's one reason I had wanted to get married. A full refrigerator makes for a full life — or something like that.

"You ready for bed, old boy?"

That was me talking to Huck, the sound of my voice sounding odd in the silence of my house. He looked up at me and wagged his tail. The two of us could get used to each other's company pretty fast, I suspected.

I shut out the kitchen light and wandered through the dark expanse of the living room, Huck swishing behind me. Halfway through, I heard a low growl and said, "Come on, pal, you can find me." The growling continued on the other side of the room where he had stopped.

So I flicked on a lamp. I was at the door of my bedroom, which was closed. Huck was sitting perfectly rigid next to the couch, his eyes open wide, his head slightly cocked, his stare shifting from me to the bedroom and back to me, growling in between.

"You want to sleep out here?" I asked. "You can sleep anywhere you want. Me, I'm going to bed."

He continued to growl — a low gurgle, really. I walked over to him and crouched down, putting my face toward his. He kept looking around the apartment, looking into the open doors that led to the dark spaces of the other bedroom, the entry hall, the bathroom. I rubbed his head, only to feel how rigid his entire body had become. He looked at me mournfully, and I said, "Do you sense my dog? Is that what it is? Can you smell Baker?"

Huck kept looking around, tense. I said,

"Look, I've got to get some sleep. You can stand sentry all night, if you'd like, but that's your choice."

He didn't budge.

I clicked off the living room light, sending the apartment into total darkness again. That's when I heard the noise.

It began softly, like a distant movement, maybe a rustle, cloth against cloth. It came from behind my bedroom door, leading me to assume I had left a window open and the drapes were blowing in the breeze.

I was about to open the door when Huck let out a low, guttural woof — more a directive to me than a warning to anyone else. I pulled my hand off the knob and looked back at him as he stared intensely at the door. His actions, or maybe they were reactions, were now making me tense.

Then another sound.

This one was more like footsteps — definitely movement, someone or something walking on the carpeted floor of my bedroom. I thought immediately of Edgar Sullivan, shot dead in a CVS a little more than twenty-four hours ago, and how unspeakably sad that really was. I thought of Joshua Carpenter, gunned down in the Boston Public Garden while he mourned his late wife. And now whoever did that might well be in my apartment, lying in wait for me.

I looked back at the dog and put a finger over my mouth, in the universal sign that requested he not bark. I'm not sure he understood, though maybe he did. Something creaked from behind the door, and then everything fell quiet.

I thought of stepping outside and calling the police. The police, at least one of them, might have been the bad guys in all this, given what I suspected Mac Foley was up to. So I put that plan on hold. I thought of calling Hank, but didn't want to leave Elizabeth Riggs unprotected. I thought of calling Vinny Mongillo, but he was stuck in jail. I thought of calling Peter Martin, but unless I planned to nag the intruder to death, that wouldn't do any good.

So I put my hand on the doorknob again. I was tired. I was frustrated. I was furious over having been unwittingly lured into the center of a lurid tale, alliteration intended. I was even angrier over the fact that people, innocent people, good people, had died. And in a more honest moment, I would probably confess that I felt more than a little guilty that I was still alive.

So without further ado, I flung the door open, simultaneously yelling, "Don't fucking move!"

I'm not quite sure what I expected to find, though it probably involved a man in a black ski hat holding a semiautomatic weapon pointed at my face. Didn't matter; I wanted to confront whoever it was that was trying to do whatever it was that they were doing. I wanted to see the face. I wanted to take a swing. Maybe, just maybe, I'd surprise him. Maybe I'd wrestle him to the ground, knock him out cold, summon authorities, and gain my biggest clue yet as to what the hell was going on.

Well, I didn't find that. Any of that.

No, what I found was a five-foot-seven-inch woman with a short mop of blond hair, and big blue eyes that were at once sleepy and surprised, wearing one of my blue oxford cloth shirts and nothing else, balancing a glass of water in her hand while she climbed into my rumpled bed. Her name was Maggie Kane, and she said to me, very simply, "I won't."

Huck, standing directly behind me, brave boy that he was, inched out in front, slowly at first, hesitantly — until Maggie called out, "Who's this?" And then he went scampering over, relief all across his face, his tail slapping against the side of the bed.

Me, I stayed in the doorway. Men might be dogs, but I didn't want to act like one here. Plus I was too tired. And shocked.

I hadn't seen her since before we were supposed to become husband and wife, meaning before she fled the Commonwealth of Massachusetts to get away from me and us, and before I had sat in Caffe Vittoria in Boston's North End and decided that she wasn't the woman I was meant to be with for the rest of my life. That seemed, by the way, like five centuries ago.

I didn't know how I was supposed to feel. I didn't know if I should feel vindicated. I didn't know if I should feel relieved. I didn't know if I should feel anger, arousal, disdain, contempt, humiliation, or overwhelming joy.

But the reality was, I didn't feel any of that. I didn't feel any of that because I didn't feel anything at all. I stood there in that doorway, looking at a barely attired woman who ninety-nine out of a hundred guys would have been jumping and screaming for joy to have found lying in their bed, and what I felt was nothing.

"How are you?"

That was me, with one of the more unoriginal questions I'd ever asked. She didn't take it that way. She looked up from the dog to me and replied, "How am I? I'm horrified. I'm depressed. I'm ashamed. I'm unspeakably sad. And I'm really, really sorry."

She kept her eyes on mine, studying me for a reaction, some hint of emotion that I'm sure she couldn't find. She was sitting up on the bed now, her arms wrapped around her knees. The dog was sitting on the floor beside her, looking up with something that approached awe.

For a passing, fleeting moment, I allowed myself some awe of my own over the situation. We were supposed to be in some five-star resort on the Pacific Ocean in Hawaii, getting pampered nonstop by a solicitous staff, having sex often and urgently, dining under the stars, looking forward to a life well lived, together.

Instead, I had the smack and acrid taste of death all around every single thing I did, to the point that it felt like it would never be any different than what it was then. And this woman, this fundamentally happy, confident, well-balanced woman, was confessing shame, humiliation, and depression.

I don't know how else to put it: Life really sucks sometimes.

But I was too tired to carry this out any further, to explore some of the not-so-subtle nuances of it all.

She asked, "How are you?" as I knew she would.

I yawned, long and hard, and replied, "I haven't slept in two days. I've never been more exhausted in my life. I've got a story that's killing everyone around me. I've more suspicions than proof. I've got little faith in anything that anyone does around me. I have no hope that anything is about to change for the better."

I paused and added, "Otherwise, I'm great."

She continued to stare at me. I snuck a glance, then looked down at the floor in silence, my arms folded across my chest. The Harvard Medical School's psychology department could do a case study in our body language here.

I quietly added, "None of this is your fault, by the way."

I snuck another glance and saw a tear rolling down her cheek. This was not what I wanted.

So I said, "I'm desperate for some sleep. Is there any possible way I can get in my own bed and go to sleep for the night, and we'll talk about this some other time?"

She asked, "Do you want me to stay or leave?"

Let's not put too fine a point on it: I

wanted her to leave. It was three-thirty in the morning. She skipped town on our wedding. She used her own keys to come unannounced into my apartment. I wanted to sprawl across my own bed for the next four hours unencumbered and unconcerned. But I didn't have the energy for the scene that her departure would inevitably require.

"Why don't you stay," I said.

Ends up, those would be just about the last words we'd ever speak to each other. Maybe communication isn't my strong suit, as Mongillo likes to remind me every time I write a story. When I got up the next day, Maggie was still asleep; when I got back to my apartment that night, she was long gone.

I climbed into bed. Two minutes later, I was already drifting off toward an unsteady slumber when I felt two paws beside me, then some tension, lifting, struggling, and then two more paws. Huck stepped methodically over my back and set himself down in the shallow valley between us, wrapping a paw over my head and resting his snout about two millimeters away from my ear.

At least something in this life was going right.

36

The sprawling lobby of Boston Police headquarters was oddly quiet when I walked through the double doors at ten o'clock on a Sunday morning for my meeting with Commissioner Hal Harrison — maybe due to the fact that Vinny Mongillo and his big mouth had been bailed out by the *Record*'s attorney about three hours before.

The silver-haired desk sergeant looked at me in silence. I said, "Jack Flynn of the *Record* here to see the commissioner." He made a little clucking sound that seemed to emanate from the roof of his mouth, snapped up the phone, and in a moment a young cadet with neither a gun nor an attitude arrived to escort me upstairs.

The commissioner's suite was empty, and I wondered if even the commissioner himself was in. The cadet asked me to sit in a little waiting lounge that looked to be designed by someone's grandmother — a grandmother, though, who had an affinity for antique, wall-mounted guns. I didn't sit, mostly because I was pretty tired of doing as told; standing was my little rebellion. Sometimes you draw your own line in life, even when no one else notices, and this happened to be mine.

The cadet disappeared, returned in a moment, and said, "The commissioner is ready to see you." No power games here, which was good.

For whatever it's worth, and maybe that's nothing, I'll note that I was feeling about as unsettled as I ever had before. Edgar was still dead, and that wasn't going to change. Elizabeth Riggs was still threatened, and that wasn't going to change, either, at least not until this serial murderer was captured. The good news there was that she still had the estimable Hank Sweeney at her side. The bad news was that in the meantime, other women might still die.

All the while, something was clattering around in the hollow spaces of my mind, little shards of information that I needed to piece into actual enlightenment — things people said, stuff they did that didn't add up, or maybe they did and that was the problem, that I couldn't do the math. Sometimes it felt like the shards were coming together, creating a whole, and then they'd suddenly blow apart, leaving me grasping at air, figuratively, if not literally as well.

"Nice of you to come in on your day off, Jack."

That was Commissioner Hal Harrison, standing behind that big oak desk of his, wearing a beige V-neck sweater and a pair of carefully pressed blue pants, the crease so tight you could cut a steak with it, and not some soft tenderloin but a thick sirloin or a well-marbled rib eye.

He leaned over his desk and extended his hand, and as we shook, I almost laughed at the notion of a day off, like I was going to kick back at home with a bag of Fritos and a six-pack of Sam Adams and watch March Madness on TV, not a worry in this delightful little world that we all share. Of course, that made me think again of the Hawaiian resort that was charging me for not being there, which made me think of the prior night with Maggie Kane, which made me happy not to be at that resort. Suddenly, work seemed good. See, life's really simple, even when it doesn't necessarily feel that way.

"Nice of you to have me," I said, the two of us maintaining the veneer of politeness.

The commissioner leaned to the side of his high-backed leather chair. I took a seat across the desk from him. He said, "Jack, you're a young pup. You weren't here back in the early sixties when this Strangler stuff was exploding around this town. You don't have a feel for what it did to Boston, to the people, to the cops like me and the prosecutors I worked with trying to get a handle on it."

He paused and looked at me, hard. I held firm to his gaze.

"I was here," he said. "I was in the middle of it. I was one of the lead detectives on the biggest, most comprehensive, most demanding investigations this department has ever undertaken."

God how politicians love the word *I,* and that's what Hal Harrison had become — a politician. You could see it all over his face. You could hear it wrapped around his every word. He wasn't so much concerned about the victims who had already been killed or those who were about to be. No, he was concerned about his own future, meaning whether this murder spree was going to get in the way of his becoming mayor.

Clank, clank, clank. There were those shards of information, bumping against intuition, almost coming together, painfully close but not quite. And then it all fell apart again, like when you can't remember someone's name even when it's right there on the tip of your tongue.

"Let me tell you, Jack, it wasn't a good time for this city. Jack Kennedy was assassinated right in the middle of it all. The Vietnam War was brewing. The country was going through huge changes. And we had some bastard, some absolute bastard, strangling women to death right in our midst."

I didn't know where he was going with any of this, so I simply sat in silence and went along for the unusual ride. I could hear church bells peal in the distance. I momentarily imagined older women in their Sunday best marching tentatively into Mass and praying for the safety of their daughters amid this murder spree. My eyes drifted toward the big windows, which revealed a gray, dank morning outside, moist, but still without any rain.

Harrison continued. "We worked like dogs. I worked. A guy by the name of Lieutenant Bob Walters, a good man, my immediate superior, worked. Stu Callaghan worked up in the attorney general's office. We worked ourselves to the bone, morning, noon, and night. I couldn't even begin to tell you how many leads we pursued, how many tips we chased, how many doors we broke down, how many suspects we interrogated, always grabbing at nothing more than straws and air."

He paused, collecting himself, surprised, I sensed, at his own eloquence. Maybe he truly was speaking from the heart. Maybe his words flowed out unrehearsed. I usually know these things, but for the moment I couldn't tell.

"And then we caught ourselves a good old-fashioned break. Jack, we got a confession. Albert DeSalvo knew those murder scenes cold . . ."

He began explaining just how well De-Salvo knew them, sharing details with me about the intricacies of the various scenes. Meantime, my brain cut out — not over something he said, but something he didn't. He did not include Detective Mac Foley on his honor roll of those who worked the case hard way back when, and given my suspicions now, this became more than interesting.

I finally cut back in and said, "Mac Foley." Hey, why not? When was the commissioner going to make himself available to me again? He stopped talking mid-sentence and stared at me, undoubtedly surprised by the interruption as well as the name. I added, "He was your colleague on the investigation. He's on this investigation now. He's one of the most successful detectives in BPD homicide. How come you didn't mention his name?"

Harrison regarded me long and hard. He ran a hand through his salt-and-pepper hair and leaned back in his chair, his fist under his chin. He suddenly leaned forward, thrusting his elbows on his desk, and asked, "Can we talk off the record?"

This wasn't necessarily what I wanted to do, but I nodded, too curious about what he might want to say to ruin the deal.

"Mac's a good man. He is," Harrison said, talking lower, his off-the-record tone, I figured. "But I worry about the quality of his work as a detective." His eyes locked on mine, as if willing me toward complicity. I showed no emotion.

"He was way off the reservation back then, to the point where I was worried about him — his psychological state, if you know what I mean. These days, he's heading to retirement, kind of phoning it in. Soon as he's gone, I think this investigation will move a lot swifter."

I asked, "Why don't you simply remove him?"

He smiled at me, leaning back again.

"Politics, my friend. Politics. City hall. Departmental. News media. You name it. You have to balance a lot of concerns in this chair."

This was interesting to me, every word, especially those about Mac Foley's psychological state. Could my wildest suspicions be right? Could he have snapped? On his way out the door, could he be killing women, reliving the toughest investigation of his career? Had he completely lost it?

Or here's another thought: Was he the Strangler way back then, kind of a police version of the firebug arsonists once so common across the country — firefighters who actually lit the infernos that they were called to put out? But if he was the Strangler back then, why would he have been ticked off over DeSalvo's confession? Could he have felt that someone else was taking credit for his work?

I was pondering these questions when my back pocket vibrated. I casually pulled my phone out and saw it was Martin calling in, and I put it back. Ten seconds later, he called again, and again ten seconds after that. The guy might have had the journalistic brains of Bob Woodward, but at the moment I wanted to wring his neck.

"What's your relationship like with Foley?" I asked.

"Nonexistent. Lord knows I've tried. We started together. We're leaving together, but he's refused to be even civil to me in the forty years since Albert DeSalvo confessed — like I was somehow responsible for his cockamamie theories not panning out on the Strangler case."

My phone vibrated yet again. I cussed Martin under my breath, pulled it out, glanced at it, and saw it was a 702 area code — a call from Las Vegas.

As I put the phone back, I felt Vinny Mongillo's thank-you note to Bob Walters folded up in my back pocket. So I pulled it out and said, "While we're off the record, you've got to see this. These charges you've filed against Vinny Mongillo are bullshit, and this proves it."

I placed it on his desk and he read it. Afterward, he looked up and said, "This will certainly factor into a complex investigation, and when we empanel a grand jury, I'll urge the district attorney to allow them to see this."

"That's garbage," I said, my voice thundering out louder than I expected. I knew his game. He was essentially trying to disqualify the *Record* from driving the story forward by making us a questionable part of it. I could see *The New York Times* headline now: "*Record* Reporter Ensnared in Serial Murder Case." It might be the only time Vinny Mongillo would be called "Mr." by his peers.

Harrison seemed taken aback, probably not so much by my assertion but by the fact someone would speak to him like that. He said, confidingly again, "So let's deal. You need me, and whether I like to believe it or not, I may need you at the moment. What else do you have?"

And there we were, at the crux of this meeting, with Commissioner Hal Harrison following the age-old adage that you keep your friends close and your enemies closer, and at that moment, I might have been the biggest enemy to his mayoral ambitions — at least in the way he perceived the world.

I ran a few scenarios through the reporting calculator that was my mind. Do I share? Do I withhold? I decided quickly, perhaps too quickly, that I was better off placing my suspicions of Mac Foley on the proverbial table, if only to see the chain of events that they might cause.

So I said, "I have some concerns about Mac Foley."

He arched an eyebrow at me and leaned back again.

I said, "You know from your underlings that I've received the driver's license of *New York Times* reporter Elizabeth Riggs, for all practical purposes targeting her as the next victim. Take a look at who she was with earlier that day."

He nodded, still saying nothing, obviously intrigued by what I was telling him.

I continued, "And you might try to ascertain how Mac Foley knew the apartment number of Lauren Hutchens over in the Fenway."

"What do you mean?" Harrison asked, his features scrunched up in thought and curiosity.

I replied, "I never gave it to him. The cops he sent to the scene said Foley gave the apartment number to them."

Harrison nodded. He was about to ask something else when there was a knock on his door on the other side of the room. Harrison angrily called out, "What!"

The same cadet who led me up walked in and said, "I'm sorry, sir, but Mayor Laird is on the line and said she needs to speak to you immediately."

Harrison snapped up the phone and barked, "Commissioner here."

Silence.

He said, "You've got to be fucking kidding me. Why are they doing this now?"

My own phone vibrated yet again. It was Martin trying to reach me yet again. This was a lot, even for him.

Harrison stopped to listen to the mayor, his brow furrowed in frustration.

"Well," he said, "you know what this is? It's fucking irresponsible. And it's fucking war. They want to fuck with me, they're making a big fucking mistake."

I stepped to the far side of the office, by the windows that held the gray hue of the dull day, and gave Martin a quick call. He picked up on the first ring and without so much as a greeting said, "Justine's finally agreed with me. She's running the Phantom's warning tomorrow — verbatim. This Elizabeth Riggs thing pushed her over the edge. You're going to write a story, and we'll put the full text of the note as a sidebar on the front page."

"Finally, some sense," I replied, then added, "I'll call you shortly."

I hung up just in time to witness Hal Harrison slamming down the phone — on the mayor.

He stared straight down at his desk for a long moment, his hands on either side of his broad head. I took a seat again in front of him. He slowly looked up at me, his eyes darker than they were before, the wrinkles of his face deeper, and he said, "You're fucking with the wrong guy, Jack."

He said "Jack" like it was also a profanity, the word propelled from his lips like an arrow.

I said, "Excuse me?"

He stared at me, his eyes as black and distant and angry as any I've ever seen. A police commissioner is used to getting his or her own way, especially when the mayor is a weak one with plans to step down.

He said, "You're fucking with this investigation. You're fucking with this city. You're fucking with this commissioner."

He paused and looked at me. It seemed like he was almost looking through me. He said, his tone as flat as the line on a dead man's cardiogram, "And if you put the contents of that bullshit note in the paper, you're going to pay."

I said, "We're going to do what we have to do, with our readers, not you, in mind."

"Bullshit!" he screamed. "Albert DeSalvo was the Boston Strangler. He admitted it. He confessed to every one of the crimes in minute detail. And now some joker comes along forty years later in the middle of my mayoral campaign, claiming to be the real Strangler, and you and your whole paper fall for it!"

His voice was bouncing off the walls and windows of his cavernous office and rising toward the high ceilings. Without warning, he picked up a binder that said "Strangler Investigation" from the top of his desk and flung it sidearm across the room. It slammed against the far wall, knocking a bronze plaque to the floor — undoubtedly a commendation of some sort. Somewhere in that act there was symbolism, but it would take a much smarter man than me to be able to say what it was.

"You're messing with my future, Jack." He was standing up now, hunched over his desk, his voice lower but no less intense. "You're messing with every dream I've ever had. You're messing with what's rightfully mine. You're digging up the past, and trying to bury me in the fucking hole. And you're wrong. You're just fucking wrong."

I stood up as well, partly in anticipation that he might come over the desk at me, partly because I realized that I wasn't going to get any more than I needed out of him, so this interview was just about done.

"Sorry you feel this way, Commissioner, but I'm going to keep doing my job as you go ahead and do yours."

I began to turn around and head toward

the door. When I took a couple of strides, he said in a voice that was at once soft and hard as steel, "You better watch yourself."

I turned around and replied, "What did you just say to me?"

"You heard me. You better watch yourself. You think some funny things have already happened? Your friend gets blown away in a CVS? Your life gets threatened?"

He caught himself here, took a long swallow followed by a deep breath, and said, "Like I said, watch yourself. You run that note, be on your guard."

I stood near the door, staring at him, incredulous over being threatened by the commissioner of the Boston Police Department, and reasonably certain that his threat included an admission that he was behind the prior attempts on my life. Edgar Sullivan's kind face popped momentarily into my mind.

As I stared, trembling not out of fear but fury, he seemed to understand what he had just said, what he had just done, the import and gravity of it all. He said in a much different tone of voice, conciliatory, yet edging toward desperation, "What can I do to stop you, Jack? What can I do?"

"Do what you're paid to do. Be a cop. Solve the damned case." And with that, I turned around and strode out the door.

Outside, I flagged a cab, got into the first one that pulled up, and slid across the backseat to the far door, which I got out of. I flagged another passing cab and got in that one. It's a little trick I once saw in a James Bond movie, or maybe it was one of the *Naked Guns,* just in case the first driver was a plant.

My first call was to Hank Sweeney.

"Everything all right with you guys?" I asked.

"Jack, this is some woman," he replied. "The hair, the eyes, the walk —"

"Hank, all right, get a grip. I'm not looking for a recitation of that which I no longer have. I'll call you in a while. Keep her safe — and you as well."

Next call was to my cell phone voice mail. I deleted the progressively urgent messages from Peter Martin — "Jack, for fricking God's sake, call me" — until I arrived at a woman's voice sounding at first strained, and then shaken.

"Jack, it's Deirdre. Deirdre Hayes. Bob Walters's daughter in Las Vegas. Listen, I was right, I found that other box I told you about."

I was nodding as if she was actually talking to me.

She continued, "You need to see this stuff, Jack. You really do."

Now I was shaking my head. It was ten-forty a.m. Good God, by the time I finished with this story, I'd have enough frequent-flier miles to get me to Bali — which might be exactly where I'd need to go to escape Hal Harrison's wrath.

"I'll see you soon," she said. "You're not going to believe it."

Maybe I would. After that little session with Hal Harrison, after learning what I had about Mac Foley, there wasn't a whole lot left in life that was unbelievable anymore.

37

The wind wasn't so much blowing as howling off the ocean as I stepped out of my car and placed my hand in front of my eyes, trying to block the cold grains of sand that felt like little needles smacking against my face. I pulled a torn sheet of paper from my pocket to double-check the address, stared at the ramshackle single-story cottage with the flaking white paint and the cracked front step, and realized I was in the right place.

It was a forlorn little structure, sitting in a yard of sand directly on the ocean's edge, part of a cramped row of similarly forlorn little structures. The difference being, all the other cottages were still boarded up for the winter; this one was not only open, it had smoke drifting from the chimney and blowing against the slate-gray sky — a pretty solid clue that somebody was home.

That somebody, I hoped, was H. Gordon Thomas, for a long while the most famous attorney in the United States, a household name, quite literally the epitome of the garrulous Perry Mason–style trial lawyer, portrayed in movies, studied in law schools, mimicked by every ambitious Young Turk who ever stepped in front of a jury trying to win a case.

And here he was living in a falling-down bungalow with mismatched shutters barely adhered to the rotting frame. I had heard that his life had taken an unfortunate turn, but I had no idea — and I don't think anyone had any idea — that the turn had been this bad.

The most recent newspaper story I had found on him said that the famed lawyer who spent decades jetting around the nation winning acquittals for some of the most notorious suspects in American history had hit drastic times. First, he began drinking. Soon after, he was sued by a suspected European drug lord whom he had represented on a trafficking case, and had lost many millions in the suit. Then he was disbarred in two states, forcing him into a secluded retirement on what was described as family property on Boston's South Shore.

I walked tentatively across the sand toward the bare front door of that family property, leaned over the one cracked step, and rapped my fist against the thin wood. The wind continued pounding, penetrating my thin coat. Tempests of sand swirled against my body and stuck in my hair. I love all those faux romantics who say they love walking the beach on a winter's day. It's like walking along the edge of hell. How can a place so warm and welcoming in the summer be so cold and lonely at just about every other time of the year?

I knocked again, and in turn heard someone moving around inside — the sound of a door shutting, unsteady footsteps, something dropping on the floor. And then the front door slowly opened, revealing a figure I had seen dozens if not hundreds of times in newspaper photographs and on television news clips.

In some respects, H. Gordon Thomas looked very much how I would have imagined — big and barrel-chested, with crystal-clear blue eyes peering through his trademark enormous, owlish eyeglasses. He must have stood six feet four, must have weighed 240 pounds, all of which belied his age, which must have been at least seventy, and probably a few years beyond that.

In other respects, he looked like his bedraggled brother, if he had one, which I'm not sure he did, but this is no time to get lost in needless detail. His long hair was scraggly, rather than slicked back in that polished way it used to be. He appeared unsteady on his feet. The buttons on his cardigan sweater were adhered to the wrong holes, and the shirt beneath it was untucked. His face, that famous face that juries used to trust so much, carried what must have been three days' worth of growth.

"Do I know you?" he asked. Not "Can I help you?" Not "Who are you?" But "Do I know you?" delivered slowly, in that famously deep voice of his that still made it seem he was performing before a judge and jury.

"I don't think so, sir," I responded. "My name is Jack Flynn. I'm a reporter for the *Boston Record.* I was hoping to get a word with you, if you had the time."

He continued to look at me, his gaze as penetrating as the sand and the wind that still cut at my body and face. He said, more quietly this time, "The one in communication with the Boston Strangler." It was an interesting choice of words — the Boston Strangler rather than the Phantom Fiend — given that he was Albert DeSalvo's lawyer many years ago and had engineered his client's confession to the stranglings.

"Yes, sir," I replied softly.

"Come in," he said as he quickly looked around the environs of his cottage, perhaps measuring its suitability for visitors. By the time he might have decided it wasn't, I was already in, so he cleared a stack of legal books from an extremely old and worn couch, pounded the cushion once, and said, "Why don't you sit here, young man." So I did.

The cottage was as threadbare inside as it was rickety outside, with just the couch I was on and a mismatched chair on which Thomas sat. Both of them were kitty-corner to a small brick fireplace, which at the moment held the last remnants of a sputtering fire. The carpet was gray, thin, stained, and old. The walls were made of cheap paneling. The ceiling had exposed beams, though not in the stylish way of an expensive downtown loft. The kitchen was nothing more than a sink, an ancient stove, and a small refrigerator pushed against a back wall. Above them, a window looking out at the churning ocean was caked in bird feces that was, in turn, covered with sand. All in all, this wasn't exactly a visit to the Naples Ritz-Carlton.

Thomas got up and tossed another log on the fire, saying, "I should have gotten this damned place winterized, but every summer I keep telling myself, 'This is my last year here,' so I never have."

He turned the volume down on the small television set that sat atop a folding table. The TV was turned to CNN. He settled heavily back in his chair in the way that old men do who carry too much weight on their tired frames.

I stayed silent. I noticed for the first time an expensive-looking bottle of single-malt Scotch sitting on an upside-down cardboard box next to his chair, and beside the bottle was a half-full crystal tumbler that was completely incongruous with the rest of the room. It was as if he carried the glass and the Scotch from his prior life, and for all I knew, perhaps he had.

He focused on me anew and said, "So you've found yourself in quite a maelstrom, young man. You're undoubtedly a very busy guy. To what does a has-been old lawyer like me owe this particular visit?"

I smiled at the way he spoke, but to myself, not to him. He was rubbing his hands together toward the fire. I kept my coat on because of the dank chill that permeated the thin walls. I said, "You better than anyone knows if the Boston Strangler is still alive today. I came to ask you if he is."

Thomas stared into the fire through those huge glasses without betraying even a hint or whisper of emotion. He stayed quiet for so long that I said, "You made reference to the Boston Strangler at your front door, as if you wouldn't be surprised if he was still alive. Is that an accurate read?"

His eyes still didn't move from the fireplace, though I thought I saw his eyebrows raise. Finally, he looked over at me and asked, "Who do you think the Boston Strangler was, young man?"

"Back then?"

He nodded.

I said, "Not Albert DeSalvo."

He laughed for the first time, looked at me more warmly, and replied, "No one with a brain in their head thought Albert De-Salvo was the Boston Strangler. Unfortunately, that includes the nice men and women of the jury who convicted him of those rapes rather than believe my argument that he was a ferocious, sociopathic serial killer who strangled so many women that they had to deem him innocent by reason of insanity."

He paused, stared straight ahead, and added, "Dumbest strategy I ever employed, and the biggest case I ever lost. I've regretted it every day since."

For the first time, he picked up his crystal tumbler of Scotch and took a long, savoring sip, almost as if it was coffee on a cold winter's morning and he was contemplating a full day ahead. He put the glass down and continued to stare at something that I couldn't see, would probably never see, that appeared somewhere above the flames.

I kept silent, again employing that old adage that you never interrupt someone in the process of giving you news.

Finally he added, softly now, "And look at what I've caused."

"How do you mean, sir?" I asked this softly, leaning toward him with my elbows on my knees, speaking in confidence, just two guys sharing some thoughts on a Sunday morn.

He shook his head, not accepting the bait. I said, "The police believed DeSalvo's story."

He laughed again, not necessarily a deep laugh but a full one, and he regarded me again with a glint in his eye, as if I was someone he could get to like. I had a gut feeling that he may not have had a visitor here in a long time, and might not have another again for a long time.

"They believed exactly what they wanted to believe, what was easiest for them to believe," Thomas said. "They had a suspected rapist who had never been within their wide orbit of suspects suddenly confessing to every one of the strangulations, sharing intimate details of the murder scenes."

He laughed again and added, "Stu Callaghan, God bless him, didn't ask a whole lot of questions — and he didn't allow anyone else to ask any, either. He merely thanked his lucky stars, got DeSalvo behind bars on the rape charges, and waltzed all the way into the United States Senate."

He paused. I recalled Lieutenant Detective Bob Walters's assertions that he was never allowed to interview DeSalvo, and that none of his men were, either.

He wasn't speaking any further, so I prodded him, asking, "If not DeSalvo, then who?"

"Young man, it could have been anyone — maybe someone we knew, maybe someone we didn't —"

"Paul Vasco?" I asked, interrupting him.

He smiled at me yet again. "You ask a lot of tough questions. You undoubtedly know that Paul Vasco was my client as well." He let forth a shallow little chuckle. "I was a busy guy back then, wasn't I?

"Vasco was a fascinating guy, brilliant,

creative, brutal, evil — a demonstrated killer with no capacity for remorse. Could he have been the Boston Strangler? I didn't allow myself to think about that at the time, because that would have interfered with my defense of DeSalvo at his rape trial. I didn't want to know, so I didn't know."

I asked, "But what about after DeSalvo's rape conviction?"

"Vasco was still my client on another case. I never asked him about the stranglings. Like I said, I didn't want to know."

I asked, "But have you thought about it since?"

He looked me over for a long moment.

"A lot," he finally said, softer than he had spoken before. "I've thought about that a lot."

His gaze shifted from me to the fireplace to the floor. A wry smile sneaked across his features as he stared down, and he mumbled, "I've thought about it too much. Thought about it as I've nearly drowned myself to death in vodka, whiskey, and gin. I played fast and loose back then, not only with my own client, who ended up dead, but with a lot of other people whose lives would never be the same because of information they might never know."

He looked up at me, almost surprised that

I was still there, listening. He said, "And the God's honest truth about all this is that I still don't know who the hell the Boston Strangler was — or maybe is."

The burning logs crackled a few times, making the sound that a cap gun might. The wind caused a loose shutter to bang against the thin outer wall.

I asked, "Do you remember Detective Mac Foley?"

"Well."

"Your impressions?"

Thomas squinted at some distant point in thought and recollection. "An odd guy. A serious guy. Adamant that DeSalvo wasn't the Strangler, as if he always knew something that no one else did. I could never get a handle on him."

I decided to leave that alone for a while and return to his heavily finessed and carefully caressed answers on Paul Vasco. I said, "Mr. Thomas, if you were me, if you were in a desperate situation, which I am, if people's lives were on the line, who would you focus on for the moment? I'll ask you this real simply: Would you focus on Paul Vasco?"

Thomas looked from me to the floor, and then down at his glass, which he lifted to his lips in another long sip, the liquid draining out as he tilted his head back and shut his eyes. He fingered the bottle for a moment, then removed his hand without ever pouring a fresh drink.

Finally, he peered over at me again and said, "You want to get it in writing, young man. That's the best advice I can give you."

Those little pieces in my mind started closing in on one another, started forming a picture that I couldn't quite see. And then the harder I thought about them, the less clear they became, until they disintegrated against a backdrop of frustration.

I looked at him hard, looked at him until he finally averted his gaze. I said, "I don't understand what the hell you're saying, and I don't have the time or the energy to be semantic here. Please, Mr. Thomas, tell me what you're talking about."

He shook his head as he stared straight down at the floor and rubbed the back of his neck with both of his hands.

"That's all I can tell you, young man. Get it in writing. You'll know what I mean."

He never looked up as I walked out his door.

38

It was two, maybe three seconds after I got into the newsroom when Peter Martin appeared at my desk the way the Japanese appeared at Pearl Harbor, which is to say without warning and certainly without apology. He was accompanied by a bald man in sunglasses who looked as out of place at a newspaper as I would at a Milan fashion show.

"This is Buck," Martin said to me.

"Hi, Buck," I said.

Buck nodded but didn't speak, which, for reasons I can't explain, didn't actually surprise me.

"What's this?" Martin said, pointing down at the black dog sitting beside me.

"That's Huck," I said. I had stopped home on my way in from police headquarters to get him, and he smacked his tail against my metal desk at the sound of his name.

"Does he bite?"

What is it with these people?

"Viciously," I replied. "Don't make any sudden movements."

Martin slowly, tentatively slid over to the other side of the desk, then said to me, "Come down to my office, would you? We need to get a definitive plan going. And why don't you leave Huck here."

That last sentence wasn't a question.

I told him I'd be right in, snapped up my telephone, and punched out the number for Deirdre Hayes in Las Vegas, Nevada. I had already called her twice — on the way down to see H. Gordon Thomas, and on the way back, leaving her messages both times. This time it rang through to her voice mail again, which I didn't like at all. I asked her to call my cell phone as soon as humanly possible.

It was Sunday, early in the afternoon, and as such, the newsroom was operating on a skeletal staff, meaning few editors, no copy editors yet, and just a handful of reporters chasing down the typical fires, car crashes, and press conferences by especially opportunistic politicians who know that the competition for coverage is always weakest on a weekend. I instructed Huck to lie down, which he did with a long groan, followed by a loud sigh, and I made my way through the long newsroom and into Peter

Martin's glass-walled office.

When I walked in, Vinny Mongillo was lovingly unwrapping what we in New England would call a tuna-fish submarine, but those in less educated parts of America might refer to it as a grinder, a melt, or possibly a hoagie. In any part of the country, this wouldn't have smelled good, so I simply tried to put it out of my mind. Meantime, Justine gave me a look that I believed to be one of apology. Martin sat at the head of the table, peering down at a legal pad peppered with notes. No one said anything, unless you counted Mongillo's soft moan of satisfaction after his first bite.

Finally, Peter kicked things off, saying, "All right, Vinny, put down the food for a minute and tell us what the hell is going on here."

Vinny put down the food, in itself an uncharacteristically selfless act. He looked around at the three of us and said flatly, "My mother was a Strangler victim in 1963. I was a baby. I never got to know her. I was ten years old when I overheard my aunt and my grandmother talking about it — right after Albert DeSalvo was killed."

He drew a breath and continued. "I studied the hell out of the case when I was a teenager. I wrote to police officers. I read books. I called prosecutors. I was convinced, like a lot of others were, that DeSalvo didn't kill my mother — that DeSalvo didn't kill anyone at all.

"When Jack received these letters, I was going to tell you — all of you. But then I decided, you know what, this is my chance to do something about what I always thought was a massive deceit. This was my chance to have an impact on behalf of the woman who brought me into this world, but who I never got the chance to know. So I kept my mouth shut. Because if I told you about my history, you rightfully wouldn't have allowed me to work on the story."

I sat there spellbound, staring at a guy who never, ever stops surprising me in one good way or another. You think you know someone, you think you're giving him more credit than he could possibly deserve, yet under all that flesh is someone who's even better, smarter, and more sensitive than you can possibly allow yourself to believe.

Peter Martin, I could see, was also enraptured, but not to the point of silence. He didn't have that luxury. He tapped his pen a few times on the legal pad that sat on the coffee table before him and said, "Thank you, Vinny. That's all very understandable.

But why were you arrested? What did you do?"

Vinny flashed me a knowing look, mostly because, well, I already knew. Then he said, "The knife. Many years ago, I was given the blood-soaked knife found in Walpole State Prison that was used to stab Albert DeSalvo to death. One of the lead detectives on the case, Bob Walters, the guy who was trying to help Jack out before he died, he gave it to me."

More silence. I couldn't peel my eyes off of Vinny, which may seem a little weird, but so be it. Justine looked from Vinny to Martin to me. Martin bounced his pen on the legal pad a few more times and said, "But Vinny, how did the cops suddenly find out in the middle of this investigation that you had the knife?"

He told them that story as well. Still more silence. Martin nodded a whole lot. He exchanged a long look with Justine Steele, but neither said anything.

Finally, Martin looked at me and said, "Jack, bring us up to date."

I shared with them my suspicions about Mac Foley — the fact he knew Lauren Hutchens's apartment number, his history of being a bitter rival of Commissioner Hal Harrison, his presence around Elizabeth

Riggs on the morning she lost her license and might have been slated for murder. I told them of my morning meeting with Harrison and his unveiled threats. I told them of my later meeting with DeSalvo's lawyer, H. Thomas Gordon, and explained how pretty much the only thing I got from him was frustrated.

I was just finishing up when Barbara, the paper's longtime newsroom receptionist, flung the glass door open to Martin's office and said, "You're going to want to turn on the television."

So Martin did, to CNN, where a rather comely reporter — a female, by the way — was standing outside Boston Police headquarters with a microphone in her perfectly manicured hand. Across the top of the screen, the slogan "The Strangler Returns" was written in bright red. On the bottom, "Breaking News" flashed in orange.

"Again, ladies and gentlemen, my Boston Police sources are telling me that Detective Mac Foley was taken into custody within the last half hour as what a high-level police official describes as, and I'm quoting him here, 'a person of interest' in the current Strangler investigation. Foley was one of the detectives on both this case and the strangulations from over forty years ago.

"Those same sources tell me that evidence confiscated from Foley's house has been tied to what has been described to me as a 'potential victim.' He has been suspended with pay by Commissioner Hal Harrison, forced to turn over his gun, and is now being questioned by an FBI interrogator who was brought in specifically to handle this aspect of the case.

"We'll update you as we know it. But one more time, a potentially major and blockbuster break this afternoon in the case of the current Boston stranglings. Back to you, Gray."

The screen quickly flashed to a commercial for adult diapers, which I thought Peter Martin and Justine Steele might need at the moment. Me, I was too stunned to speak or even think, though I did wonder what kind of parents name their kid Gray.

As far as the story went, part of me felt vindicated, that my suspicions had panned out, that the cops had apparently found something in Foley's house tying him to Elizabeth Riggs. Part of me was quietly elated that the case appeared to have been cracked, that the letters with the driver's licenses of recent victims would stop. Yet another part of me, the one with those little shards of information knocking around my brain, felt uneasy about it all, like there was something else at play here. But the bigger part of me, maybe an embarrassing part of me, was fuming that I had just watched the whimpering end to this enormous story on a national cable network, rather than having broken it myself on the pages of my *Boston Record.* I got the letters. I saw the victims. I did the investigative work. I felt the guilt. This was my story, from beginning to its presumed end, and I didn't want to see any part of it broken on TV.

Sitting there, my aggravation turned to controlled fury. I was the one who developed the intuitive suspicions about Mac Foley. I passed them along to Hal Harrison. And then he burnt me to a crisp, leaking to CNN what should have been mine. If there's one thing a newspaper reporter hates most, and trust me, there are a lot of things a newspaper reporter hates a lot, it's watching a story that he or she has owned get advanced by some blow-dried, over-powdered light-weight on cable TV.

Martin looked at me and said in an unusually high-pitched voice, "Jack?"

Before I could answer, my ass started vibrating, not out of anger, but from the phone call that I seemed to have been receiving. I glanced at the cell and saw it was a 702 number, so I said disgustedly, "Let me just take this first."

I gave it my usual "Flynn here." A woman's voice said, "Jack, it's Deirdre Hayes. I never got to thank you for that money you left on the counter. So, well, thank you. You're a really sweet guy."

I could listen to compliments all day — except today. So I said, "Deirdre, you've caught me in the middle of a bunch of things." Like my complete and total career demise. "Tell me what you have?"

"You've got to see it, Jack."

I was quickly losing patience, and the truth was, I had very little left to lose. "Deirdre, I'm in Boston."

She said, "So am I. I brought the stuff out here to you. Least I could do. After my shift last night, I jumped on a red-eye through Chicago, and now I'm in the *Record* lobby."

"This *Record*? My lobby? I'll be right down."

As I turned to walk out, Mongillo, Steele, and Martin were all still mesmerized by the television coverage. I called out, "Be right back." I paused at the door as something struck me. "Hey Vinny, did you ever get results from those DNA tests before you were arrested?"

He smiled a knowing smile at me and

said, "Ah, Fair Hair, someone finally posed the question I was waiting to be asked. Good on you for doing it."

I said, "Well?"

He picked up the remainder of his tuna sub in one of his hairy, oversize mitts. "Not yet," he said, staring down at it. "But any minute, I hope."

It's probably more important to note what Deirdre Hayes wasn't dressed in rather than what she was. She wasn't wearing that miniskirt or the skintight tank top she had on the day before, or the dark eyeliner that made it look like she charged by the hour rather than by the drink. She was turned out on this Sunday afternoon in a pair of jeans and an expensive-looking sweater, and her fabulously wavy auburn hair was pulled back in a bun pinned to the back of her head. All of which is to say that today, she looked like someone you could introduce to your mother, which made her appearance of the day before even more of a turn-on. If this is hard to understand, that's because it should be.

She jumped up from one of the settees that sat in the floor-to-ceiling windows and gave me a kiss on the cheek, as if we had known each other a long time, rather than exactly one day. I gave her arm a squeeze and thanked her profusely for flying all the way across the country to deliver whatever it was that she had. She explained that her father would have wanted it that way, and that I was too nice to leave that money on the table for her. I told her she was way too kind. We could have gone on and on, but I didn't have the time. Nodding at the folder she was carrying under her left arm, I said, "So let's take a look at what you have."

She sat back down, and I sat down beside her. Reaching carefully into the folder, she said, "I knew there was this other box. I just knew it. So I went down into the cellar late yesterday afternoon before my shift and looked for it. Dad had another trunk that he kept down there. I had to break the lock with a hammer, and sure enough, there was a small box inside."

By now she had pulled out a small sheath of what looked to be old papers, and she handed them to me, saying, "He never told me about these. He never told anyone in the family. But this makes it a whole lot easier to understand why he was so tortured by this case."

She paused, her eyes welling up, and added, "I wish I had known."

I put the stack of about nine sheets of

paper on the glass-top coffee table in front of us, then picked the first one up carefully in my hands. It was a sheet of lined notebook paper, the kind you might pull out of a wired binder, and indeed, the left side had the little broken circles that showed that was exactly what was done.

The date was scrawled in black ink, in crude, adolescent penmanship, at the top of the page: "June 15, 1962."

Below, written in the same hand, the note read, "Detective Walters, You were supposed to find Yvette before anyone else. Next time, I promise. I killed her in the kitchen. When she was dead, I dragged her into the living room. I had sex with her on the floor. Others will die. The Phantom Fiend."

I put the sheet down and picked up the next one. On the same lined paper, in the same pen, by the same hand, the date "July 2, 1962" was scrawled at the top. Below it read, "Detective Walters, Her name is Paulina. I strangled her in her own bed. You need to go save her sorry soul." It then gave her address, in the Dorchester section of Boston. It was signed, "The Phantom Fiend."

And so it went for seven more letters, all of them addressed to Detective Walters, all of them signed by the Phantom Fiend, most of them alerting him to the presence of a body that had yet to be discovered, a couple apologizing that they had been found by someone else.

My head, for every obvious reason, was spinning or swimming or whatever heads do when they can barely process the staggering, earth-shaking information flowing into them. How did the news media not know about these letters? Why did police keep them quiet? Were there handwriting samples taken? Fingerprints? Anything to tie these letters to Albert DeSalvo?

I immediately thought of Bob Walters sprawled across his bed when I visited him the week before. *In this case, we held something back that was pretty big.* That's what he'd said, and I never probed him on it. If I had, I probably would have found out about these notes days before.

All of which brought me back to H. Gordon Thomas's line earlier that day. *You want to get it in writing, young man. That's the best advice I can give you.*

This, I assume, is what he meant. Or was it?

I did a quick calculation, and these notes seemed to further open the possibility that Detective Mac Foley could have sent the current notes to me, because he would have been in a position to know about the old ones. Or maybe he had sent the old ones as well, which brought me back to that old firebug theory of the arsonist who extinguishes his own work.

Or it could mean that Paul Vasco sent the notes then, and was sending them now. Or that the Strangler of old, if it wasn't Vasco, is the Strangler of new.

I turned to Deirdre, who was watching me partake in these mental calisthenics and gymnastics, and I said, "I can't thank you enough."

"What's it mean?" she asked.

"I have no idea, but damned if I'm not about to find out." Then I added, "Come on upstairs for a moment. We owe you a courier fee for your services."

Peter Martin was about to pay through the nose.

39

I was staring at a blank computer screen, which is something that no writer, never mind a reporter on a deadline, likes to do, when Peter Martin parked himself in a chair at a neighboring desk and wheeled it toward mine.

Problem was, he wheeled it directly over Huck's tail, unpleasantly rousing him from a deep slumber. Huck bolted up in shock. Martin scrambled from the chair and leapt over my desk to escape what he believed would be the unmerciful wrath of a ferocious animal, and I sat there momentarily contemplating what my life would have been like if I'd taken the LSATs.

"You've got to get that thing in a cage," Martin said.

"He's confined in the same cage that we all are," I replied. I thought that was pretty profound. Martin eyed me like I had lost my mind.

Rather than respond, he said, "Every network, every newspaper, every blogger, every radio station, every mainstream website is going whole hog on the cop-as-murderer saga. *Newsweek* put out a story on its website quoting victims' families from the sixties saying they always thought Mac Foley was an odd guy. FOX News is reporting that the White House is preparing an invitation to Hal Harrison for dinner with the president, in hopes of luring him into the Republican Party. CBS Radio is quoting defense lawyers all over Boston describing the shoddy investigative methods Foley used to employ in convicting other murderers. 'Other murderers.' They actually used that term, like Foley was already convicted."

I shook my head. I'm the one who started all this in a typical negotiating session earlier that morning with the commissioner of the Boston Police. And here I was, just a few hours later, already sucking the fumes of other news outlets' progress, as if I had suddenly become irrelevant to the entire tale. I didn't like it for that reason. I liked it even less so for the nagging uncertainty that Mac Foley was truly, actually involved.

Martin continued, "We have to run big on this, every conceivable angle, and then some. We're still printing the Phantom

Fiend's miniature manifesto. In the main-bar, which you're writing, play up the initial suspicions of Foley, what you said to Hal Harrison to kick this whole thing off. The Elizabeth Riggs driver's license deal. Touch on the Vinny Mongillo allegations, just in case others do. We were at this thing first; we want that to be easily apparent in our coverage."

I only nodded. Peter Martin's every instinct was exactly right, as they almost always are. But my instincts were holding me back, preventing me from going full bore on Mac Foley in the story. Was it because of the fact I lost the initial newsbreak, and now wanted to be counterintuitive, because in the end, that's mostly what reporters are — at least good reporters — counterintuitive, obstinate pricks? Or was it because of my dealings with Foley, in which I never got a whiff of anything especially wrong? Or was it these little pieces that still floated around in my head, nothing ever quite coming together?

"I'll do it," I said.

"You don't sound excited," Martin responded. "Jack, this is huge. We've been the paper of record on this story; we have to remain the paper of record. Whomp it up. While you're writing, I've got Vinny and about four others working the phones for anything we can learn about the investigation, and anything we can learn about Foley's life and career. Let's do it."

He clapped his hands together and walked away, nearly skipping toward his office. I looked down at Huck; Huck looked up at me.

"I wouldn't mind switching places with you right about now," I told him.

He struggled slowly to his feet from his long and deserving nap. He licked my knee, then casually placed two paws on my lap as if he was about to climb onto my chair.

"I didn't mean that literally," I said, laughing. He groaned again as he flopped back down on the floor.

At seven o'clock, Peter Martin approached me gingerly, less because of the dog than the hour. It was deadline, after deadline, even, and he had been watching from a safe and secure distance for the past four hours as Jack Flynn — that being me — did what he did best: write stories.

Vinny Mongillo fed me great details on, among other things, the cops raiding Mac Foley's house, and how they found Elizabeth Riggs's wallet in the trash can of a next-door neighbor. A couple of other

Record reporters, Linus Pershing and Cray Dalton — no one in this business is named Billy and Bobby anymore — fed me reaction from Strangler victims past and present. As I finished the story, I begrudgingly began to like it, if not for content than for style, proving that old newspaper adage that the best story a reporter's ever done is the one he or she just wrote.

Still, I felt uneasy. I felt uneasy about the fact that Mac Foley was still being detained, even though formal charges had yet to be filed. I felt uneasy that Hal Harrison hadn't even hinted at what those charges might be. I felt most uneasy of all about my own role, essentially leading Harrison to Foley's house, where some incriminating evidence was discovered — or perhaps planted. Now, there's a thought.

At that point, I was talking myself out of the story all over again, still nagged by all those disparate pieces in my head refusing to form a whole.

"You ready to let go?"

That was Martin, three paces away, looking at me expectantly. I clicked a button on my computer that transported the story from my queue to his, essentially taking it out of my hands. I should have felt good about that, another deadline successfully behind me, a blockbuster front-page story ahead. I felt anything but.

"All yours," I said. And Martin, to his considerable credit, was as sober in his departure as he was in his arrival.

"All right, Fair Hair, I'm thinking of the thinnest-crust pizza we can find, with fresh mushrooms, maybe a little oregano, the cheese melted just perfectly so, all of it washed down with a Chianti so peppery, so authentically earthy, so absolutely Italy, that you're going to start thinking you have a Vespa parked out front."

That was, of course, Vinny Mongillo, parking himself in a nearby chair while he tossed one of Huck's tennis balls high in the air, catching it effortlessly himself. "What are you thinking?" he asked.

"Of you leaving me alone."

"Oh, come on, my little amigo. So we didn't have it first. Get over it. We'll have it best. We've got a million other things in that story that no one else will have."

I sat in silence, watching Huck watching Vinny toss his ball.

Vinny asked, "Did you remember to put a noun and a verb in every sentence? Did you remember to put skinny Vinny's byline right up high, preferably on top? If you did that, the story's going to sing like a diva in Las Vegas."

My phone rang. God bless my phone.

"Flynn here."

"Sergeant Ralph Akin, Boston Police Department. This call is not on a recorded line, and I'm assuming yours isn't either. We met overnight when you came to visit your colleague."

"Hello, Sergeant. Nice to hear from you."

"Same. Listen, I have a proposition for you. My very excellent friend, Mac Foley, is currently being detained as the commissioner and his lackeys cook up some bullshit charges. Mac would like to chat with you, in person, in the lockup."

I asked, "What's the proposition?"

He hesitated. I wasn't meaning to be difficult, but sometimes I just am. Okay, more than sometimes. Sergeant Akin said, "Could you come over here ASAP and meet on the sly with Foley? That's the proposition."

"I'm on my way."

"Call this number from your cell phone when you near headquarters. Enter through the rear delivery door."

We hung up and I turned to Vinny and said, "Hold the oregano and watch the dog for me. I've got a little more reporting to do tonight."

As I hustled through the gloomy newsroom, I could hear Vinny saying to himself, "Christ, a guy can starve in this life."

As I walked up to the darkened delivery bay in the rear of Boston Police headquarters, a garage door rolled up about four feet off the ground and a lone arm extended from the dark environs, beckoning me inside. I crouched down and did as told.

Inside, Sergeant Ralph Akin, a.k.a. Ralphie, was there to greet me, with precisely none of the frivolity he had displayed earlier that day when I was meeting with Vinny Mongillo. In fact, he looked and sounded deadly serious. "Mac Foley is my friend," he said. "He's a fantastic cop. Ask anyone in the building. The commissioner is trying to stick it up his ass on the way out the door."

We walked across the cavernous delivery bay, through a set of double doors, and down a narrow, fluorescent-lit hallway. Akin cut me off, flung open a door on my side of the corridor, and guided me into a tiny room that looked to be the observation area on an interrogation room on the other side of a two-way mirror.

"You'll have some privacy in here," Akin said. "I'll go get Mac." He paused at the door and said, "The brass is out to dinner.

You won't have a whole lot of time. Listen, Jack, and I think I can call you Jack. Any friend of Mongillo is good enough to be a friend of mine. Like I told you, they don't make them any better than Mac Foley. He really needs your help."

I didn't say anything, though I don't think he expected me to. In a moment he was gone.

Less than a minute later, the door opened and Mac Foley came walking in, looking far more pissed off than panicked, his expression bringing me back to the prior Monday night, at Hal Harrison's retirement dinner, when Foley shot me an icy stare from across the crowded ballroom. Who knew then that this is where that brief relationship would lead: a clandestine meeting in the bowels of police headquarters while one party — fortunately not me — stared down the barrel of multiple murder charges.

There were four chairs in a semicircle facing the wall of glass, and Foley sat in the one closest to the door. I sat in the farthest. He said, "Jack, I don't know what Hal Harrison is telling you I did. I don't know yet what charges they're going to file. But you've got to understand, you've got to believe, whatever it is they're saying I did, I didn't do it."

It was odd, having a cop plead with me like this, turn to me as the ultimate arbiter, understanding the odd power that the *Record* held on this most bizarre of stories.

I said, "Detective Foley, they found Elizabeth Riggs's purse crammed away in your neighbor's trash can. Are you going to say this was a plant?"

He shot me a look of surprise, and then the heat faded from his eyes as he slowly gazed up and down the darkened glass, then at the tile floor in front of him, and finally at the backs of his hands.

"Whatever they're going to say that I did, I didn't. Please, you've got to trust me on that."

He didn't answer my question. It's also worth noting that his line of argument was painstakingly selected. He wasn't denying having done anything wrong, only denying doing what they were going to say he had done. It was interesting, if slightly confusing. Though maybe not.

"What are they going to say you've done?" I asked.

The question came out perhaps a little louder than I had intended, more aggressive than I might have meant, but truth be told, it was how I felt. Yeah, my gut told me that Boston Police Detective Mac Foley wasn't one of the bad guys in this case. And maybe some oblique part of my mind told me the same thing. But the facts didn't speak particularly well for him at the moment, and thus, neither would I.

"It's a setup, Jack. They're making me a scapegoat. They're trying to do to me what they did to Albert DeSalvo forty years ago — pin the whole thing on someone, make all the unpleasant facts go away, and then ride it all to whatever victories they're chasing."

I asked, "Did you kill Jill Dawson or Lauren Hutchens or Kimberly May?" Their names rolled off my tongue like those of old friends.

He was standing now, pacing the short part of the room by the door.

"I didn't kill anyone," he said, though he said this while staring down at his shoes.

"Did you steal Elizabeth Riggs's license?"

Silence. He continued to pace. He looked up at me and said, "You need to talk to Paul Vasco. Have you talked to Paul Vasco?"

"Last week," I said, the words encased in anger as they slipped out of my mouth. I added, "You didn't answer my question. Did you steal Elizabeth Riggs's license?"

Abruptly, he slapped his fist against the back of his chair, sending it toppling over.

"You're asking the wrong questions." He yelled this more than he said it, his voice bouncing off the hard walls and glass and ricocheting around the room. "You're asking the wrong fucking questions of the wrong fucking people."

"Did you steal Elizabeth Riggs's license?"

He plunked himself down in the next chair over from mine. He looked me hard in the eye. "Jack, I've done nothing wrong. You've got to talk to Vasco again. You've got to tell him that I'm at risk of being charged. You've got to get to the bottom of this story, the killings now, the killings then."

His voice was growing panicked now, his eyes turning wild. "Please, Jack, talk to Vasco. Please."

There was a firm knock on the door, and then it pushed open. Sergeant Ralph Akin looked at Foley and said, "The brass is back. They're coming down to see you in a minute. I've got to get you back into lockup. Fast."

Foley hung his head in defeat. I asked him, "Were we on the record here?" Granted, it was a little late to be asking the question, but better then than never.

He was shuffling toward the door, his face still aimed at the floor. "We're whatever you want us to be," he said, his tone deflated.

At the door, he turned around and looked at me and said, "But Jack, before you destroy my life, before you ruin what's left of my career, before you destroy my wife, my daughter, my whole reputation, please put it to Paul Vasco. Do it for me, do it for yourself. Do it for all those people, Jack, the hundreds of people whose lives have been ruined by the Boston Strangler.

"Please, Jack."

It was then that Ralph Akin grabbed his elbow and pulled him out of the room.

40

We were rounding the corner onto Bulham Avenue in the Charlestown section of Boston, Vinny and I, when the Muzak I was listening to on my cell phone abruptly clicked off and my ear was suddenly filled with the familiar voice of Boston Police Commissioner Hal Harrison.

"Sorry to keep you on hold, Jack," he said, though I doubt he really was. "It's bedlam over here. That was a good tip you gave me on Mac Foley. That thing has paid off in spades."

Beside me, in the passenger seat of my Honda, Vinny Mongillo was barking into his cell phone at another police official, "You've got to be shoving the private parts of a donkey right in my coffee-colored eyes. You're sure you have it locked down? You're telling me I can go into print and feel good about this?"

I glanced over at him, unable to get his

unfortunate imagery out of my head. I wheeled the car up to the curb in front of Paul Vasco's halfway house. It was 10:00 p.m. Huck was sound asleep in the back.

"Yeah," I said to Harrison. "I've been watching these spades all over CNN and FOX News. You capitalized on my tip, and then spoon-fed it to everyone else in the world but me."

Harrison replied, "Jack, I would have loved to have held that for you. But Christ almighty, this place is swarmed by press. I've got cops leaking left and right. There was no way —"

I cut him off and said, "I need something else, something fresh, something they don't have. You owe me."

It was deadline — after deadline, actually — for the first editions of the next day's *Record,* and though I had many fat paragraphs of exclusive information in the story, I wanted to advance the investigation with something that would force the networks to give chase. In this business, you never settle for what you have, because there's always something else to get. And if you don't get it, someone else will.

Harrison said, "Let me talk on background for a moment, as a law enforcement source."

I liked the direction this was headed. "Go ahead," I said.

"My guys are in the process of executing a search warrant at Mac Foley's house. They're still over there. But my lieutenant at the scene just called to say they've already found something of extreme interest. Again, not from me. You have to protect me. But I want you to have this."

He paused. I said nothing. He continued, "They found Kimberly May's driver's license in one of his dresser drawers."

Kimberly May being the third victim, the one identified via the video taken by her killer in her apartment.

I reflexively drew a deep breath, and in Harrison's brief, intentional, and dramatic silence, I quickly tried to sort through my feelings. First, I was thrilled to be in possession of this nugget, which could probably take over the lede of my story. This essentially and truly implicated one of the most respected homicide detectives in Boston, all based on my initial tip.

The second emotion I felt was relief, that maybe, really, truly, the Phantom Fiend was caught and would spend the rest of his life behind bars, never to torment my city, or me, for that matter, ever again.

The third emotion, and this is where the

reporter side of me rears its occasionally ugly but often pragmatic head, was doubt. I just didn't, couldn't, maybe wouldn't believe that Mac Foley was involved in the murders of three young women now, and perhaps eleven victims from forty years before. It wasn't that I liked him so much. It wasn't even that I knew him. I just had this nagging sense that there was something — or maybe someone — else involved.

The facts, of course, belied my intuition. Mac Foley with Elizabeth Riggs's purse. Mac Foley with knowledge of Lauren Hutchens's apartment number. Now Mac Foley with Kimberly May's license. Much as I was hesitant to believe it, the raw details made for an excellent newspaper story.

"Right now, we're charging him with interfering with an investigation," Harrison began anew. "That gives us the ability to hold him. We'll seek high bail from a judge, get a DNA sample, and compare that with possible samples from the crime scenes. Again, you can use this, but not for attribution. We're scheduling a full press conference for tomorrow morning."

By now I was jotting notes down. Mongillo was still spewing into his phone, alternately laughing and uttering exclamations like "C'mon, zip it back up." At another point, his tone got deadly serious and he said to whoever it was on the other end of the line, "This one's personal to me. My mother was one of the victims all those years ago."

I thanked Harrison, hung up the phone, and stared out the front windshield through the raw March night at the hulking house that held Paul Vasco, who suddenly didn't seem all that relevant to my story.

Or did he. Something just kept telling me he was. Maybe it was the photographs of the victims on Vasco's wall. Maybe it was that satanic smile of his when he talked about the crimes. Maybe it was the look on Foley's face, one of desperation, but perhaps one of honor as well.

Before you destroy my life, before you ruin what's left of my career, before you destroy my wife, my daughter, my whole reputation, please put it to Paul Vasco.

Mongillo hung up the phone.

"You get what I get?" I asked.

"The license?"

I nodded and asked, "A good source?"

Now he nodded.

I snapped open the cell phone and dialed Peter Martin, who answered, as always, on the first ring. I relayed the information. I read him a quote that was to be attributed to a law enforcement official involved in the investigation. His tone was nearly giddy as he hung up to make the changes for the paper's next edition.

Mongillo nodded toward the darkened house that loomed over our car. "Still worthwhile?" he asked.

"Something tells me it is," I said. We both opened the doors at the same time.

Just like on our visit two days before, the front door was unlocked, and the downstairs lobby, such as it is, was unguarded.

Vinny and I made our way up the dark staircase and walked along the decrepit wooden floors on the second story until we arrived simultaneously in front of Paul Vasco's door. I reached out and softly knocked.

Inside, I heard movement, and judging from the slight squint he gave, so did Mongillo, but no one answered the door. So I knocked again, this time more firmly. More noise, like a muffled shuffling, but still Vasco didn't come to the door.

I knocked a third time, a firm rap now, which was met by utter silence. Mongillo put his face against the door and called out, "Paul, it's Vinny Mongillo and Jack Flynn. Can you let us in for a minute?"

Nothing. So I tried the knob. It was open.

I mean, think about that for a moment. The door was open — in a halfway house filled with supposedly reforming criminals. Shocked doesn't begin to describe how I felt. Neither does pleased.

I looked at Mongillo; he held up a single fat finger, and I'm pretty sure we were both thinking the same thing. If we walked into this room, we would at that point be trespassing, and Paul Vasco, a convicted killer with a confessed lust for the act of murder, could rightfully gun us down in our woeful tracks. A jury would not only acquit him, it'd probably award him damages for the pain and suffering of having a couple of jerk reporters mucking around in his life.

I shut my eyes for a second, furiously trying to figure out a course of action. Vinny motioned for me to slowly push open the door, which I did, a crack, and Vinny called out, "Paul, it's Jack and Vinny. We need to come in for a second. Is that all right?"

No sounds, no movement, no answer.

So I edged the door open another few inches. Mongillo looked at me and I motioned him aside. I stepped through the narrow opening, my arm first, figuring if that was shot off, I still had another. Then a leg. Same theory.

"Paul, it's Jack Flynn. I really need to see you."

And then my face. One hard bulb illuminated the room, and what I saw was absolutely no one. That is, until I saw the shoe resting on its side, half under the bed — a workboot, actually, with dried mud caked on the treads of its soles.

It's funny how the mind works in a crisis, or at least under pressure. It's funny how the dots connect faster, how the synapses fire harder, how every sense is cut and clean and grabbing at every little detail it can find, and even some it can't. A mere shoe. Paul Vasco, I quickly understood, did not have an extra pair of shoes. You don't come out of prison like Imelda Marcos, carrying a duffel bag full of various pairs of shoes — the loafers for a lazy Sunday afternoon, the workboots for the week, the sandals for those times at the beach when nothing else will do. No, if the shoes were here, then so was Vasco, so I called out, "Paul, I just have another quick question for you. There's been a break in the case that I think you're going to be interested in."

As I said this, I eyed the boot carefully, though at the moment I wasn't sure why. And then I was. Connected to the boot was a sock. I'm no Sherlock Holmes, hell, I'm not even Columbo, but the sock, I deducted, covered an ankle. The ankle belonged to a person hiding under the bed. The person hiding under the bed was undoubtedly Paul Vasco.

I stepped back, beckoned Vinny into the room with my hand, gave him the shut-up sign by placing a finger to my lip, and said aloud, "We missed him. He's not here. Let's get back to the newsroom, fast."

Granted, I probably wasn't ready for my Broadway debut, but I didn't think this was bad.

I motioned Vinny out the door now. He left. I carefully stepped up on the one wooden chair in the room, summoning every bit of my athletic ability to remain as silent as I could. I leaned over and shut the door firmly.

My thinking was as follows: If I assumed that Paul Vasco was armed, and I had to assume that Paul Vasco was armed because it seemed like every single person I'd come across in the last week was armed, then I wanted to grab him while he was undertaking the awkward motion of emerging from under the bed.

Something else also pecked at my suspicions as well, and it was as simple as this: Why was Vasco hiding? And what did he have to hide?

I quite literally held my breath. Thirty seconds passed, and the boot didn't move. Sixty seconds passed, still nothing. I let out little breaths through my nose and sucked in air through my mouth. I began to think he knew I was there. Either that or maybe sometimes a boot is just a boot, and all my deductive reasoning was out the window.

Two minutes in, I was furiously contemplating my next move. Do I look under the bed and risk being shot in the head? Do I simply grab at the boot? Do I step down from my makeshift pedestal and leave? And that's when the boot moved, not anything subtle, but it virtually rolled over, and then a hand emerged from beneath the bed, grabbing at the top of the mattress, pulling the rest of the body out.

The form fully emerged from under the bed, facing away from me, still having no idea I was in the room. He was carrying something in his hand that wasn't a gun. It looked like a sheath of paper. I had no time to think, let alone strategize. So what I did was pounce.

I leapt off the chair and on top of the guy's back, slamming him down against the side of the bed, and then the floor. He let out a long, hard groan. I grabbed his neck in a headlock and slammed my fist into his gut. I'm not sure why I did this. Maybe it was all the violence that had touched me over the last week. Maybe it was rubbing off. I wouldn't be telling the whole truth about this situation if I didn't say it felt a little bit good.

Amid the cacophony, Vinny Mongillo flung open the door and raced into the room.

"Grab Vasco's legs!" I yelled to him. I didn't want the guy somehow kicking some particularly sensitive part of me while I tried to hold him down.

"I can't," Vinny replied.

I continued to hold Vasco down, his head facing away from me as his body furiously squirmed in an attempt to get free. "Why the hell not?" I asked, looking up at Mongillo.

"Because Vasco's not here. This isn't him."

I pushed the guy away from me, down onto the floor. He had long, stringy hair, an unkempt beard that was born of nothing more than laziness, and needle marks up and down his skeletal arms. He was looking at me wide-eyed, truly frightened, and he blurted out in a panicked tone, "Vasco's gone. He told me I could take some of this stuff. He really did." I noticed for the first time that the sheath of papers, now strewn across the floor, was a collection of pornographic photos that the guy had obviously pulled off the wall.

I clenched my fist, raised it in the air, and said, "Where is he? Where's Vasco?"

The guy blinked long and hard in anticipated pain and said, "He took the train. I don't know where he went."

"How do you know he was on the train?"

"I was with him when he left."

The guy was still on the ground, his head raised a few inches off the filthy floor. I was kneeling above him. Mongillo stood behind me.

Mongillo barked, "When?"

"This morning. We went to the train station this morning. We were supposed to be going to work together for the first day, and he said he had somewhere else he needed to go."

"Which train station?" I asked.

"I don't know."

I clenched my fist harder, causing him to flinch. They probably don't teach this interview technique at Columbia University's ever-famous journalism graduate school, but nor do they probably teach young reporters-to-be what they're supposed to do when everyone around them keeps dying. Or maybe they do; I don't really know. I barely got a bachelor's degree.

I asked, "How the fuck do you not know?"

"I don't know this city, man. I don't. I'm from Detroit. I really don't know."

Mongillo and I remained silent for a moment, both our minds rushing to devise our next step. In the quiet, I glanced over at the wall that held the photographs of Jill Dawson, Lauren Hutchens, and Kimberly May, and saw with a start that their pictures were no longer there. I scanned the floor quickly, and they weren't there either. I don't know why this was important to me, the fact these pictures were missing, but it was.

"You're coming with us," I said, grabbing him by the front of his dirty white T-shirt and lifting him up.

"I can't, dude. I can't."

I hate the word *dude,* though that's not entirely why I clenched my fist once again, gritted my teeth, and whispered to him, "If you don't, I'm going to kill you."

"I need a fix."

Mongillo, intuitively and literally understanding where we were going with this, said, "We'll get you one — right after."

I asked, "What's your name?"

"Marcus."

"Marcus, we're going to go for a little ride,

and as soon as we're done, we'll set you up with whatever you need."

He nodded, hopeful for the first time in this encounter. The three of us walked out of the room, down the dark, dingy hall, down the stairs, and out into the street. He wasn't wearing a jacket; I didn't particularly care.

The goal was to retrace their route. I'm not completely certain why this was so important to me, but it falls in the same category as conducting an interview in person rather than by phone. You always get more from facial expressions, from body language, from being in the same room. You always get more from just showing up.

In the car, Vinny got in the driver's seat and I sat in the back beside Marcus, with my man Huck squishing over against the door. Before we pulled out, we discerned that Marcus and Vasco had walked to a subway stop. The subway stop was next to where the Celtics played, which meant North Station. They did not switch subway lines. They did not take the subway directly to the train station. They got off the subway and came aboveground at a busy intersection with a large park, then walked to the train station behind a tall glass skyscraper.

I said to Vinny, "Sounds like they took the

Green Line to Arlington Street, and walked to Back Bay Station. But why the hell didn't they just take the Orange Line from North Station right into Back Bay Station?"

Mongillo said, "Maybe Vasco doesn't know the subway lines well."

"He's a genius." I paused and said, "Drive over to Arlington Street."

We did. Marcus said it looked familiar. I started feeling like I should work for Scotland Yard. He pointed in the direction they walked, which was toward the train station, and Vinny slowly followed the route.

Marcus, sleepy now rather than feisty, pointed casually out the window and said, "Paul went in there."

It was a Kinko's copy store, still open because it was always open.

"He stopped in there?" I asked, incredulous. "For long?"

"No. Five minutes."

"Then where?"

Marcus said, "We went to the train station."

I insisted on following the route. It was ten-thirty at night; the streets were virtually void of traffic, giving us the luxury of driving at our own slow pace.

Marcus said, "We took a left here."

Vinny banged a sharp left, down the

wrong way of a one-way street, but that's all right. What wasn't all right was that it suddenly didn't make complete sense, this route, because it took them a block out of their way.

"Marcus, think hard. Where else did you stop?" I said.

"Nowhere. That was it."

Vinny pulled up to the next intersection, driving the wrong way.

"Think, Marcus. Any little stop. Any short detour. Think."

Marcus casually pointed out the window and said, "Right there, but just for a second."

I whirled around in my seat. He was pointing at a U.S. post office, the Back Bay annex. Suddenly things started fitting together in my head like they never had before, pieces creating a whole, the whole being a picture of Paul Vasco mailing a letter to me because he was the Phantom Fiend, and probably the Boston Strangler.

"What happened?" I asked, nearly yelling. Huck sat up for the first time.

Marcus was staring out the back window at the post office. Vinny had pulled to the curb. "Paul handed me an envelope. The building was closed. There were three mailboxes on the sidewalk, and he told me to go put it in the middle mailbox. He said he'd give me twenty dollars if I did. He kept walking toward the train station."

I asked, "Did you mail it?"

He nodded. "Then I had to run after him. I met him outside the station. He gave me the money, said he had to take another trip, and told me to get to work and not tell anyone what we had done."

I let out a long breath. Vinny looked back at me and I looked at Vinny. I reached into my pocket, pulled out a pair of twenty-dollar bills, handed them to Marcus, and said, "You're a man of your word. Thanks for your help. Don't tell anyone about us."

"I won't," he said as he got out of the car, looking back nervously as he shut the door.

I snapped open my cell phone and dialed Peter Martin. "You've got to hold that Mac Foley story," I said. "I think we're wrong."

Martin replied, "You think, or you've got something else you can write in its place?"

Good question, as usual.

"Give me an hour," I said, having only some idea just what an hour it would be.

41

At ten forty-five on a raw Sunday night in the middle of a dismal March, the Pigpen lounge in Chelsea was exactly how I expected it to be, which is to say peopled by some of life's most exquisite losers — beer-bellied guys with tree-trunk necks wearing ill-fitting black blazers, desperate-looking women in caked-on makeup with skirts that revealed things that no normal man would want to see, coked-out servers who had neither showered nor shaved in days.

The place reeked of stale cigarettes, cheap whiskey, and fresh urine, not necessarily in that order. That potpourri actually represented an improvement on the drugstore-quality colognes and perfumes worn by the patrons. If Charles Darwin had ever been able to stop by the Pigpen for a Scotch and a beer chaser, I think he'd have quickly remade his entire theory.

I marched through the front doors and

yelled out, "Everyone freeze. Massachusetts Health Department. I'm here to enforce the state's no-smoking laws."

Actually, that's not what I did or said. I didn't have the luxury of time or humor. Rather, I barged inside, spied old friend Sammy Markowitz sitting in his usual rear booth, and made a beeline for him.

I almost got there, too, but for the two bodyguards who looked as if they had just escaped from the primate exhibit at the Franklin Park Zoo. They stood side by side, blocking my path, their bodies about the width of a football field, and one of them said, "Nobody goes back dere."

"You must be mistaken," I pointed out to them. "There are people back there now. So if you'll excuse me."

The guy who had spoken to me glanced over at the silent one, as if he was looking for some sort of explanation of what I had meant. He didn't get one. Then a voice called out from behind them, "He's good, gentlemen. He's good."

The men hesitated, then awkwardly parted in silence. To me, the voice said, "Jack Flynn in the Pigpen. To what do I owe this rarest of pleasures?"

That was Sammy Markowitz, bookmaking kingpin, Pigpen owner, and one of the oldest, most valuable sources of information in my legendary stable. We'd befriended each other years ago when I was reporting out a story on the scope and breadth of his enormously successful criminal enterprise. Desperate for me not to write, he leaked like a sieve about anyone and everyone all around him, from cops to mayors, providing me fodder for a series of stories that nearly — but didn't quite — win a Pulitzer Prize. We'd remained in occasional touch ever since.

I hadn't seen him in years, and Father Time had not necessarily been kind. Not exactly Tom Brady to begin with, Markowitz's jowls now hung so low that they almost rested on the table. His eyes were so bloodshot that I think even his pupils had turned red. His teeth were the color of caramel, most likely from the Camels that were ever present in his mouth, like the one that hung on his bottom lip at that very moment.

He ran his syndicate from this corner booth, and he was sitting there alone with open green ledger books bathed in the soft light of an old-fashioned banker's lamp, a highball glass of his trademark Great Western Champagne sitting within easy — and constant — reach.

"A favor," I said, sitting down across from

him. "I only come when I'm looking for favors, and I apologize for that. This one I need real bad."

"Every time you come in here, you need it bad," he replied, looking at me with that deadened stare.

"I am sorry —"

"I say that as a compliment, kid," he interjected. "Believe me, you're me, there are pains in the asses that are shuffling through here seven goddamned days a week looking for this and looking for that. It never ends. You show up, I know it's important. Go ahead."

So I did. Mongillo and I had checked the pickup times on the mailboxes, and saw that all Sunday mail was retrieved by four o'clock. That meant the envelope from Paul Vasco was most likely sitting inside the locked and darkened brick building. I needed to get into that post office, and I needed to get in there fast.

I remembered that years before, the U.S. attorney had leaked word that Sammy Markowitz was about to be the subject of a multiple-count indictment on a battery of far-reaching charges that, if proven, could send him to prison for the rest of his life. The crux of the charges, as with the crux of many federal indictments, involved mail fraud. So when a key U.S. Postal Service inspector in the Boston office lost a laptop computer and a box of critical evidence, the entire case fell apart before the grand jury ever took a vote. Supposedly, that inspector now owned a lavish oceanfront spread on Nantucket, courtesy of Sammy Markowitz. I was hoping to hell he was in Boston now and willing to help out.

This is what I told Markowitz. He looked at me, forever flat, the butt drooping off his bottom lip, his eyes sagging into the bridge of his nose, and he said, "That's all you need, a U.S. Postal Service inspector to allow you to commit a felony on government property on five minutes' notice?"

He let that hang out there amid the swirl of fresh smoke, the acrid smell of old beer, and the tinny sounds of the jukebox that at that precise moment was playing Huey Lewis and the News. I didn't say anything, because there was really nothing I could say.

"No problem," he added, with just the hint of a smile at the edge of his lips. He leaned over and picked up the receiver on an office-style phone that rested on his table, placed a pair of reading glasses across his eyes, and carefully dialed a number.

"Barney, Sammy," he said into the phone. "Oh, did I wake you . . . How's the island been . . . ? You're using sunscreen, I hope, on that fair skin of yours . . . Your wife ever ask after me . . . ? Listen, I'm in the market for a favor and I need it now . . . You're going to have to go over to the Back Bay post office . . . I'm sending a guy over there, name of Jack. He's like my son, but not as good-looking. He needs to go inside . . . Huh . . . ? What . . . ? Yeah, inside the post office. He's looking for something. Do whatever you can to help him out . . . Call me sometime from Nantucket. I want to see if you really can hear the waves from your porch."

And that was that. I rapped the scratched tabletop twice with the side of my hand as I got up to go.

"Wait a minute," Markowitz called out after me.

I turned around and he said, "What the hell do I get out of the deal?"

Good question. I replied, "You got the opportunity to do something really good."

He shook his head in mock indignation, pulled the cigarette off his lip, and said, "What the hell good is that? You owe me, kid. You owe me."

He was right, I did. As the old saying goes, when you're looking for a pig, you don't search the cosmetics counter at Saks. Or something like that.

I slipped out the door, from fetid air to fresh, snapped open the passenger door to my idling car, the dog still asleep in the back, and told Mongillo, "Back to the post office."

And we were off, one more stop amid a long day in an awful week in an increasingly uncertain life. One way or another, I suspected it would be our last.

42

When my cell phone rang, I snapped it open so hard I almost snapped it apart. "Flynn here," I said.

Mongillo was deftly steering my car over the Mystic-Tobin Bridge, the mostly darkened towers of Boston's Financial District spread out in the near distance below. Huck was snoring in the backseat, oblivious, virtuously so, to all that was wrong in this world.

"Sweeney here." Hank Sweeney, to be more precise. His voice, as always, was soft, velvety, and welcomed.

"How's things?" I asked, my pulse slowing for the moment.

"Well, two goons, both newly hired employees of *The New York Times,* just picked up Elizabeth Riggs, escorted her to the airport, and are getting her out of this crazy town via a company-hired jet. So you should feel good about that."

"I do." At least I thought I did. I had to

further process the fact that she was gone, though safe, before I could make that same declaration to myself.

"Which frees me up to spend a little more quality time with you," Sweeney said. He paused, gave me that purring chuckle, and added, "Of course, anytime you and I spend together is quality time."

"How about we begin anew in about five minutes, in front of the Back Bay post office. I need some help committing a felony — all toward a good cause."

"Such a coincidence," Hank replied. "I just happen to be feeling very felonious." And like that, the line went dead.

Vinny Mongillo glided up to the front of the post office, a hulking brick building that sits on the corner of Stuart and Clarendon Streets in the shadows of the tallest building in Boston, the John Hancock Tower.

I said to him, "You don't have to do this. You can watch the car, stay with the dog, and I'll slip in there with Hank."

"Don't be an asshole," he said. "By the end of this night, we're going to know who killed my mother, one way or another, and I'm going to be front and center in bringing that information home."

I wasn't about to argue with that.

578

Hank was waiting outside, dressed in black, looking like little more than a silhouette. I told the dog to guard the car, though he didn't so much as open an eye in acknowledgment. As Vinny and I joined Hank outside, my cell phone rang yet again.

"Flynn here."

"I'm the guy who's helping you."

I couldn't be so sure, especially since the car that at that precise moment was rolling slowly past on Stuart Street bore a striking resemblance to a vehicle parked two spaces behind us at the Pigpen. Thinking even more quickly than usual, I asked, "What did Markowitz tell you to wear plenty of in your last conversation?"

Silence, and then, "Sunscreen. What's that have to do with breaking into the post office on my watch?"

"Nothing." And everything, but I didn't have time to explain. That same car idled about half a block down. I hit Hank on the arm and pointed, and Hank pulled a pair of what looked like opera glasses out of his coat pocket and peered down the street.

"The garage door is rolled up about three feet in the middle loading bay in the back alley. Use that as your entry point. I'm watching the building from a distance. When you're done, flash the lights of your car once before you illuminate them for good. The overnight managers start coming in around eleven-thirty, so you have to be out in the next ten minutes. When you're inside the building, keep all lights off at all times."

And he hung up. I turned to Hank and asked if he brought flashlights.

"Does the pope carry a rosary?" he replied, then handed small lights to Mongillo and me. As I led them around back, Hank said, "What are we doing here? Are you missing your Publishers Clearinghouse Sweepstakes form this year, or is there something larger at stake?"

Mongillo laughed. I didn't. I told them both, "We're looking for any envelope addressed to me. We're probably going to find it in an incoming mail bin that's yet to be sorted, but who really knows? It was dropped off in one of the front boxes earlier today. I'm just hoping it hasn't been brought down to the main headquarters for sorting already."

Neither of them said anything, though I suspect I knew what they were thinking: this was like looking for a hunk of manure from a specific horse on a sprawling farm field. Or something like that. The face of my cell phone read 11:15. I said, "And we've got ten minutes to get in and out of the building, no lights allowed."

Mongillo asked, "Would it be any easier if we were all bound and gagged as well?"

I ignored that, but Hank laughed. Apparently this was anything-goes night on the humor front.

As advertised, the garage door on the middle bay was rolled up about three feet from the bottom, leaving a gap that I slid under easily enough, and Sweeney did with just a little more effort. Mongillo, that's another story, one that involves some pushing and pulling and a rather uncomfortable moment when I thought we might have to abandon him directly under the door. Once inside, Hank rapped softly on a regular exit next to the garage and said, "Mong, use this on the way out."

So we were in, the three of us. My cell phone said it was 11:17 p.m., giving us about eight minutes of search time before we had to get out, and another five minutes to alert Peter Martin as to what we'd found.

"Look anywhere and everywhere," I said, "for anything addressed to me."

The place was as dark as the Black Forest on a moonless night, though I confess the closest I've been to Germany is a slice of German chocolate cake that I had at an absurdly overpriced New American restaurant about six months before.

Suffice it to say, the place was dark — extremely dark, can't-see-your-hand-in-front-of-your-face dark. It was also moldy and more than a little musty, and it made me understand for the first time why UPS drivers are always so cheerful: because they don't have to work for the post office.

The three of us fanned out across the first floor of the building — at least I think we did, but I couldn't see them very well. A moment later, I did see a couple of slices of penetrating light from their flashlights, and I illuminated mine as well.

The place was lined with various canvas pushcarts. Little warrens were separated from one another by mesh netting. There were stacks of envelopes and piles of boxes stuffed in every possible crevice. It made it seem all the more extraordinary that a letter could be delivered to the most remote outposts in America in just a few days.

I quite literally stumbled across a row of those aforementioned pushcarts, each of them identified by zip code. I shone my light on the various labels until I found my code on the waterfront, and I reached into the deep basket and pulled out a fistful of envelopes.

I quickly shuffled through them with one hand, shining the light on them with the other, dropping each envelope back into the cart after I had scanned it. I got to the end without finding anything with my name.

So I went to the cart that bore the *Record*'s zip code, only I found hundreds more letters. I called out in a loud whisper, "Guys, over here, I could use some help," and I flicked my light around the room. In a moment they were both by my side, and the three of us divvied up the contents of the basket. I was fairly sure we'd find it there.

We didn't.

I checked the face of my phone — 11:21. Sweeney said, "Follow me, I found a bunch of white boxes with postmarked mail. I'll bet it's in there."

Mongillo and I followed Sweeney across the cluttered floor, stumbling more than a couple of times but ultimately arriving safely. I should have taken Hank's bet, though, because after we divvied up about six hundred envelopes and shuffled through them, we didn't even find so much as a phone bill bearing my name.

Now it was 11:23, time to give up. Mac Foley would be toast in the morning *Record,* in a story under my byline. I briefly tried to convince myself that he deserved it, but both my conscience and my gut told me otherwise.

My hands, by the way, were starting to cramp, probably from lack of food, lack of water, lack of sleep, lack of sex, lack of joy, lack of humanity, lack of virtually anything that normal people have plenty of in their refined and enjoyable lives.

That's what I was feeling — self-pity — when the first gunshot rang out, the report slamming off the concrete floors and walls and ringing in my ears. I'll repeat that: a gunshot. A real live honest-to-goodness gunshot, right there in the Back Bay U.S. Postal Service Annex in the dark of a crucial night. When I thought about it for any more than a fraction of a second, it started to make perfect sense, because that's just plain and simple what happens in the increasingly absurd life of intrepid reporter Jack Flynn.

It's what I heard after the gunshot that really frightened me. A crash, very near me, as if someone crumpled to the floor not from the sound of the shot but from the impact. I dove for cover, then crawled furiously toward the sounds of despair, which now also included a voice muttering, "Fuck. He got me." It was, for the record, Vinny Mongillo's voice.

I extinguished my light so I wouldn't be a

sitting duck, or in this case, reporter. I crawled headfirst into a metal desk, then a tall trash can, grabbing the former before it tipped to the floor. In about twenty seconds, I felt the form of Mongillo lying on his back between a desk chair and a canvas bin.

"Vinny, it's Jack," I whispered.

"The fuckers got me," he said. His voice was more angry than panicked, especially when he added, "Right in my stomach."

I flicked on the light and circled both my palms around it as I shone the bulb onto Mongillo's vast abdominal area, which was not unlike trying to hit the continent of Asia with a dart. I didn't see any bullet hole in his plaid shirt. I didn't even see any blood. I whispered, "Show me where it hurts," and he took his big, beefy hand and drew little circles in the air above the right side of his lower stomach.

I shone the light and saw the truth: he was grazed with a bullet that might have cost him an old shirt and a little bit of skin, but it hadn't penetrated any flesh, or for that matter caused any lasting damage, at least not of the physical kind.

I whispered, "Vin, I think the bullet skimmed your gut. You've got nothing worse than a scrape."

He replied, "Oh, God, man, anywhere but

my stomach. Don't take away the one true pleasure I still have."

I don't think he was talking about sex.

I shut my light off and told Vin to stay down and keep his light off as well. I set off across the room in search of that which I didn't yet know. I stole another glance at my cell phone: 11:25 p.m. We were about to be late.

Hank Sweeney, it's important to note, had virtually disappeared. Last I saw of his light was a full minute earlier, before the shot was fired, when he was futilely searching the last envelopes in the postmarked bin. As I crawled along the gritty floor, my heart was heavy with failure. All my soaring optimism coming in was seeping out. I was pretty resigned that my new goal wasn't finding the letter, which would have been the proof I needed for a story I hadn't written. Rather, it was simply the three of us getting out of there alive.

And then came the crash. It was surprisingly close to me, a few yards ahead, a fierce, sharp collision, as if something had just been flung across the room. Immediately afterward, a gun discharged. It was so close that I could see the flash of light from the muzzle. I could smell the explosion. Then silence. I was flat on the floor, holding my breath to mute any sounds.

About twenty seconds later, I heard commotion about ten yards away, a strange voice yelling some indecipherable words, and then another gunshot, followed by a scream of agony. Out of the mayhem, Hank's voice cut through the darkness. "Hit the lights," he yelled.

I bolted for the door, the narrow band of my flashlight illuminating the way. I stumbled across one cluster of boxes, and then another. When I got to the wall, I felt frantically around for a switch, found several, and flicked them all upward. Immediately, the room was bathed in harsh light, revealing Hank Sweeney kneeling atop a middle-aged man sprawled haphazardly on the ground, his head pushed against some empty boxes, his left thigh oozing blood.

Hank looked hard at the guy and said, "Wait a minute, I know you." He still had that smooth voice, though his next motion didn't seem quite so calm. He raised his fist and cracked it down on the guy's nose, causing a veritable explosion of blood. The man was actually reduced to tears as Hank called out, "Let's go."

Vinny Mongillo was already up and about, seemingly recovered from his close call. The three of us got to the back door in unison. Hank flicked the lights back off and we all filed outside. My cell phone said 11:27.

On the loading dock, I asked, "Who was that?"

Hank replied, "Goddamned police captain, one of the commissioner's top yesmen. Maybe I should say henchmen. Seems like the commish has been going to extremes to block your story."

As I let that little shard of information sink in, Mongillo asked, "No luck with the letter?"

I shook my head. Hank said, "We've got to give it up." He pointed to a car turning from Clarendon Street into the alley and added, "The writing's on the wall. We've got to get out of here."

The writing's on the wall.

This jarred something deep inside my head, or maybe it wasn't that deep. Maybe it was something that had been precariously floating along the surface of my mind, something I couldn't quite piece together.

All truths are easier to understand once they are discovered.

That was Paul Vasco, in his miserable little room on that miserable Friday that Edgar Sullivan died at the hands of a gunman in the Beacon Hill CVS, and I was just now starting to sense what Vasco meant.

You want to get it in writing, young man. That's the best advice I can give you.

That gem, courtesy of the famous H. Gordon Thomas, pretty much summarized what I had been trying to do right here. But it occurred to me that I had the wrong execution of the right idea. It was as if I had just heard a clap of thunder in my brain.

I turned to Hank and all but yelled, "What's the zip code of police headquarters?"

The car was pulling down the alley now, into a space in front of the bay.

Hank told me.

"Hold this person off," I called out as I slipped back under the garage door.

I could hear Hank hissing, "Wait," as I groped my way farther inside.

Once in, I flicked on my penlight, got myself to the row of canvas baskets, and found the one marked with the zip code at police headquarters. There were about a hundred envelopes inside, and I furiously picked up a stack and sorted through them, throwing the ones that I didn't need onto the floor. No luck.

So I scooped out another stack. I couldn't hear anyone at the door. I couldn't hear anything at all but my own heavy breathing.

And that breathing got a whole lot heavier when I came upon a plain white envelope with "Detective Mac Foley" typed in a familiar font. I tossed the rest of the mail back in the carrier and set out for the door.

I slammed into a desk, stopped for a moment to get my bearings, and shone my light across the room to determine an easy flow to the door.

Click.

That sound, though, stopped me cold. It occurred right in front of me, in an open area of the room unencumbered by furniture or tall baskets. I shone my light onto the floor, and about ten feet away, in my path toward freedom and what I strongly suspected was a magnificent story that no one else would ever have, that middle-aged man with the bloody thigh was aiming a handgun directly at the bridge of my handsome nose.

"Drop it," I said. I had no authority to command this. Well, maybe moral authority, but not a whole lot else. I had no weapon. I had no easy hiding place. I didn't even have the power of persuasion, because by the time I'd use it, I think I'd already be dead.

The man, dressed in a pair of jeans and a sweatshirt, was trembling as he held the trigger up around his eyes and took aim at my face. I had watched Hank Sweeney grab the guy's gun, but apparently, like the perpetrator in the CVS, he was hiding another. Actually, I shone my light on his face and realized he was the same attacker as in CVS, a thought that didn't exactly thrill me because it meant he had no compunction about killing.

"You don't want to do that," I said.

I said this mostly to buy time, to play out my options, to give Hank or Mongillo or the postal inspector or the Easter Bunny time to walk inside this goddamned dank post office and shoot this nutcase in the back of the head. Problem was, I didn't see any of the above — and didn't hear them, either.

The gunman, by the way, didn't reply to my assertion. He just kept pointing, trying to get his bearings, shaking all the while.

I said, "I can help you with that wound. I can drive you to the hospital, drop you off at the emergency room, get you taken care of, and no one will ever know why you or I were here."

Again, nothing.

I shone my light more directly on him, and noticed what his hesitance was in shooting me. He was slowly gathering his body,

591

arduously lifting it upward against the pain of his own wound. He was obviously trying to position himself to be able to flee once the gunshot rocketed through the room and I lay dead on the floor. Sweat was pouring down his face as he tried to move, hampering his vision.

"Get that fucking light down," he said, his Boston accent thick, his voice craggy and tough.

I pushed the light off to the side, and in the process saw the glint of a metal object on the desk that I had just slammed into. It was a letter opener, long and sharp, just sitting there for the taking.

So here's what happened next. I sized up the gunman's position, and then mine. I flicked my flashlight off, leapt over the desk, grabbed the handle of the letter opener, and flung it directly into his temple, kung-fu style, killing him instantly.

Well, all right, that's what I was trying to do, anyway. Would have been good, even if I wasn't.

Here's what actually happened. I flicked off my flashlight. The split second I did that, he began firing, the bullets passing so close to my face and shoulders that I could hear them scream past in the air.

I dove for cover, paused for about ten

seconds, picked a basket filled with mail up off the floor, and heaved it in his direction — one, then another after that, and still another. After the third one, the gunman groaned in agony. Suddenly the lights sprung to life in the room. Sweeney raced toward us with his weapon drawn. The perpetrator lay on the ground, still as a statue, his gun just out of reach of his hand. Sweeney approached frantically, kicked the gun farther away, lifted the guy's head off the concrete, and announced, "He's out cold. You must have hit him in the head with this basket."

Brings new meaning to the USPS motto of "We deliver for you."

"I've got to run, Hank."

"So do I," he said.

We bolted for the door. Outside, Mongillo was talking to a pair of postal workers like they were relatives. Actually, as we were leaving, one of them called out, "I promise, cousin, nothing but silence."

At my car, I flipped open the driver's door and climbed in beside a sleeping dog named Huck, who had crawled into the passenger seat. I flicked on the dome light, calmed my nerves for a second, gently opened the envelope that I had risked my life to get, and held its contents in my sweating hands.

I unfolded a single sheet of paper and bore down with my eyes to read it.

"Back again," it said. "Still more to follow."

On a separate line were the words "The Phantom Fiend."

It was written in that same typeface as the notes I had received at the *Record*. In my other hand I was holding something else, something that it literally hurt me to my core to feel: the driver's license of a thirty-four-year-old woman named Jennifer Cooper who was listed at an address on Commonwealth Avenue.

Jennifer Cooper, I said to myself, rest in peace.

I snapped open my phone, saw it was 11:35, and hit the speed-dial button for Peter Martin. He picked up on the first ring.

"Peter, you've got to kill the Foley story," I yelled. "You've got to kill it now. It's wrong. I've got the facts right here in my hand. I can write another story identifying the Phantom Fiend."

"Who is it?" Martin asked.

"Paul Vasco. He's definitely the killer now, I'm betting he was the killer then. I've got it good enough to go with."

"You're telling me that with all we have on Mac Foley, that he's not guilty?"

"Peter, he's guilty," I replied. "He's guilty as hell. He's just not guilty of murder."

Martin said, "I don't know what the hell you mean, but I trust that you'll make it clear in print. Now get in here and do your job."

Mongillo was still standing on the curb with Sweeney when I threw the car into drive. It was the first time in a week that I was about to write something that I really wanted to say.

43

The turquoise waves rhythmically rolled against the soft shore — breaking, foaming, retreating — as I stretched out in a comfortable chaise lounge on the khaki-colored sand, drifting in and out of the most deeply satisfying slumber of my entire sheltered life. Tropical birds chirped in the distance. The gentle sun caressed the pale features of my tired face. I swear I could hear dolphins splashing offshore.

"Are you going up to the beach bar?"

That was the voice of Vinny Mongillo, who happened, not by coincidence, to be lying on the chaise beside mine.

I opened one eye, then the other.

"What'd I do that made you think I was going up to the bar?"

Vinny said, "Well, it's hot out here. If you were hot, I thought you might be thirsty. If you were thirsty, you might be going for a drink."

I said, "I was sleeping."

Vinny said, "I'm just saying."

I closed my eyes again.

"So you're not?"

Okay, I guess this is what I get for bringing my friend and colleague on vacation to a five-star beach resort halfway around the world from where we began. It ended up that the hotel wouldn't give me a refund on my honeymoon; the manager, who I'm betting was still on his first wife, said I had canceled too close to our arrival date. He offered me a credit instead, so here I was, accepting it — Vinny, as usual, along for the free ride. I mean, you can't bring another girl along on your canceled honeymoon, right? Answer below.

Seventy-eight, by the way. That was the temperature of the water I'd been wondering about just before the shots rang out in the Back Bay annex of the U.S. Postal Service on that night four weeks earlier when the *Record* broke what may be the most closely followed story that Boston has ever known. More on that in a moment.

My reverie broken, I said to Vinny, "How long do you want to live?"

"Is that a threat?"

"No, it's a serious question." And I meant it.

"Just one more day than I need."

Interesting answer, though all his answers are usually pretty interesting. I sat up and looked over at him sprawled topless in his chair, clad in a pair of flowered surfer shorts, slathered in baby oil, his skin as dark as the inside of that post office ever was, his hand wrapped around a cell phone that I'm not even sure worked this far away from home.

"Need to do what?" I asked.

He looked at me. Even his cocoa-colored eyes seemed to have darkened in the sun.

"You know — whatever. Win a Pulitzer. Start a family. Achieve some sense of inner peace."

I was about to say something, though what, I'm not really sure, when he cut in, "That's the problem with you, Jack. You almost had what you always wanted, and then it got taken away. Now you're too hesitant to do something that's not planned down to the most minute details. You're too protective — of yourself. Maybe it's just that you're afraid."

For this I got woken from a quiet reverie involving marine mammals and cockapoos. Or maybe that's cockatoos.

"Treat life like a story," he said. "Let it unfold. Kick your feet up and go along for the ride. Manipulate it where you can, enjoy the parts that you can't."

A nice thought, even if I wasn't entirely sure what he meant.

I slammed the Paul Vasco story out of the park that night. As I sped back to the *Record,* I dispatched Mongillo and Hank Sweeney to Jennifer Cooper's apartment and they found exactly what I expected, which was her body, dead about a day.

I jumped on the phone and called the Boston Police Department's holding cell and had them put Detective Mac Foley on the line. I told him what I had, which was an intercepted letter from Paul Vasco to him. I told him what we found, which was a dead woman highlighted in the mailing. And then I told him what I believed, which was that Paul Vasco was sending him the driver's licenses and other clues leading him to recently strangled women, just as the Boston Strangler had done with Bob Walters some forty years before.

And just like four decades previous, higher-ups in the department wanted to keep the correspondence under wraps. So Foley in turn forwarded them on to me, knowing they would generate enormous publicity and immense public pressure around the case, just at the time that the buffoonish commissioner was running for mayor.

In what may well be the most extraordinary on-the-record interview of my career, Mac Foley admitted to all this and more. He said he was so frustrated with the lack of publicity that he devised that mini-manifesto, and that when the *Record* didn't immediately publish it, he stole Elizabeth Riggs's driver's license and sent me the note that essentially said "Or else." He never intended to kill her. That's what he said, anyway. I guess I believe him, but maybe not.

Foley was being hailed as a hero throughout BPD, a whistleblower of the highest order. Soon enough, though, he'd be an indicted one. Word is that the Suffolk County District Attorney is looking at charges of evidence tampering, obstruction of justice, and interfering with an investigation. With a good lawyer, my bet is that he can keep himself out of jail.

The entire journalism world was chasing us the next day, and just when they thought they'd caught up, we came out the day after that with the results of DNA testing from Mongillo's long-hidden knife. The irrefutable findings: Albert DeSalvo was not the Boston Strangler. More bedlam, like it couldn't get any worse, until the morning after that when we carried the story, based on the cigarette butt that we had pulled from that dismal little room, that Paul Vasco's DNA was tied to at least five of the murders from the early 1960s.

Hal Harrison ended his mayoral campaign that very day, not with a bang but with a press release. He needed to spend more time with his family, he said. I didn't quite get that, since he was divorced and his kids were off in college. What was he going to do, attend keg parties with them? I never had the heart to ask.

Of course, Mongillo, Sweeney, and I committed at least one felony, and probably multiple felonies, that crucial night we came up with Vasco's letter. Fortunately, it hadn't been postmarked yet, and no one ever pressed us on the interception. The *Traveler* carried a story a couple of days after the fact reporting that Captain Carl Gowan, one of Commissioner Hal Harrison's top aides, was wounded in a mysterious attack just outside the Back Bay post office, and had crawled inside seeking help. The case remained under investigation. We're all holding our collective breath for the results.

As Hank Sweeney told me in no uncertain terms, it was Commissioner Hal Harrison who wanted me dead throughout the story. Soon as I get back east, I'm going to pursue that theory, not for myself, but in the memory of Edgar Sullivan, the man who single-handedly kept me alive.

Don't bother hanging around the courthouse waiting for Paul Vasco's murder trial to begin. The guy's long gone, I suspect never to be found again. Believe me when I say that Boston doesn't do fugitives particularly well.

What else?

Maggie Kane. Never heard from her again, nor has she heard from me. I was half tempted to call her from our room and describe the view that she opted never to see, but decided it would have been more rude than funny, and really not that funny at all. I have to draw the line somewhere, odd as that might seem. And the truth is, I'm a little embarrassed about the whole thing — embarrassed for me, embarrassed for her, embarrassed for us, embarrassed that we believed something was there that never really was, and embarrassed that we walked away from it in the manner we did. That's life, even if it shouldn't be.

Huck? Great dog, and no one's ever taking him away. He was staying at Peter Martin's house for the duration of my Hawaiian vacation. Their first day together, Martin called me no fewer than twenty times asking questions about "this surly beast." The second day he called another twenty times to say the dog was growing on him. I got a call on the third day asking for advice on getting one of his own. People surprise you all the time, even when they don't.

Which brings me to Elizabeth Riggs. She gave a ring two weeks after she fled Boston to congratulate me on the story and to let me know that she was moving from San Francisco to Chicago. She joked, though maybe she didn't, that it was her way of meeting me halfway. I explained that if I went and did the same thing, that would leave me in Pittsburgh — a perfectly nice city, but was that really where we wanted to spend the rest of our lives? She didn't really laugh, and I can't say I blame her.

"So you're really not going to the bar?"

Mongillo again. He gets something in his mind, especially involving food or drink, and he's incapable of letting it go.

"Mother of Christ," I said, slowly rising to my feet. "Just to shut you the hell up, I'm on my way. What do you want?"

"Surprise me," he replied.

I'd make certain of it.

The open-air bar had a thatched roof, a

603

particularly facile server, and at this precise moment, a rather stunning brunette in a backless yellow sundress, sitting on a corner stool and sipping a frozen strawberry margarita that she held in her tanned and manicured hands.

"Hello, Jack," she said, looking up at me over her drink.

"Hello, Elizabeth," I said.

Then I added, "Of all the gin joints in all the towns in all the world, she walks into mine."

"Actually," Elizabeth Riggs replied with that crinkle-eyed smile of hers, "you just walked into mine."

She was right, actually, so I didn't argue the point. Instead I said, "This is a long way from Chicago."

"It's a long way from everywhere."

A long way indeed. I thought of the panic I felt when I held her driver's license in my trembling hand, the sheer, unadulterated relief when I found her alive in the lobby of the Copley Plaza hotel, the empty sadness when I learned she had understandably fled town.

I glanced back at Mongillo, who had this stupid look on his big face as he looked back at me, and I thought of his simple request: Surprise me. I thought too of Elizabeth's spot-on analysis in the San Francisco airport that night, that the dead keep on dying in my life.

"Can I help you?" the bartender asked. He was a big suave native guy with biceps roughly the size of my thighs.

I said, "I think it's time I helped myself."

With that, I took Elizabeth by the hand. She stood and followed me, surprised and delighted at the same time, followed me across the tile floor, across the sandy beach, and into the shallow surf, where the warm waves rolled against our legs.

I leaned in and kissed her on the lips, and she kissed me back. I pulled away, just a few inches, and said, "Pittsburgh may not be so bad."

She kissed me again, neither long nor hard, but it was perfect. "Neither's Hawaii," she whispered. "It's just a matter of paying attention to who's around you rather than who's not."

Not for the first time in this life, the woman was absolutely right.

ABOUT THE AUTHOR

Brian McGrory was a roving national reporter for the *Boston Globe,* as well as the *Globe*'s White House correspondent during the Clinton administration. He is now a columnist in the newspaper's Metro section. The author of three bestselling thrillers — *The Incumbent, The Nominee,* and *Dead Line* — he lives in Boston. Find out more at www.brianmcgrory.com